PRAISE FOR YVONNE JOCKS AND *THE RANCHER'S DAUGHTERS*!

PROVING HERSELF

"Fans of western romance will enjoy this novel, seek previous *Rancher's Daughters* books, and look forward to the other tales by Yvonne Jocks."
—Amazon.com

FORGETTING HERSELF

"A tender, sweet story that carries a powerful message readers will not be able to ignore."
—*Romantic Times*

"A wonderful, can't-put-it-down read, *Forgetting Herself* is a welcome addition to my keeper shelf."
—Amazon.com

"Ms. Jocks shows promise, and she obviously did her research."
—*All About Romance*

BEHAVING HERSELF

"Yvonne Jocks has written an engaging novel with warm, wonderful characters her readers will give their hearts to. Nicely done, Ms. Jocks."
—Amazon.com

"Compelling characters and rich description add up to a savory read."
—*Romantic Times*

NIGHT SECRETS

Somewhere off in the distance, a coyote yip-yipped at the moon, as if to agree about ghosts. Victoria stepped just a little closer to Ross—even if she'd spent her whole life hearing coyotes at night. Even if she knew what little cowards coyotes were.

It seemed as good a reason as any.

He stiffened beside her. "You . . . " Then he swallowed. "Best get inside, where it's safe."

She looked up at him and nodded, not about to go inside yet. She was enjoying this excited, warm, tingly feeling of being close to him far too much. "Is that all you wanted to know? Ross?"

He had to tip his head downward to see her, they were standing so close. As ever, the movement seemed graceful, cautious, contained. "For now."

She felt like shivering, and not from wet petticoats. Only when she spread her hand on his arm—to catch her balance, to catch her breath, to feel his hidden gun—did she realize that he was shaking too. A fine, almost imperceptible trembling. She had to know.

"If you asked me out here to kiss me . . . I'll let you."

His eyes, lingering on hers, seemed so very sad. *Haunted.* Like the rustler ghosts. "I shouldn't," he said.

So *she* kissed *him.*

OTHER LEISURE AND LOVE SPELL BOOKS BY YVONNE JOCKS:
THE RANCHER'S DAUGHTERS: PROVING HERSELF
THE RANCHER'S DAUGHTERS: FORGETTING HERSELF
THE RANCHER'S DAUGHTERS: BEHAVING HERSELF

THE RANCHER'S DAUGHTERS:

EXPLAINING HERSELF

YVONNE JOCKS

LEISURE BOOKS NEW YORK CITY

A LEISURE BOOK®

May 2002

Published by

Dorchester Publishing Co., Inc.
276 Fifth Avenue
New York, NY 10001

ISBN 0-8439-4996-1

Printed in the United States of America.

Visit us on the web at www.dorchesterpub.com.

To everyone who has sought out and
embraced a second chance.

(And for Toni, Kayli, Matt, Deb, and Mo:
Thank you for this.)

EXPLAINING HERSELF

Prologue

"Rustling," repeated Jacob Garrison in a low drawl.

Laramie waited for the accompanying accusation. When none came, he relaxed—some. Garrison wasn't much of a fellow to ever truly unbend, and a man would do well to keep his guard up around the white-bearded cattle baron.

But it surely did help that Garrison hadn't recognized him.

"All the markings," Laramie agreed finally. He shifted in his saddle to glance over the neat, white outbuildings that flanked the two-story house, protective-like. The house itself had flower beds, shade trees, and a picket fence. Four girls of varying sizes added bright, calico color to the back porch. Sweet place, this. No wonder someone figured the family could afford to lose some beef. "Good brand burner."

He *expected* suspicion, after that comment. It spoke

1

well of the rancher that he merely challenged, "You'd know the difference?"

Laramie said, "Yep."

There had been a time when the weight of Garrison's steely, hat-shadowed gaze would have shaken him. No more. Nothing shook the man called Laramie nowadays.

"Looking for work?" the rancher asked.

Other, darker reasons had drawn Laramie back to the Big Horn Basin in northeastern Wyoming. But finding that cow, with its botched brand, seemed lucky. Laramie needed a place to bed down while he pursued his plans. And of all the local ranchers, he reckoned he trusted Garrison more than anyone.

Which wasn't saying a whole hell of a lot.

"Maybe." For an extra touch of honesty, he forced out a complete sentence. "I take issue with rustlers."

Garrison's gray eyes burned into him. "How big an issue?"

"Not big enough to make it yours."

The rancher studied him a long moment more, then nodded. "Won't have a hand what's cruel or belligerent. If you're lookin' for killing, callin' it frontier justice, you won't do it on my pay. This ain't a frontier no more."

The way he said that last part sounded almost sad, reminding Laramie of men he'd met in jail or at Robber's Roost, men who lamented the passing of the older days of Jesse James and Billy the Kid.

Of course, there was that train-robbing syndicate Laramie had declined to join, in favor of his personal vendetta. And here sat proof of cattle rustling. Laramie figured the frontier wasn't dead just yet, but what he said was, "Fair 'nough."

"Bed down in the bunkhouse. I won't have folks wonderin' who hired you."

Laramie nodded in grudging respect.

"No drinking, gambling, or the like, less'n you go into town for it," instructed his new boss. "Anything illegal or immoral, don't come back."

By the time Laramie got around to the illegalities, he wouldn't need the job anyway.

When Garrison turned away, Laramie thought the interview was over. Then the rancher reined his buckskin back and leveled a final, leather-clad hand in his direction. "And stay away from my girls."

Laramie said, "Not a problem."

The cattle baron nodded one last time, then rode away, business done. He didn't know who he'd just hired. Laramie aimed to keep it that way. Garrison'd had the reputation of a stand-up man when Laramie was a boy—a boy with a different name, a different life.

Of all the men Ross Laramie might end up having to kill this summer, Garrison was the one he most hoped would prove innocent.

But he'd kill him all the same, if he had to.

Chapter One

Victoria didn't wait for her father to reach the fence. She hopped off the back porch where she was washing clothes with her sisters and crossed the yard to meet his horse, catching its bridle. "Who's that you were talking to, Papa?" she asked, as he dismounted. "The man on the black gelding. He's not from around here, is he? He looked tired. Did you hire him?"

Papa paused, one scuffed boot on the first step to the porch, to stare at her. One would think, after almost eighteen years, he would be accustomed to her. He said, "None of your affair, Victoria Rose."

He climbed the steps, tugging one of nine-year-old Kitty's brown braids and ruffling six-year-old Elise's blond curls in passing. But he didn't stop to talk.

As if *anything* about Victoria's family wasn't her affair, no matter how old-fashioned Papa was about that.

Vic's third younger sister, fifteen-year-old Audra,

watched from the hand-crank washing machine. She was old-fashioned, too.

"He's staying a spell, anyhow," guessed Vic, glancing over her shoulder as she followed her father across the porch. "He's unsaddling his horse."

Now that the stranger had dismounted, she saw that he was exceptionally tall. Instead of a cowboy's rolling lankiness, he moved with a tight, contained grace that made her wonder where he'd learned it—and how. His only awkward move, a slight hitch when he first lifted his saddle, caught her attention. Was he hurt?

Had Papa hired him?

Her father sighed. "Where's your mother?" When *he* wanted information, he did not hesitate to ask *her*, Vic thought grumpily.

"She's upstairs. What's wrong with him?"

Papa stopped, to squint at her in suspicion. So the stranger had hidden his injuries from her father? Interesting!

"The steer, I mean," Victoria added quickly. "Why'd you pen it? Is it sickly?"

"Best finish your work." Papa palmed off his hat as he disappeared into his wife's clean, modern kitchen.

"It is not polite—" started Audra almost immediately after he was gone.

Victoria had heard it too often. "—to pry into other people's doings." Not that finishing other people's sentences was polite, either, but they were sisters; politeness didn't carry the same weight between them. "Well, if folks don't want me to sneak around, they should tell me more. How else am I supposed to know what's going on?"

Audra shook her head with a Papa-like sigh. The girl still wore her strawberry-brown hair in a long, neat braid, but once she started putting it up she would look just like the schoolmarm she meant to become.

A small, dainty, *prim* schoolmarm.

Victoria's hair, darker than any of her five sisters', was already escaping its knot and curling around her face in the heat of the day. *Prim* was not a word she would use to describe herself. She stayed too busy to worry about appearance. Busy doing chores. Busy writing columns and setting type for the local newspaper, three days a week.

Busy keeping informed about what went on around her.

Another glance told her that the tall stranger had shouldered his saddlebags and bedroll and was headed toward the bunkhouse. He no longer looked injured, but maybe he just hid it very well. And the bunkhouse meant—

"Papa *did* hire him!" And he'd gone to tell Mama about it. "Wait here," Vic told her younger sisters, dropping a wet shirt back into the washtub with a splash and drying her hands on her apron. "I need something upstairs."

And she did. She needed to know what was being said.

"Oh, Victoria!" protested Audra while Vic slipped into the still air of the kitchen, then up the wooden stairs.

"—I'll watch for him," her mother was promising in the upstairs hallway. "But I trust your judgment, Jacob. You picked *me*, didn't you?"

Her father's silent answer wasn't unusual. Nor was Mama's soft laugh. "Don't give me that look, boss. You did *so* choose me. I just may have chosen you first. . . ."

Victoria usually enjoyed hearing her parents talk like this. Unlike her older sisters, she'd never met a man who made her want to blush or smile the way Mama did around Papa, and it intrigued her. But this was *not* what she'd risked getting caught eavesdropping to hear.

"Ain't your boss," drawled Papa finally.

"And don't you forget it, cowboy," teased Mama.

Then, just as Victoria began to back down the steps in disappointment, Mama said, "Now, go on—you've got an empire to run and bad guys to corral." Papa must have given her another of his *looks*, because Mama added, "Rustlers are so bad guys! Ask anyone. Except the rustlers, maybe; I imagine they would be biased."

Victoria caught her breath. Rustlers on the Circle-T? What *idiot* would rustle cattle from her father?

"Ain't no empire, neither," Papa chided.

Victoria tiptoed back down the stairs. This wasn't good news . . . but it opened a whole new, wonderful box of puzzle pieces. Had *rustlers* hurt the tall stranger?

Outside, Audra was still accepting wet clothes from Kitty and wringing them through the wash-rollers. Her young mouth was set. While the two littler girls didn't ask what Vic had discovered because they didn't know she'd eavesdropped, Audra wouldn't ask from sheer principle.

It was hard for Vic to stay silent as Papa clumped across the porch to leave. "Take care, Papa," she called innocently.

He shook his head and went to his horse, his expression sour. "Curiosity killed the cat, Victoria Rose."

That's why they get nine lives, she thought in retort. She watched him ride out toward the mountains and wondered what had hurt the stranger, and why he hid it, and why he was here, and what was so important about the steer they'd penned.

As soon as she finished here, she meant to find out.

*　　*　　*

7

The problem with stopping, reckoned Laramie, was that's when a fellow remembered to hurt.

And oh, did he hurt. Hole-in-the-Wall, where he'd been recovering for the last few weeks, was a long day's ride—and a lifetime's—away from this place.

Surveying the empty bunkhouse from caution more than interest, he eased some of the pain in his shoulder by lowering his bedroll and saddlebags onto a bare bed. He kept his '95 Winchester in hand. That the bunkhouse seemed clean and well-furnished— with shelves and a footlocker at each bed, two washstands and mirrors in the corner—he noticed only peripherally.

Six windows. He circled the room, glancing out each to make sure nothing dangerous lay outside to trip up a fellow in a hurry. One door. Good.

Only then did Laramie add his rifle to his small pile of belongings on the bed. He let his shoulders sag, took a deep breath—and winced at the hot, sticky pain in his side.

Damn, gunshots healed slow. But they put things into perspective, too. If he'd died after that nasty business last month, he would never have kept his promise. All he'd lived for since childhood would be a lie. No, he'd ridden out the fever, and here he stood. If barely.

And he had no idea what to do next.

So he tended his wounds.

Laramie carefully unbuttoned his dirt-stiff shirt and, gritting his teeth, shrugged it off. Then he unhitched and peeled down his union suit so that its once-white sleeves hung along his trousered thighs. He gingerly unwrapped the bandages from his left shoulder, and the ones around his middle, then—gritting his teeth— peeled back the stained wads of cotton beneath them.

Just more proof of what bullets could do to flesh.

Like he'd needed that.

8

He went to a water barrel in the corner and scooped shade-cool water onto his face and fingered it through his hair. It felt good. He splashed it onto his chest and arms, then dribbled it more carefully onto his wounds, hissing at both the pain and his inadequacies.

He was here. He'd come back. What now?

"He was rich," he muttered. This was an angry recitation that had gotten him through so many nights of hell, so many days of misery. "A rancher, maybe. A bachelor . . ."

When he dried his torso on a surprisingly clean, flour-sack towel, his seeping wounds left little yellow stains; something else to clean up. "*Maybe* a bachelor," he conceded, since he knew more of the world now. As a child, he'd never figured his sister could be seduced by a married man. But he hadn't been a child since . . . forever.

Whoever had seduced his sister had destroyed their lives, seen his father killed, reduced Laramie himself to . . . this.

And the bastard had gotten away with it for too long.

Laramie's hands didn't falter as he bandaged his wounds with more rags from the saddlebag. He could handle wounds almost as well as weapons by now; it was people who gave him trouble. How did a man go about exhuming secrets from over ten years ago without revealing his own?

Ask questions, he reckoned. Talk to people. But—

A light knock at the bunkhouse door caught him by surprise. He spun, dropping the end of a bandage to flare his left hand—then clenched a fist to keep from going for his revolver when he saw who peeked in the doorway.

A girl. No . . . a *lady*.

"Oh!" Seeing that he wasn't wholly dressed, she

9

spun away and covered her eyes. "Golly. I should have waited for you to say 'come in.' "

Laramie didn't know how to answer that, so instead he quickly finished binding his shoulder, using his teeth to hold one end of the bandage as he tightened the knot with the other. A lady shouldn't be here at all.

This had to be one of the daughters. He could tell that much by the cut and yoke of her yellow calico dress and the ruffled white apron she wore over it. She'd tied the apron in a big bow, the ends of which trailed down from her waist like rivulets of water, running into and out of the bright folds of her skirt. He could tell by the neat way she wore her hair up, despite the dark-brown curls of hair that trickled across her ears and the bare nape of her neck. Laramie had seen nice girls before—bosses' daughters, or hired girls—but never this close. Proper married women, yes, but not young ladies. He sure hadn't spoken to them.

And even if he were better with words, he felt odd— his throat tight, his skin prickly—just looking at this girl's neck. She looked so . . . *clean!*

"I brought some salves," spoke the lady toward the door, and lifted a pail with one hand. "And some of my mother's soup. I wasn't sure what was wrong with you."

What was wrong . . . He pushed his arms back into the sleeves of his union suit, started fumbling buttons into place. When his gaze drifted downward again, to where the lady's apron ties dipped in and out of her skirt's flounces, even more of him felt tight and prickly. It embarrassed him.

The last thing Laramie was, was clean.

The lady peeked over her shoulder, her eyes quick, her lashes dark. Fingers still on his union suit, Laramie felt himself flush to be caught staring.

"Aren't you going to put on your shirt?" she prompted. "I can hardly ask you questions like that."

Questions? At least that explained why she would have wanted to help him. Laramie scooped a clean shirt out of his saddlebag, tugged it on—and missed his sleeve on the first try. "What questions?"

"Are you decent?" She'd turned away again.

"No." He was still tucking.

She started talking anyway.

"Well, first off, I was going to ask if you were all right. I saw how stiffly you moved, like maybe you'd hurt yourself. That's why I brought the salves and the soup. Here." She put the pail on a shelf by the doorway.

He guessed he should thank her, except that she had no business in the bunkhouse. Even *he* knew that much.

"Then I figured on asking your name," she continued, still speaking toward the door as Laramie finished tucking. "Since Papa didn't tell me that. I'm Victoria Garrison, by the way. Sometimes my family calls me Vic."

When he still said nothing, she peeked over her shoulder again. Luckily, this time he was decent.

Fully dressed, anyhow.

She turned to face him. "So what's your name?"

"Laramie." Some folks knew it for an alias as soon as they heard it. All Victoria Garrison said was, "What's your first name?"

He didn't like this. He didn't like the risk of being alone with the boss's daughter. He didn't like that she'd seen his bandages—so much for hiding his injuries from Garrison. He didn't like how odd he felt at the sight of her skirt's flare or her bare neck, and he didn't like anything distracting him from what he'd come here to do.

Even if he wasn't quite sure how to do it.

11

He'd given her a handle to hang on him. She was rude to demand more. And yet, when she smiled with encouragement, he couldn't drum up enough energy for annoyance. All his energy was going into the prickly, tight feelings.

The lady had pretty eyes. Gray, if the shadows of the bunkhouse weren't fooling him. Laramie liked how her lips turned when she ducked her head to slant a smile up at him, as if to be less threatening that way.

Not that a little thing like her had to duck.

"Some—" He cleared his throat. "Some folks call me Ross." It had once been Draz, but his parents wanted him to sound American. Since almost before he could remember, he'd been Ross—except sometimes to his momma. Draz had died years ago, not long after his father, his brother, his sister. It was Laramie who stood there with water dripping off his hair and onto the collar and shoulders of his shirt.

"Pleased to meet you, Ross Laramie," said Miss Garrison brightly. Unsure how to answer her, he just nodded. They shouldn't be here together, but since she blocked the door, he wasn't sure how to get out . . . unless it was to dive through one of the bunkhouse's six windows.

Stalling, he strapped on his gunbelt. Normally he would check his rounds, but it seemed unnecessarily threatening in front of a lady.

"Welcome to the Circle-T," she went on cheerfully. "I've already guessed that Papa hired you. Is it because of the rustlers?"

Laramie squinted at her. She knew about the rustlers?

"I saw the steer," she explained, while he slid a knife into his boot. "At first I couldn't understand why you and Papa would pen it, since it looks fine—not sick, anyway. Then I noticed the brand. I *think* it's a brand. It almost looks like the steer had a Circle-T and doesn't anymore, although how a person would erase a brand I have no idea. I'd think a rustler would just put a new brand over the old one. Though really, what design would fit over a Circle-T? If it were just a bar, that would be one thing, though I guess that's why not many ranchers use just a bar. But a T is uneven already, and when you put it in a circle . . ." She shook her head. "But this isn't even that. It's like it's erased. That's what I can't figure out."

Laramie wasn't staring at the gentle flare of the lady's skirt anymore, or even other, less proper curves. He found himself watching her mouth. He'd never heard so many words come so quickly out of one mouth.

She widened her pretty gray eyes, and he guessed she'd meant that last to be a question. His brain lurched back into motion like a spurred horse.

"Blotted," he offered.

She blinked. "Pardon?"

Laramie swallowed. Now she wanted an explanation—about changing brands? He should have said nothing at all. But she cocked her head and looked so interested . . .

"Brand 'em through a piece of wool blanket," he explained. "Wet one. Blots over the old brand."

"Really?" She considered that. "It's not particularly convincing, is it?"

It was when *he* did it. Likely this rustler got interrupted, or distracted. Nobody who regularly botched a job like the one on that steer could be doing enough damage that Jacob Garrison would hire himself a range detective.

Laramie wouldn't have said all that even if he could, though. Neither did he offer that any brand could be changed by a man skilled enough with a running iron, who was hungry enough for easy cash. Heck, he could think of three possible counterfeits for Circle-T right

13

off. But it was better that people not know the extent of his education on the topic.

"I should leave," he said, pushing his belongings into the chest at the foot of the bare bunk, hoping she would head out first. Not that he really needed this job. But he preferred to stay in one piece until he did what he'd come to do—and Jacob Garrison didn't seem the type to tolerate a man philandering with his daughters.

"Don't forget the salves," she offered. Drawing a mason jar of what looked like soup from the pail beside her, she then offered the pail to him.

Laramie risked stepping closer to her, long enough to take the pail and add it to his chest of belongings, then shut the lid. It was a rare ranch hand who would poke into another man's things. Short-lived, too.

"Got to head out to work, huh?" she asked, stepping outside. But she waited for him, holding the door open. "What is it you're doing for Papa, anyhow?"

He picked up his rifle. "Working."

She narrowed her eyes at his cryptic answer, though with apparent good humor. "Well, I hope you enjoy it here. It's probably pretty different from Texas."

He stopped beside her and narrowed his eyes down at her. *Texas?* She was wrong—but disarmingly close.

She smiled delightedly up at him, as if he'd greeted her announcement with praise instead of suspicion. "You've got a Texas saddle," she explained. "Not that you couldn't have bought it off someone, but your hat has a Mexican look to it, too. And your spurs. Definitely Spanish."

It occurred to Laramie that Victoria Garrison saw a lot more than she should. The pretty little lady might prove dangerous, and not just to his composure.

It didn't help that he could smell her, she stood so close. She smelled as clean and warm as she looked, like cinnamon and Chinese-laundry soap. Maybe this was why men made such a fuss about women. Since it was usually about whores, Laramie had never fully understood the draw. Money bought little more than a brief pleasure that hardly seemed worth the smell, sweat, and embarrassment. Now, standing this close to a neat, shiny-haired lady who'd even smiled at him, he wondered if some fellows pretended that instead of a whore, they were with . . .

His body felt more than tight, and he had to get away from this particular lady, *now*!

He wasn't clean. He wasn't decent. And there was still the chance he might have to kill her father.

"Stay away from me, Miss Garrison," he warned, and her upturned eyes widened. He noticed again just how small she seemed beside him, the top of her head barely reaching his breastbone, and yet how curvy she was. He didn't like that she looked scared of him, even if it *would* keep her away.

But he didn't like a lot of things. "Please."

"Oh." She blinked, regaining her composure so quickly that it unnerved him. He was armed, and a stranger . . . and a killer. She should probably be at least a *little* scared. "I'll try. My apologies for intruding. Here."

He suddenly found a jar of soup in his left hand.

"Good day, Mr. Laramie," said Miss Garrison, and— glancing both ways as if to make sure nobody had seen her here—she strode away, her skirt swinging with her enthusiasm.

She took her soap-and-cinnamon smell with her.

Laramie felt unnerved—and strangely relieved that she'd not called him Ross.

Chapter Two

"Then he said to stay away from him," complained Victoria three days later, typesetting at the *Sheridan Herald.* Her friend Evangeline Taylor, reading Vic's editor's story, passed over metal type from a partitioned case. Vic slid the letters into an open-sided composing stick, holding them in place with her thumb. Whenever she finished a line of type, she transferred it into the press's chase, or frame. "Flat out. Except for the please."

And after I brought him soup.

Evangeline glanced nervously toward the newspaper's owner and editor, Mr. L. E. Day, clacking away on his typewriting machine across the room. He often allowed Evangeline to help, as long as she used the back door. He said it gave Victoria someone to talk to who wasn't him. Evangeline took that to mean he did not like his and Victoria's conversations, but slim, pale Evangeline worried too much.

"He was fascinating, though," Vic remembered. "Not Mr. Day—he can't hear us anyway. Mr. Laramie." Even without the wounds, which she hadn't mentioned, the man would have intrigued her. Something about his taut stillness put her in mind of the air before a storm.

Evangeline turned her silent concern to Victoria.

"Not that kind of fascinating," insisted Vic with a laugh, pausing to make sure a *b* wasn't an *r* before she continued adding on letters to form the word *Robbers.*

Not that Ross Laramie wasn't handsome, in his tall, black-haired, *dangerous* way. His face had seemed to be all angles, from the sweep of his eyebrows to his sharp nose and long jaw. His mouth had looked hard, set. And his hooded eyes . . . Well, if eyes were the window to one's soul, Victoria wasn't sure she should open those windows. She had a feeling they led to a haunted place.

But Laramie certainly didn't make her smile or blush, or anything else Evangeline should worry about. Vic knew better than to go sweet on a stranger, much less one who could buckle on a heavy gunbelt without once looking at it—like it was part of him.

Very low, lest Mr. Day hear over his typewriting, Evangeline said, "He doesn't sound very proper." And she handed Victoria a three-em spacer and a lowercase *s.*

Proper? Victoria remembered Mr. Laramie's bandages and how she'd managed to catch sight of them. She wished she hadn't turned away in such quick mortification. How many chances would she have to see a man's naked chest? "He's proper enough for Papa to hire. I just wish I knew for sure what he's hired on *as.* He seems to stay separate from the other hands."

Evangeline's eyes widened. "You've been watching him?"

"No more than I have anybody else. Practically. Anyway, I still think he's a range detective."

"Like that awful Idaho Johnson?"

"He couldn't be a bad man. Papa wouldn't hire one." Victoria finished typesetting the line, confirmed with a glance that Mr. Day wanted it separate from further text, then slid in a piece of wood furniture. At Evangeline's look she repeated, "I said, I'm not that kind of fascinated." She paused. "Although really, I think after Mariah and Laurel, I could probably take up with an outlaw and Papa wouldn't be surprised."

Her father had not wholly approved of her older sisters' choices in husbands.

"He would still mind," insisted Evangeline solemnly.

Vic sighed. "I suppose he would." Running a finger along the type, with its reversed lettering, she frowned, then read it.

Robbers Still at Large.

Sitting there in her leather printer's apron, she shivered. She loved that feeling, as if in the midst of a pile of confusing puzzle pieces she'd suddenly glimpsed a hint, just a little color or shape, of something that might make sense. "May I see that story for a moment?"

Evangeline gave her the typewritten sheet, and Victoria quickly skimmed Mr. Day's article. This seemed to be the summer for train robbery; just the previous week, the Colorado Southern had been held up in New Mexico. But the outlaws Mr. Day referenced had robbed the Union Pacific Overland Flyer more than a month earlier, right here in Wyoming. Despite the biggest manhunt in Wyoming history, no suspects had been captured.

If the famous Miss Nellie Bly lived in Wyoming— and if the lady reporter hadn't given up her writing career to marry—this was the sort of mystery at which she would have excelled. The writer had gotten herself locked up in an insane asylum to expose the horror within its walls. She'd traveled around the world, beating a fictional eighty-day record. Victoria could only imagine to what lengths Miss Bly would have gone to uncover train robbers.

Greater lengths than Vic herself ever would.

Still, there could be nothing dangerous about a little investigation from the safety of the *Sheridan Herald*!

"Mr. Day?" she called. "Do you have a description of the bandits suspected in the Wilcox robbery?"

Her employer didn't stop typing on his marvelous machine. "The June twenty-fifth *New York Herald* published pictures."

Wyoming's bandits were even big news in New York City?

"You don't think . . . ," whispered Evangeline, while Victoria went to shelves stacked high with various newspapers from the previous month.

"No!" But Vic still relished the excitement of digging until she found the right one. "Papa wouldn't hire a train robber. I just want to—"

Make sure Papa wouldn't hire a train robber?

"—to know more," she finished, turning pages. New York City certainly did put out larger papers than Sheridan, Wyoming, did! "Here."

And she read the descriptions of the suspected outlaws, a "wild bunch from Brown's Park," including Flat-Nosed George Curry, the Roberts brothers, the Sundance Kid, and—

"Buck Cassidy?" That didn't sound quite right.

"They must have gotten it wrong," murmured Evangeline.

The newspaper had printed drawings of several of the outlaws, based on prison photographs. Victoria felt more relieved than maybe she should have that none of the pictures or descriptions matched Mr. Laramie: The only man described as "tall" was the Sundance Kid, and he was apparently fair-haired. In fact, many of the bad men seemed to have a history of horse theft or rustling.

As an enemy of cattle rustlers, didn't that make Ross Laramie the opposite of these desperadoes?

"Customer," called Mr. Day. Since he supplemented the newspaper's income by doing printing jobs, another of Victoria's responsibilities was that of a shop girl.

She looked up as the door opened and actually gasped.

It was Laramie himself!

He stood there, almost too tall for the door, and surveyed the room. His clothes were dark for this time of year. He was not wearing a gunbelt, but then, carrying firearms was illegal within the city limits. Victoria noticed a slight bulge on his lower leg, under his dungarees, which made her think he was still wearing his boot knife. He looked contained, in control . . . until his hooded gaze, sliding across the room, tripped over her.

He didn't know I would be here, she thought.

Only belatedly, with pressed lips and a ducked head, did he take off his hat. His hair wasn't wet this time, but it was still very black.

"May we help you?" called Mr. Day, glancing in confusion toward Victoria. As her boss's words drew Laramie's attention, Victoria took action.

"Move that paper," she hissed to Evangeline.

"What?"

"The one about the R-O-B-B—" Victoria stopped spelling to smile innocently when Ross Laramie's gaze darted back to her. Luckily, she heard the sound of a newspaper being rapidly folded behind her.

Not that she thought Laramie was in any way involved.

The man blinked, as if momentarily disoriented by

her smile. Then he swung his attention back to Mr. Day. "You keep old papers?"

"Ours, or other folks'?" Mr. Day grinned. Then, maybe because of Laramie's expression, his smile weakened. "We've got everything from '86 on. Why do you ask?"

"Can . . . ?" Laramie looked down at the plank floor, scowling. Victoria noticed that his left hand was working nervously. At least it wasn't his gun hand—was it? Although his head was down, his eyes slid back up. "Anyone read 'em?"

"Yes, indeed! Miss Garrison?"

Laramie's head swung toward her.

"Yes?" Victoria quickly went to them, rolling more questions through her mind. Why would he want old papers? How old? What about?

"Would you please assist this gentleman . . ." Mr. Day hesitated. "I'm sorry, sir. I didn't catch your name."

"Laramie," said Vic's father's new hand, his eyes narrow.

Mr. Day raised his eyebrows. "Miss Garrison, perhaps I should assist in Mr. Laramie's search myself."

Him? The first time she truly *wanted* to do assistant duties, and Mr. Day meant to take over? "Don't be silly, sir," she insisted, catching a startled Mr. Laramie by the hand. It was slim and hard and warm. "I'd be delighted to help him. He works for my father, you know."

"He . . . ?" Mr. Day looked from her to Laramie and back.

"We're friends," insisted Vic, hoping it was true, and tugged gently on the stranger's hand. Her *friend's* hand, she corrected silently. "And you have that editorial to finish writing."

She noticed peripherally how startled Evangeline looked. Mr. Laramie hid it better, but he seemed startled too. Still, he followed her toward the cabinets.

She couldn't wait to see what he wanted to read.

She was holding his hand.

Until Victoria Garrison's small, warm, ink-smudged fingers captured his own, Laramie had mainly been thinking that he should have known better than to visit a newspaper office. Now he wasn't thinking at all.

Why was a lady like her holding his hand? Why had she called him her friend?

It took him a moment to see past her brown curls, pretty face, and clear gray eyes, to think past her touch and the smell of soap and cinnamon and ink, for him to understand. She was lying to get her way.

He relaxed some. Suddenly Miss Garrison did not seem quite so removed. Laramie felt a strange tightness in his cheek and realized that he'd almost smiled.

He also let her draw him toward the back of the room, nowhere near as reluctantly as he should. Then she asked, "What date are you looking for?"

And he remembered that he should have known better.

In trying to decide how to pursue his old vengeance, Laramie had thought, with something close to surprise, to attempt everyday routes of investigation first. Hearing another cowboy read from a newspaper the other night had suggested to him one route. Back when the crimes first took place, he had not exactly been reading about the murders.

He'd been sitting in jail for committing one of them.

Still, if he'd known he would find Miss Garrison at the *Sheridan Herald,* he would never have taken the chance. She looked sweet in her oversized leather apron, a smudge of ink across her otherwise clean cheek. The strings that tied her heavy, stained smock played in the folds of today's pressed blue calico dress, just as he remembered. Over only a few days, he'd remembered that sight often.

He'd forgotten to remember his questions.

What date was he looking for? November 1888. But he wasn't about to say that, and in a flash of cleverness, he realized how he could keep his secret. "What year did the train come through?"

Of all the growth that Sheridan had seen since his childhood, the train seemed the biggest.

Miss Garrison paused, clearly disappointed. "The train?"

He looked patiently down at her—if jail taught a man anything, it was patience—and found that he very much wanted to wipe away the smudge on her cheek. With his bare finger. He clenched his fist, the one not in her hand, instead.

The other girl, tall and pale, cleared her throat. Laramie noticed her attention move meaningfully from their still-clasped hands back to Miss Victoria herself. He let go, too reluctantly. "I like trains," he explained.

Was it his imagination, or did her eyes widen at that? She looked away quickly enough. "The railroad came through Sheridan seven years ago, Mr. Laramie, in 1892," she said, and turned to one of a whole set of cabinets that lined the back wall. "We'll find enough written about it to keep you reading all afternoon."

He watched her open a drawer and made note of how the papers seemed to be organized. If that drawer was 1892, then one above it would likely be the drawer he wanted.

"Don't—" he insisted when she lifted a third newspaper out of the drawer.

She looked up at him, more flushed and bright-eyed than seemed necessary. He liked how she waited for him to frame his words. "Don't take them all out," he managed. "I can get more as I need them, yes?"

She put the papers onto a table by the cabinets and gestured to a stool. "Certainly. But you'll ask for assistance if you need further help, won't you?"

He considered that, considered the girl with the smudged cheek. "What are friends for?"

She blushed.

Laramie liked how the pink tones warmed her lively face. He liked standing this close to her, feeling tight and prickly. He liked that she'd recognized him, liked her saying his name. Then he remembered how dangerous liking anybody and anything could be.

Better the hardness, the anger that he'd carried in him since well before the train came to Sheridan. That anger was his friend. It kept him alive. It reminded him of his promise—and that meant not letting Miss Victoria Garrison or anybody else know who he was. So he turned away from her and sat at the table, looked at the first paper, then looked up. She hadn't left.

"May I ask you something, Mr. Laramie?"

He knew it might be trouble, but he nodded.

"What connection is there between the railroad and whatever you're doing for my father?"

Of course, this had nothing to do with the job he'd been hired for. But all Laramie said was, "It's secret."

The way her eyes brightened at the word "secret" told him his mistake. But it was too late.

"Well, enjoy your reading," she said. Then she went back to her counter, by the monstrosity of a printing press, and picked up what looked like a small wooden box. The blond girl, after some hesitation, began handing her bits of metal and Miss Garrison, with one last smile for him, began sliding them into the box.

Friends?

Laramie felt the tightness in his cheek again. Then he looked at the table in front of him and knew how little he wanted to read about the railroad coming through Sheridan.

Still, if he was anything, it was patient.

He waited almost half an hour before he stood, went back to the drawers, and put away the papers Miss Garrison had retrieved for him. Then, hoping his body would block his choice from prying eyes, he tried another drawer, then another, and found the dates he wanted.

The ones he sought, anyway.

Nobody would *want* to be reminded of November 1888.

Chapter Three

If Ross's father had not been clever, they never would have reached the West. So many immigrants from old-world villages had set out for the Land of Opportunity that Americans had coined a derogatory word for them—*Bohunks,* short for Bohemian-Hungarians. It didn't matter that many were from neither Bohemia nor Hungary. Not to the Americans, who figured that one Eastern European peasant was the same as another. Not to the immigrants, many of whom started new lives by forgetting old ones. And not to the factory representatives who met them at the docks, speaking their language and offering jobs and places to live.

Most of the newcomers, overwhelmed by the confusion that was New York City, clung to such familiarity and generosity. Ross's poppa did not.

Ross's poppa, Josip Lauranovic, had educated himself. He spoke some English, and he could do math. He insisted on understanding American money and law before signing his family into such wondrous employment. From what Ross had since learned about the factory slums in New York and Chicago, that wariness had very likely saved all their lives.

Extended them, anyway.

Instead of slaving in a slaughterhouse or mill for inhuman hours at cruel wages, the Lauranovic family found enough employment to save pennies and educate the children as Americans—Filip, Julije, and Drazen became Philip, Julia, and Ross. By 1884, the family called themselves "Laurence," leaving off the telltale "itch" sound at the end. Joseph Laurence filed for a homestead in what was then part of Johnson County, near the new town of Sheridan. And like most people in Wyoming, they'd tried raising cattle.

They'd started small, although Poppa had the usual dreams of profiting from the beef bonanza. He'd recognized the signs of a bad winter the year of the Big Die-Up. Because of his foresight, the Laurence family's losses were slight and the next year saw them on their way to real success.

The kind of success that won them enemies.

Blinking out of his memories, Laramie stared down at the paper in front of him. *RUSTLERS LYNCHED!* proclaimed the headline, and he did not want to read it. At that moment, he wanted to do almost anything else—take another bullet, dance in public, kiss Victoria Garrison in front of her threatening father—except read that newspaper article.

At that last unexpected thought, Laramie slid his gaze toward the lady. She was still working with the wooden frame and the metal bits, dwarfed by her canvas apron. Sunlight through the plate-glass window reflected off motes of dust, surrounding her in golden sparkles. Her curling brown hair reflected the sunlight

27

back in twists of copper. He was starting to think he'd never seen so pretty a girl.

And she'd held his hand!

But she lived in that sweet, white-with-blue-shutters ranch house—in a whole other world from Laramie's. If she went to the sheriff complaining of a crime against *her* family, people would believe her. If she were discovered doing something that looked illegal . . .

Damn it, he might as well read about that night. He could never forget it—and yet he still wasn't sure who, in the end, was most to blame. This article might offer names or information that Laramie—having been young, confused, and imprisoned at the time—could not have known. And if not . . .

He did not know what to do if this didn't work, but he would think of something. He'd thought of this.

Pained by more than his still-healing bullet wounds, Laramie began to read:

RUSTLERS LYNCHED!

The foothills outside of town became a place of death Thursday night when rustlers who have been terrorizing the open range for several years were captured and brought to vigilante justice. According to Sheriff Howe, he received information about the outlaws from a leading member of the community who asked to remain anonymous; and a posse, largely composed of ranchers, including Boris and Bram Ward, Hayden Nelson, Jacob Garrison, Colonel and Alden Wright, rode into the perilous foothills to see justice done.

The men split into two forces to better cover ground. The group including the Wrights, the Wards, Nelson, and Deputy Butler got the drop on the stock thieves in a small box-canyon before the desperadoes could escape.

To the surprise of all, the rustlers were themselves local ranchers—the so-called "Joseph Laurence" and his sons. The immigrant family, whose real name is Lauranovic, had earlier brought unfounded complaints of rustling to the sheriff. Now, with proof of the Lauranovics' crime surrounding them—including running irons and stolen cattle, many from the Wards' Lost Pines ranch—the enraged posse took the law into its own hands, lynching first the father and then the older brother. The younger boy might have met the same fate but, instead, the night saw further tragedy. During the lynching of his seventeen-year-old brother, Phil, the youngest Lauranovic grabbed a rifle, shot Boris Ward, and held the group at bay before the rest of the posse arrived and negotiated his safe passage to jail. The Big Horn Mountains would see no more vigilante justice that night.

The twelve-year-old outlaw, formerly known as Ross, is actually named Drazen Lauranovic. He is being held in the town jail for cattle rustling and attempted murder. The head rustler, Mr. Lauranovic, is also survived by a widow and one daughter.

Boris Ward, whose only crime was protecting his livelihood, is not expected to live through the week. There will be a prayer service for him at the church tonight as the town unites in its support of this well-respected member of the community.

Laramie wasn't sure at what point he stopped reading the article and instead began to stare across the room. He was remembering that little box-canyon in the pale light of a full moon, the hiding place for all that stolen stock. He was seeing the Lost Pines brand on the hip of a rangy longhorn in front of him, smelling acrid, burning hair as he used a wet piece of wool blanket to blot the changed brand back to his family's own Double Mountain mark. He'd felt angry that night, at the Wards' blatant theft of his family's cattle and at Sheriff Howe for doing nothing about it. And he'd been uneasy because his older sister had wheedled him into describing their hideout. Julie had been acting oddly for some time, confiding to him that she was in love with a man who would, she said, put them in a big house, buy her pretty clothes, "make everything better."

As if Ross had cared about love and such. He'd cared only about getting their cattle back. But it had been important to her.

He heard a rock skitter down the arroyo wall, heard Deputy Butler demanding that Ross drop the hot iron and step away from the steer. Then he'd felt afraid.

Ross hadn't known what to do until his poppa gently repeated the deputy's request. "Do what they tell you, Drazen," Poppa had murmured, calm and clever even yet. "This is America. The truth will come out at our trial. Look at all our proof."

So Ross had obeyed. He'd dropped the running iron and backed away from the fire until a large man grabbed him and twisted his arms behind his back. When he'd cried out, his older brother had tried to lunge to his rescue, but two more men grabbed him. More of them aimed guns at Poppa as they stepped nearer, pawing him. As if Ross's poppa would hide weapons!

It was Boris Ward, the rancher who'd been stealing their cattle all along, who said, "Stupid Bohunks. What makes you think you deserve a trial?"

Only then did Ross notice the rope being slung over a tree branch. At that moment it seemed as if not just a handful of men but all of Sheridan, all of Wyoming, all of the United States of America, had turned against them.

30

*   *   *

Laramie blinked, startled from his memories by . . . a woman? Victoria Garrison was watching him from across the room, her head cocked in concern.

How long had she been doing that without him knowing it? Would he have returned to himself if she'd approached, or were the memories destroying even his long-developed survival instincts?

As his eyes focused on her and the present once more, she mouthed, *Are you all right?*

It was the second time she'd asked that. How long had it been since anyone cared if he was "all right"? Not since he'd watched his life destroyed. And now, if he had to—

No, he would not imagine destroying her happy world while remembering the end of his. Instead he blinked, then nodded at her. He did not try to smile.

She looked unconvinced, but turned back to her work.

Laramie cupped his jaw with a hand, leaned on his good elbow, and knew he hadn't been all right in years. He'd watched his father and brother bound, watched them pushed up onto horses, watched the nooses draped over their heads, first Poppa, then Phil. He'd screamed and screamed, sometimes words, sometimes sheer anguish, but the posse had not stopped. He'd watched the horses bolt and the bodies drop; watched his father and brother dangling and kicking and soiling themselves. And he'd heard laughter.

Later, people had said the Lauranovic boy did it to keep from hanging. But at that moment, Ross could not have cared less whether he lived or died. What he'd wanted, needed with every beat of his wounded heart, was to save his family. Part of him already knew it was too late, but that part was no longer in control. He'd squirmed loose of hard, gripping fingers and he'd grabbed Deputy Butler's shotgun—not a rifle, as reported, but a double-barreled shotgun—and he'd made them slowly, finally stop laughing.

At that moment, a shotgun held in his shaking young hands against half a dozen armed killers, Ross had found a power he would never, never forget.

"Cut them down," he'd said, and when the men just stared at him, he'd raised his voice. "Cut them down!"

And at that, old man Ward—Boris, not his bully of a son—said, "Sonny boy, they's already dead and in hell, where they belong." And he'd laughed again.

So Ross shot him.

He'd set the shotgun against his shoulder, and he'd pointed it, and he'd squeezed the first barrel's trigger slow and gentle, just like Phil had taught him. It spat out a dreadful explosion, and kicked something awful, but Ward stopped laughing. The rancher's chest darkened wetly, and he crumpled onto the rock-strewn ground in the moonlight and the firelight.

And it had felt good.

That's when Ross guessed he really became a killer, because although he should have regretted taking another man's life, that moment freed him. It wouldn't save his poppa or his brother. It might not even save him. But he hadn't been scared anymore after that.

At that moment he'd wanted to kill all of them. He longed to shoot them, one after another. He knew it would feel good, better than anything he'd ever known.

If only he'd had more than one round left.

God only knew what he might have done if he'd gotten hold of a thirteen-round carbine instead of a shotgun.

He'd aimed at Bram Ward, who'd dropped to his knees beside his gunshot father, his face crumpling in horror. Then he saw that the man was crying.

The full-grown bully was crying because Ross had shot his father, and all Ross could do was point that shotgun and *want* to kill them all—not looking at the bodies still swinging from the tree branch—until he'd heard horses approaching and knew he was losing his chance.

The rest of the posse arrived then. Later, people would say that Ross surrendered to Sheriff Howe because Howe had promised him a fair trial. He had not. Ross had surrendered to Jacob Garrison, because Garrison—looking over the carnage in the box canyon—had done two things right.

First, he'd shaken his head at the sight of the two hanging bodies.

Then he'd looked at Ross and said, "You don't want to do this." Somehow, as the moment passed, the rancher had been right. Ross might be a killer—but it had been a momentary bloodlust.

Even back then, Garrison was considered a stand-up man. So Ross had given him a small, frightened nod. The rancher had crossed the canyon to where the boy stood, walking right into the line of fire. And when he'd held out a leather-gloved hand, Ross had given him the shotgun.

The rest of the posse had started to surge in on them then, but Garrison had spun, the shotgun upraised. "Promised a trial," he'd drawled firmly.

Some of the others had protested, especially Bram Ward. "He killed my pa!" the bully screamed, pointing his own rifle at both Ross and the cattle baron.

But Garrison didn't flinch. He merely said, "An' you kilt his. Built the jail and courthouse for a reason."

Ross had ended up with his hands tied, mounted on the horse that had helped hang Phil, taken to jail to await trial. He hadn't cared what happened to him after that.

A whole lot of other people had, though.

Of course, he'd been locked up, alone, for three days before he learned that he hadn't been deserted—

the sheriff just wasn't letting his momma in. He'd found out when Garrison's wife marched into the jail and said: "Mrs. Lauranovic says you won't allow her to visit her son, but I assured her that our sheriff could not be so unjust and irrational. Do not tell me I was wrong."

So Momma was allowed in. She'd reached through the bars of the cell to hold him, kiss him, cry onto him. Poor boy. Why had his poppa done this to them? Had Philip died quickly? Julia would not come from her room since hearing the news. Someone had thrown stones through their windows.

Momma was so frightened, she hadn't even asked if he was all right. Few people had since, either, until . . .

Laramie shook his head, sneaked a glance toward Victoria Garrison, and thought, *She resembles her mother.* Then he made himself go back to the newspapers.

He could torment himself with mere memories anytime.

Boy Held for Trial, announced one article. It only gave what the ranchers said was the truth.

Sheridan Mourns Boris Ward, read another, and in smaller print, *Drazen Lauranovic Charged with Murder.*

He remembered. People had quickly forgotten that his family was American. They wanted the villains to be foreign. Ross—despite having no accent and few memories before his family's arrival on American shores—had not corrected them. Clearly, his family wasn't American. Not American enough for justice, anyway.

All he had to do was look at the papers to be reminded.

Mob Demands Lauranovic Boy, reported another headline. Laramie remembered little of that frightening night, the shouts, the stones. The sheriff facing down the angry crowd.

Four pages in from that he found *State Prisons Unfit*

for Children, an editorial by Mrs. Elizabeth Garrison, which seemed to have prompted later letters of outrage that she would call a murderer a child. Then came another editorial—*Self-Defense Isn't Murder*—resulting in even more fury and, to Ross's surprise, a few lonesome letters agreeing with her.

It made sense. The only reason he'd finally gotten justice was Mrs. Garrison. The cattle baron's wife, despite carrying another baby under her apron, had for some reason adopted his cause and hired him an excellent young lawyer, all the way from Chicago. Ross had overheard the sheriff and the deputy talking, so he knew it wasn't the cattle baron himself who'd done all that. "Says she has her own money," Howe had snorted. "Can't say as I'd let *my* wife have her own money. Even if she did, I wouldn't let her make a fool of me and the town with it."

At the time, Ross had seen the woman as a goddess, an avenging angel. He'd been too young to question motives. Now he had to wonder.

Not here, he told himself, glancing across the room.

The headlines told the story. *Trial Starts Today.* Then, *Witnesses Admit to Lynching.* And later, *Darrow Argues Self-Defense for Drazen.*

But then had come the worst blow of all.

He'd woken in jail to someone brokenly calling his name from the alley outside his high window. To see out, he'd had to draw himself up by the bars—and there in the night shadows stood his sister Julie.

He hadn't seen her since his arrest, not at the jail, not at the trial. Now he barely recognized her. Her dark hair was a tangle. Her dress hung loose and wrinkled on her, and smelled sour. Meager light reflected off her wet, swollen cheeks.

"Ross." Her voice sounded worn. "Ross, I'm sorry."

"Julie?"

"I'm sorry," she repeated. "I'm so sorry. It's all my

35

fault. I killed them—Phil and Poppa. Oh God."

"What—?"

"I told him," she insisted. "He said he wanted to help, that when we married you'd be his family too. He said he had to know where you took our cattle, so I told him—but he didn't help! He *didn't*. And now Poppa and Phil are dead and he won't see me. Ross, he won't even talk to me!"

At first he simply hadn't understood. "Who? Julie, what's wrong?"

She covered her face with her hands, so that he could see only the top of her head and had to strain to hear her.

"He said he loved me." Her shoulders shuddered. "He loved me and he would help. Now he won't talk to me, and his family has threatened me if I don't stay away. He never loved me at all." She began to sob outright, her voice filled with devastation. "He just wanted Poppa. He just wanted Poppa, and Phil, and you, all for some stupid cows. And I gave you to him. God help me, *Draz.* . . ."

By then he had begun to understand, even at twelve, and horror was rapidly loosening his grip on the window bars. His horror and mounting fury had needed only direction. "Julie, who? *Who?*"

She'd backed away then, shaking her head, her arms sliding down to hug her middle. Her next words came out a soggy squeak, her eyes closed, her face dripping. "I'm so sorry, *Draz.* I'm so sorry I killed Poppa. . . ."

Then she'd turned and staggered back up the alley.

"WHO?" Ross had screamed. *"Julije,* who was it?"

But she didn't come back to tell him. And two days later—well, the newspaper in front of Laramie said it all:

RUSTLER'S DAUGHTER SUICIDE!

She'd hanged herself. Ross wondered if she'd been

mimicking Poppa's and Phil's deaths. He knew her guilt—guilt like a blow, like a fall, like a scream choking the throat. He knew because Julije had told her lover their secrets, but Ross had told them to her. If she'd helped kill Poppa and Phil, he'd killed them and her, both. Them, her, and the baby that the undertaker said she was carrying.

He'd barely noticed the trial going on around him after that. He'd barely cared that his excellent lawyer had gotten him paroled to a special boy's ranch down in Texas. When his mother stopped answering his letters, not three months later, he hadn't hesitated to break his parole to go find her—only to discover that, lost without her family, she'd left town and all but vanished.

He'd never found her. Finally, a fugitive from justice, he'd taken up with men who admired his ability with cattle and a running iron, men who taught him guns and anger, and he'd comforted himself every night with one thought: Of six fearful, ignorant men who had killed Poppa and Phil, only one had forged those deaths—his sister's lover. And that man deserved vengeance.

Sometimes Laramie believed that was the only reason he'd survived: to avenge his family, once and for all.

His instincts had not entirely deserted him. When Victoria Garrison stood and started toward him, Laramie caught the edge of another newspaper and smoothly turned it over the ones he'd been reading.

Butch Cassidy's face stared up at him.

It wasn't a very good likeness.

Miss Garrison arrived in a whisper of petticoats and curvy innocence. "Are you finding everything you want?"

With him sitting and her standing, his eyes were at

a discourteous level to her smock-covered bodice. He realized how badly he hurt—in new ways now. If he leaned forward, he could rest his head against her front. He could wrap his arms around her, borrow softness from her just for a while, just to rest for a little while from all life's hardness. The thought of it made his throat ache.

Before he could force an answer, she stiffened. Had she read his thoughts? Had he done something rude?

"Miss Garrison?" asked Laramie, but she said nothing.

She was staring at the newspaper with its picture of a misnamed "Buck" Cassidy. Butch would hate it that his very picture could frighten ladies.

"Are you all right?" Laramie asked.

With a quick breath, she turned her face back to him. Smiling. "I'm fine! Why wouldn't I be? I only meant to say that if you don't find what you want, Mr. Laramie, just let me know. I'm very good at finding things. Ask anybody in Sheridan."

She was lying about being fine, but he feared that her ability at finding things—more aptly, finding them *out*—was pure truth.

"Thank you," he said softly. "No." He relaxed some when she smiled at him again, more honestly, before retreating back to her work. But only some.

At least it gave him a chance to move the recent paper aside, to focus again on the older, darker story.

"He was rich," he muttered to himself, moving his lips more than adding voice. "A rancher, maybe. A bachelor."

His family has threatened me if I don't stay away . . .

"*Maybe* a bachelor."

Bram Ward had been a bachelor, of course, but he hadn't been any richer than the Laurence family. More importantly, Julie had despised the man; he could not have been her lover. Alden Wright, though,

38

or Jacob Garrison's boy Thaddeas, or Hayden Nelson. They'd been single, too. And wealthy.

He would somehow learn about them first. And if he found nothing to implicate them . . .

It could still be Colonel Wright or Jacob Garrison.

All the more reason to stay away from the daughter with the ability to find things out.

Chapter Four

Victoria enjoyed sneaking peeks at where Ross Laramie sat curled over the table. It added a definite pleasure to her workday. He had a secret.

He'd flat out said so when she asked what today had
to do with the rustling. And though she wasn't sure
which newspapers he was reading, she'd noticed him
exchange the ones from '92 for previous issues—and
apparently for the one she and Evangeline had read
earlier about Butch Cassidy.

Why was he reading about train robbers?

Maybe he was considering the outlaws' former ex-
ploits, piecing their previous rustling together with
their current crimes? She'd heard of Pinkerton detectives investigating stranger connections than that.

Maybe Ross Laramie was a Pinkerton detective!

Where was Nellie Bly when you needed her?

Beyond the intrigues and excitement, though, Victoria simply liked the man's presence. She enjoyed

looking across the room at him, having someone to
meet Evangeline's near-panicked gaze about. She
liked the olive undertone to his tanned skin, and how
sunlight reflected silvery off his black hair. She liked
the deliberate, slightly raspy quality in his voice. When
she asked questions, she liked the unwavering way she
looked at her with those haunted, hooded eyes of a
sort of green-brown color.

He was clearly pursuing outlaws, which made his
secrets all the more appealing. She would be foolish
to pursue a *bad* man's secrets!

"Mr. Day," she asked deliberately, toward the end
of the afternoon. "If I learned something about the
train robbers, I could write about them. Couldn't I?"

Mr. Laramie did not look up from his reading.

Neither did Mr. Day look up from his wonderful
typewriter. "If you learn something about train robbers, Miss Garrison, tell me and I'll let you know."

"Let me know if I can write something?"

Now he glanced up at her, over the rims of his spectacles—still typing. "Let you know if you should go
immediately to Sheriff Ward," he clarified.

Now Ross Laramie looked up.

Before she could decide how to pursue further
questions, Victoria's older brother arrived.

"Howdy, Lester," greeted Thaddeas, looking very
proper in his brown suit, despite his cowboy boots.
"Miss Taylor," he added politely, toward where Evangeline stood near the press. "Are you ready to go
home, Vic?"

Was it already quitting time? She loved almost everything about the newspaper, from its smell to its purpose. She loved being a modern, working woman. But
today seemed to have hardly begun.

"Almost," assured Vic, fumbling behind her back at
the strings of her printer's smock. Then she had a
clever idea—her favorite kind. "Thad, have you met

41

Mr. Laramie? Papa hired him this week."

Mr. Laramie's dark eyes had found Thaddeas as soon as he came in, but they narrowed at the name. He unfolded from his chair, his gaze never leaving Vic's brother.

"Thaddeas Garrison?" he asked quietly.

When he stepped forward, spurs jingling, Laramie stood taller than Vic's brother. But Thad was clearly older. Her half brother by her father's first marriage, Thad had been an adult for nearly as long as Victoria could remember.

"Do I know you?" Her brother shook Laramie's hand, but both men seemed unusually wary. *"Laramie?"*

Laramie said, "No."

Vic shifted her hips a little, to get a better grip on her knotted apron-strings, as she spun her plan. "Perhaps we should ride back to the Circle-T together. Since we're going the same way."

Thaddeas shrugged and nodded. Some days, her own brilliance thrilled her.

"I'll clear my things." Laramie, his gaze sliding from her to her brother, turned to the cabinets.

"I'll help you!" Victoria bounced slightly in her struggle with the knots. "It's my job!"

At least it was when she wanted to see what someone had been reading! But Laramie ignored her request, turning his back to effectively hide which drawers he was opening.

Desperate, Victoria looked toward the type case. "Evangeline, could you . . . ?" But nobody was there.

"She slipped out while we were talking," explained Thaddeas. Turning Victoria around by the shoulders, he began to work at her knots himself. "Unusual girl, your friend. Stand still."

She's madly in love with you, you blind oaf. But that was yet another secret Victoria must never reveal—not to

42

either of them. Thad was a respected lawyer with political ambitions who hardly remembered Evangeline's name, except to be polite. And Evangeline, for all her efforts at propriety, came from the wrong side of the railroad tracks.

Wyoming was too old-fashioned to see past that. So were the male Garrisons. Vic's only comfort was that Evangeline understood; that was why she'd left.

"Stop wiggling," scolded Thaddeas. "There."

And she was free. But Mr. Laramie had already collected his black hat from the now-clear table, and Victoria had lost her chance to learn more about the mysterious stranger. For now.

The ride home would provide another lovely opportunity. And it would even be safe. And proper!

Her big brother would be there.

Then again, when Thaddeas held a handkerchief in front of her face and said "Stick out your tongue," then wiped a black smear off her cheek, she had to wonder if that was really a blessing.

Could this be the man who'd seduced and abandoned Julije, who'd destroyed his family?

The heir to one of the oldest ranches in the Powder River Basin, Thaddeas Garrison would have been about nineteen or twenty years old at the time—certainly old enough to ruin a girl. He had money, and he wasn't bad-looking.

His body humming with revived memories, Laramie felt particularly conscious of the rifle scabbard hanging off his saddle, heavy with his Winchester; the Bowie knife in his boot; the holdout derringer strapped to his good arm, under his shirt. If this man deserved to die, Laramie had no doubt of his ability to send him to hell.

But Laramie was also aware of the rifle stowed under the Garrison buggy's seat—and the lady perched upon it next to her brother, acting like this was a picnic.

Worse, he couldn't remember if Thaddeas Garrison had even been in town at the time of the murders, much less been secretly courting his sister. Laramie wondered how—besides physical threat—a fellow went about getting that information.

"Mr. Laramie," Miss Victoria announced pleasantly to her brother, "says he likes trains."

Laramie squinted at her, startled, but Thaddeas seemed to take it as some kind of conversational cue.

"That so?" he asked, glancing across from his view of his harness horse's rump.

Laramie didn't care about trains. What he really wanted to know was what Garrison had been doing in 1888.

Flat-out asking seemed less than circumspect.

"He was curious about when the railroad came through Sheridan," continued Victoria brightly, as if she had an endless supply of words to do her bidding. Then she teased Ross with a smile. "Though he won't tell me why."

"Exciting time," agreed Garrison. Only then did Laramie recognize the glimpse of opportunity Miss Garrison had just given him.

"You were in Sheridan in '92?" he asked, casual-like.

"Yep. That's the year after I graduated college."

College. One more reason Thaddeas Garrison sat there in the buggy, and Laramie rode a cow pony.

"Thaddeas went to William and Mary, in Virginia," explained Victoria. "Now he's a lawyer. Do *you* have a preferred profession, Mr. Laramie?"

The lawyer elbowed his sister lightly in the side.

"Not lawyering," noted Laramie dryly. *A lawyer?* And the sheriff's name was *Ward?* Had *all* his family enemies gone into law enforcement?

But if Garrison had been away at school before '92, likely he'd left Julije alone. Right?

"That must take some time," Laramie noted—then regretted the attempt. The words sounded foolish in his mouth, even when he tried to clarify. "College."

"Five years, in all," agreed Garrison, clucking at his carriage horse. That put him in Virginia in '88. *One down.* "It sure seemed longer, though."

"It *was* longer," insisted Victoria. "I was a baby when you left home, and I was nine when you came back to stay!"

Thaddeas grinned at her. Only when the expression startled him did Laramie realize how strongly the lawyer, though brown-haired and clean-shaven, resembled his cattle-baron father. Rumor was, Old Man Garrison never smiled.

He felt suddenly relieved not to have to kill Thaddeas.

"Victoria should go to college herself," teased the lawyer. "She's got the mind for it."

"Nine years old," she repeated firmly.

"Don't forget, I quit for a while," her brother reminded her. "During that bad stretch after the Die-Up."

The Die-Up. The bad winter of '86–'87.

Thaddeas Garrison might have been in town long enough to woo Laramie's sister after all, damn it.

He should know better than to ever feel relieved.

"Have you heard of the Die-Up, Mr. Laramie?" asked Victoria. He wanted to reply that, hell, folks in South America had heard of it. But he didn't. She continued. "You never did say if you're really from Texas, like your saddle. You don't *talk* like you're from the South."

"Vic," warned Thad. Then he added to Laramie, "Please excuse my sister. She's nosy with everyone."

She was that. And she was good at it.

"I was just making conversation," the girl defended, as if folks had ridden her about it before. Laramie reckoned they probably had. Out west, an overzealous curiosity could be a shooting offense. For men, anyhow. But ladies . . .

Miss Garrison turned and faced Laramie, almost as a dare. "If I was prying, I apologize."

She didn't add *so there*. It was implied. Laramie found his cheek tensing in a hint of a smile again. "No need," he assured her, the words sliding out almost effortlessly. "I admire how easily you do it."

Her eyes widened at his unexpected response, and he looked quickly away, across the rolling foothills, past a heavily wooded creek line and then into the mountains. He was starting to form an idea, and it troubled him. Deeply.

But she *was* damned good. Here he rode, within spitting distance of a man who might have destroyed his family, and he couldn't learn a thing. It was Victoria who had clarified that Thaddeas may have been in Sheridan in '88—and she hadn't even known it was information Laramie needed!

How well might she ask questions if she knew what she was looking for? *I'm very good at finding things*, she'd said.

People even expected it of her!

When Laramie slid his gaze back to the buggy, she was watching him with bright gray eyes, a smile twisting her lips. She seemed to sit up straighter after his praise. "Thank you."

You're welcome. But that momentary ease with words had deserted him, so he ducked his head, touched his hat brim.

Thaddeas Garrison groaned. "Don't encourage her."

Now it was the lawyer's sister who did the elbowing. Laramie's gelding tossed his head and snorted at some flies that were hovering near its face. The sun felt hot on his shoulders, and the air tasted dry and dusty—another reason he'd learned to keep his mouth closed. But maybe his best reason was that the last time he'd told a woman a secret—even a woman who meant well, a woman he could trust—she'd gotten their poppa and brother killed.

No.

Laramie concentrated on how the straps of his hold-out were rubbing his bare arm, under his shirt, and on the nearness of his rifle. His bullet wounds hurt, pulsing and sticky even after so easy a day as this. But no matter what he focused on, he could not ignore the teasing between Thaddeas and Victoria Garrison. They weren't quite bickering, weren't quite laughing. But their easy affection made him ache as badly as his injuries.

He resolved then and there to spend as little time around the Garrisons as possible. It wouldn't make the killing of either the son or the father any easier, should his quest come to that. Nor would involving Victoria.

Yet he liked hearing her chatter along the ride, until they rode into sight of the Circle-T spread itself. The white farmhouse, with its flowers and porch swing, still looked like nothing bad ever happened there.

Maybe it hadn't. Maybe that's why Victoria asked questions so easily. Maybe she'd never gotten an answer that threatened to tear her life apart.

When they reached the stables, Laramie was particularly careful in his dismount, in unsaddling Blackie, lest anyone notice his stiffness. He longed to go to the nearby creek and just lie in it like he had in the Blue Creek, outside Hole-in-the-Wall, letting the cool of the water draw the fever out of his hurting body. He was so distracted by that prospect, while he gave the gelding a rough once-over, that he almost forgot Victoria Garrison until she started toward the house—right past him.

She didn't look at all hot or stiff; in fact, she looked as cool as he imagined the creek would feel. Her lively step swung the skirt of her pale-blue dress, offering glimpses of white kid shoes. White!

They matched her ruffle-edged parasol.

He figured she would pass him with little more than a nod, but instead she slowed her step. "I hope you found what you were looking for at the *Herald* office."

He stared at her, with her bright face and her unruly, upswept hair, and he no longer knew if he had or not.

Before he knew it, the quiet words slid right out of him. "Where can we talk?"

Maybe he was hoping to scare her off. But rather than give him a cutting glare and march away, Miss Garrison blinked, then sank to one knee fussing with her shoe.

There didn't look to be anything wrong with her shoe. But he liked this view of how her hair clung to her damp neck. He admired the curve of her spine.

"There's a big rock by the creek," she said, low, without looking up at him. "In a willow grove. Nate Dawson knows where. Be there after supper."

Then she finished dusting the nonexistent speck from her shoe and stood. Or started to. Her air of intrigue suffered when she stepped on her hem and almost fell.

Laramie caught her arm, and she caught his. She even *felt* clean and cool. And soft, impossibly soft.

He quickly let her go, but it wasn't soon enough for her not to notice the holdout under his sleeve. He could tell from the way the hidden derringer jammed

48

into his arm as surely as how her gray eyes widened up into his.

Now she knew he'd been armed all day.

When she hurried away toward her safe, neat house, he wondered if she would meet him now, after all.

And he wondered which he would really prefer.

Chapter Five

As she left the house that evening, Victoria doubted she was thinking clearly. Her palm still tingled, either from the memory of Ross Laramie's touch or the gun she'd felt under his shirt, she wasn't sure which. He'd been secretly armed all day? That didn't seem quite right.

And yet he wanted to talk. To *her*.

Slipping into the twilight-shadowed trees bordering Goose Creek, Victoria tried not to remember that her sister Laurel had used the rock in the willow grove for romantic trysts. Just because she'd agreed to meet with Laramie privately did not mean Vic had fallen into some sordid, Garrison-girl custom. Mr. Laramie showed no sign of being sweet on her, except for sometimes staring. And that could have something to do with her staring first.

Not that she was sweet on him, either. Just intrigued.

Victoria picked her way along Goose Creek—rushing with cold water from the looming Big Horn Mountains—for no worse reason than to discover things. Who Ross Laramie was. Why he'd come here. What he knew about train robbers and rustlers.

She would stay in shouting distance of the house. What could go wrong?

Still, when she reached the willow grove and heard a splashing over the gurgle of the creek, she slowed her step enough to carefully peek around the big rock first.

Ross Laramie's long form crouched on the dirt bank, his dark shirt wetly reflecting the sheen of purple light still in the sky, his black hair dripping. As she watched, he scooped a hatfull of mountain water and poured it down his chest. Head bowed and shoulders sinking, he sighed.

Vic cocked her head, noting how his clinging shirt defined the long line of his back. His hair dripped into a curled point between his shoulder blades.

He did it again, this time pouring water over one shoulder, and she finally understood. His injuries, the ones she'd seen bandaged, must be hurting him.

"Hasn't the salve—" she started to ask.

But he spun, dropped onto his flank, and in a snap aimed a derringer at her before she could get "helped" out.

Victoria had never had a gun pointed at her in her life, much less one that came right out of a man's sleeve. For a long moment, it downright silenced her.

Laramie opened his mouth as if to say something— a defense, or an apology—even as he slanted the weapon downward. She saw that of course he hadn't intended to shoot her, even though he made no sound. And in the meantime—

"Your hat!" she exclaimed, and started down the creek bank after the Stetson he'd dropped during his

51

quick draw. She knew it was silly. She should take him to task about the derringer, not try to fetch his hat.

But hats were necessary. She doubted he had more than one. And this was, at the moment, the easier choice.

The hat spun and bobbed like a black felt boat while she skirted the edge of the creek. In a moment, Mr. Laramie strode past her on those long legs of his. He glanced over his shoulder as he did, his eyes questioning and silent and . . . apologetic?

The gun had vanished again. But she noticed that, unlike the rest of his shirt, his left sleeve was dry.

And there went the hat! Vic pointed. Laramie broke into a run. She picked up her skirts and ran after him, remembering a fallen log farther downstream.

Laramie waded in, then went down on one knee with a splash and a grunt. The current swept him several feet before he could brace to a stop. The hat dodged him.

Victoria balanced her way out onto the log and knelt precariously. Almost as a gift, the creek twirled the hat right to her. Snatching it from the water, she grinned at Laramie, wading toward her, knee-deep in rushing creek.

He ducked his head with something like chagrin. As he got closer he said, "Figured you weren't coming."

Which only explained the wet shirt. "Who did you think I was, that you might have to shoot?"

He lifted his gaze to study her face, looking up at her for once. "No one person," he admitted.

Then his eyes went cold and he lunged at her.

He pulled her off the log and into the creek—in her white shoes!—and swept her behind him with one wet arm. His hip felt hard and wet against her mostly dry dress. The current swirled her skirt tight against her leg on one side, floated it up around her knee on the other. With what felt like impossible slowness, Victoria realized that Mr. Laramie was not hurting her at all.

Then she recognized the echo of the clicking she'd already heard earlier that evening—a drawn derringer.

Slowly, she peeked around Laramie's side and followed the point of his aimed weapon to a dusty, skinny cowboy standing on the bank of the creek.

He looked like a drifter, maybe part Indian. He wore a gunbelt, a rifle scabbard, two boot knives, and a sly expression in his black eyes that she didn't trust.

Instead of trying to pull away from the wall of Laramie's body, Vic pressed closer to it, bracing her cheek against his upper ribs—since she *did* still want to see what was happening. She felt very aware his arm looping around her back, his hand spread on her hip.

"Whoa there, friend," said the stranger, shaking his head. "Ain't meant to surprise you. Let's not get spooked."

Laramie just stood there and silently pointed his gun.

So Victoria said, "What are you doing out here, mister? It's almost dark."

The man's smile bothered her. "Not what you was doin', I guess."

"Chasing a hat?" She shivered, but that was because rushing mountain water chilled her feet as it tugged past, even in late July. The wet shelter of Laramie's body was warm in comparison.

The man's smile widened. "My mistake, miss. I was just fillin' my canteen." Lifting a dripping canteen in proof, he noted the derringer aimed at him. "You got my word, *mister*. I don't mean either you or the lady no harm."

Victoria guessed Laramie believed him, because he

slowly lowered his gun hand to point down at the water.

But she felt just as glad that he didn't push it back up his sleeve yet.

"No offense meant, friend," added the stranger, kneeling on the bank to finish filling his canteen. "But anyone ever tell you you're a touch quick on the draw?"

Victoria said, "You should ride up to the house. We've got a perfectly good pump, and maybe dinner too."

"We're not that close to the ranch house," noted the stranger. It was true that, even if they left the trees, they wouldn't be in immediate sight of the house anymore. Darned hat! But only one rise separated them from it.

"You're closer than not," she challenged.

"True enough." The stranger looked at them both with sly eyes. "Miss, wouldn't you like to stand on dry land again? I'm surprised your feller here ain't helped you out."

"I'm fine," she insisted—still pressed against Laramie, even if he wasn't "her feller." She felt safe this way. She liked that he kept his attention on the stranger. "What's your business at the Circle-T?" she asked.

Laramie's hand twitched against her hip, as if maybe he didn't like the question. But it wasn't his family's ranch.

The stranger's eyes slid from her up to Laramie. "I'm lookin' for someone I heard tell rides for the brand."

"Why?"

"Figured I might have some business with him."

"What kind of business could you have that you couldn't visit during the day? Why wait until night?"

Laramie was definitely nudging her.

The stranger laughed at her protector. "She sure does know how to fan them questions, don't she?"

When Laramie said "Yes," his chest vibrated under Victoria's fingertips. Where her cheek pressed against his ribs, she could hear the comforting sound of his heartbeat.

"Miss, you may have a point," agreed the stranger. "I guess I'll just get word to my friend to meet me in town. Maybe at one of the saloons. You know of any to recommend?"

Her? She drew a breath to protest the insult, but then Laramie answered, "The Red Light."

So maybe the stranger hadn't been asking her at all.

Victoria corrected him anyway. "I've heard that's not a very nice saloon. The Buffalo Bill's the nice one."

When the stranger grinned again, his teeth seemed whiter because the shadows were getting deeper. "This is business for a not-very-nice saloon," he admitted. "So I'll have this feller meet me there. That would be better than sneakin' about on a fine ranch like this, don't you reckon? Less chance of folks . . . talkin'."

Folks talking, or her? Victoria could keep secrets; heaven knew she collected enough of them. But she also had responsibilities as a Garrison to be sure that nobody connected with the ranch was doing anything illegal or immoral.

"Who is your friend?" she asked. Now Laramie's heel found her toe, under the water, and pressed slightly.

"Miss." The stranger tipped his hat and turned away. Then he paused and looked over his shoulder. "If I was you, mister, I *would* get a handle on that quick draw of your'n. Could be you'll pull down on someone you ought not have."

55

Laramie, of course, said nothing. But when Victoria called, "Wait," he tensed against her.

"Ma'am?" called the stranger.

"May I ask *your* name?"

The stranger grinned, and he was definitely part Indian. "Sure, you can ask."

Then he tipped his hat to them both and vanished into the shadows. Barely a moment later, she heard a horse riding away. She thought she should take one last look—

Except that she still stood in Goose Creek, tugged by the current, holding herself against Ross Laramie's long, lean body in ways that were wholly inappropriate.

And to her surprise, she was enjoying it.

Laramie wasn't sure at what point during his standoff with Lonny Logan he'd noticed Victoria Garrison pressing her warm, curvy self against his back and side. He did know that he began to have trouble thinking clearly.

Not a wise state, around outlaws.

Then again, Lonny didn't fascinate him like Victoria did. Lonny only worried him. But that was enough reason to watch the youngest Logan brother, even while Laramie's blood swirled and eddied, playing with him like the creek had played with his hat, hot as the creek was cold.

She felt so soft and round in some places, tucked and firm in others. And warm and dry, where he was wet. And at that moment, he would have given anything to keep her safe.

So what level of fool *was* she, to ask those kinds of questions to a bona-fide train robber?

Only once Lonny had said his piece and rode off could Laramie breathe again—and then he felt downright weak. Not that he figured even a Logan, especially Lonny, would hurt a lady. But if anybody would, why not a desperado? *Damn!*

In one long movement and a solid click, he eased his derringer back into its holdout. That comforted him some. In another, he turned and lifted Victoria right out of the water, took three dripping steps, and set her onto the bank—even if pain did clutch into his wounded arm and side when he did it. Then he stared at her from the creek, eye-to-eye now, furious and afraid, and still too aware of his eddying blood and her soft, warm curves . . . and again, he did not know what to say.

Should he say, *Don't do that?*

How could she have not known not to do that?!

"Golly!" Victoria exclaimed, her hands still on his wet forearms where she'd planted them in midair. That meant she must feel the holdout's rigging—but she'd seen it in action, so it was hardly a secret anymore.

Laramie liked her fingers, her soft palms on him.

She seemed to be too excited, her eyes bright as moons, her face aglow even in the shadows, to notice minor details like deadly force. "Did you see all his guns? I don't think that man was up to any good at all, do you?"

Laramie stared at her. *Of course he was up to no good!*

Hell, Laramie had been doing much the same thing, until Victoria showed up and startled him near senseless, and he wasn't up to any good either. He'd even drawn on her!

"I wish we'd seen his horse," continued Victoria, squeezing his arms. "I wish we knew who he was meeting, so we could discover if anything nefarious is going on. If I were a man, I think I'd go to the saloon myself and see who he meant to meet!" At least being a girl would stop her.

Laramie looked down at his submerged feet, braced

against the now-dark current. "Could be trouble."

"Well, if I stopped doing what needs doing just because it could be trouble, I'd make a sorry reporter." She let go of his arms to take his left hand in both of hers, then tugged. "Or human being, for that matter. But now I have to tell Papa, and that *will* be trouble!"

"No." Whether he was protecting his secrets or her world, Laramie wasn't sure. Likely himself. But he'd brought the trouble here; he had to deal with it. "I'll visit the Red Light."

He'd be meeting Lonny there anyway.

The way Victoria lit up, like he was doing her a grand favor, pained him. So did the relief with which she said, "Oh, good! Once we know more, then I can better decide how much to tell Papa."

Laramie climbed out of the creek, water sloshing off him and out his boots, and hoped she told Papa nothing. He did not need outraged fathers distracting him from his real job here in Sheridan, and he was already risking it. He'd kept the lady out after dark.

"I'll walk you back," he offered reluctantly, glancing in the direction Lonny had gone.

"Well, as far as the rock, anyway," she agreed, taking several squelching steps up the path that paralleled the creek. When Laramie started wetly after her, she slowed down so that he practically had to walk beside her.

Not that this was a hardship.

"But we can't go in yet," she continued, grasping her skirts to flap them a little, shaking some of the water out. "We aren't at all finished."

He tried not to stare at the quick little glimpses of her high-shoed ankles as he thought, *We aren't?*

"You still haven't told me why you asked me to meet you," she continued happily. "Why *did* you, Ross Laramie?"

Ross. He began to ache again, somewhere deep that

58

he didn't want to know about. Meeting her had been a bad idea. He'd drawn on her. He'd put her face-to-face with a train robber. Now he was lying to her about the Red Light Saloon.

And because she called him Ross, it suddenly mattered.

She stopped walking, so suddenly that Laramie almost bumped into her. Staring down into her shadowed face, he remembered what she'd felt like pressed against him, more intimately than either of the gals he'd known sinfully, and he felt guilty for such common thoughts, too. Why had he asked to meet her?

"I forget," he lied, and felt like a damned idiot.

He feared she saw his lie, but all she said was, "Since we're here, then, will you answer a question for me?"

He shrugged one shoulder, wary. He owed her.

"Why would a stock detective spend the day looking through old newspapers?"

To his relief, he could answer that with marginal honesty. "Been rustling here before."

Victoria Garrison clapped her hands together. "I *knew* you were a range detective! I just *knew* it!" And he recalled again just how good she was at finding things out.

Good enough to not just be helpful.

She was good enough at it to be dangerous. To both of them.

Chapter Six

"Just a cowboy tracking rustlers," said Ross Laramie, sounding defensive.

But Victoria knew better, just as she knew he could not have forgotten why he asked her to meet him . . . which made the real reason all the more intriguing. "That means there *are* rustlers!"

Anyway, a range detective was more than that, a cowboy whose *purpose* was to track down rustlers. Though the term was sometimes used for hired guns, a real range detective was practically a lawman. And meeting a *lawman* by the creek wasn't so bad. "You were reading about old rustlers?"

He shrugged that one shoulder again. "Folks involved once . . ."

Might still be involved! That was smart thinking. "You mean some rustlers from before are still around? They aren't arrested, or dead, or run out of town?"

He stared at her in the darkness, and she guessed

that meant yes. Rustlers from the past might still be walking the streets of Sheridan!

Life surely had gotten interesting since he rode in.

"Do you think that man by the creek was a rustler?" She shuddered to think that, and felt glad that Laramie had been beside her—well, in front of her—the whole time. Considering that it was dark, she felt glad he still was.

"No." He sounded vaguely angry. "He wasn't the type."

"There's a type? Tell me how to recognize a rustler, then, please? Maybe I can help you."

He shook his head and started walking again, his spurs jangling with each step, so she followed. Light from the rising half-moon bounced off the creek and lit them from two sides. She found herself noticing Laramie's denim-clad backside.

She guessed she should think of him as Ross now, after how she'd clung to him earlier.

It should seem strange to admire *that part* of a man. Maybe she just felt ready to admire all of him, after this evening, and that's just the part she was facing. He was tall, after all. And his dungarees were still drying.

When he reached the big rock, where they'd meant to meet in the first place, he sank onto it and she decided the front half of him was fairly admirable, too. Then, hitching one foot up so that his tapering fingers could reach the top of his wet boot, Ross drew his long knife from it and distractedly began to dry it on his sleeve.

Dangerous.

Victoria leaned back against a tree while he chewed over whatever he'd gotten riled about, happy to watch. "When do you suppose they'll meet?"

His lashes lifted as he looked up at her again.

She persisted. "The rustler and the ranch hand?"

"He was no rustler." Oh no. Not the *type*.

"Likely tomorrow night," she guessed. "Maybe the night after. They'll need time to make arrangements, won't they?"

He shrugged.

"You'll tell me what you find out, won't you?"

"Shouldn't involve you," he insisted, looking right at her with those haunted eyes.

"I want to help. And I'll be curious whether you tell me or not. Maybe if you *do*, I'll get in your way less."

His troubled gaze sank back to the knife, which he was caring for like a boy would fuss over a favorite toy.

Victoria went over to the rock and propped her elbows on it, then leaned over her arms to be closer to him. It felt right, being closer to this man . . . maybe because of the safety being *close* to him had already carried, just this evening. "And if you tell me what you're doing, I'll tell you what I'm doing, and maybe you can help keep me from putting myself in danger."

Goodness, but that was one big knife.

Ross was looking at her again, somehow reluctantly.

"I don't put myself in danger on purpose, you know," she insisted—almost by rote, considering how often she'd had to explain it to her father, her mother, her older brother, her sisters. Her brothers-in-law. Her teachers. Her editor, Mr. Day. "I just want to know things."

"To write about them?" he challenged.

"Partly. But I've had to know things long before I worked for the paper. I need to know because, well . . ."

Did he really want to hear this? He was watching her as if he did, so she forced herself to consider it.

"It's almost like it hurts, not knowing something," she tried explaining, pressing a fist to her chest. "In here. Not book learning; if that were it, then I would want to go to college like Thad. But the things I want to know aren't about far-off lands or scientific inventions or even books. The things I want to know are about people, and what they're doing, and why they're doing it."

At least he wasn't caressing his knife anymore, though he hadn't put it away. He'd drawn his knees up, where he could drape his forearms across them, and continued to watch her as if what she had to say really mattered.

For once.

She reached down and fidgeted with her skirt, though it and her petticoats were finally starting to dry. "Some secrets seem to hurt people. Have you ever noticed that? Not like us meeting here," she added quickly, when his cheek worked in that way she'd begun to think of as a ghost smile. "Big secrets, about *important* things. Like the bad times Thad mentioned, after the Die-Up. I was only five or six, but I remember sensing things had happened that we weren't allowed to even know, much less talk about."

Ross Laramie's eyes narrowed, and again she thought: *Dangerous.* But she had to be wrong. Why would her father hire a dangerous man?

She didn't know how to explain those bad times, not without revealing things about her family she oughtn't. The secrets weren't about the blow to the ranch. The Great Plains may have lost seventy-five percent of their cattle in the Die-Up, but the Circle-T, which had already started stocking in extra hay, survived better than many. No, the secrets had more to do with the dead baby.

Vic had known what her mother's round tummy meant. She'd recognized the grown-ups' panic in one word, *early.* Since she'd never met her impossibly tiny, dead baby brother, she didn't really mourn him. But she'd felt the grief that poured from both her parents, even from Thaddeas, home from school. She'd watched her father tirelessly carrying firewood out near the big elm tree, in sight of the new house, so he could build a bonfire. When she asked, Thad explained that they had to thaw the ground to dig a grave, and she'd understood that, too.

It had been the months afterward, when spring came and the carnage of the blizzards was cleared, which frightened her. Her mother still kept crying, through her chores and over her daughters, until Papa seemed drawn with worry. Every time Vic had asked Thaddeas or her older sisters what was wrong, they'd say not to ask. Sometimes she would ask Mama, who said, *I can't tell you. It's just something inside me. I can't explain.*

Vic thought of that stretch as the Big Silence, and it had scared her. Things hadn't gotten noticeably better until shortly before Mama's tummy started to swell with Kitty. By then, Vic was secret-shy.

Maybe she thought that if she could have helped Mama explain, things wouldn't have gotten so bad. But she'd hated secrets like that ever since.

Laramie—Ross—was still sitting there on the rock, knife dangling forgotten from one long hand, waiting.

"That wasn't a good time," she simplified, and lit on something she *could* tell. "Or when my oldest sister, Mariah, took up with a sheep farmer. They met, courted, and got engaged before anyone knew about it, even me. That hurt my father something awful. Well . . . that, and Stuart MacCallum being a *sheep farmer,* but still. Secrets like that never seem to do any good."

"No," agreed Ross.

"It's as if . . ." Victoria sank onto her folded arms so that she half lay on the rock, her chin resting on her fists, although her feet were still on the ground. "As if keeping secrets, the *big* secrets, is an insult. It means you don't trust people."

Ross let out a sharp breath, almost a snort. "Some folks oughtn't be trusted."

"Maybe not with your money, or your horse, or your daughters. But everyone should be trusted with the truth—especially about politicians, and laws, and government, which is why I love the newspaper so much. Otherwise, how do you know who people are, what they're really after? You can only see who people really are if you have all the information. Otherwise, you just see make-believe."

Ross searched her face with his dark, deep eyes.

"Especially people you *should* be able to trust," she added, remembering Mariah. "People you love."

Love? Suddenly she wished she didn't talk so much. Ross still hadn't confessed why he'd wanted to meet her. Vic felt tempted to hide her face. Instead, she watched his.

"Yes." He agreed that simply, and suddenly she liked him. A lot.

It felt warm, and tingly, and exciting, and it made her want to smile. And blush. Now she looked down, in case he could read her eyes, and said, "That's why I want to help you. If someone's stealing other people's cattle, then folks should know about it. Not just my father. Everyone."

It felt like a vote of trust, if strangely off topic, when Ross said, "Is Bram Ward the sheriff?"

Letting her help made her like him, too. "Oh, yes. Last five or six years, not that I think very highly of him. Do you think *he* knows anything about the rustlers?"

He quirked his mouth, shrugged that one shoulder. "What about Hayden Nelson?"

"Nelson . . ." Victoria considered the name, pushing back up off the rock a little. "Oh! Him. He sold out and moved back east a long time back, not long before the railroad. The Triple-Bar bought up his land,

and Mama said they would've had to pay a lot more if they'd known about the railroad."

"Wrights still own the Triple-Bar?"

That, she thought, was an odd way to phrase it. Did they *still* own the Triple-Bar? They'd owned it all along!

"Sure they do. Colonel Wright, and his wife, and their son and daughter. I don't much like them, either," she admitted. "Colonel Wright hired a range detecti—I mean, a gunman to run my brother-in-law out of town. The sheep farmer, you know. But the Wrights wouldn't rustle cattle."

Ross sat still, considering.

"They have plenty," she assured him.

Scowling down at his knife, he asked, "Ever hear tell of a local family named Laurence?"

Laurence. She shook her head. "Should I have?"

He finally returned the knife to his boot. "They were lynched as rustlers some time back."

OH! She pushed all the way off the rock, standing straight again. "That's awful! But they couldn't be involved now, if they were lynched. Accomplices, maybe."

"Or ghosts." Ross slid off the rock beside her.

Right beside her. Almost like when he'd been standing between her and a suspected bad man. His nearness felt warm and safe. He smelled good, like leather and herbal salve.

He'd listened to her.

Somewhere off in the distance, a coyote yip-yipped at the moon, as if to agree about ghosts. Victoria stepped just a little closer to Ross—even if she'd spent her whole life hearing coyotes at night. Even if she knew what little cowards coyotes were.

It seemed as good a reason as any.

He stiffened beside her. "You . . ." Then he swallowed. "Best get inside, where it's safe."

She looked up at him and nodded, not about to go inside yet. She was enjoying this excited, warm, tingly feeling of being close to the range detective far too much. "Is that all you wanted to know? Ross?"

He had to tip his head downward to see her, they were standing so close. As ever, the movement seemed graceful, cautious, contained. "For now."

"You'll tell me if you have more questions?"

He nodded slowly.

"Promise?"

"No." Wonderingly, he lifted his fingers to her lips. His fingertips felt soft, oh so careful. His gaze searched her face as he whispered, "I can't promise you anything."

"Will you promise to try, then? Please?" She felt like shivering, and not from wet petticoats. It suddenly seemed more important than rustlers or bad men.

To her relief, Ross nodded. Only when she spread her hand on his arm—to catch her balance, to catch her breath, to feel his hidden gun—did she realize that he was shaking too. A fine, almost imperceptible trembling. She had to know.

"If you asked me out here to kiss me . . . I'll let you."

His eyes, lingering on hers, seemed so very sad. *Haunted.* Like the rustler ghosts. "I shouldn't," he said.

So *she* kissed *him*.

Her mouth felt even softer against his lips than it had under his fingertips, and Laramie sank into that softness like he would into rest, peace, sanctuary. He breathed her in, savored her breath on him—and closed his hands into two fists, desperate not to do more.

Until this moment, he'd never fully understood the appeal of kissing. The few times he'd tried it—

No. He wouldn't think of paid women around her again. This was nothing like those frenzied preambles to embarrassment and release. This was a preamble to nothing.

Victoria Garrison's kiss was whole and holy, a completion unto itself. And in only a moment, it was gone.

She dropped back onto her heels, and only then did Laramie realize how Vic had drawn herself up high enough to reach him by pulling on his arms; he hadn't even felt pain under his shoulder bandage. She looked up at him now, somehow awed and confused and . . . thinking.

Always thinking. "That's not right," she said softly, the smooth skin between her eyebrows creasing.

"No," he murmured, his senses swirling like the creek. "I . . ." Then he registered what she said. "It isn't?"

But of course it wasn't. Her world was safe; his was dangerous. He'd done enough tonight without kissing her.

"It was nice," she rushed to assure him, ducking her head. "I . . . liked it. But that's how my parents kiss when we're watching." Did she know how they kissed when she *wasn't* watching? "I thought . . ."

Laramie could not have guessed what she'd thought if she'd turned his own gun on him. That she drew her hands down his arms, onto his fists, didn't go far in helping him piece anything together.

"You're shaking." She pulled gently at his curled fingers, until his palms opened for her. She didn't look up—all he saw of her was her curly dark hair—when she asked, "Didn't *you* like it? Should . . . should I apologize?"

Her apologize? "I liked it," he whispered honestly.

Only then did she tip her face up, her palms pressing into his, and she smiled. Laramie found himself staring into bright eyes, an angel's face, soft lips— pure beauty.

"You did?" she asked, shy and pleased at the same time. "Oh, good."

Then he took a quick step back from her, before he forgot himself again. What were they doing?

"You need to go home now," he told her. He winced inwardly at the pain that glanced across her expression then. But of course she wouldn't leave it at that.

"Why? What's wrong? You said you liked it." She took a step forward.

He took a step back. "Shouldn't have."

Her eyes widened with dismay he would rather have not seen. "Are you *married?*"

The idea startled him enough to not back away any farther. "No!"

"Well, thank goodness for that!" She poked out her lower lip and blew a heavy breath upward, so it moved the dark hair that fell across her forehead. "Are you *engaged* to be married?"

He shook his head. Of course not.

She smiled then, teasing. "Are you a priest?"

Laramie stared at her.

Victoria folded her arms, which had the effect— fortunate or unfortunate—of plumping her bosom beneath that prim blue calico of hers. He ought not be noticing, but could not look away. "Then I don't understand. Don't you like *me?*"

He did not know how to answer so primed a question as that, except with more truth. "Yes. Now go home."

"Why?"

Because I am not a good man. Because you would not like my world. Because I vowed to kill somebody, and he might end up being someone you love.

Her family had troubles the year of the lynching; she'd said so herself. And why *had* Mrs. Garrison concerned herself with an immigrant boy's welfare after-

69

ward? Had she spent her money from guilt about her son? Her husband?

"You're keeping secrets," Victoria accused. "That means you don't trust me."

But he *couldn't* trust her—any more than he'd been able to trust Julije. And he'd known Julije so much better. She'd been family.

"You cannot trust me, either," he reminded her.

"Oh." She blinked. "Well, then. I guess that's that." And, gathering her oddly wrinkled, drying skirts up around her white-shoed ankles, she squelched out of the clearing.

Laramie ached, but not because of his wounds. He wished she hadn't kissed him, because now he knew what it tasted like. He wasn't sure he could stand a lesser woman's mouth against his again. It would seem blasphemous.

He felt startled, hopeful, worried—more reactions than he could ever have corralled—when Victoria Garrison spun on him and demanded, "You'll tell me what you find out about the Red Light, though, won't you?"

The woman had a mind like a Texas Ranger's. Maybe that's why it was getting increasingly hard to lie to her.

That, and the kiss. And her calling him Ross.

"If I can." It would not be a matter of what he would know, after all. Just what he dared tell her.

She nodded. "Meet me here on Friday, then."

And foolishly, he nodded. After that kiss, he might agree to meet her in hell, if she told him to, even with her angry at him.

Actually, he felt safer with her angry at him.

So he saw it as unfortunate when she stopped scowling and lifted her chin. "Thank you for standing between me and that stranger, Ross."

But any man worth his salt would have done that much. She hadn't had to kiss him for it.

Ross Laramie stood and watched the trees where she vanished up the path for far longer than he probably should have. Then he left for the Red Light Saloon in Sheridan—to meet up with one of the Wilcox train robbers.

The train robber who'd saved his life.

Chapter Seven

Victoria left her damp shoes and stockings on the mud porch, then padded barefoot into the parlor where the rest of her family was comfortably settled. Most of them, anyway.

She was used to Thaddeas living away in town. But in the last two years, Mariah and then Laurel had moved out too. It felt odd sometimes to see just her parents, Audra, Kitty, and Elise. It felt even odder, with the memory of Ross Laramie's kiss on her lips. And yet this was still home.

The room smelled of floor wax and fresh-cut flowers, as usual. Her weathered father still kept busy; tonight, he had leather traces in his lap. Her younger sisters amused themselves with their own pursuits, Audra with a book, Kitty practicing scales on the piano, Elise playing with her dolls and their newest dog, Duchess. And her mother, sitting quietly in a comfortable chair toward the edge of the room, was somehow the center of it.

Despite having borne six children—seven, counting the baby buried under the elm—Elizabeth Garrison had thus far retained her dark-haired beauty and her tenaciously pleasant ways amid the hardness of the frontier. Mama loved the niceties of life, the iced lemonade and the electric lights and the cut flowers, almost as much as she clearly loved her husband. Papa, thought Victoria, would give her the world if he could—and had come pretty close to doing so.

But just because he accepted Elizabeth's progressive ways did not mean he tolerated them in his daughters. "Throw a shoe, Victoria Rose?" he asked.

"No, sir. Just got them wet." Victoria sat on the settee beside Audra, so she'd appear better-behaved by association. "So what are you reading tonight, Audie?"

"It isn't a dime novel. You wouldn't like it."

"Hard on footwear," noted Papa, looking back at the leather in his lap. He was fixing a bridle, Victoria decided.

"Yes, sir," she said. "Just water, though." Only when she noticed him slant a gaze toward her mother did she realize a lecture was coming.

"It's late for you to be out alone," noted Mama, who was sewing lace onto a piece of pink silk.

Victoria sat up, unwilling to argue with her parents—especially in front of her sisters—but somewhat affronted. True, she hadn't exactly been behaving herself out by the creek. But she wasn't in school anymore. If she were a boy—

"Of course, you're practically a grown woman," added her mother before Victoria worked herself into a froth. "And you're gainfully employed. You *should* have more freedoms than the younger girls. But

73

you're our daughter, and we worry, all the same."

Mama's eyes danced slightly when she said "we worry," so Victoria knew that *we* was mainly her father. She glanced back toward Papa, but he was scowling down at the broken bridle—and listening intently.

"Yes, ma'am," Vic said.

"Your father and I discussed it," added Mama, still smiling at her sewing. "I was all for barring your windows and locking you in the house, not letting you leave without an armed escort at all times, but your father thought that was a little extreme."

Papa looked up from the bridle to stare at his wife, as if to protest that neither of them had said any such thing.

Mama noticed, and laughed.

Papa sighed. "Take the dog with you after dark."

"Duchess?"

The dog, a black-and-tan Alsatian, lifted her head at her name. Though barely a year old, she resembled a small wolf in size and, as she'd shown more than once when protecting the family, in temperament.

She was more Papa's dog than anybody's, since Papa trained her. He disliked allowing a dog in the house at all. But since her mother insisted—on the dog, on the fishbowl, on the canary, on the three cats that sprawled about even now—he would at least have a *well-behaved* dog in the house.

Not that Victoria thought Duchess would tattle on her, but . . . how would the dog have reacted when Ross Laramie drew his gun on her, or when the stranger surprised them?

Things could have gone badly—and not just for Laramie or the stranger. If Victoria got the family dog killed . . .

Such guilt didn't bear considering.

"I think she's happier here with Elise," said Vic

quickly. "She doesn't need to come out just because I feel like walking by the creek."

"Or *in* the creek," murmured Audra, staring at her book.

Victoria surreptitiously kicked her.

Audra surreptitiously kicked her back.

Duchess huffed out a long-suffering sigh, remarkably similar to Papa's, and dropped her head back down again, beneath little Elise's ministrations.

"Duchess loves me," declared Elise, petting the dog's flank with a china doll.

"Reckon you can spare her of an evenin', Elise Michelle," declared Papa firmly—and that was that. To protest further would be highly suspicious. And futile.

"Yes, sir," said Victoria. "I understand."

Papa stared at her, because she *was* Victoria—gainfully employed or not—so she repeated for him: "If I'll be out after dark, I'll take Duchess with me."

He nodded and went back to bridle-mending.

"*We* will feel much better, thank you," said Mama, amused. But a great deal amused Mama. "Now, haven't we had enough daughters falling into creeks lately?"

"No, ma'am. I . . ." She might be the only Garrison daughter who managed to lie successfully, but that didn't mean she *always* succeeded. "I saw something, so I waded in."

With a handsome stock detective, who was dripping wet at the time . . .

Suddenly she had a clever idea—her very favorite kind. "I thought maybe it was treasure—loot from that train robbery. Do you suppose outlaws ever come this direction?"

Audra looked up from her book, and Elise from the dog. Kitty's fingers faltered to a stop on the piano keys.

75

"The robbery wasn't even a week's ride away," Vic pointed out. "And I've heard the hoot-owl trail runs right though Johnson County. Do you think desperadoes would ever ride through here?"

"We've had suspicious visits now and then," said Mama, who—unlike her daughters—hadn't looked up from her sewing. "There was a time half the ranches in the area had Butch Cassidy on their payroll, so he wouldn't rustle from them."

Vic guessed it wasn't "Buck Cassidy" after all. "Really? Did Papa?"

Papa, looking from Victoria to her mother and back, seemed annoyed with them both. *"No."*

"So did he rustle stock from us?"

"Not that we ever caught him at, of course," answered Mama. "But probably. Kitty, I think we've heard enough piano music tonight; why don't you come sit by your father?"

Kitty obediently lowered the hinged cover over the piano keys and went to Papa's side. He moved the bridle aside long enough for his second-youngest daughter to climb into his lap, even if she was almost nine years old.

Victoria felt bad. "Kitty, I didn't mean to scare you. You know outlaws would never bother us—Papa and Duchess wouldn't let them." *Nor would hands like Ross Laramie.* "I was just wondering, is all."

"Was it treasure, Vic?" asked Elise, pretending her doll was shouting that into Duchess's ear. "What you saw in the creek? *Was* it?"

Victoria felt increasingly bad about the lie, especially after what she'd said to Ross about not trusting people—not loving them like one should. Even if this wasn't a big secret. "No. Just pyrite, so I threw it out."

Audra said, "There's a reason it's called fool's gold."

"Doubt train robbers would've ridden this far with a surplus of gold," noted Papa dryly, and did something to make Kitty smile. "Hard on the getaway horses."

"I was just wondering, is all," insisted Victoria.

Wondering who that stranger was, by the creek. Wondering how he might know one of our ranch hands. Wondering just what's going on at the Circle-T.

"What if it *was* treasure?" demanded Elise. "What would you buy, Victoria? Would you buy me a bicycle? Would you buy me a camera?"

Victoria already owned the first, and was ordering the second with her wages from the newspaper. Like her mother, she enjoyed newfangled things.

"She'd give it to its rightful owners," said Papa firmly. "There's right, and there's wrong."

And that was that, to his way of thinking.

"Well . . ." interjected Mama. "Occasionally there's a pretty broad spectrum connecting the two."

Papa scowled at her, clearly annoyed.

"In a few matters," added Mama quickly, her smile broadening. "Personal, relative matters, I mean."

She had not soothed him yet.

"But not," she finished with a dramatically firm nod, "in matters of stolen loot. No, in that there is *clearly* a right and a wrong, Elise. You listen to your father."

Papa continued to glare at her, as if he suspected he was being mocked. And Victoria guessed he was, somewhat.

But the way Mama smiled back at him, as if she'd teased the glare out of him on purpose, held no real disrespect. Victoria watched them, more intrigued than ever now that . . .

Well.

Her hands tingled where she'd pressed her palms into Ross Laramie's. Her lips tingled, too. He'd fought that kiss so hard, he'd been shaking—and yet he said he'd liked it.

That made two of them.

Not that she was foolish enough to think herself in love after one kiss! Not the kind of love her parents had.

But it was kind of nice to know she could blush, too.

The Red Light Saloon sat on the outskirts of Sheridan. All the better for Laramie. Men from the Circle-T took more pride in their job than to come this far past the tracks.

Anonymity was all but guaranteed—and not just for him.

He didn't see Lonny Logan when he first pushed through the swinging doors of the saloon. He didn't expect to. Instead, Laramie made his way past several customers and one buxom whore to the bar long enough to order a rye, then moved to the farthest table from the front he could find, where he sank wearily into a scarred chair.

Damn, but he hurt. It had been a long day.

From habit, he surveyed the room, noted the exits, the back hallway, the stairs up to second-floor rooms. Not a great place to be trapped, should trouble find him, but not the worst, either. For a dump.

Laramie had never much liked saloons, with their noise and booze and desperation. Most rebellious boys *escaped* to the world of saloons and vice. Laramie had been exiled here. Tonight, in particular, the contrast from the willow grove and the pretty lady who'd stood with him, talked to him—*kissed him*—was downright depressing.

At a familiar whistle, Laramie saw Lonny heading down the stairs, tucking in his shirttails. Had he been watching for Laramie? If so, what had he been doing in the meantime, shirt untucked, that he could stop so quickly?

Laramie tried not to think of the upstairs windows

overlooking the street. He didn't want to contemplate whores in any fashion tonight. It was an insult to nice ladies like Victoria Garrison that such women even existed—or that men like himself partook of their services.

With a corner table, both men could sit with their backs to the wall. "Howdy," greeted the half-breed outlaw, slumping into a chair, and grinned. *"Feller."*

"Thank you for not knowing me." Laramie owed his companion that much, at least.

"Bits of calico as nice as that don't come along every night," agreed Lonny. Laramie tensed at the implication, but that was it. Maybe because this was a Logan, despite the fact that the newspapers were calling them "the Roberts Brothers." Harvey "Kid Curry" Logan was the meanest of them, but Lonny had been known to hold men at gunpoint while Harve had at 'em.

Luckily, all Lonny said was, "Buy you a drink?"

"No, thank you."

"I'm feelin' pretty flush lately." Considering that he and the others had gotten about $30,000 off the Union Pacific, he should be.

"Money gets traced," warned Laramie. "Thanks anyway."

The barmaid brought his rye, and Laramie paid. Lonny pointed at the glass as his own order, then left the subject alone. "When I heard you was in town, I figured I'd warn you. Think twice afore you ride back to New Mexico."

Victoria Garrison had come close, guessing Laramie had come up from Texas. But Texas had better law enforcement than New Mexico, so Laramie had spent his last year on William French's WS Ranch. After getting shot up last month, and deciding he had things to finish before dying, he hadn't much thought about going back.

He'd taken too long keeping his family promises already.

Still he asked, "Why?"

"You hear 'bout that trouble they had the other week?"

The only trouble big enough to reach Wyoming was the holdup of the Colorado and Southern. "Near Folsom?"

"That's the one. McGinnis was involved. Word's out he got shot up pretty bad."

Damn. Laramie liked Mac McGinnis, who more often called himself Elzy Lay. Next to Butch Cassidy—who went by "Jim Lowe" on the WS—Mac had to be the most popular man in the whole outlaw bunch. Laramie had met them long before his latest stint cowboying on the WS, working their own cattle and others. They trusted each other, more or less. He'd even been invited to join their more lucrative ventures, banks and trains. So far, he'd had reasons to turn them down.

Until he got past his life's job—serving justice to the son of a bitch who'd betrayed Julije, Poppa, and Filip—he wasn't much drawn to anything else, including big money.

Keeping company turned dangerous enough. Riding with Butch and Elzy—or Mac—was what brought Laramie back to Wyoming. Riding with the Logans was what got him shot.

Then again, Lonny had risked his own life to drag Laramie back to Hole-in-the-Wall, down in Johnson County. Better than letting some liquored-up posse lynch him before he'd recovered enough to protest his innocence. With a sheriff dead—compliments of Harvey Logan—folks might have forgotten why they had a jail and a courthouse.

As Laramie knew, the line between good men and bad men, out on the range, was a tenuous one at best.

Here sat Lonny, calling Laramie "friend" and venturing into town at least partly to warn him off of the WS Ranch.

Laramie could only wonder what the other part was.

So Mac had gone and pissed where they slept. Now folks in New Mexico might connect Laramie to the outlaws.

Speaking of which . . . "Was, uh, *Lowe* involved?"

"Nah. Mac hooked up with some locals for this one."

Well, that was something, anyhow. Butch was likely hurting over it, though. He and Mac were as close as pards could get. If Mac didn't pull out of this, who would Butch turn to as his *segundo*? Longabaugh?

Better than a Logan.

"Guess I'm not going back," said Laramie. He finally took a sip of his rye. It tasted sour and hot—and soothing. A fake comfort, but better than none at all.

"Finer things around here, eh?" asked Lonny, downing his whiskey as if he liked it. "Like in blue calico?"

Laramie narrowed his eyes in warning. "Unfinished business, is all. Then I'm riding on."

Where to, he had no idea.

"Think you might be up to some fun, then?" asked Lonny.

A burly, blond-haired man pushed through the swinging doors into the saloon, and something about him raised the hair on Laramie's neck. Something familiar.

Still, he challenged Logan, "Fun?"

From the nearby train tracks a long whistle blew, and Lonny grinned. "Burlington and Missouri fun?"

Laramie swallowed another mouthful of rye, watching the burly blond man from the back, willing him to turn around. Unlike better saloons, there wasn't much of a mirror over this bar. "*Lowe's* breaking promises."

81

Word was, Cassidy's promise not to pull jobs in Wyoming had gotten him his pardon from Laramie City prison in '96. It was why Laramie believed Butch hadn't been in on the Wilcox job, even if he'd planned it.

"That was only for cattlemen and banks," insisted Lonny. "Anyhow, he's not leaving New Mexico 'til Mac is safe out." Maybe noticing Laramie's distraction, he added, "We can wait 'til she crosses the line to Montana."

Still, Laramie didn't look away from the big, burly guy. *Turn around,* he willed. "Don't tell me this."

It was the safest way to say "not interested" to this kind of offer—and not just to a Logan.

"C'mon. We're out McGinnis and Lowe. Bob Meeks is doing time in Idaho. We could use a good shooter."

Turn around, damn you.

"I'm busy," murmured Laramie. He had rustlers to track, vengeance to seek. He'd even somehow promised to meet Victoria Garrison by the creek this Friday, to report something—anything—about this very meeting.

It made for a helluva full plate.

The burly blond man finally turned around, and for a long moment Laramie thought he was seeing a ghost.

The ghost of the man he'd killed.

Then he noticed the star pinned to the man's vest, and his plate got fuller.

Chapter Eight

It had to be here.

Victoria turned another page from another news-paper, this one from 1890. She read about events as large as statehood and as small as Bram Ward becoming deputy.

It had to.

The delicious scents of old paper and ink filled her nostrils. Someone said something, like the buzzing of a fly, but she ignored it to turn another page. Then another. She put that paper aside and picked up the next.

"Miss Garrison!"

She looked up, blinking at the momentarily blurry image of her editor beside her. "Mr. Day?"

"Don't you have anything better to do, Miss Garrison?"

"The type's set for the next issue," she pointed out, rolling some of the kinks from her shoulders. To think that Ross had done this for half a day, and he was injured!

He must be very dedicated to his work.

Mr. Day said, "Yes, but—"

"And after my pieces on Alice Wright's new engagement, and the coal interests, and the temperance movement, you asked me not to write anything else this week." She touched the paper to hold her place. "So I'm doing research."

"Research on what?"

"Cattle rustling." She lifted another page.

Mr. Day planted a hand in the middle of it. "Rustling?"

Victoria blinked patiently up at him. Hadn't she just *said* rustling? "Yes, sir."

Mr. Day pushed his spectacles up on his nose. "Miss Garrison, you do realize that rustling is something for Sheriff Ward to investigate, and not the *Herald.* Don't you?"

She nodded. Although it was also an issue for her father's range detective to investigate—especially if it involved Circle-T cattle. But why split hairs?

"Okay, then." With a shake of his head, Mr. Day went back to his own desk. "Carry on, Nellie."

Grinning, Victoria went back to the newspaper from nine years ago. Nothing. She turned the page. Nothing.

Despite her best efforts, the idea of meeting with Ross Laramie tonight began to distract her all over again.

Four days had passed since they'd talked—and, yes, kissed. Four days of wondering what he'd learned about the stranger at the saloon. Wondering what he thought of her. Wondering why she'd kissed him in the first place, and if they might do it again, and whether that would be a good thing. She could barely sleep last night, from thinking, which was when she decided to find the issues of the newspaper that Ross had been reading and better her understanding of past rustlers, perhaps even impress him by mentioning something he didn't know, like—

Sheriff Ward?

Pushing her thoughts from kisses and wet clothing, Vic turned back to the previous issues. This one? No, that one. March, nine years ago. *Bram Ward Appointed New Deputy.*

She read it more carefully. Apparently the sheriff— then deputy—felt strongly about justice because his own father had been murdered by a cattle rustler.

"Yes," whispered Victoria, savoring a happy shiver. It felt like a puzzle piece clicking into place. "But when?" Seeing nothing in the article, she asked, "Mr. Day, do you remember when Sheriff Ward's father was killed by a rustler?"

He looked up from his reading. "I didn't know his father *was* killed by a rustler."

Ten minutes later—most of them spent getting her printer's apron off—Victoria was striding up Main Street toward the jail, wishing she had her bicycle. She got within a block before she noticed her friend Evangeline beside her.

"Oh! Golly, Evangeline, say hello or something!"

"Where are you going?" asked her friend, her eyes darting.

"The sheriff's office."

Now Evangeline's eyes widened. "Don't do that!"

"I just want to ask him some questions, is all."

Evangeline shook her head so hard that some of her pale hair fell out of its upswept braid. She had fine hair; it was difficult to keep up properly. "Please don't."

Victoria slowed her step. "Why not? I realize he's not the nicest man in the world, but he's a public official and I'm the public, female or not. Why shouldn't I talk to him?"

Evangeline looked both directions, seemingly frightened. When Victoria looked, she saw nothing but the everyday hustle-bustle of Sheridan's Main Street.

But she hadn't been friends with Evangeline Taylor for three years without learning to respect the girl's sensitive nature. So Victoria took her hand and drew her farther down the block. "Let's go where we can talk."

Evangeline followed—until she saw where Vic was headed. Then she stopped, so suddenly her hand pulled loose.

Victoria looked from Evangeline to her brother's lawyer office back to Evangeline. "Don't be silly. We'll go upstairs; he won't bother us."

Then she noticed Evangeline look down at herself, and realized the problem. Her friend wore a plain, butter-yellow work dress. She was barefoot. Her hair had fallen.

She doesn't want Thaddeas to see her not at her best, she thought, and felt a sudden surge of sympathy. Hadn't Victoria chosen her own white sailor-dress this morning, specifically with the intention of looking nice when she met Ross Laramie tonight?

She also felt a surge of annoyance at her brother.

"We'll go up the outside steps," she promised, catching her friend's hand again, and chose her words carefully. "We won't be in the way of Thad doing business at all."

After a moment's resistance, Evangeline trailed her to the building where Thad kept his office, his name etched in green and gold on the front window, and past it to a flanking wooden staircase. He kept an apartment upstairs; although he had usually stayed at the family's in-town house, he didn't always want to wake them if he worked late.

It was, as ever, unlocked.

"So why shouldn't I talk to the sheriff?" Shutting the door behind them, Vic headed to the little pantry to see if Thaddeas had cakes or cookies set aside. He did. The number of ladies who brought him baked goods was amazing.

Evangeline said nothing, and when Victoria looked over her shoulder, she saw her friend staring at the bed.

Oh!

Victoria looked quickly away, blushing. Was Evangeline imagining Thaddeas in that bed? He was Vic's *brother!* Modern women or not, there was a certain propriety to maintain.

Wasn't there?

"Would you like a macaroon?" Victoria asked, loudly enough that Evangeline jumped—and, blushing, quickly shook her head. "So why shouldn't I talk to the sheriff?"

And Evangeline, nervously smoothing her butter-colored skirt, told her.

By Friday evening, Laramie doubted he was thinking clearly. Slipping into the tree line by the creek, he tried not to dwell on thoughts of Victoria Garrison— her shiny eyes and her swaying skirts and the way she said "Ross."

He failed, which explained why the dog startled him.

"Duchess!" commanded Victoria over fierce warning barks, and he rounded the rock to see her with both arms wrapped around the large animal's neck. "Duchess, *quiet!*"

The dog stopped barking. It growled instead.

"*Sit,*" she ordered, and it sat.

Laramie looked from it to her. Then he dragged

his attention back to the less dangerous of the two—the dog.

"Duchess," said Victoria, slowly standing, "this is Ross. He's my friend. Ross, this is Duchess."

Ross again. It sounded more like an alias than *Laramie*. But he liked hearing the name from her, a reminder of what could have been, all the same. It was a sweet hurt.

"Hello, Duchess," he said carefully, noting how the dog's ears perked; *she* knew *her* own name. So as not to leave out the lady, he rasped, "Hello, Victoria."

She smiled with undiluted sweetness, maybe the prettiest thing he'd ever seen. She wore a white dress with dark blue sewn to its edges and far more material in the sleeves than seemed practical. She had her hair up again, poofy-like the way ladies did, and little curls slipped out over her temples, across her neck. Her hair looked so soft. So did her neck. She wore the same white shoes as before, dry again and polished, and he was a fool to have come.

"Papa didn't like me wandering around in the evening without protection," she explained, as if she could read his thoughts. "So . . ."

"Duchess," he finished. The dog's ears turned to him.

"Exactly," Victoria agreed. "You can pet her, if you like. She's safe, unless Papa's trained her to attack beaux—" Her eyes widened, and she covered her mouth. "I mean, not that *you're* here for . . . for any reason but to tell me . . ."

Wasn't he? He'd gone by the barbershop for a shave, bath, and haircut from simple courtesy, not foolish aspirations. And yet why did he have to step closer, just to exchange information? "Why would your father train her to attack beaux? Do you . . . Do many men . . . ?"

Do you have many beaux? Do you let other men kiss you?

Explaining Herself

If I were part of your world, would I even have a hope?

But he was not from her world. This tryst was just pretend. He let the dog sniff and then lick his hand.

"You haven't been in town long, or you'd have heard about my sisters," she explained, eyes shining up with seeming gratitude at the distraction.

He closed his gun hand into a fist so as not to reach, to touch, nowhere near distracted enough. *Her sisters?*

"Sheep farmer," he remembered. "Engaged in secret."

"That was Mariah," agreed Victoria, clearly pleased. He liked pleasing her. He was a fool. "Then Laurel married up with a remittance man."

"An Englisher?" Poor Garrison.

She nodded. "Papa calls Collier 'His Lord God Pembroke.' And of course with Stuart MacCallum . . ."

Laramie nodded. A cattle rancher would dislike a sheep farmer on principle. But he was watching her mouth far more closely than he was listening to it. Compared to him, the boss would likely welcome a whole army of foreign sheep farmers descending on his remaining daughters.

She took a deep breath that did wonderful things to her bodice. "But that's not why—I mean . . ." She bit her lip, then let it go. "Did you go to the Red Light Saloon? Did you see the stranger? Who did he meet? Is he up to no good?"

Then she waited, hopeful and excited, and all he had to do to make her happy was to tell her something. Just that one thing, of so many that he had to hide.

It was why he'd come tonight, wasn't it?

"I did not see him meet anybody," offered Laramie with marginal honesty—then saw her disappointment. She'd given him some information about Nelson and the Wrights; he was paying her back. But surely he did not owe confessions!

"You saw him, though?" Victoria asked.

Did he feel *guilty?* He nodded, truthfully this time.

"Do you know who he is?"

If he said Roberts, she would immediately connect Lonny to the Wilcox robbery. "I think he goes by Logan."

That clearly pleased her, anyway. "First name or last?"

Ross bent to scoop a stone from the ground. The move pulled the bullet wound in his side, but somehow that didn't hurt as much as having to lie again did. "I don't know."

"Still, that's something," encouraged Victoria, as he tossed the rock. "You're sure he didn't meet with anybody?"

"Nobody I saw." But he couldn't help remembering that to her, in particular, secrets were an insult. "He left not long after the sheriff came in," he offered inadequately.

Victoria stood straighter at that, with a bounce that startled both him and the dog. "The *sheriff?*"

Laramie remembered Bram Ward's face, so like the man's pa, and that blasphemous lawman's star, and he nodded. He'd forgotten how much he'd hated the Wards, how much he would welcome a chance to kill the sheriff. But Julije had not betrayed them to Bram—the Wards were no better off than the Laurences back then, and there would have been no family to threaten Julije away after the lynching. Unless Laramie meant to hunt down the entire posse, he had no justification for killing Ward outside pure meanness.

Far more likely that he would have to kill Thaddeas or Jacob Garrison.

"Ross?" asked Victoria as he stood not three feet from her, thinking about killing her loved ones.

But only the one who deserves it.

He said, "I'm sorry. I should go."

"Go?" She stepped closer, as if to head him off. "You can't go yet. We haven't finished talking."

He wondered what it would feel like, to be that innocent, that trusting. He doubted there was any pain in feeling like that. Any gut-wrenching guilt. Any regrets.

She took his fisted hand in hers. "Don't go. I haven't told you what *I* found out about the sheriff."

Suddenly he didn't care about the sheriff anywhere near as much as his burning guilt and her cool, innocent touch. She ducked her head, showing him her curly hair and the bare nape of her neck, and drew her own hand over his. Now it wasn't just his hand clenched. It was his whole body.

He hadn't come here to talk at all. He should go.

"Why do you do this?" she asked wonderingly, stroking his closed fingers.

So I won't touch you, he thought. *So I won't make any sudden moves. So I won't overreach myself.* He wasn't innocent *or* trusting, and he understood regrets.

Like before, she slid her hand over his, her gentle fingers easing his own out of their fist. He did not fight her. But this time, once his hand was open, he couldn't fight himself, either. He had to fill the empty hand.

So he reached out, slid his hand around her waist, and used it to draw her up against him, soft and sweet.

He wasn't barely thinking at all now, just feeling. He *felt* as if here was an untainted piece of the world and that maybe her purity was such that it could cleanse him. Just enough to make the hurts stop haunting him. Just for a while.

More amazing yet, Victoria Garrison wrapped her arms around him in unexpected, silent welcome—and God help him, it worked. Even before he kissed her, for one long, blissful moment, him holding her innocence tight against his aching, weary body worked like magic.

Then his own want of innocence won out.

Ross surprised Victoria by pulling her firmly against him, closing his long, hard arms around her, but she did not fight it at all. She guessed she'd been expecting . . .

Hoping . . . ?

And they *were* within shouting distance of the house.

He smelled good, like leather and hair tonic, and felt so warm, so solid. She felt safe with him, and excited.

"I can tell you later," she offered breathily. So much for Sheriff Ward.

Ross held her as if she were something precious, something he needed—and Victoria leaned into that need. Maybe it *didn't* make sense. They didn't know each other well enough for her to be precious to him. He was a tall, strong man who shouldn't need anything, especially not her.

But despite all that reality, she felt his need like a tangible thing and she longed to soothe it.

She leaned her head against his chest and sighed her own pleasure as tension seemed to ease from him. Ross laid his cheek on her head and she heard him swallow, heard him breathe, as if even that little bit of humanity had to be forced past almost inhuman control. Only after a brief forever did Ross turn his head, nuzzle into her hair. Victoria stretched into the sensation, lifted her face to better see him. His eyes were closed, his lashes two black smudges against his cheeks. His hold on her tightened until one of his shirt buttons dug against her bosom, until her hipbone bumped against his holster, through her petticoats.

For once, she had nothing to say.

Ross's eyes opened then, dark and hot, and when he covered her mouth with his, it wasn't like their other kiss at all. His hard lips had no caution to them, no wariness, just need. She didn't try to draw back—could she have?—so he kissed her mouth again, then her cheek, then her ear, then her jaw, then her throat, not stopping. . . .

Victoria sank into the sensation of it, of a man's mouth, *this* man's mouth, touching her where even his hand shouldn't. If he hadn't been holding her so tightly, she might have fallen. Instead, she slid her cheek across his own, marveled at the rasp of it, smiled at the cool vulnerability of his ear and then the thick softness of his freshly barbered hair.

She could hear Ross's breath fight out of him in little gasps. Her hand slid down his back, his ribs. When she reached his waist, he gasped a little. Landing on something hard and smooth and cool, her fingers closed around it in inquiry. His hold on her eased, as he caught her hand by the wrist and drew it off of what she realized was his gun. But still he kissed her. His kisses seemed to be searching, desperate, needful. She wished she could sate such needs. And yet . . . this couldn't be right.

She tried to draw breath to ask what was wrong, but he covered her parted lips with his own, kissing around the edges of her open mouth. He startled her with his tongue on her lower lip, hot and improper and wonderful.

Now *she* had trouble breathing, trying not to remember why this wasn't right. She felt dizzy, confused, pleasured, frightened. He seemed to want this so badly. Moans ground out of him with each breath. He held her so tightly. . . .

And she wanted this too. Didn't she? Even if she'd never known she did until now, how could she not?

Victoria let Ross frame her face with kisses, bless her

eyelids with kisses, trace a necklace of kisses across her throat. She savored the pressure of his fingertips against her scalp as he buried a hand deep into her hair. She liked the feel of *his* hair, thick and clean, when she mimicked the gesture. She held his head still so she could stretch upward on her toes to kiss his mouth some more, to see what it felt like to touch *his* mouth with *her* tongue.

He tasted warm, and salty, and he shuddered against her. The hand at her waist slid behind her, lower, to where she should not have felt him through all her petticoats, but she did, and of course this was not right. Somehow, with more effort than she'd ever had to give a single word, she forced a question from her throat into his mouth. "Why?"

And she wasn't even certain what she meant.

The word he groaned back was "Please."

He sank with her to his knees then, in the dirt and dry willow mulch. Trapped in his embrace, she sank with him, unable to fight, not wanting to. She ached to be whatever it was he needed, to do that, be that, dissolve into him.

But she had an existence outside him, too.

Her lips felt swollen under his greedy kisses; his cheek rasped against hers. And something else, something short and furry, bumped Victoria's elbow and whined.

Ross drew his hand upward, toward other forbidden parts, and of course she wasn't him at all. She was Victoria Garrison. And no matter how good it felt, *this was wrong.*

"Wait," she gasped, muffled from kissing Ross.

He wasn't waiting. He was cupping the curve of her breast, over her white frock, and it should have frightened her. It didn't. How good it felt—*that* was what frightened her.

She twisted her head sideways, to escape his kisses, and repeated more firmly, *"Wait!"*

And Ross fell still.

He still held her, very tightly, and that should have frightened her too. So should his gun, his boot knife. So should his size, his strength, his hardness, his very maleness, and the certainty that if he wanted to push her to the ground and muffle her cries . . .

But he didn't frighten her at all, and not just because of Duchess standing beside them, looking concerned. The idea of what he *could* do didn't frighten her because he was Ross, and he wouldn't. Something instinctive, deep inside of her sensed something vulnerable, deep inside of him, and she trusted it at least as much as she trusted herself.

Which wasn't implicit.

He was still cupping her breast, after all. And she was, she realized, arching into that touch. *Heavens!*

Feeling clumsy and lost, she planted her hands on his shoulders and pushed back from him, pushed him off her. He sat back in the dirt, staring downward. His eyes burned, but not at her. His mouth worked, but no sound came out.

Victoria sank back against the big rock's support, dizzy and flushed and excited about what had just happened, even if it shouldn't have. Even if it must not happen again.

Ross Laramie, sitting on the ground, looked mussed, and lean, and handsome. Even now her palms, her fingertips, tingled with the memory of him. But he did not look excited.

When finally he lifted his burning gaze to hers, he looked hurt, accusing—and almost suicidal.

Clearly, she would have to speak first. She licked her lips in preparation—and tasted him on them. *Golly.*

Words had never failed her before, and they did not this time. Not exactly.

"No wonder you clench your fists."

Chapter Nine

Laramie stared at her for several long, shuddering breaths before he was sure he'd heard her correctly. Even once his ears were sure, his mind wasn't.

His lips felt strange, traitorous as he tried to shape them into a word. His voice only half complied. "What?"

Wasn't she going to slap him? Sic the dog on him?

If she sat up, reached across to him, drew his pistol and shot him with it, he doubted he would fight her. It was a double-action. She wouldn't even have to cock it.

What had he done? Worse, what *would* he have done if she hadn't stopped him? Clearly there was no purity powerful enough to cleanse him—only more innocence for him to ruin.

"The way you clench your fists when we get close." Victoria pushed brown curls from her face, and Laramie truly saw what he'd done to her hair. "You were trying not to let yourself do just this, weren't you?"

Trying *not* to?

His breath rasped from his chest, the rush of his blood nearly deafening, and what he felt—

What he felt . . .

He'd been safer feeling nothing, because this was just too much. *Soft hair and skin and lips and tongue and starched, white dress and round, warm curves*—and that was just from *her.* The sensations that surged up from inside him, past the discomfort where her fingers had clutched at his wounds, past the ache he'd never admitted, deep in his chest . . . past the needs that had surged up from inside him were hungry and greedy and debased.

It was far too much, so he only let himself feel numb. He'd learned long ago how safe numbness could be. He could think through numbness. And what he thought was, *I've been trying* not *to let myself do this?*

For a reporter, Victoria Garrison wasn't always terribly observant.

"I have to go," he murmured, rolling onto his heels. He didn't know where. He didn't care. He just had to get away from this, his latest and most monumental mistake.

He had to get away from her before he destroyed her.

"Go? Don't be silly. I'll just let you keep your hands closed from now on. Now that I understand. I agree— of course we can't be doing this. We hardly know each other, and even if we did, there's a right way and—"

She blinked, looking startled, but he didn't know why. She looked down at her lap and seemed to notice the bits of willow mulch stuck to her skirt at knee level. She brushed futilely at them, forging on. "If you were to call on me, then maybe . . . well . . . Not that I'm assuming you would want to court me. But certainly, that's the only time something like this should ever happen again. Assuming it *could* happen, with a chaperone, even if we were allowed, and I doubt we would be. On the one hand, I'd think I'd be embarrassed to behave so . . . so . . . ."

Ardently? Graciously? Irresistibly? he thought.

"Well, to kiss a man like that with someone looking on. Except maybe Duchess."

The dog, sitting beside her, cocked its head with a worried expression. Laramie glared at it. Did it realize just how miserably it had failed in its duties?

"But I guess we should be embarrassed even without someone looking on, shouldn't we? It's amazing how quickly I started to forget, well . . . everything."

Laramie stood and swayed unsteadily. He had to go. *Now.*

"Is that even normal?" demanded Victoria Garrison, tipping her head entreatingly up toward him. With her hair half down, it made for a strange image—an enchanting image, here in the grove, against the rush of the creek. "Is that normal, to stop thinking and just . . . just . . . ."

Dark or not, he could see her blushing. Had he allowed himself to feel, he might discover he was blushing too.

He must never allow himself to feel again.

"Not that I assume you would know," she added quickly, with a fetching little laugh. "I thought you seemed to, well, understand what . . . and . . . but that doesn't mean . . . well, does it? Not that you have to answer so personal a question. I'm just curious. You may have noticed that about me."

He'd also noticed that she was still talking!

How could she be talking to him after how he'd treated her? How he'd almost . . . almost . . .

Clearly it was her way of comforting herself.

Clearly he'd left her with a great need for comfort.

Laramie had to swallow, twice, before he could even manage two more words. "I'm sorry."

Then he turned and strode from the grove as fast as he could. Willow leaves snapped across his exit, like a whip.

"Where are you going?" called Victoria.

Keep walking, he told himself. The kindest thing he could do for her, for *himself,* was to stay the hell away. He would quit the job with her father—he wasn't making good on it anyway, hadn't found the rustler. He would stay someplace else until . . .

Until he was finished in Sheridan.

But it wouldn't be that easy; she was following him. "Wait! Don't be sorry—or if you have to be, let me be sorry too, but at least stop and talk to me. You haven't even heard what I found out about Sheriff Ward!"

Laramie's pace slowed.

Keep walking, he urged himself even as his next step faltered, even as he glanced over his shoulder, against his will, toward a flash of shadowed white. *Get away from her. Now. She's more important than your vendetta.*

But she was not.

Clearly, she was not. Because despite what felt like his final dregs of decency, Laramie stopped and turned, and he waited on the path for her and her dog to catch up.

When she did, casually pulling pins from her hair so that it spilled evenly across both her shoulders, Laramie's hands remembered its softness. They longed to feel those locks again, to feel even more of her. Given too much chance—

No, if Victoria Garrison really mattered to him, he would tell her good-bye, right now, and mean it. Instead Ross asked, "What about the sheriff?"

If for no other reason, this was why he must never behave so familiarly with her again. Because God help him, even a sweet beauty like Victoria Garrison wasn't more important than vengeance. And that made Laramie no better than the man he hunted.

He'd waited for her.

Something that felt like panic eased when Vic saw Ross standing in the path, his hands loose at his sides, his gaze steady—waiting. He wasn't leaving her after all. Not yet.

He'd stopped to hear Sheriff Ward's secret.

If only for that, Victoria would love Evangeline Taylor forever. "He's corrupt."

Ross stared at her, his haunted eyes showing no surprise. That was disappointing.

"He's *corrupt*," she repeated, in case he hadn't understood. "He takes bribes! Can you imagine it?"

She never would have thought she could want to simply touch someone as badly as she wanted to touch Ross—to make sure he was all right, to silently ask if he thought *she* still was. Her fingers ached for wanting him, almost as much as her mouth did. But she and Ross must not behave that way again.

She made herself stop several feet from him and linked her hands behind her. But instead of exclaiming "You must be crazy" or "How do you know?" Ross just said, "Yes."

"Yes?" He really wasn't the most forthcoming man in the world, was he? Except when it came to kisses.

Victoria squared her shoulders and tried not to think about kissing. "Yes, you can imagine it?"

"Yes," he agreed with her. "I can imagine it."

Oh. "Well, I have a friend whose mother—well, word is that he charges the, umm, *working girls* to do business. It's illegal for them to do . . . what they do." His eyes were widening on hers, so she glanced away, toward the creek. "But he lets them, for a fee. And really, if something is legal it should *be* legal, and if it isn't, then it shouldn't be. Right? I do realize that

100

some foolish laws exist—not that *those* laws are foolish, of course . . ." Oh dear.

Victoria did not approve of what little she knew about prostitution, but the memory of touching her tongue to Ross Laramie's mouth—of how quickly she had started to forget, well, *everything* in his arms—flustered her with thoughts about not casting stones.

Still, little though she respected the idea of women renting out their bodies for money, or men paying for it, she saw a gaping disparity between that and the immorality of a lawman demanding money to look the other way.

When she peeked, Ross was still staring, wide-eyed.

She wanted to know what he was thinking badly enough to not say anything for what felt like forever.

It did not work. He just kept on staring.

Finally she asked, "What?"

"How do you know this?"

Hadn't she mentioned the friend with the fallen mother? "I talk to people."

"You talk to the *wrong* people."

She cocked her head. "Oh. You think she's mistaken?"

Ross spun away from her, shaking his head. "No!"

So he must mean—oh! "For mercy's sake, Ross, I haven't been talking to those women myself! Just to someone who hears things." More things than she'd ever expected. "I thought you would know what to do about it."

"Do?" he repeated, bowing his head over one fist.

"About what I know. It's not right!"

"No." His agreement relieved her; she'd *known* she could trust him! "But it's none of your business."

Or perhaps not. She put her hands on her hips and circled him, so she could see his face. Not her *business*?

Wasn't it her town? Wasn't she a woman too?

He shifted his weight, coiled and balanced as ever.

101

She noticed, again, the big gun hanging off his left hip. "This sort of thing happens," he told her. "Everywhere."

"You're *defending* him?"

His eyes widened again. "No!"

"Good. Because it's indefensible. What I would *like* to do is write a newspaper article about it, but that would be difficult. I can't exactly interview fallen women." Nellie Bly might—but Nellie Bly hadn't had to live in Sheridan, Wyoming. With Victoria's father. "And I doubt Sheriff Ward would admit anything to me. But I can't just do nothing."

Evangeline had even said Ward abused the women who couldn't pay.

"Yes," insisted Ross Laramie softly, meeting her gaze. "You can. You should not be involved in any of this."

Victoria caught her breath. "*Any* of this? Oh, Ross, do you think he's taking graft from other lawbreakers too? Like the rustlers!"

Ross blinked, clearly startled. "From the rustlers?"

"If Sheriff Ward demands bribes to allow one crime, why wouldn't he do the same for another?" Then she remembered why not. "Unless his father hardened him against rustling."

"His father," repeated Laramie, his interest so tangible she could almost feel it burning in him.

It wasn't as enjoyable as him holding her, kissing her—but for now, she would take it. Until she could convince him to pay a call on her, what else could she do? So she savored the drama of her next announcement. "I found out that the sheriff's father was murdered by a rustler."

Strangely, *that* was the news that made him go pale.

Working cattle was a slow process, done right. Riding the Circle-T's south pasture that next week, meeting with ranch hands and examining heifers' hooves, gave Laramie plenty of time to think about Victoria Garrison.

And about him being a murderer and a rustler.

He'd already felt sick, the other night by the creek—sick at his obscene loss of control, sick with wanting to lose control again. And once she mentioned Bram Ward's father that way, *murdered by a rustler,* he'd felt heartsick as well.

No matter how much he admired Miss Garrison, and no matter how familiarly she'd behaved with him, he could never change that he was that killer, that rustler.

At a sharp whistle, Laramie looked up. He spotted Nate Dawson waving a hat at him, one slow arc, and reined his gelding patiently in that direction.

Riders who moved fast around cattle only spooked them, and spooked cattle weren't easy to work. Maybe a fellow should work folks the same way. It would better justify that he'd been in Sheridan two weeks now and still had no idea who had seduced his sister, who had betrayed his family.

Slow and steady. He'd waited almost a dozen years for this. A few more weeks, even months, wouldn't change things. He could live with the guilt of not keeping his vows a while longer, as long as he stayed away from the boss's daughter.

Kissing Victoria, holding her, he'd been able to forget killing. It shamed him now that he'd wanted to forget.

That, the memory of her in his blood, he wanted to.

Laramie made himself focus on the two heifers and five steers grazing some ways from Dawson's roan. He was no closer to finding the bastard who'd ruined Julije than he'd been when he got here. But at least he understood cattle—and bad men.

"The dun-colored cow," directed Dawson, as Laramie eased his gelding closer to the knot of cattle. The animal lifted her head to watch his approach, while the other critters ignored him. "I remember thinkin' she was favorin' her right-front, some weeks back, but she moved quick enough when I got close. Next time I saw her, she was fine."

Laramie dismounted with a creak of leather and walked toward the cow. It turned to amble warily away from him.

Dawson, still on horseback, roped her in one toss. As if resigned, she stopped, even with the rope slack. Still, Laramie made quick work of checking her hooves for burn scars, then her udder to guess when she'd lost her calf.

"You're right," he called, straightening. "She's been hotfooted."

"What kind of sorry son of a bitch burns a mama between the toes so's she can't follow her baby?" protested Dawson.

Laramie lifted the rope off the poor old girl's neck, scratched behind her furred ears with his leather-gloved hands, then returned to Blackie. "That's four so far."

"Four on the ranch?" asked Dawson.

"South range." Mounting, Laramie dug a folded piece of paper and a pencil stub from his pocket and drew another X on his roughly sketched map. In the last few days, he'd narrowed his search to the west range, in the direction of the mountains.

It wasn't the revenge he wanted. But, as Victoria had pointed out, Bram Ward might just be in cahoots with the rustlers, turning a blind eye. If so, maybe Laramie could get a lesser form of revenge on the sheriff who grated on him so badly, by finally exposing him for the low-down rustler the Wards had always been.

He might not kill the man, like he would kill whoever had betrayed Julije. But this was a start. It was something he could manage. And he was being paid to do it.

Besides, Victoria wanted him to.

Laramie tried not to ponder that part too closely.

Dawson was still sighing over the cow. "Bad enough to swing a wide loop. But to torture animals in doin' it . . ."

Now, that was interesting, and Laramie glanced up from his crumpled bit of map. "Rustling's rustling." Wasn't it?

Dawson looked startled by the low proclamation. That reminded Laramie that, though they bunked together, he was still the hired gun. Dawson was the honest hand.

"I'm not defending the one," the honest hand now insisted. "But it's still a different thing from t'other."

Like Victoria's opinion on graft being worse than prostitution. A lot of folks around here had an interesting habit of weighing crimes.

When Blackie's head came up suddenly, and Dawson's roan followed suit, Laramie saw someone riding nearer who, he guessed, would see things in black and white—whether they were talking about rustling or the man's daughter.

Dawson rolled a cigarette while they waited for Garrison to reach them. "Boss," greeted the hand.

"Boys." Laramie got the feeling Jacob Garrison had been calling his hands "boys" long before his hair had turned white. His steady gray eyes, in the shadow of his black Stetson, slid from Dawson to Laramie—and lingered on Laramie. "Keepin' busy."

His voice didn't go up at the end, but Laramie recognized it for a question, all the same.

This couldn't be the man Julije had given herself to. Surely, even eleven years ago, he'd been too old for her!

It was Dawson who said, "Laramie here was just lookin' over another hotfooted heifer."

Garrison's solemn expression didn't change. His eyes shone with something like anger, though. Over the theft, or the purposeful injury to the animal? "Who is it?"

Laramie shrugged. Anybody could burn a cow.

The boss's eyes narrowed, as if to ask what he was paying Laramie for if not to find the rustlers.

Laramie thought about kissing the man's daughter by the creek—and carefully maintained his poker face. "Workin' out of the foothills," he offered instead.

Garrison nodded as if he'd figured as much—but hadn't wanted to hear it, all the same. The foothills offered too many good places to hide.

Dawson said, "Boss, that's where Miss Laurel and that Marmaduke of hers have their horse ranch. I don't like to think what she might do if she comes across some rustlers."

Garrison said nothing.

"I could ride out there and give her a warnin'," Dawson offered, and Laramie wondered just how deep the cowhand's concern for the married Miss Laurel went.

"I'll go," announced Garrison, and looked back at Laramie. "In the mornin'. You'll come with me."

It had been two weeks since the rancher hired him. Laramie guessed the boss would want an accounting sometime.

He nodded, wishing he knew how to get his own accounting. *Have you always been faithful to your wife? Do you remember a young immigrant girl, hanged herself over ten years back? How well did you and your son know her?*

Like trying to hurry cattle, questions like that would only scatter what he needed to learn.

He wasn't Victoria.

But when Laramie led Blackie up to the pretty ranch house's picket fence, after breakfast the next day, Victoria was the first Garrison out the door—and she was wearing an extra-long riding skirt and leading a child by the hand.

He hadn't seen her since the Friday before—since he'd all but mauled her and she'd somehow forgiven him. She looked pretty as the morning, her eyes shining, her lips smiling to show barely crooked teeth, her curly brown hair drawn back in a frothing ponytail.

"I'm coming along!" she announced happily.

Holding her gaze, Laramie couldn't begin to corral all the things he didn't know how to say to that. *How'd you talk your father into this? What about your job? Why would you even speak to me?*

During his silence, Victoria led the smaller girl, also brown-haired, to the fence where he stood. "So's my sister, Kathryn. Kitty, this is Mr. Laramie."

The younger girl wore spectacles, which gave her a fragile look. Or maybe she'd already been fragile, and the spectacles just emphasized that. Laramie felt particularly aware of the weight of his hip holster, almost embarrassed by it, even if they *were* riding into rustling territory.

From inside the house, an incredible howling started up—but Victoria just kept walking. After some hesitation, Laramie followed, leading his gelding. "That's my sister Elise. She's upset because she can't come along."

"She was naughty." Kitty reached a little hand toward Blackie's muzzle. "You have a pretty gelding."

The howling from the house stopped abruptly, and the little girl's eyes widened behind her glasses, as Laramie quickly asked, "Would you like to ride him?"

Why he said it, he didn't know. But the way Vic flashed an appreciative smile at him, he felt glad he did.

"Isn't that nice of Mr. Laramie, Kitty-kat? You can sit on Blackie while we're saddling the other horses."

Kitty's hopeful expectation when she nodded and lifted her arms unsettled him. She wanted *him* to . . . ?

He slid his gaze briefly toward Victoria, but she was still beaming at him—a reaction that ruffled him in even more pleasant and unexpected ways. So he took a breath, gritted his teeth against the pain in his side and shoulder, and lifted Kitty Garrison up into Blackie's saddle. Her yellow calico dress rode up to her knobby, white-stockinged knees, showing high-buttoned shoes that came nowhere near the stirrups. She grabbed the saddle horn, then graced him with a smile surprisingly like her older sister's.

Suddenly, she was pretty too.

"What do you say, Kitty?" prompted Victoria—and Laramie caught his breath. How many years had it been since he'd heard someone ask that?

What do you say to the nice storekeeper, Julie? Ross, what do you say to your brother?

"Ross?" Victoria's use of his Christian name, his Anglicized name, startled him further. "I mean—Mr. Laramie?" She glanced toward Kitty to make sure the girl was distracted by the horse. "Are you all right?"

He looked over his shoulder at the two-story ranch house, with its porch and its blue shutters and its flower beds. A swing hung from a tree in the yard. A small, single gravestone stood amid another bed of flowers under an elm, some distance from the house but clearly in view.

This was how a family lived. Little girls. Home. High-buttoned shoes. *What do you say, Kitty?*

It wasn't his world, the world of rustlers and killers, and that hurt.

"You're welcome," he said to Kitty's polite thank-you, and led Blackie the rest of the way to the stables. He felt unbalanced, out of place, a blight on their world. It bothered him enough that he did not try to find the words to ask Victoria any of the questions still haunting him.

Knowing her, she would tell him anyhow.

Chapter Ten

It was a beautiful August day for a ride into the thickly wooded foothills of the Bighorn Mountains, and Victoria could not be more pleased by the company.

She'd feared Ross was avoiding her after last week, especially since she'd made it clear that they mustn't indulge in similar behavior unless he were actually calling on her, like a respectable man would. He'd disappointed her by not offering to call. But he was here now, and he'd been kind to Kitty this morning.

And watching him ride was its own kind of joy. He sat his horse as if born to it, and although he wore pointed Spanish spurs, she did not see him touch his horse with them once.

"So Papa, Mr. Laramie," she said, to make conversation. "If you were rustlers, where would you hide?"

She'd expected Papa's doubtful look—her literal father did not play the "if" game very well. She'd forgotten how fearfully Kitty might react.

"They aren't hiding *here,* are they?" the girl asked from her secure seat in front of Papa, as if bad men would step out from behind the next copse of pines, bandannas pulled over their faces and pistols smoking in their hands.

Then again, to judge from the revolver on Ross's hip, and rifles holstered on both his and Papa's saddles—as well as the way Ross stiffened at her question—maybe they might.

"No," assured Papa, narrowing his eyes in warning.

"No, puss, not here," Victoria assured her. "We use this path too often. Right, Mr. Laramie?"

His gaze, when he slanted it toward her, smoldered with an upset she couldn't even guess. It took her a long moment to realize that Papa, too, was waiting his answer.

"Maybe to the north," Ross offered finally, so softly that they almost didn't hear him over their horses' slow hoofbeats. "There's arroyos, box canyons."

"Been rustlers there before," noted Papa, returning his attention to the path in front of him.

All Ross said was "I've heard."

Victoria, however, sat up straighter in her sidesaddle. "*I* haven't. When were there rustlers up here?"

Papa ignored her to bend closer to Kitty's ear, whisper something, and point. Kitty's face lit up at the sight of the rabbit he'd spotted for her. He was good at ignoring Vic.

But the way Ross was still staring at Papa's back, eyes narrowed, intrigued her. Something *else* to find out.

"A family outfit," Ross finally offered, low and bitter—he must really dislike rustlers. "Immigrants, yes?"

"Yep," said Papa.

Kitty said, "Families *rustle* together?"

It surprised Victoria too, though maybe it shouldn't. Families worked together in so many other businesses—even crime, like the Roberts brothers who were still at large after the train holdup. Why not rustling?

"Jest the menfolk," Papa assured them.

Ross asked, "*Were* there women?" If she hadn't spent as much time with him already, maybe Victoria wouldn't have noticed the odd note in his voice. But she did, and the undercurrents of his question drew her like a fly to blackberry cobbler.

Papa glanced back at him, unreadable. "Not rustlin'."

The silence that followed lasted for some time. And Victoria knew they weren't close to telling her everything.

Just watching Victoria Garrison ride, primly sidesaddle, was enough to remind Laramie how ill-qualified he was to court one of the rancher's daughters. If he needed further proof, he got it at the horse ranch Collier Pembroke was building with Victoria's older sister, Laurel.

The homestead wasn't terribly imposing at first. Their footpath joined into a wider track, not large enough to be called a road, and over the entrance hung a sign announcing "The Lorelei Ranch." But that title was burned into a wooden board and hung between two lodgepole pines. Nothing fancy.

When the original homestead came into view—a rough corral of split logs, a lean-to for riding horses, a small claim shack with tar paper tacked around it—Laramie thought he could do better than that.

But then they rode around another copse of pines and into a finer reality. At least four corrals were nestled among the trees, so new that the end of the log rails hadn't fully weathered. A long, formal stables was painted to match a new, two-story house. It had glass windows, a shingled roof, white wood siding not yet stained by rain or winter, and blue—no, purple shutters.

"It's so beautiful!" declared Kitty happily, so he guessed it was new to the family as well.

"They only built it this June, after rounding up the wild horses," explained Victoria, which relieved him. She'd been awfully quiet for the second half of the ride. "It's a mail-order house; it came in pieces, and a whole bunch of us got together and built it in just one weekend."

They reined to a stop by the original homestead's corral, and Laramie knew that, even mail order, he could never build such a house. Somehow, that bothered him.

"Laurel and Collier married last November," Victoria continued, dismounting from her gelding's sidesaddle before anybody could offer assistance. "At first Laurel wanted a cattle ranch, but then they decided to raise—"

The bugle of a horse—unmistakably a stallion—interrupted her, and everyone looked uphill. Sure enough, a paint mustang paced his corral, clearly watching the new arrivals. As if to show off, he lifted backward onto his rear legs, pawing the air, trumpeting again.

A blond man stood in the corral as well, some distance from the beast, and raised a coiled rope in slow greeting.

Jacob Garrison growled something under his breath.

"He's not *that* close to it," defended Victoria, waving back. As if there was such a thing as being a safe distance from a stallion, much less what looked like a *wild* stallion.

Laramie glanced at her, annoyed by her innocence, noticed Garrison doing the same thing, and looked away.

A second figure strode toward them from the stables. She wore a man's hat and a man's shirt over a split skirt, and she resembled Victoria, maybe older. Her face wasn't as round, and she had straighter hair. "Hi, Papa!" exclaimed Laurel Pembroke. "Kitty-kat, come here! Hi, Vic!"

It took longer for Collier Pembroke to safely skirt the stallion, duck through the extra-high rails of the fence, then hike down from its more isolated corral. Victoria easily filled the time. After hugging her sister, she introduced Laramie to Mrs. Pembroke. She told about helping her sister homestead in the tar-paper cabin the previous summer. Mrs. Pembroke explained that they were breeding thoroughbreds with mustangs, for polo ponies. Then Victoria explained how they'd captured not just the bandit stallion, off in the high corral, but his band of almost thirty horses, most of which they'd sold for extra funds.

"Nobody will buy the stallion," Laurel Pembroke explained, taking her story back from her younger sister. Laramie saw her gaze settle on his gunbelt, though she said nothing of it. "So Cole's trying to gentle him."

Garrison snorted.

"If anybody can, it's Collier," insisted Mrs. Pembroke. "We can still, well, *alter* him if we have to, but Collier thinks it would be kinder to put him down than do that. So we'll try this first."

In his years of ranch work, Laramie had castrated more bull calves and yearling colts than he could count, much less remember. It was a necessity of raising livestock, no more, no less. But those animals were usually young.

He again glanced uphill toward the stallion, magnificent despite its mustang size, and he thought, *Collier's right.*

"*Kill* him?" exclaimed Kitty. Laramie wasn't sure the child even knew what "altering" meant; it unsettled him that her sisters did. But she clearly understood "put down." "Why don't you just let him go again, if nobody wants him?"

Garrison snorted again. This was clearly a topic of some contention between him and the Pembrokes.

"Because mustangs have a price on their head," explained Victoria patiently. "There's a reward for them, like outlaws. You know how the jail has Wanted posters that offer money for bad men, dead or alive?"

Eyes wide, Kitty shook her head.

"Oh." Victoria winced toward her father in an apology that did nothing to dispel his glare. "Well, there are. Since they're bad, like train robbers, a cash reward is offered to the person who brings them in. And there's a reward for the bandit stallion too, but only if he's dead."

Laramie wondered how many of his old companions had just such prices on their heads, and he liked the Pembrokes for not killing the mustang stallion for the bounty.

Kitty asked, "Is he a bad horse, then?"

"Yep," said Garrison firmly.

"No," protested Laurel, scowling at her father. "But I guess he is a thief, because if he's loose he'll just steal other people's mares again. He doesn't understand that they don't belong to him. It's his nature."

Garrison stared at her. "Don't make him *good.*"

The Englisher, a remarkably good-looking man, arrived with handshakes and hugs. He sounded pleasantly like Laramie's old boss from the WS Ranch when he spoke. The family sent Kitty off to the stables to see the foals, so that they could discuss the rustling without frightening her, and headed for the fine new house.

But Laramie glanced uphill again, to where the stallion watched them, and he thought the Pembrokes were making a mistake trying to tame a wild creature like that.

Jacob Garrison was right. Whether a critter was bad from its upbringing, or its lack of understanding, or its nature, didn't matter.

Bad was bad.

Victoria had loved homesteading with her older sister, living by themselves, chopping wood and patching leaks and even shooting rattlesnakes on their own. It had been the first time in their lives they couldn't just call for Papa—not quickly, anyhow—when things went wrong. She'd felt frightened, and excited, and capable, and . . . and *free*.

Then she got her job at the newspaper. Laurel married up with Lord Collier. And it all seemed over. Now Laurel was leading her guests into her sparsely furnished front parlor and asking if anybody wanted lemonade. Laurel the cowboy. Laurel the homesteader. Worse, when Papa said that would be fine, Laurel said, "Come and give me a hand, Vic?"

It wasn't that hot a ride. The refusal had almost reached Vic's lips before her confused gaze glanced by Ross Laramie again. He still stood uncomfortably in the front foyer, as if unsure he qualified for the parlor, hip-shot and head down. His boots were awfully dusty. Back when he'd lifted Kitty onto his horse this morning, Vic had noticed the briefest wince, so she knew he was still hurting from whatever had been bandaged two weeks ago. And he'd ridden all this way without complaint.

Suddenly, she wanted him to have lemonade. So she spoke to the men instead of Laurel. "Don't say anything important."

The men looked innocent—except Collier, who subtly caught his wife's hand as she passed, trailing their palms off to their fingers and then letting go.

When he noticed Vic noticing, Collier raised his eyebrows in seeming innocence, even while Laurel vanished into the kitchen. The Pembrokes loved each other; that much Vic knew.

Maybe there were other ways to prove one's independence than to live alone, at that.

As soon as they were alone, Laurel said, "So tell me."

Normally her family wasn't so curious. "About . . . ?"

"About my new skirt; what do you *think* about?" Laurel made a face since, of all Vic's sisters, she was the least likely to want to talk about clothes. "Tell me what's going on? Why'd Papa bring a *pistolero* up here?"

As if Ross were simply some hired gunman!

"Well, it is a daring skirt," teased Victoria, picking up a pitcher to fill with water. It was daring—practically like wearing dungarees, but with a great deal more fabric. Dungarees *disguised* as a skirt. "Collier doesn't mind?"

"Collier ordered it for me." Laurel went to the pantry, then started rolling lemons across the floor at Vic. "Talk!"

Laughing, Vic stopped as many lemons as she could with her feet, kicking several gently back at her sister before she began to press them, one at a time, beneath her boot so Laurel could squeeze more juice. "He's not a *pistolero*."

"Well, he's better armed than a cowboy."

"His name is Ross Laramie, and he's a range detective. Papa hired him to catch rustlers."

Laurel paused in squeezing lemons. *"Rustlers?"*

"Not just that." Victoria fetched the sugar. "Mr. Laramie thinks they're hiding in the foothills, and Papa seems to agree. That's why we've come—to warn you and Collier not to bother anybody who might seem suspicious."

"Not bother them? Some low-down, stinking cow-thieves sneaking around my foothills, and I shouldn't *bother* them?"

While Laurel spooned in sugar, Vic fetched the cut-glass tumblers the Pembrokes had bought for their fancy guests from England a month before. "I may be wrong, but I doubt Papa will like that reaction. How about Collier?"

Laurel scowled at her, but stirred the lemonade. "He'll tell me to stay out of their way too, darn it. But the British are extra civilized, don't you know."

"Then you ought to think up a different response," suggested Vic, lifting the tray of glasses.

Picking up the pitcher, Laurel paused by the door from the kitchen. "What is it you always say?"

"I understand." The beautiful thing about that response was that it didn't promise not to do anything, just that she comprehended why she perhaps oughtn't.

Laurel nodded. "Maybe, since I'm not you, I can try that."

All three men, even Ross, rose at their entrance. Collier took Victoria's tray to set on a low table, but he spoke to Laurel. "Hullo, dearest. Your father and Mr. Laramie were just explaining a rather disturbing situation."

Vic *knew* they would discuss important things—although she had to wonder whether her closemouthed father or the closemouthed range detective had done most of the talking.

Collier was doing the talking now, explaining what Victoria already knew. She liked listening to his British accent. Normally, as pretty as Collier was, she liked watching him, too, but this morning she found her attention sliding appreciatively back to Ross. *He's taller than Collier,* she thought loyally, noticing how his shiny black hair caught the sunlight in silver highlights through the parlor window. *He's more . . . more . . .*

The word escaped her for almost a full minute, during which time she sank into a ladder-back chair and accepted a full tumbler from Laurel. Ross was different, perhaps even more attractive, though in subtler ways. She could feel the difference of him across her skin and deep inside her; she just couldn't quite label it. It had something to do with his dark, deep-set eyes and his serious mouth, with his angled face and his sculpted hands and the revolver still slung dangerously off his hip. His difference felt . . . sharp. Fierce, even. Controlled—always controlled.

She tried not to blush. Almost always.

Intensity, she realized. That's what he had that the polite, shiny Lord Collier Pembroke did not. Ross Laramie was the most intense man she'd ever met, and she liked that.

He seemed downright startled in his chair when Laurel handed him a glass of lemonade, then he nodded nervous thanks. His gaze slid over to Victoria, then quickly away.

She liked him very much.

"So we have been requested," finished Collier, "to stay out of these men's way—should we actually come upon them—and allow the law to handle the matter."

"The law?" Laurel sat rather abruptly on her settee, beside her husband. "Papa, you can't mean Ward!"

Ross seemed to deliberately avoid Vic's gaze. He looked down, took a sip of the lemonade. After a pause, he drank more—several swallows—and she felt glad he liked it.

"Sheriff," noted Papa pointedly, meaning that if the man held the post of sheriff, he deserved some respect. Just like President McKinley demanded their respect simply as the leader of the nation, even if he *was* a Republican.

"*You* hired an outside man," noted Laurel, about Ross.

"He works for me," warned Papa. True outside men generally weren't forthcoming about who hired them.

"A range detective, then. *You're* not sitting back and letting the law handle it."

Papa sat straighter. *"My cows."*

"He does have a point, dearest," interrupted Collier, before this could escalate into another of Laurel and Papa's arguments. "If the scoundrels were stealing horses, then perhaps we could hunt them down like vermin, eh?"

"You're no help," accused Laurel.

Collier only smiled his lopsided smile—the only thing about his face that wasn't perfect—and said, "That is exactly the point. We aren't to help."

Because she'd been keeping track of Ross on the edge of her vision, even while watching Laurel's husband, Victoria immediately noticed when Ross's head came up. She saw him frown. Then, before she could ask what was wrong, he put down his glass and stood, and everyone noticed.

Then, in the silence that fell over the parlor, even Victoria heard it through the open windows—the scream of a horse. It didn't sound hurt. It sounded somehow . . . angry.

Laramie bolted for the door on those long legs of his, only bothering to call a single word—"Trouble"— over his dark-shirted shoulder.

Papa and Collier were up then, Collier darting to the fireplace for the sleek rifle hanging over it.

Was it rustlers? Victoria stood, still confused, and looked to Laurel for clarification. A mountain lion? A bear? But Collier, leaving with the rifle, called, "The stallion!"

Nobody would steal a wild horse that, thus far, the Pembrokes could not give away. That's when Victoria realized there could be other kinds of trouble than theft, and she followed Laurel out by a heartbeat.

Papa turned to point a stern hand at his older daughters. "Stay."

But then Victoria's ever-searching gaze stopped, frozen, on a flash of yellow in the stallion's corral. She could not have looked at anything else even if she wanted to. Just that. Yellow. Close to the ground. Yellow like calico. Yellow like a dress.

Then not even her father could keep her from breaking into a full run after Ross and Collier.

Chapter Eleven

Of course, Laramie heard it first. He'd lived his adult life watching, listening, waiting for trouble. It still surprised him when trouble came. But he'd kept alive staying ready for the surprise.

When the feeling came upon him in that fine parlor—like a hum of danger, deep in his gut—he didn't question it. He was on his way out even as the others fell quiet enough for him to hear the horse. A horse, even in distress, shouldn't give him this cold clutch in his chest, this itch in his gun hand. But he knew better than to question it, so he kept going.

When Pembroke called, "The stallion!" Laramie knew which direction to head, his shoulders tight, his pulse rushing. Something felt wrong, smelled wrong, sounded—

Then he saw the rearing stallion, and the flash of its deadly fighting hooves. He saw the heap of yellow calico lying beneath those hooves.

His hand moved even faster than his mind, so quickly did he have his left arm extended, his aim taken, his trigger finger squeezing. Once. Twice. Three times.

With the first shot, the stallion dropped to four feet and turned, startled. At the second, it staggered back. With the third, it shuddered—he was hitting it, he knew he was hitting it, and yet still it hadn't gone down.

Too far away. Even as he ran, it was too far away for the accuracy of a damned six-killer. But he fired again.

Someone screamed, behind him. He hoped it wasn't Victoria, and he fired again.

The horse was stumbling now, red starting to mark lighter patches of its coat—and Laramie's revolver clicked on an empty chamber.

Men who rode with a sixth bullet tended to lose toes, but he would have sacrificed toes for this. *Click!*

He spun on the man he sensed beside him. "Damn it!"

And Collier Pembroke, with the finest rifle Laramie had ever seen, fired the shot that took down the rogue stallion for good. The Englishman did not look handsome at that moment. He looked ill. But he did it.

In the midst of tragedy, that counted for something.

Then everyone was rushing past them—Laurel and Victoria, their father moving faster than any old cowboy Laramie had ever known. And the two younger men were left standing in a sharp cloud of gun smoke, staring at a corral that looked to be too full of death for a kinder world.

"Kitty!" At Victoria's wail, a cry so full of grief it hurt to hear, Laramie felt sudden fury. Not at her. Not even at the damned horse.

Bad is bad.

He felt furious at the world, at God, for letting this happen. He'd always known—well, learned early

123

enough—that he didn't live in that kinder world.

He hadn't realized until this moment how much comfort he'd taken from the belief that Victoria Garrison did.

Papa's hat fell off as he swung himself between the corral rails. Victoria noticed that. Though hurrying, he didn't cry out or stumble, but his white hair seemed oddly vulnerable, without a hat.

Then he was gathering Kitty's frail little form up into his arms and carrying her out. The hat stayed, in the mud by the dead horse. *I should get his hat,* Vic thought numbly. But that was so she wouldn't think the worse thing.

Then she saw the broken spectacles, also in the mud, and she thought the worse thing anyway, and she pressed both hands to her mouth to keep any noise, any words from escaping and making this horrible thing real.

Not Kitty. Not little Kitty.

Collier was in the corral then, rifle in hand, checking to make sure the horse was dead. It was Laurel, the bravest of Vic's sisters, who flanked their father as he strode back toward the house with his precious armful and somehow asked what needed asking. "Papa? Is she . . . ?"

Papa answered so low that Victoria, still standing where she'd stopped, couldn't hear. Laurel started to cry—but she didn't stop walking with Papa and Kitty. She even ran ahead to the house, got the door.

What had he said?

Still not moving, Victoria wasn't sure she wanted to know. That depended on the answer. But want to or not, she *needed* to know. As Ross Laramie came to her side and took her arm with a gentle hand, she turned to him as her only hope. "What did he say, Ross? Did you hear? Is—is she . . . ?" She couldn't face the worse question, any more than Laurel had, so she again begged, "What did he say?"

"He said she's breathing," answered Ross in that low, even way of his. She longed for his containment, his control. Collier jogged past them toward the house, while Papa carried Kitty inside, but Victoria could only search Ross's face, see the truth of his words—and feel her heart begin to beat again. "Breathing?"

He nodded, the most beautiful answer she ever could have received.

"She's alive?"

He nodded, tugged at her arm. "They'll need you."

She glanced toward the corral—at what she could see of the dead stallion—and she imagined poor Kitty's terror as the beast reared up, struck at her. "Why? Ross, why? Why would anything hurt a little girl?"

He framed her face in his hands, as if to make her hear him. The warmth and steadiness of his touch felt like salvation, like the only thing that kept her head from exploding. She was safe with Ross. She always had been. "Victoria," he repeated, "They need you."

She nodded. Yes. Poor Papa. Poor Laurel.

Kitty . . .

When Ross drew his fingers off her cheeks and held her shoulders instead, turning her toward the house, she let him. She blessed his ability to move, when she couldn't. That thought, mixed with the gun smoke still lingering like a blue cloud, reminded her of another blessing.

"You were so fast," she marveled, remembering how quickly he'd drawn, how quickly he'd fired. She hadn't realized he'd done it until the third shot. "You saved her life. How did you ever learn to shoot that fast?"

125

But, urging her toward the house, Ross didn't answer.

Victoria's innocence frightened him, and Laramie didn't know what to say. How could he be the one to tell her that death didn't always come fast? Life could be gruelingly tenacious in its good-byes; maybe that's what made the taking of life so profane. Even a man gut-shot by a rustler could linger for days. Even a little girl, trampled by a wild horse.

How could he tell her that instead of saving her baby sister's life, he might have only prolonged it?

He couldn't. And the hope on her face as she quickened her step, tugging him by the hand she would not release, found its way into his heart just to break it.

By the time they reached the house, Collier Pembroke was heading toward the stables, his face drawn. "I'll bring the doctor," he promised as he passed. "Victoria . . ."

But then he shook his head and hurried on.

He thinks it's his fault for keeping the stallion, thought Laramie. Maybe the Garrisons would blame themselves for not watching the girl more closely, or their mother would take fault for not coming along, or keeping her home. None of them knew what it *really* meant to be responsible for someone's death.

That was yet another reason he didn't belong here.

He felt blasphemous walking into the grieving household. Laurel was running up the stairs as they came in, and Victoria followed, dragging Laramie with her. He had to actually grasp her wrist to free his hand from hers, before she tugged him right into the sickroom.

He didn't deserve to be in there, with the family.

Instead, Laramie watched from the doorway while Mrs. Pembroke used sewing shears to cut Kitty's torn, muddy dress off her broken little body, so as not to hurt her further. And it *was* broken. Right off, Laramie recognized the flash of white bone amid the bloody mess of one leg. One of her arms wasn't lying natural anymore, either. And something seemed wrong with her shoulder. Even once her father drew blankets over the child's near nakedness, they couldn't hide the blood already soaking into a pillow from the side of her head. Laurel Pembroke pressed a bandage against the wound, then made Victoria hold it while she darted out, past Laramie, for more supplies.

"What can I . . . ?" His words did not come easily, and she'd gone before he finished them.

The minutes stretched into bandages, soap and water, spiderwebs to stop bleeding, a hopeful bottle of brandy waiting to be used as a painkiller. All the while, Victoria was biting her lip, and Laramie wondered if it was to keep from saying anything wrong. Her older sister seemed more used to a sickroom, white-faced but grimly determined. And their father worked as smoothly and efficiently as if this were any injured animal he'd found, running his hands over the child's body, pressing at her gut, listening to her chest. He seemed almost unnaturally calm. Only his sharp eyes showed his agony—and that, only because Laramie knew how to read a man's eyes.

It felt like a blow when the man finally lifted that raw gaze to Ross. "Fetch two lengths of wood," he instructed, hoarse. "Flat."

"For her arm," guessed Laramie.

The rancher nodded, already turning back to Kitty.

As Laramie started down the stairs, Victoria must have released her lip. Suddenly he heard her asking, "But what about her leg, Papa? How will we ever set her leg?"

Laramie drowned the rest under his boot heels on

the stairs. Kitty's leg was clearly ruined; best that they leave it for the doctor. If it came to amputation . . .

He'd seen plenty of men torn, bleeding—by accident, or due to poor companions and poorer choices. Hell, a posse's mistake had sent two bullets ripping through him just that June—the most basic of doctoring, in an outlaw's hideout, had hardly prettied his wounds. But this was the first *child* he'd seen in such shape. It sickened him, deep down where he'd thought he'd gone numb years ago.

Nobody should have to amputate his own child's leg.

Laramie hid from that sick feeling by focusing on the task. When he got back upstairs with the wood, Victoria hovered in his spot in the doorway herself, her shoulders hunched, her bloody fists pressed against her chin as if to stop her mouth from trembling. He hoped she hadn't gotten herself expelled from the sickroom for her questions; God knew a girl who took comfort in answers must feel a powerful need to be asking them.

Despite the risk of exposure, he slid a hand down her spine as he ducked past. The look she sent him— grateful, hopeful, terrified—broke his heart a second time.

Garrison accepted the wood, then lifted the blanket off the girl's bad arm. "Best do it while she's out."

"But she'll come to, won't she?" That was Victoria again, desperate to know something, anything.

Laurel sounded cross when she said, "We don't *know.*"

The arm didn't look so bad, now that they'd cleaned her up. Oh, it was broken—arms just weren't made to turn like that—but Laramie had seen worse.

"I'll set it," he offered. "If you'd like."

But Garrison did it himself, as if turning and readjusting his daughter's thin little arm wasn't tearing his guts out. It was, surely. But he did it anyway.

Just as Laramie began to regret thinking he could help, the rancher said, "Fetch my wife. I—" He stopped then, in the midst of adjusting the wood split over the now straight little arm, and swallowed. "We'll need my wife."

"Yes, sir."

But before Laramie had reached the stairs, Garrison added, "Take Victoria."

"What?" Vic's eyes widened—a reflection, Laramie thought, of his own.

Her sister said, "Do you want Mama to hear this from a stranger, Vic? No offense, Mr. Laramie."

"No," he agreed, understanding now. "We'll get her."

Then he headed down the stairs again, surrounded by the scents of new wood, new paint, and fineries that meant nothing when a little girl lay up there hurting, maybe dying. He waited at the bottom until Victoria followed, her gray eyes still glazed with fear. Then he took her elbow and led her to the kitchen.

"Wash the blood off," he instructed, working the pump handle until water began to gush out, then guiding her hands into the flow. "Smell might spook your horse."

One of the hardest parts of riding to safety, after he'd been shot, had been handling his goddamned horse.

"I hate horses," she said—and suddenly he wanted to laugh. It wouldn't have been a good laugh. He swallowed it.

Instead he said, "I know."

"Give me Papa's saddle," she called, as he headed out the kitchen door, and he nodded.

He'd saddled her gelding by the time Victoria arrived, and she adjusted her father's stirrups to her leg length while Laramie tightened Blackie's cinch for himself, all in silence. When he turned to help her mount, Vic surprised him by suddenly leaning her head against his ribs, wrapping her arms around his waist, and crumpling into him, shaking.

Startled, he instinctively drew her more tightly against him, taking a bitter comfort in just the holding of her. He wished he could make this better, wished protecting life were as easy as taking it. But all he could do was stand there and try to absorb some of her misery.

"I don't understand," she said, her words slurred like maybe she was crying. Even when he tucked his chin to his chest, he could only see the top of her head—so he stroked a hand across her hair. "She should have known better than to go in there. And that horrible horse—she couldn't have been a threat to it! Why did it happen to her? She's so good. Of all of us . . ."

You're good, too. He doubted she wanted to hear that, and he didn't know any other answers, so he just held her.

"Tell me she'll be okay." Now she tipped her face toward him, her wet eyes bright with desperation. "She will, won't she? Papa's taking care of her, and Collier's fetching the doctor, and we'll bring Mama back, so Kitty *will* be all right, won't she?"

But this time, he couldn't lie. Not even a lie that she needed so badly to hear as this one. Only God knew if Kitty would make it.

Assuming God cared.

Cantering along the wooded path that would eventually take them to the ranch road, wishing Ross—in the lead—would spur his horse into a full gallop, Victoria felt guilty for not leaving sooner. She shouldn't have stopped to wash her hands and face, even if that had calmed her. She shouldn't have let Ross hold her, even for those few brief minutes, even if that had helped far more.

Nothing should matter but getting Mama back to Kitty—until Ross's horse reared back, even as Victoria registered a sound too familiar, today.

A gunshot?

Another gunshot?

Ross wheeled his horse back at her—"Get down, get down!"—but she didn't understand. Was someone hunting? Had someone made a mistake?

Still, she slid from Papa's worn saddle to the safety of the rocky ground, tugging poor Huckleberry hurriedly back up the path where Ross, leading Blackie, was crowding them. When Ross looped his gelding's reins over a tree branch, Victoria did it too, for lack of a better idea.

"Stay here." He spread his hand, the one not carrying his rifle, as if that could hold her back, then started up the path on foot, without her. But not for long.

"What's going on?" she whispered as she followed him. "Who's shooting?"

"Shhh!" He waved a hand backward at her. "Stay there."

When she shushed, she could hear what sounded like men's voices arguing from the trees beyond them, then the nicker of a horse.

Ross hunkered down with a slight wince and started to take off his spurs, one-handed. She stepped closer to him, put her hand on his hard shoulder and leaned very near his ear to whisper, "Why would anybody shoot at us?"

He widened his eyes at her, one finger—and a handful of leather and spurs—to his lips, and sank lower behind some brush. He left the spurs on the ground to reach up for her, catch her arm, and draw her abruptly down beside him.

131

Suddenly, after this awful morning, Victoria felt glad to be kneeling so close to the safety of Ross Laramie—even if someone *had* shot at them. Surely nobody had *meant* it! And in the meantime, his warmth and his smell and the lean hardness of him somehow reassured that she would be fine.

Though if it hadn't been an accident, if it had been *bad men* . . .

When she parted her lips again, he covered her mouth with his hand. She almost protested. But the way he then used that hand to gently draw her head toward his, then pressed his cheek against her hair and his lips near her ear, felt so intriguing that she did not want to interrupt.

"They *shot* at us," he whispered into her ear, and she shivered at the sensation. "But they didn't *aim* at us."

How did he know that? His hand muffled her attempt to ask the question. In the meantime, she heard the lowing of a cow from the same direction as the voices.

Was it rustlers? Of course, they *were* in cow country; there were more cattle around here than humans. But the shooting part, that did seem significant.

Laramie whispered, "Speak. Very. Quietly." And she felt guilty again. His words shouldn't tickle like that. Not when they were in a hurry. Not with her sister hurt.

But they did.

When she nodded, he slid his hand from her mouth.

She rose on her knees to brace her jaw on his shoulder, brush her lips against his ear. Her whisper was barely a breath. "Do you think it's the rustlers?"

His nod was an awkward jerk, his shoulder tight.

"How do you know they weren't aiming at us? Maybe they're bad shots."

132

When she drew back, she saw that Ross had closed his eyes. After a moment, and a long breath, he opened them and bent back to her. "Gut," he admitted breathlessly, with a one-shoulder shrug. "And I did not hear the bullet hit."

Oh. She returned to *his* ear. "Then why shoot at all?"

He nuzzled her hair again to answer. "Warning. They heard us coming."

When she leaned back to him, his sleek, soft hair tickled her cheek. She liked his scent, even the gun smoke that still clung to his clothing. He may have saved Kitty's life, fast as he could shoot. She would always admire that about him. "Are you going after them?"

He looked from her to the sound of the fading voices, clearly torn. She wondered how many minutes they'd been crouched in the underbrush. Three? Five?

"If you think it's safe, I'll ride ahead and tell Mama what happened," she continued quickly. "You can see who they are, why they're shooting at us."

He wove a hand into her hair and all but buried his face in it to hiss, "What if it isn't safe?"

"I'll go anyway," she whispered firmly, and didn't shy from his disapproving stare. The rustlers weren't aiming at them; he'd said so himself. And she had to fetch Mama.

Ross sighed. Hard. "Take the rifle," he instructed against her ear. "Go back for your horse, but make noise once you get there, and while you're riding. Let them know you're just a woman."

She drew back far enough to flare her eyes at him— well, *really!*—and he grinned.

Ross Laramie grinned.

It was beautiful. He quickly ducked his head, as if embarrassed by his own behavior. Then, his hand still in her hair, his fingers steadying against her scalp, he drew her head close to his jaw again. "If they know you are no threat, you'll be safe. And if they think you are alone, I can keep better watch to make sure of it."

By now they were kneeling to face each other, cheek to cheek, so she didn't have to move to whisper, "You won't try to capture them?" They had to get Mama back to Kitty!

"Not today."

She drew back to search his dark, angled, *intense* face. She didn't want him trying to capture the bad men for other reasons, too. "But you'll catch up?"

"Yes."

"Promise?"

At that, he used the hand in her hair to turn her head and he pressed a kiss to her lips—a kiss she'd wanted since the previous Friday, a kiss she'd *needed* since she caught that glimpse of yellow in the corral. His kiss begged her to be careful, promised mysterious possibilities that *had* to mean things would turn out all right.

But of course they would. Ross was here.

Too soon, he wrenched his mouth from hers, leaned his forehead onto her shoulder, breathed shuddering breaths.

"Ross," she whispered, and he faced her again, his dark eyes burning. So she kissed him. She didn't know how to do it as well as he, but his lips felt just as firm even so, tasted just as good. Then she drew back and asked, "Did you reload your gun?"

He stared at her for a long moment, no expression on his face and worlds of emotion roiling deep in his dark, brown-green eyes. But all he said was "Yes."

"Then be careful," she whispered. On second thought, she picked up his Spanish spurs, where he'd left them on the ground, showed them to him, and folded the leather straps over to squeeze them into her skirt pocket. Then she crept back toward where her horse waited.

She needed to get Mama for Kitty.

She trusted Ross to handle the rest.

Chapter Twelve

Laramie wasn't sure what he was doing.

Obviously he was creeping like an Indian, if a stiff one, through the wooded foothills; but for once, he wasn't the one hiding. He was the one in pursuit of the "bad men," as Victoria called them. How the hell had that happened?

But he knew how. Not his current job. Not even that they'd shot at him, bad aim or not. They'd shot at Victoria. For that, they deserved . . .

They deserved tortures that would take more time than he had, just now. More important matters waited at the Circle-T and the Lorelei.

Behind him and slightly uphill, Laramie heard Victoria say, "Well, Hucky horse, I guess someone must be hunting. Papa sure will have something to say about that! How about we try not to look like a deer again, huh?" Then she even raised her voice to call, "Hello? Whoever you are out there, I'm not a deer!

I'm Victoria Garrison, and I want to go home now, so please don't shoot anymore!"

Laramie felt that amused tightening in his cheeks again. Somehow, she made even talking to *herself* sound easy and natural. She made quite a bit of sound that way.

Did you reload your gun?

He had, of course. But that even Victoria wanted him to stay armed had to make it less reprehensible, didn't it? And she'd kissed him, full deliberate, which somehow made *that* less reprehensible too.

Laramie shook his head and continued creeping. Now was no time to think about kisses, even kisses that lingered on his lips, making serious headway into parts of his heart that he'd thought scarred over years ago. For now, he'd best concentrate on the shooters who, if they had a lick of sense, were hightailing it as far from the main path as possible. It might be easier to look for where they'd crossed, then follow their tracks. But they'd be watching behind them, and he preferred not to get shot. For now, Laramie moved stealthily through the trees, toward what sounded to be an unhappy cow—and angry voices.

"—that again, I'll kill you myself," warned a man with a gravelly voice.

A younger voice said, "She didn't see us, did she?"

"No, but she'll surefire tell her pa. And I don't want the boss thinkin' I was shootin' at one of his girls."

The boss? "She. Didn't. See. Us."

"I don't want the boss thinkin' *anyone* in these hills was shootin' at one of his girls, 'cause he might just come lookin'. And he might just not stop."

"You'd rather she *did* see us? A hundred more yards and she woulda, you know. This steer might make her wonder—"

"Hush!"

Laramie went still. Apparently the two men—and it

sounded like only two—did as well. The cow, for its part, moaned out another protest at its situation.

"What?" asked the younger voice after a long moment.

"Thought I heard somethin'," admitted the other man. Then his pitch changed, maybe for the cow. "Get on, you."

Laramie crept closer still, each footstep a well-considered choice. As he shadowed the rustlers, he saw how the bank shifted here—the rustler's path sloped downward, but a nearby stretch climbed upward. Either he had a hunch or a years-old memory, but Laramie chose the incline. Sure enough, after some hunting he found a rock that jutted out over the rough track. He crawled out onto it, first on all fours, then—gritting his teeth—low on his belly and elbows, and waited as two mounted cowboys eased a steer into tree-dappled view.

The problem with lying so high was that he could see only the top of them—hats and shoulders, not faces. But he could tell from their size that neither man was Sheriff Ward. Surely the lawman wouldn't be doing his own rustling anymore, even if he *was* reaping profits from it.

Ward knew as well as anyone, except maybe Laramie, the dangers of being caught with a stolen cow.

Frustrated, he looked for clues he *could* see—noticed clothes, horses, hints of a brand. Something distracted him, something that felt foolishly like . . . impatience?

Laramie had seen more men die from impatience than from bullets or knives combined. That wasn't his cow, and this wasn't the reason he'd returned to Wyoming. So why was he considering swinging himself into the path, drawing down on these men, and ending the situation right here? What had happened to his usual composure?

He didn't have to think hard. *Victoria.*

She'd made him promise to catch up, as if he mattered. As if in this small thing, she needed him.

Laramie could confront the rustlers and maybe survive, maybe not. Or he could follow them wherever they were headed, and lose the afternoon. Or he could accept that they were well off the path, and would pose no more threat to the Garrisons this afternoon, and just hope he got back to this part of the woods while he could still find tracks.

It was a harder decision than he would have guessed.

It was hard not to gallop headlong down the hillside; only strict training about abusing one's horses kept Victoria from giving Huckleberry his head. She told herself she wasn't scared of the rustlers, and maybe that was so. But she was scared.

She was scared Kitty might yet die. She was scared she would say the wrong thing and add to Mama's fears. She was scared because Ross had gone after the rustlers alone.

And every time Huck stumbled or scattered rock, Victoria was scared she wouldn't get home fast enough.

By the time she left the woods and rode down the grassy swell of foothills toward the ranch road, Victoria felt downright ill from worry. Before she got in sight of the buildings, she drew Huck to a full stop and wondered if she tried hard enough, whether she could vomit right now and get it over with.

She wanted to be strong for Mama, and Audra, and Elise. Maybe if she threw up now, she wouldn't do so in front of them. But her stomach refused to cooperate.

Desperate, she arched her neck back, stared at the sky, which was blurred with tears, prayed for extra

strength to do what she had to do in the best possible
way.

That's when she heard the hoofbeats.

They came on her fast, faster than folks should ride
except in a race, and she remembered the rustlers and
train robbers and bad men. Suddenly, Victoria was
scared for herself after all.

But she had to get to Mama anyway.

Dazedly, reaching one hand behind her to touch
the rifle stock, she turned in Papa's saddle—and finally felt something other than fear. Because she recognized the black horse galloping out of the hills,
recognized the rider leaning low over its outstretched
neck, a point of darkness before a cloud of dust.

It was Ross Laramie, catching up.

What she felt then was sweeter, deeper, fuller than
anything she could remember feeling in her life. *He'd
kept his promise!* Now she didn't have to ride into the
ranch by herself. Now she wasn't alone.

Because of him.

She turned Huck toward Ross's approach. Ross
slowed Blackie as he neared her—no need to spook
her mount—which only gave Victoria more time to sit
there, grateful and relieved and . . . and sweet and
deep and full.

Full of him.

Her reins were in her left hand, so she reached her
right hand out to him, fingers spread wide as if that
alone would bring him closer, faster. As he neared,
Blackie walking now, he reached out too. Their hands
closed around each other's, fingers weaving together.

She wished she were holding more than his hand.
She wished she could lean out and wrap her arms
around him, slide out of Papa's worn saddle and into
Ross's arms.

As ever, she made do with words. "You made it."

He nodded, not trying words at all. Poor Blackie,

blowing and lathered, needed to walk this last bit of road; one more reason to ride on.

That, and to tell Mama what had happened.

Ross looked a mite lathered himself, his eyes bright with excitement or pain, strands of black hair stuck to his neck and his jaw and his high cheeks. His shirt was damp—but she remembered liking him damp.

Huck decided the issue by shifting position, which forced Vic and Laramie to either release their grip or tug one or the other out of the saddle.

Vic felt herself starting to lean out before their hands drew reluctantly apart. Like a greenhorn, she actually grabbed the saddlehorn to catch her balance.

In more ways than one.

"I'm glad you did," she admitted, reining Huck toward the ranch. "Oh, Ross, I don't know how to tell Mama. I don't want to alarm her, but I can't lie either, and it *is* alarming. It is, isn't it?"

When she dared look toward him, his brightness had darkened some. "Yes," he agreed.

"What will I say?"

"You'll know," Ross assured her with that even, controlled certainty of his.

"Do you think so?"

He nodded. She wished they could hold hands again, but they were topping the last tall rise, in sight of the ranch house now.

"You always know what to say." He ducked his head and added, "It's something I admire about you."

Victoria caught her lower lip between her teeth. He'd said that before—did she dare believe him? For years, she'd been called a chatterbox, a blabbermouth, a magpie. Was it possible that her words could be admirable?

She could see the distant figure of her mother in the yard, hanging laundry with Audra, not far from the elm tree with its lone grave. Both women seemed to look up at Ross and Victoria's approach. Mama stepped around the laundry to see them better.

Did she always know what to say?

"Tell me about the rustlers," she begged Ross. "Later on, I mean. Once I know Kitty's all right. You'll do that, won't you? I want to have something else to think about, in case . . ."

But she'd run out of time to focus on anything but how her mother had broken into a run to meet them, clearly recognizing that Victoria was alone with a ranch hand—and riding her father's saddle.

"I'll tell you," promised Ross. "Once you know."

Victoria found the right words. Mrs. Garrison, beyond a certain waxen-faced shock upon hearing of the accident, responded with more competence than many women—or men—might. She asked Laramie to get fresh horses so that they could return to the Lorelei at once, and she set about collecting what she might need to save her daughter.

Laramie roped and saddled horses for the ladies, chose another mount for himself from the ranch's stock, explained—haltingly—to the foreman what had happened, and sent for Nate Dawson. Now that they knew rustlers might cross that path, they would ride with guards.

Not long after Laramie and Victoria arrived at the Circle-T, they were leaving it. Laramie rode point, then Victoria, then Mrs. Garrison with Elise, then Audra. Dawson took up the rear. Duchess, the dog, tended to run ahead on the path, then double back whenever it suited her.

They arrived in the early afternoon to the sight of the doctor's horse, hitched to the porch. Ross helped Victoria down this time, despite the sharp tug in his side, and felt guilty for how much he wanted to leave his hands around her waist, wanted to draw her against him and hold her through this. While everyone dismounted, Laurel Pembroke rushed out of the house with what little news she had. "She hasn't woken up yet."

Laramie thought she was putting a great deal of hope in that "yet." But he'd kept silent for far worse reasons than not kicking that hope for this frightened family.

Mrs. Garrison ordered her daughters to stay downstairs—even Mrs. Pembroke—and went up to take over the nursing duties. Then the waiting began.

Everyone except little Elise had a haunted look—more fearful, thought Laramie, than the look of someone facing down a shotgun barrel, because this fear held increasingly less disbelief, increasingly more resignation. Whenever he and Victoria caught each other's gaze, her gray eyes begged him to say something to make it right, but of course he could not.

Not even the most eloquent words could bring comfort right now, much less his. Not without lying. And he would not lie to her about this.

The ladies distracted themselves with work, cooking and cleaning. Laramie and Dawson saw to the horses and tackle, then any other chores they could find. Thaddeas Garrison arrived, breathless and tight-mouthed, to no further news than they'd had; after briefly seeing Kitty and their parents, he made himself useful by taking Elise out to see the foals. Collier Pembroke, who'd sent the doctor ahead, returned with an attractive blond woman, a baby lying on a pillow across her lap, and Laramie learned that this was the oldest girl, Mariah MacCallum.

She left the baby with her sisters and went upstairs as well, then came down with red eyes and helped cook.

Laramie found Collier Pembroke seeing to his own

mount and asked, "Where should we bury the stallion?"

Pembroke looked up, his otherwise pretty features pinched. "The stallion," he repeated tightly.

Laramie hesitated to offer advice to this fancy man, a respected ranch owner, maybe nobility. But the burying had to be done, and if he could get past his guilt long enough to think about it, Pembroke would see that.

"It's a warm day."

Pembroke took a long, shuddering breath, then nodded and turned away from his sparse, English patch-saddle and pointed. "Up higher, I suppose. That stand of aspens out there, just before the land turns, if it's not too rocky. It seems fitting."

Laramie had the strangest urge to put his hand on the Englishman's shoulder, to tell him the accident wasn't his fault. All stallions were dangerous, not just wild ones, but a horse ranch couldn't exist without them. The child knew better than to get close. She'd been little, but Laramie could tell she'd been—*was*—smart.

From the looks of that separate corral, and the extra-high rails, Collier Pembroke hadn't been negligent in the stallion's keep. He'd kept it out of kindness. He ought not be suffering for that.

Yet Laramie was just a hired hand—and barely that. Pembroke didn't know him from Adam, and certainly had no cause to find comfort in his reassurances. So all Laramie managed was, "It'll give us something to do."

After that, throughout the afternoon, the men took turns with two shovels up on the point. First Laramie and Dawson, Laramie silently gritting his teeth against how that hurt his still-healing wounds. Then Thaddeas Garrison and Pembroke arrived, deepening the grave. Some hours later, a stocky young man who was introduced as Stuart MacCallum arrived at the ranch and hiked up to join them, taking his turn at the shovel.

He seemed a good man, even for a sheep farmer.

They stopped for a midafternoon dinner, though nobody was hungry, washing up at a horse trough. God knew there was enough food. And they learned that there had been no change in Kitty's condition— or so they thought.

Victoria surprised Laramie on the porch, drawing him around the corner of the house long enough to whisper, "The doctor wants to cut her leg off."

He didn't bother to ask how she knew that when her older siblings didn't. Instead, he stared down at her tear-bright eyes, noticed how she was clutching her middle, and wished he knew what to say to make the hurt stop for her.

He didn't have those words, so what *she* said next was an accusation. "You knew."

He shrugged, inadequately. She glared up at him, her dark hair spiraling into tight curls around her face from all that time in the hot kitchen. No matter why she'd told him, she demanded more than he'd given in response.

"It looked bad," he admitted, finally.

She bit her lower lip, still hugging herself.

"I'm sorry," he said. Then, almost against his will, he lifted his hand and drew his thumb gently across her poor, trapped lip.

Her teeth let it go. "The doctor thinks it's bad too. That's why he wants to cut it off. Mama's fighting him on it. She says that if they set it as best they can, and just keep the infection out, there are doctors in Chicago and New York who can fix it better once she's well enough to travel. But the doctor says the infection could . . . It could kill her. And Papa doesn't know what to do."

Tears began to slide from her eyes, down her

cheeks, and Laramie drew his thumb across those, too. "I'm sorry."

Her shoulders began to tremble, so he put his arms around her, drew her to him tightly and surely, held her as best he could while her arms slowly fell to his side and she cried against the front of his shirt—wet from the horse trough. He still had no words of comfort, but he hoped this somehow helped soothe her.

Strangely, it soothed him.

He lost track of how long they stood there like that, Victoria soft and tired and frightened in his arms, him doing little more than being strong and less visibly frightened and . . . and *there.* The noise of the screen door slapping shut, on the porch around the corner, startled them both apart. He didn't breathe until he heard footsteps heading in the direction of the stables.

Damn! Laramie pushed a hand through his hair, angry at himself now, angry at the world. He felt suddenly cold. He had no right to be the one holding her, comforting her.

Victoria's gray eyes narrowed, as if she'd thought the same thing. But what she said was, "You'll tell my papa you mean to call on me, Ross Laramie."

He blinked at her, startled.

She wanted him to not just ask the boss, but *tell* him?

"You've been wonderful today, and I need you, but I deserve better than to hide it," she declared, swiping the back of her hand across a cheek. "You deserve better, too."

As if she knew what he did—or did not—deserve.

All he managed was a single, broken question. "Now?"

She laughed then. It wasn't a pretty laugh, and sent her digging for a handkerchief—she found and gave back his spurs, with another sniffle—but it relieved him some anyway. "Of course not now. Not while Kitty . . . while she . . ."

He put a hand on her back and waited while she wiped at her face. Then she looked up, drier but no less determined. "You will, though, won't you? I wouldn't ask, except I've gotten the impression you were . . . You . . ."

Who could blame her? A less observant woman than Victoria could not have missed his interest. In a different world—one with a future, without his past— Laramie would be on Victoria Garrison's doorstep in a heartbeat. But their worlds were different. "I don't think I can."

"You never know until you ask." At least she backed off of the idea of him *telling* Garrison anything!

"I don't have . . . prospects," he explained weakly.

"But you can find some."

He stared down at her, wishing he knew how to explain. If he trusted anybody with his secrets—the promises he'd made, the sins he'd committed—he guessed it should be her.

But he wasn't sure he had the nerve to watch her face when she learned who he was. *What* he was. That he wasn't one of the good men at all.

Apparently he stayed silent too long, because Victoria said, "Oh," and turned sharply away. "Never mind."

He'd hurt her, the last thing he'd wanted to do. Panic burned in his throat, and his hand squeezed tight enough around his spurs to jab himself on the rowels. "Victoria."

But she was circling the house. "My mistake!"

And the fact that she had other, more important worries than him tonight did nothing to belie the fact that she was right.

Half right.

It had been both their mistake.

Chapter Thirteen

Vic hated being wrong, even about little things, but being wrong about Ross hurt. Maybe he *did* enjoy holding her, kissing her. But he clearly didn't intend to court her. And since he *had* kissed her, and she had kissed him, that must make her, well . . . loose.

Which was nowhere near as bad as what it made him.

She paused on the stoop outside Laurel's kitchen, hurt and confused. She'd thought she understood him, that she'd sensed a *goodness* in him, a real caring.

How could her instincts have been so wrong?

The door from the kitchen opened and Audra stepped out, her pretty face drawn with the same edge of fear the rest of the family wore. Victoria opened her arms, and they held each other. Audra was barely two years younger than she, but it seemed like a long two years.

Especially tonight. Well-behaved Audra would never

act the way Victoria had with Ross Laramie.

"Have you heard anything?" asked the younger girl tentatively. Audra didn't normally approve of Victoria's nosy ways; clearly she was desperate.

Vic wasn't about to burden her younger sister with the doctor's dire warnings about possible gangrene and amputation. "I'm sure they'll tell us if anything important happens."

Audra nodded, trembling.

"And Mama came down to fetch supper," Victoria reminded her. "They wouldn't be eating if they thought the situation was too desperate, would they?"

"No," whispered Audra. "No. I guess they wouldn't."

Victoria gave her a squeeze and, arm in arm, they went inside to join Laurel, Elise, Mariah, and little baby Garry.

She had more important things to worry about than Ross Laramie's sincerity—or lack thereof.

When the menfolk finally returned from burying the horse, Collier moved immediately to Laurel's side. Stuart went to Mariah, lifting little Garry from her lap into his thick, working-man arms. Thaddeas scooped Elise up and put her on his shoulders. Vic held hands with Audra.

Ross Laramie and Nate Dawson stayed out on the porch, in the late-slanting sunlight of this never-ending day. Then Papa and the doctor came downstairs and she forgot about everything else.

Papa stood behind Vic and Audra, putting a steadying hand on one of their shoulders each, while Dr. Crowley announced, "Your sister is a very lucky little girl."

The exhalations around the room were audible.

"She's awake, with no serious damage to her head or spine. That, however," he warned, "is the good news. She also has a broken arm and some broken and cracked ribs. The injury that most concerns me"—

149

his gaze lifted to Papa's—"concerns *us*, is her left leg. It is badly broken, and I fear that at the very least she may need crutches or even a wheelchair for some time. Possibly the rest of her life."

Now the room hung silent except for baby Garry's gurgles from Stuart and Mariah's joined arms. Victoria noticed that Collier had leaned his head onto Laurel's shoulder, to hide his face, as he held her from behind.

It was Papa who added one firm word: "But . . ."

"But," agreed the doctor reluctantly, "that will be a matter for physicians more experienced than myself. In the meantime, I will return daily, for at least a week, to monitor her progress. Mr. and Mrs. Pembroke, I suggest you prepare yourselves to have guests for some time."

"We're glad to," said Laurel immediately.

And as if they'd just gotten out of church, everyone started talking at once. Collier assured the doctor that he could still reach Sheridan by twilight and offered to accompany him. Stuart, after a quick discussion with Mariah, insisted that he do it—he should get back to their ranch, and he trusted Thaddeas to bring Mariah and Garry safely home the following day. Audra hugged Papa so hard that her long, strawberry-brown braid started to come loose, and Elise wanted to know when she could see Kitty, and if Kitty got a wheelchair, could she ride in it.

"You can take turns seein' her," allowed Papa.

When Victoria noticed her father silently watching her, and met his gaze, he said, "Awful quiet, Victoria Rose."

His stern, gray eyes teased her. That, more than anything, reassured her that Kitty would get well. Victoria traded hugs with her father, and her sisters, and her brother and brothers-in-law. She gave Mariah's darling baby a happy kiss and, waiting her turn to go into the bedroom, asked questions of the others as they left.

When her turn arrived, she kissed her sister, promised to read to her, and began to think she could finally relax.

Then Kitty asked, "Is Mr. Laramie still here, Vic?"

Victoria lifted wide eyes to her father, who looked surprised but not upset. Mama said, "You should rest for now, baby. You've had a lot of visitors."

"But you always say that thank-you's and sorries are best said right off," protested Kitty, an edge of determination in her wan voice.

Mama smoothed her hair gently back. "You're right. We do say that. But only if you feel well enough."

"Best said right off," insisted Kitty.

So Victoria said, "I'll . . . fetch him." But she wished, more than ever, that she hadn't all but begged the man to court her. Or that he hadn't refused.

Now that she wasn't quite so worried about Kitty, she wasn't sure which part of that combination bothered her the most.

When Laramie first heard the news from the porch, he almost didn't believe it. Even after being trampled by a stallion, Kitty would survive?

Hell, if Mrs. Garrison had her way, the child might even walk again. What was it Victoria had said? *Doctors in Chicago and New York.*

Must be nice, he thought wryly—then frowned at his own bitterness. Watching the family through the parlor windows, seeing them hold each other and weep and laugh in shared gratitude, made him feel lonely, was all.

Either that, or he was a bigger shit than even he had realized. After all, he knew some men who would be glad to have a fancy lawyer defend them on murder charges, too. Mrs. Garrison had hired a professional for him, too.

But why? Why would a rancher's wife spend so

much money on an immigrant boy? Was it from guilt over her family's involvement? Would he ever know?

Through the window, he watched Jacob and Thaddeas Garrison exchange nods while Thaddeas hugged Victoria. Their sister was alive. Sometimes God cared after all. But his own sister was still dead. Worse yet, he'd been in Sheridan for weeks and done nothing to keep his promise to her.

Worst of all, he was no longer certain that he could.

Without a word to Dawson, Laramie swung off the porch and strode through the last dregs of sunshine to the old homestead cabin, the one Victoria said she'd helped renovate. Leaning against a tar-paper wall, he tried to imagine her chopping wood or toting water. The only way he could picture it was to see her talking at the same time, which made him want to smile. And *that* unnerved him.

Whether it should or not, something was happening, had already happened between them. Something important, which he would have to honor, though not the way she wanted.

He still couldn't court her.

But he also wondered if he had it in him to kill Victoria's brother or her father—even if one proved to be the man he'd sworn to destroy. Whoever had betrayed Julije still deserved death, or worse. And yet, if it was a Garrison, how could he deliberately put Victoria through what he'd watched her go through today?

The sacrifice wasn't what she wanted from him.

It wasn't even close to what he wanted for her.

A sharp whistle drew his gaze to the house. Victoria stood with Nate Dawson on the porch. Dawson beckoned.

But Laramie watched Victoria as he returned, reluctant to face her anger, and surprised by her request.

"Kitty wants to see you," she said, focusing on his chest instead of meeting his eyes.

Laramie looked at Dawson, but the hand shrugged.

Laramie looked back at Victoria and nodded. Then, since she hadn't seen his nod, he said, "All right."

And he followed her upstairs.

Kitty Garrison looked fragile in the Pembrokes' big feather bed, even with her mother sitting on the bed beside her and her father standing stern guard by the window. Her bandaged face had swollen, making her lopsided. Her hurt arm hung in a gingham sling. Laramie couldn't see her bad leg, but the shape of the blankets indicated that someone had propped up the covers to keep their weight off of it.

He hesitated in the doorway, feeling guilty that he could resent anything, no matter how briefly, about such a child's recovery. Then Mrs. Garrison beckoned him nearer, so he came to the bedside.

"Miss," he said, confused. "I hope you feel better."

The words sounded foolish to his own ears. She had to be feeling like hell.

The little girl looked up at him with eyes pinched either from pain or poor vision. Likely both. "Thank you, Mr. Laramie, for saving me from the stallion. I'm sorry I made you do that."

He blinked, unsure he'd heard correctly. "You're . . . ?"

She looked down at her covers now, her good hand fidgeting with the sheet. "If I hadn't gone where I wasn't supposed to, you wouldn't have had to *do* that," she explained with warbling solemnity. "I feel just awful that I got him killed."

Behind him, Victoria protested, "Oh Kitty, no!" Laramie felt her nearness—even if she wasn't there to be near *him*.

"I *did*," insisted the child, her voice climbing in pitch. When she tipped her head back to stare at Laramie again, he recognized the pain and guilt in her blue eyes.

From a mirror, long ago.

He'd gotten good at hiding those feelings, but if anybody could still see them, it was him.

"At least, I helped," she added tearfully, actually grieving for the horse that had tried to kill her. "And because of me, you had t-to shoot him. And that must feel just awful. So I'm s—*sorry.*"

Then she began to cry too hard to continue, despite her mother's steadying hand on her thin shoulder.

Laramie carefully sank to a crouch beside the bed so he could look at her straight on, his heart pounding. "That's not how it is," he told her evenly. "That horse was bad."

She shook her bandaged head. "Nooo!"

"Maybe he wasn't born bad," he insisted, unsure where all these words were coming from—maybe Victoria, standing so near that her skirts brushed his hip, had a lingering influence. He didn't question it. He just talked. "Maybe if his world hadn't changed, he would have been fine. But things do change. He couldn't have his world anymore. There was a bounty on his head. He had to be captured or killed, and the Pembrokes—they figured capturing him was the kinder thing. But there he was in that corral, his mares sold away from him, and I don't guess he wanted to live that way. Critters that get trapped, they turn mean. They hurt so bad inside that they don't know anything else but to hurt other critters. And whether they intend it or not, that makes them bad. Do you understand?"

She nodded, her pinched gaze now locked onto his.

Laramie didn't look away either, mainly because he was afraid to see what anybody else in the room thought of his speech. That had to be more words than he would sometimes string together in a month.

"So . . ." The way Kitty bit her lip looked familiar to him now. "So you think maybe he didn't mean to hurt me?"

"I guess maybe he didn't want to live in that corral anymore, and you gave him a way out." He hesitated. "Maybe it was a kindness."

Kitty reached out her good hand then and laid it on his own. His left hand. His gun hand.

"I'm still sorry I made you and Collier help," she whispered. "I'm sorry you hurt now, too."

Laramie stared at the contrast of their hands, and all he could manage was a nod.

"And that," interrupted Mrs. Garrison firmly, "is enough for now. It's time for your pain medicine, Kitty."

The little girl nodded. "My heart doesn't hurt so bad anyway," she announced unevenly, patting Laramie's hand once with her own before he managed to draw away.

And he did draw away. When he stood, it was so quickly that he almost stumbled.

He had to get out of here.

Mrs. Garrison looked up at him, a strange calm in her searching eyes. "Thank you for that, Mr. Laramie."

He had to get out of here *now*.

Somehow he managed not to bump into Victoria as he spun to leave. He shouldn't be in this house, this room. He shouldn't be talking like this to a little girl, and he damned well shouldn't be thanked for it!

"Good night," called Kitty, but he didn't slow to return the wish. He wasn't sure why he felt so panicked—so *trapped*—but he did, and instincts were instincts.

As he descended the stairs, he could see Garrisons sitting in the parlor and Garrisons on the front porch—but he knew the escape routes. He cut out the back way, through the kitchen, instead. Only on the stoop, noting that the sun had finally set, did he slow his steps, let his head fall back. This long day had nothing to do with him. He shouldn't have let it. This was the Garrisons' world, not his, and Kitty's guilt over the death of a wild stallion didn't—

Damn it, it *did* matter. It shouldn't, but it did.

Then, just to add to his evening's confusion, he heard the screen door behind him open, then shut. Maybe he smelled her. Maybe he sensed her. Maybe, after sneaking through the underbrush with her, he knew the sound of her petticoats. No matter how, he recognized Victoria without turning around, before she even started talking.

And she did start talking.

"I *wasn't* mistaken!" insisted Victoria, circling Ross Laramie to see his face. "You *are* a nice man."

Nobody could say those things to Kitty, the way he had, if he weren't deeply decent.

"Don't count on it," he warned, his expression blank.

"I'm not counting on anything, I'm just . . ." *Following my instincts. Justifying my earlier behavior.* "I'm trying to understand you."

"Don't."

She folded her arms. "I try to understand everything, Ross Laramie. You're not likely to be an exception. Still, I . . . I shouldn't have said what I did earlier. I didn't mean to herd you anywhere you didn't mean to go. I just thought I should be, well, clear on what I expected." She felt herself blush. "Or what I *should* expect, anyhow."

He didn't say anything.

"I'm sorry for getting angry over it," she added.

He shrugged one shoulder, as if to say he didn't care. The tension in his back said differently.

"I was upset at myself, too," she continued doggedly.

"For thinking I'd misread you. And then you were so nice to Kitty, upstairs, and I knew I hadn't misread you at all. You *are* a nice man. So something else must be going on, and I didn't give you a chance to explain, and I'm sorry for that. Everything—" For a moment she almost lost her train of thought, under remembrances of him holding her, kissing her, whispering in her ear. *Everything*, for sure. "Everything else aside, you've become a friend, and I want to help."

He said nothing, so she put a hand on his tight, taut arm. "I want to help with whatever's got you trapped."

"Like Kitty helped the stallion?" he demanded.

His anger confused her more than his words. "What?"

"She heard us talk about putting it down, so she tried to set it free. *That's* why she was in the corral. *Helping.*"

Victoria blinked up at him, stunned by his insight. Of course! Why else would well-behaved Kitty do something so strictly forbidden as to climb into the stallion's corral, unless she thought she had no choice?

She felt embarrassed that she hadn't figured it out herself. "She wanted to save it."

"And in appreciation, it tried to kill her."

Critters that get trapped turn mean. His description of the stallion had given her chills. Now—she didn't know why—she got chills again. *They hurt so bad inside that they don't know anything else but to hurt other critters.*

"And you saved her," she reminded him.

"Pembroke's the one who killed it."

But she wouldn't let him duck that. "And you're the one who heard it first. You're the one who shot it the fastest—you kept it from hurting her more. You saved her."

When Ross closed his eyes, as if fighting something,

it looked strangely as though he were praying. His words came out low and tight. "I am fast for a reason."

That made her look at his gun, solid against his dark thigh—and suddenly it wasn't there anymore.

Vic blinked, startled. In one smooth movement of his hand and his hips, Ross had skimmed the weapon from its holster and pointed it toward a tree behind the house. In another flex of his arm and flick of his wrist, he dropped it neatly back into the holster, as if he'd never moved.

"Golly," she breathed.

"I am fast," he repeated bitterly, "for a reason."

"I haven't seen anything that fast since Mr. Cody came to lunch. But Papa told him to put his piece away." Buffalo Bill had done so, too. Her parents felt strongly about using weapons as tools, not entertainment.

Ross scowled at her reaction. "That wasn't fast." He lifted his foot onto a nearby stump, long enough to tie strings from his holster around the inside of his thigh. Then he stood again. "This is faster."

This time he didn't move his hips. She didn't even see the gun go from holster to hand—one moment he was standing still, the next moment he was aiming at the woodshed.

Then he rolled it back into its holster.

Then—like magic—it was back in his hand.

"This part," he told her evenly, spinning the pistol backward, then forward over his hand, then finally into the holster, "is just show. Because I've had time to practice."

"Like Buffalo Bill," she told him.

"Like a man who is too familiar with guns," he corrected her. "This is why I cannot court you."

What? "Because you know guns?"

"Because nice men don't generally know guns this well." As if to prove his point, he drew the revolver

158

again, popped its cylinder, and dropped the bullets into his palm, one-two-three-four-five. They clinked together like hard candy. "Nice men don't have the leisure to learn this."

Then he pocketed the bullets and really started to play—fast draws, backward draws, tossing and twirling the revolver from hand to hand. Every now and then he stopped and pointed the weapon toward something—a tree, a stump, a boulder. Never at her. Never once at a living thing.

He *was* a good man. Maybe he just didn't realize it. "Lawmen know guns," she reminded him.

His cheek went tight, his ghost smile, but it didn't reach his eyes. "A badge doesn't make a man good."

"And a gun doesn't make a man bad."

He shook his head, fed the bullets back into the revolver, and returned it to its holster. Then he reached under his thigh and undid the strings. He looked sulky, as if his show hadn't accomplished what he'd meant it to.

Victoria decided that a little courage was in order. "So you're some kind of gunslinger," she accepted, low. "That's probably a good thing for a range detective. And maybe . . . maybe it's a good thing that you don't want to court me, too. But I meant what I said. You've become a good friend, to my family and to me. So if something's wrong, if you've got some kind of trouble, I want to help."

"You don't just want to help," he accused, bitter and resigned at the same time. "You want to understand."

And he was right. So she nodded.

Ross closed his eyes, his lashes sooty on his high cheeks, and again he looked as if he were praying. He looked like he was praying hard. And when he opened his eyes, he looked as if God hadn't answered.

He nodded as if a decision had been made—even if it was, somehow, one that would damn him.

"Maybe you can help me, at that."

Chapter Fourteen

His best chance at controlling how much she learned was to tell her himself. To tell her some part of it, anyway, and to pray that she never learned the rest.

Glancing to make sure they were alone, Laramie headed toward a sheltering brace of quaking aspen, not far behind the house. Victoria paused only to whistle boyishly for the dog, then followed. So did Duchess, loping around the corner of the house to join them.

"It's night," she explained needlessly. "I promised." And unlike him, she kept her promises.

Laramie reminded himself that, in all likelihood, the man he hunted was no Garrison. He could still avenge Julije, and Victoria could still help him—if only he could manage the words. He watched her wrap her arms around a tree trunk and pillow her cheek against it. Even in the shadows of mountain dusk, he could see the shine in her eyes, the curve of her face. She *wanted* to help, and she was beautiful.

"I made a promise too," he confessed over the whispering of the leaves. "Long ago. And I need . . ."

But the words wouldn't squeeze out of him, not even for her. He looked down, discouraged.

"What kind of promise?" prompted Victoria—but how could he answer? *I promised to kill someone.*

She considered him, worrying her lower lip. Then she tried, "To whom did you make the promise?"

Which gave him an idea. "A boy," he responded—not honestly enough to face her while he spoke the words, but far more honestly than he'd feared.

"From around here?"

"Once. He was . . . sent to Texas."

"Which is where you met him," she guessed. And he did lose track of the boy he'd been, sometime between jail and Texas, while turning into the man he'd become. So maybe they'd met.

"Well . . ." Victoria leaned back, hanging from the tree trunk, as if stretching into so enjoyable an activity as asking questions. "Does he have a name?"

"A foreign one," admitted Ross, low. "Lauranovic."

"Lor-ah-no-vitch," she repeated carefully, and it startled him to hear the name out loud. His family had been the Laurences for so long, before the lynchings. They'd only become Lauranovic again when they became outcasts.

He nodded and made himself speak what he hoped, tonight, would be the worst. "Folks say they were rustlers."

She straightened. "The rustlers Papa mentioned today?"

Laramie nodded, startled by how quickly she'd pieced that together, afraid she would suddenly guess the rest. *YOU are a Lauranovic, Ross-alias-Laramie! YOU are a rustler!*

"But—" Victoria cocked her head. "He was just a boy?"

He sank carefully into a low, cowboy crouch and picked up a twig to poke at the ground between his boots. "He was twelve when his father and brother were lynched."

"Lynched!"

"Your father kept the posse from hanging him too." Yet another reason to spare Jacob Garrison. "Your mother hired the lawyer who got him sent to Texas instead of to prison."

"Which is where you met him," she finished mistakenly, clearly absorbing all this. "Oh my."

Laramie crouched there and said nothing. He expected the worst when Victoria bent down beside him. Cowboys could hold that easy crouch for an hour at a time. Ladies, from sheer modesty, weren't so good at it. She didn't try; she just swept her skirts aside and knelt in the dirt.

Now he couldn't look away without being rude.

"It wasn't a regular ranch, was it?" she asked solemnly. "If he was sent there instead of prison, it must have been some kind of . . ."

"A boy's ranch," he admitted, knowing she would grasp the judicial overtones of that euphemism. It had been one of the earlier models for what were called reform schools.

"That's why you haven't told anybody about your connection to him," she guessed—and he realized his mistake. Even trying to hide his delinquent childhood, he'd somehow confessed it to her! And yet . . .

He felt confused to see nothing but sympathy in Victoria's shadowed gaze. Concerned sympathy. For once, Victoria Garrison did not ask something.

She did not ask why he'd been at a boys' ranch. He felt certain she wanted to know. That was how Victoria gauged trust, after all. Intimacy. *Secrets.*

But she also respected his privacy. So all she asked was "What did you promise him? This rustler boy?"

At that moment, he thought her the finest woman he'd ever met—a woman whose eyes he dared not meet for this part. "His older sister pointed the lynch mob to them," he admitted, keeping his voice desperately even. "She was in love with a local rancher, and confessed her father's hideout. That rancher betrayed them all. Then he abandoned her, and she hanged herself."

Even when Victoria gasped, he did not look at her.

"That's when folks learned she was with child," he finished, ugliness on top of ugliness. "And the boy—"

"Lauranovic," she said, and again the name tickled down his spine like a ghost of memory—or identity.

"He believed his family was innocent. He—" Laramie swallowed. "He claimed that the Wards were rustling their cattle, and his father and brother only stole them back. His only purpose—hope—was . . ."

How could he ask this of her?

But now that he'd told this much, how could he not?

"He had to know who betrayed them. Someone in Sheridan seduced, then abandoned his sister, destroyed their family, and he must—he *needed* to know who."

"And you promised to help him find out?"

"I—" How could he explain that part? "Yes."

Only when Victoria said nothing did he slide his gaze warily back toward her. She was fidgeting with a heart-shaped leaf in her lap, her dark brows drawn together in concentration. When she lifted her eyes, he wasn't prepared for the demand in them. "So that's what you've really been after, all along."

He stared, trapped. He hadn't thought of that.

"You didn't come to Sheridan for work, even as a

range detective," she continued, piecing it together even as she spoke. "You came here to uncover an old injustice."

For once, he could not hide behind ambiguity. He nodded, watched her shadowed face, and awaited the worst.

Instead, she nodded, then cocked her head again. "But you're a very *good* range detective."

Confused, Laramie sat back in the dirt. He doubted he could hold his balance if the conversation kept going like this. Every time he thought she would make an accusation, see his dark truths, she somehow managed to praise him instead. He was a good range detective?

Only Victoria. Only his sweet, hopeful Victoria.

"Only for the same reason I'm good with a gun," he warned her, his voice an uneven rasp.

"Well, I'm good at detecting other things," she assured him. "And if this happened some time ago—when was it?"

"Eighteen eighty-eight."

"Well, then maybe folks won't be so touchy about discussing it with me," she continued easily.

He stared at her. She meant it? She would help?

"Or maybe folks won't remember it at all," he said.

She dismissed such pessimism with a wave of her hand. "A scandal like that? They'll remember. *Especially* the man who was to blame. Anyway, it never hurts to ask."

He almost smiled again. Almost. "Yes, Victoria," he insisted quietly. Using her first name felt intimate, stolen. "It *can* hurt. At the very least, it can hurt reputations."

And at the most, for the man he was after, it could hurt far, far more.

"Don't worry so much. I'll try to keep people's

names out of it as much as possible. The past is past, right?"

He stared at her and thought, *The past is everything.*

"I'll say I'm curious because of the rustling," she continued, warming to her ruse. "And really, Ross, since I'm curious about everything, people might not get suspicious at all. Once we find out who misused that poor immigrant girl, you can send word to the boy—"

Then she paused, frowned. "I guess her brother's not a boy anymore, is he?"

Laramie said nothing. In the woods behind them, an owl hooted, coyotes called. The aspen leaves whispered warnings.

"Well, send word to your *friend* anyway. And you'll have kept your promise. All right?"

It wasn't all right. She didn't know what he meant to do with that information. His promise had not been simply to learn who misused Julije. His promise had been to avenge her. As desperately as he needed to do that, even now, he also knew that many people would think him wrong for it—including, he suspected, Victoria Garrison.

If she discovered what he had not, finally found him the name he needed, he would have used her to help him commit murder. She might forgive him for spending time in a reform school, but she would never forgive him for that.

He wasn't sure he could, either.

Victoria didn't tell even her best friend everything she'd learned from Ross Laramie. Especially not what she'd learned *about* Ross Laramie.

She didn't mention that he'd spent time at a boy's ranch, because Evangeline would wonder why—and Vic hated to admit that, like with his wounds, she hadn't asked. When Ross trusted her, wholly trusted

165

her, he would confess the rest on his own.

Wouldn't he?

She didn't tell Evangeline that Ross was a faster draw than Buffalo Bill Cody, since Evangeline already thought of Ross as dangerous. Evangeline had to be wrong there, too. Ross had saved Kitty's life. He'd held Victoria, quiet and strong, when she'd desperately needed holding. After they'd separated on the trail, he'd caught up with her just as he'd promised to, and later that night he'd even recounted what little he'd seen of the rustlers he'd followed.

Ross was a good man. She knew it, *felt* it, even if she couldn't prove it.

So Victoria summoned unusual reserve in what to reveal to Evangeline about Ross Laramie. And even there, her friend did not approve.

"Where were your folks when he told you all this?" asked Evangeline as they both sat in the back of the *Herald* office during Victoria's noon break, flipping through newspapers from 1888. Mr. Day had gone upstairs to take his meal with his wife; that usually meant a long lunch.

Together, the girls had gotten as far as October and found nothing about a lynching. The continued lack of proof made Victoria uncomfortable, but, well, maybe Ross or his friend had been mistaken about the year. Or maybe the lynchings had happened in December.

He hadn't lied to her.

"My parents were upstairs with Kitty. Stuart had gone home by then. Collier was on the porch with Laurel, and Thaddeas was in the parlor with Mariah and the others."

Evangeline did not look up, but her thin, pale brows drew together. "And you were behind the house together?"

Oh. Now Vic knew why she'd asked. "Duchess was

there. And we sat under some trees and talked, is all."
They'd done nothing more *that* night, at least. No
matter how solid Ross's hand had felt when he'd
helped her to her feet afterward, the barest flicker of
his eyes revealing that he was still healing from . . .
from what? No matter how tall and warm he'd felt
beside her before he let her go. And then the thirsty
way he'd stared at her, his head tucked as if to better
see her eyes . . .

Well, they'd done no more than that at the Lorelei.
He *had* refused to court her, after all. And she *did* have
a father, brother, and brother-in-law dangerously
close.

Evangeline said nothing, just turned pages.

"You're starting to remind me of Audra," teased Vic.

"Audra's a proper young lady." Evangeline said that
as a compliment, almost wistful.

"Or of Thaddeas," added Victoria. "Overprotective.
You know, you should come to dinner with us while
I'm staying in town." Papa was running his ranch from
the Lorelei for at least a week, while Mama tended
Kitty. Victoria, because of her job, had temporarily
moved into their in-town house with her older brother
until her parents returned to their own ranch. "I only
wish you could spend the night. The house seems very
empty without my parents or my sisters there."

Evangeline stopped turning pages, and Victoria saw
her friend's cheeks had color now, anyway. Spend the
night with Victoria and Thaddeas and *nobody else*?

"But I don't suppose that would be proper," Vic
added.

"No," said her friend in a small, choked voice.

Victoria put aside one newspaper and picked up yet
another one. November 1888. She tried to ignore her
rising uncertainty. Ross would not have lied to her.
And surely something as dramatic as a lynching and a
suicide would make the newspaper!

She just had to keep looking. "I told you Ross went after the rustlers when they shot at us, didn't I?"

"Yes," said Evangeline.

"He said he just has to watch for them now." And she believed him.

Evangeline nodded and reached for another paper. As she moved it, Vic saw the headline of the issue beneath it and let out a squeal of excitement. "Look!"

It said, *RUSTLERS LYNCHED!*

She snatched the paper to her breast. Ross was telling the truth. Of course, she'd *known* he was telling the truth—he was a good man. But still, after the quick draws and the boys' ranch and the refusal to court her, she couldn't deny her relief at having his story confirmed.

"Oh," said Evangeline softly. "Goodness."

"Here, I'll read it and you take notes." She cleared her throat. " 'The foothills outside of town became a place of death Thursday night . . .' "

But her reading soon slowed, and her voice thickened the worse the story got. Lynchings were wrong, especially in a township that had law. These lynchings, of a man and his older son, seemed even worse. Would the posse really have hanged the twelve-year-old, too?

Unlike the most dramatic dime novel, it had really happened, right here in Sheridan.

Just like Ross said it had.

"Look," she noted, touching the paper toward the bottom. "Part of it's missing. It says, 'The twelve-year-old outlaw, for—' and then it's rubbed out until it starts, 'named Drazen Lauranovic.' "

"That's a funny name," said Evangeline.

After looking at the back of the page, where she saw no reason for the deliberate smudge, Vic shrugged and continued reading until she neared the end.

" 'The head rustler, Mr. Lauranovic, is also survived by a widow and one daughter.' "

"The daughter must be Julie," she decided. "The one who got herself into trouble with a rancher."

"How does Mr. Laramie know it was a rancher?"

"I'm sure he has his reasons," insisted Victoria. But she found herself wishing she knew what those were. "I'll ask him, the next time I see him."

Whenever that would be. Papa refused to let her live alone at the Circle-T, so she had to choose between town, with Thaddeas—and her job—or staying at Laurel and Collier's ranch, with the recovering Kitty. Either choice neatly kept her away from Ross. And she *missed* him.

They'd spent a whole, long day together—him comforting her, protecting her, telling her his secrets, sneaking through the brush with her in pursuit of bad men. She would have thought that would sate her desire to spend time with a person. Instead, it whet her appetite for more.

Even if they *weren't* courting.

"Your mother wrote an editorial," noted Evangeline, looking in another newspaper. Victoria made do with the distraction. She was doing this for Ross, after all.

And maybe for the poor immigrant girl who had been so ill-treated. Maybe for the service of truth.

Helping Ross Laramie was just an added benefit.

Before Mr. Day came down from his long lunch, Vic and Evangeline read about Boris Ward's death, and the trial of young Drazen, and the Chicago lawyer whom Mama had hired to defend him. They read Victoria's mother's editorials, and Vic wished she'd managed to ask her parents about all this before leaving with Thaddeas. At the time, Kitty had been the only thing on their minds.

This weekend, she would ask.

They'd just found the paper that told about Julije

Lauranovic's shocking death when they heard Mr. Day coming down the outside stairs.

"I'd better go," said Evangeline, standing. "I don't want to wear out my welcome."

"Oh." Vic made herself look up from this latest headline—*RUSTLER'S DAUGHTER SUICIDE!*—which was no mean feat. "All right. Will you come by tomorrow?"

"You don't work tomorrow." Evangeline edged toward the back door. She felt it was better for business if nobody thought the newspaper was employing her.

"Then come by the house. I can show you the camera I ordered." When Evangeline shook her head and almost panicked, Victoria sighed with impatience. "You've come by the house hundreds of times!"

"When your mother is there. Not—" But whatever Evangeline meant to say, she stopped. "Victoria?"

The look in Evangeline's eyes silenced Vic's answer. Instead of asking *what*, she followed her friend's gaze past the printing press itself and out the front window.

Three cowboys were riding slowly down the street, drawing the attention of most of the passersby. One of them, on a buckskin, was Jacob Garrison, Victoria's father. One, on a black mustang, was Ross Laramie, looking as dark and dangerous as ever.

And the third, riding between them, had his hands tied together and hitched to his saddle horn. Papa held the man's reins like a lead rope. Ross seemed to have the man's gun, unless he'd taken to carrying an extra gunbelt over his shoulder.

"Oh my," said Victoria, stepping closer to the window to watch them pass in the direction of the sheriff's office.

They'd caught themselves a rustler.

Chapter Fifteen

Capturing the young rustler had been easy. It was delivering him to the sheriff that was hell.

It wasn't just because Laramie thought the sheriff was a son of a bitch, either. No, what had him on edge as he sat tall in his saddle, head defiantly up, was that he'd spent too many years trying not to be ridden into towns in just this way. He felt like he was on the wrong horse. He felt like a fraud.

But the boss had insisted. And when Jacob Garrison insisted on something, it generally went his way. That's how the rancher had been present when Laramie and two other Circle-T hands caught this fellow with a stolen steer and a running iron in the first place. It's what had Laramie accompanying the rancher into town with their prize.

That Sheridan was a much larger city than in '88 was more obvious, riding down Main Street at midday, than it had been skulking into a saloon on the edge of town. Laramie already knew the outskirts had an electric lighting house, flouring mills, brickyards, even a soda-water manufactory. Downtown, he counted three blacksmith shops and two livery stables, along with more stores than he could name. Far more people turned to watch from the boardwalks, or came out of shops to look, than he might ever have recognized. When he did occasionally place the face of an old undertaker here, a once-friendly storekeeper there, his gut cramped at the unpleasant sensation of past meeting present. After all, if he recognized them, they might just recognize him.

He could end up sitting on the other horse, even yet.

Riding a rustler into town like this—as if he were some kind of lawman—felt like he was *asking* for that kind of set-down. He resented Garrison for making him do it.

Then he saw Victoria.

She came out of the newspaper office in the same way that other folks were emerging from the tonsorial parlor, or the dry goods, or the millinery—her eyes wide and her lips parted in surprise. But unlike the rest of the townsfolk, she recognized him—as Ross Laramie, anyhow. And she knew just what this fellow had done to be tied up this way.

Unlike the rest of the townsfolk she also began to hurry along the sidewalk, sometimes dancing sideways to look again at Laramie and her pa as she went, following them toward their destination. She seemed to be trying to send Laramie messages with her bright eyes—looking at the rustler, looking at him, smiling encouragingly. Sometimes she bumped into people, seemed to make a quick apology, and kept right on shadowing the small parade. Laramie realized she was so packed with questions that she couldn't have stood still anyway, and he felt a smile of understanding pull at his mouth, threatening his mask of indifference.

Likely he would regret having told her so much about his real purpose in Sheridan, even under the clumsy guise of a third party. But for the last few days, he'd felt better able to concentrate on the rustlers, knowing that Victoria was investigating the older crimes.

Had he sat tall as a defense against anybody thinking poorly of him? After a block of Victoria following, sweeping her skirts and printer's apron this way and that as she dodged other folks, Laramie found himself sitting straight from a different motivation entirely.

In capturing one of the men who'd been stealing her father's cattle, he'd pleased her. That may not have been why he'd done it. It was what he'd been hired to do. But still, knowing he'd pleased her somehow pleased *him,* deep down where he'd never expected it.

Deep inside where he thought he might be dead. Or frozen over, anyhow. That was happening a lot lately.

When they reached the new brick building marked JAIL, Laramie dismounted, then stood back and let Garrison pull the rustler off his horse. He waited for Victoria.

It gave him the chance to step between her and the prisoner when she reached them, before they even went in.

"Is he a rustler?" she asked, then leaned past Laramie. "Excuse me, sir, but are you a cattle rustler?"

The rustler—a freckled fellow who said his name was Harry Smith—got that startled look about him that Victoria tended to provoke. "Miss?"

"Get back to work, Victoria Rose," drawled her father, one gloved hand nudging the cattle thief inside the sheriff's office.

"But this *is* my work, Papa," she insisted, following

173

him as he followed Harry, leaving Laramie to take up the rear. Partway in, safe behind her father's back, she spun around to beam at him for a quick, private moment of shared triumph. Then she turned back. "It's news. And I'm a newspaperwoman."

Whether Garrison thought better of that battle or dismissed her as dealt with, Laramie couldn't tell. But he could tell that the man sitting behind the sheriff's desk—one of the few folks on Main Street who hadn't come out to see the excitement—was *not* Bram Ward. The star he wore said "Deputy," and Laramie's gut feeling was that he was one of those lawmen who weren't necessarily good.

Though he might be basing that too much on the fellow's long, toothy face, or the interest with which he looked at Victoria as he belatedly stood. "Why, Miss Garrison," he greeted, glancing with less interest at the rancher and his prisoner. "Boss. Ain't this a surprise?"

"Franklin," greeted Garrison. "Where's Ward?"

"Out takin' lunch." Finally, Franklin's gaze glanced across Laramie. "You takin' up with bounty hunters, boss?"

"Found the boy changin' a brand," said Garrison instead.

Victoria, nearly bouncing with her need to ask questions, tried leaning around Laramie. He angled himself more firmly between her and the prisoner.

As well as the deputy.

She scowled at him.

Finally, Franklin was impressed. "On a Circle-T cow?"

Garrison's scowl was darker than his daughter's. As if he would ignore a rustler blotting someone else's brand? "Steer," he corrected dryly.

"I reckon this fellow's lucky to be here at all, then." Franklin scooped a ring of keys from the desktop and unlocked the closest cell. "That's a damn—excuse me," he added quickly when both Garrison and Laramie turned sharply to him. "A *dang* unhealthy profession around here."

Victoria tried to use the distraction to angle around Laramie's other side, but in a single step he cut her off.

"Yessir," said Harry. "That is, it would be, if that's what I was really doing. But see, it's all a mistake."

He was around Laramie's age in years, but not in experience. Harry's astonishment that anybody had even discovered his hideout had made his capture easy.

Laramie only wished they'd caught his gravelly-voiced partner—or someone more important. This couldn't be Harry's operation. He wasn't smart enough, and he hadn't fought hard enough. He was hired help, at best.

But he was a start.

Victoria asked, "How was it a mistake?"

Poor Harry hadn't even figured up a good answer for that, so he blushed.

Garrison looked disgusted. "Judge decides that."

"I won't do it again," insisted Harry, as Franklin closed and locked the cell behind him.

"Well, that's easy to say when you've been caught," Victoria pointed out, from the other side of Laramie.

"Ma'am?" asked Harry.

"If you really, truly meant to reform—" Victoria leaned more determinedly to one side, then dodged to the other direction. Laramie extended a hand that would have planted itself firmly against her waist had she not stopped first. Her eyes laughed at him, teasing. Beautiful.

He glanced quickly toward her father, who, thank God, was still scowling at the man who'd stolen his cattle. Looking back, Laramie saw Victoria do the same thing.

"If you truly meant to reform, you would have done it before you were arrested, wouldn't you?" she asked. As if reforming were that simple. As if a fellow didn't need a damn—*danged*—good reason to try it.

Like the reason standing right in front of Laramie, pulling a small notebook and pencil stub from the big pocket of her big leather apron. "I'm sure the readers of the *Herald* will be interested in both sides of the story," she assured Harry, then looked encouragingly at the other men. "It is all right if I ask some questions, isn't it?"

Garrison sighed, as if he knew full well the futility of trying to stop her now.

"Miss Garrison," said Deputy Franklin, wiping a hand on his dungarees, "you can ask all the questions you want."

Then Laramie and Garrison both sighed.

Victoria got most of her information out of Harry Smith, the alleged rustler—who, she thought stubbornly, did not look like any *type*, no matter what Ross had said.

Papa tended to give little slivers of answers, like when she asked why he'd hired a range detective at all and he'd held her gaze a moment, then said, "To detect."

Ross might have been more forthcoming if they were alone. For that reason, she planned to find some privacy with him very soon. But for now, in the sheriff's office, his answers weren't much better than Papa's.

"So you knew how to find the rustler's trail from the other day, when they shot at us," she prompted.

He nodded.

Harry Smith, from his cell, said, "I'm real sorry

about that, miss. I had no idea you was a woman until you started talkin' to your horse."

Papa gave her an odd look, but she ignored him to ask more questions while they still let her. "So you just kept watch on things until the rustlers showed up again?"

Ross nodded. Then maybe he saw something in her expression, because he said, "Yes." No great improvement.

"So what did you do when one did? No offense, Mr. Smith," she added toward the cell. "I should probably say *alleged* rustler, but that's a mouthful, don't you think?"

"Yes, ma'am," he agreed. He seemed nice enough— if a little depressed.

"Mr. Laramie?" she prompted in the following silence.

"Fetched some Circle-T men," Ross admitted. "Your pa came back. Went after him."

Thank goodness he was a range detective, because he would never write dime novels telling a story like that. But she kind of liked him strong and silent.

She turned to the rustler. "Mr. Smith? When did you first realize you were in trouble?"

Mr. Smith sat on his cell's single cot, his elbows on his knees and his head hanging, but he looked up quickly enough at her question. "Miss? It was when I heard that fellow there cock his six-shooter behind me. That's a fairly impressive little noise. I pretty much knew it then."

"That fellow there" was Ross, of course. Victoria had a very hard time not smiling proudly at him. At moments like this, she truly wished he would call on her properly.

But she'd asked. He'd refused.

In the meantime: "So what brand were you changing the Circle-T *to*, Mr. Smith?"

"Miss?"

"You were blotting out the original brand, and you had running irons. What did you mean to change the brand to?"

The rustler seemed to be blushing. "Cain't rightly recall, miss."

Papa made a rude sound and stood. "Best get back."

It took her a moment to realize that for once he meant himself and not her. He really *was* making an effort to let her be the newspaperwoman she wanted to be.

Through her pleasure at that realization, she had a clever idea—her favorite kind. "Papa, may Mr. Laramie stay while I finish my interview?" she asked. "You'll want someone to talk to Sheriff Ward when he gets back, right?"

Ross wasn't the sort of man who would widen his eyes, but he did go strangely still at that.

Papa nodded once. "Sendin' Thaddeas," he warned, so she'd know her time was limited. Then he opened the door—almost on top of Mr. Day, Victoria's boss.

Oh. She hadn't exactly asked permission to write this particular story, had she?

"Mr. Garrison," greeted Mr. Day. "Just the man to talk to. I hear you caught yourself a cattle rustler."

Papa stared at him a moment, slid his gaze toward Victoria with that way he had of knowing too much— and disapproving of most of it—before he looked back at the editor. "Yep," he said, and left.

Mr. Day watched the cattle baron go, then looked at Victoria, then moved on to Ross. "You're Mr. . . . Laramie, wasn't it?" He said the name oddly, as if it had some hidden meaning. "Working for the boss?"

Half the town called Papa "boss." Victoria suspected her mother had something to do with that.

Expression blank, Ross nodded.

"I assume you helped capture this rustler?"

Ross nodded.

Mr. Day frowned. He didn't seem particularly pleased when Victoria said, "Since I was here to see my father, Mr. Day, I took the liberty of asking questions. I have all my notes here, if you'd like to look at them."

"If that wouldn't be too much trouble," said the *Herald*'s editor.

She tore the pages of notes from her pad and handed them to him, but made sure to keep the pad.

The door to the jail opened again, and it was Sheriff Ward. Finally. "Had us some excitement?" drawled the lawman, looking over his visitors. He touched the brim of his hat toward Victoria, and barely noticed Ross before focusing on the cell. "Well, well, well. Looks like you've got yourself in a heap of trouble, sonny boy."

Ross stiffened so subtly, Victoria felt sure nobody else had noticed. She did.

"Sheriff," said Mr. Day. "May I ask you about what this rustler faces from our modern legal system? Miss Garrison, may I borrow that pad of paper? I don't think you're using it anymore."

She wouldn't get to write the story after all. Quickly, Victoria wrote something, pocketed it, then handed the pad to Mr. Day. "I probably have typesetting to do," she said stiffly, and glanced hopefully at Ross.

He was still staring at Bram Ward.

So much for subtlety. "Mr. Laramie?" she asked, which seemed to startle him. "When you've spoken to the sheriff, would you walk me as far as my brother's law office?"

He blinked at her for a moment, as if he wasn't even sure who she was. Then he nodded and said to the sheriff, "Found him changing brands. Boss is pressing charges."

Then he opened the door for her. That, apparently,

was his version of talking to Sheriff Ward.

But the sheriff seemed to have finally noticed him. Victoria had the strangest feeling that, if she waved her hand between them, the intensity might burn her.

Sheriff Ward asked, "Do I know you, boy?"

Since Ross said nothing, Victoria said, "This is my father's new range detective, Sheriff. *He's* the one who caught the rustler." *The rustler you couldn't catch,* she didn't add.

"Says his name's Laramie," added the deputy, grinning.

"Fancy that." And Sheriff Ward kept on staring.

So did Ross.

Something was going on that Victoria didn't understand, and she hated that. She swept past Ross, then waited sternly for him to join her on the sidewalk.

He took longer than seemed right.

"What's the matter?" she asked after he came out, looking from him to the now-closed door and back. "I know we may not feel . . ." She lowered her voice, and he had to bend nearer to hear her. "We may not think the sheriff is wholly honest, but we oughtn't antagonize him."

It took him a long while to say, "No."

Something *was* the matter. But she could see Thaddeas coming their direction, lifting a hand in greeting. She'd run out of time to ask questions *and* slip Ross the note she'd written him.

She chose giving him the note, in a handshake. "Well, Mr. Laramie, thank you for your time and your insight."

He looked vaguely confused by her words and her handshake—but to his credit, he gave no indication of having received the crumpled bit of paper at all.

Then she turned to greet her brother and let him walk her—as was only proper—back to her place of business.

*   *   *

The sheriff even had his dead father's voice.

Even out on the boardwalk, Laramie felt shaken by his first up-close look at the lawman. Big and blond, Bram Ward had grown into the spitting image of his murdering pa, a ghost come back to haunt him.

Sonny boy.

He felt ill, and worse, Victoria had noticed. Had he thought he'd pleased her? His pretense of being a range detective had pleased her, not him. Never him.

So her pressing a note into his hand, smoothly as a three-card monte dealer, took him by surprise. Then she turned and called, "Thaddeas! Mr. Laramie was walking me to your office. Did you hear the news? Isn't it exciting?"

"Thanks, Laramie," said the lawyer, somehow harnessing his sister's excitement long enough to get her hand on his arm, even while he ignored her. "I'll take her from here."

Nothing proprietary colored his statement—not like that newspaper editor back in the sheriff's office—but Laramie felt the dismissal sharply all the same. If life had turned out differently, he could have walked her back to her job, even walked her home of an evening. If he himself had turned out differently . . .

But he hadn't. So he shrugged his unnecessary consent, said "Ma'am," by way of a good-bye—and felt the hidden piece of paper crackle intriguingly in his palm until they'd gone far enough for him to risk looking at it.

Cemetery, she'd written. *Five-thirty.*

He frowned at her pretty handwriting. *Cemetery?*

Maybe he would never be free of ghosts. And yet the gaze he felt on him, then, was of the living. Slowly—dangerously—he looked up.

The last person he expected to see across the street, watching him leave the sheriff's office, was Lonny Logan.

Chapter Sixteen

While many people still believed a young lady oughtn't *walk* unescorted down a city street, few disapproved of her taking a leisurely afternoon bicycle ride. So as soon as Thaddeas saw her home, Vic mounted her ladies' drop-frame bicycle, adjusted her skirts to make sure the weights pinned to her hem to keep her skirt from blowing were evenly balanced, and pedaled out toward Mount Hope. The cemetery lay on the edge of town, though closer than when it was established in—

Oh dear.

Victoria was already coasting toward the cemetery gates when she realized the extent of her gaffe. Mount Hope didn't exist until at least a year after the lynchings.

How could she have made that mistake?

Still, Blackie stood hitched by the lamppost, near the street, and Ross Laramie waited in the shadows of the McCrae family's tomb, and Vic could not wholly regret her error. At least they were meeting.

Ross straightened, eyeing her bicycle warily as she pedaled toward him, and she felt so very glad to see him again that she couldn't regret much of anything.

"Hello," she called, dismounting to walk the rest of the way in, then leaning the bicycle against the back of the tomb, out of sight from the main road. "Thank you for—"

She stopped talking when he bent down and kissed her.

His lips were seeking, tentative, wonderful. Too soon he straightened from her, his head down.

"I'm sorry," he started to say. "All day I've been—"

She reached up, captured his cheek with her palm, and guided his mouth back to hers.

He came willingly.

Was there some reason she shouldn't be kissing him? She let whatever it was stay vague as she arched herself eagerly into Ross's hard arms, stood on tiptoe, and met his next kiss with her own. Gathering her against him, he turned to sandwich her neatly between him and the marble wall of the tomb, beside her bicycle. He braced himself with one arm, as if afraid he would fall, but his free hand cupped the nape of her neck, and his thumb stroked her cheek as he kissed her. He was so tall, and dressed so darkly, he seemed to block the light. She didn't care, as long as he didn't stop.

He didn't. Another kiss followed. Then another. She sensed that he was holding himself back—physically. His hands were not wandering as they had by the creek; his hard body sheltered more than crushed hers. *Controlled*. But his kisses . . . his kisses, he gave freely.

Happily, Victoria looped her own arms up over his shoulders and hung on. When his mouth explored her lower lip, she pouted for him, so he would have more of it. When her head sank sideways, her neck oddly weak from the sleepy, seductive feelings running through her, he angled his to match her. At one point he suddenly drew back, and she feared he meant to end this. But Ross only gasped a mouthful of fresh air and then ducked back to her, and she caught a hint of his smile before he was kissing her some more.

They stood there and kissed until her lips felt wet and swollen beneath his, until her breasts felt heavy against his chest, until the rest of her was starting to feel unusually heavy too. They kissed until only Ross's arm, sliding in increments more firmly around her despite his control, kept her from sinking right down the tomb wall and into the grass. His thigh brushed her hip as he shifted to prop a knee against the wall.

She was, she decided happily, a wanton woman. The idea just made her lean more eagerly into him, made her open her mouth to him so that soon he was not just kissing on her mouth, but in her mouth—and she his.

She began to feel shaky from expectation, curiosity, hope. She felt feelings she didn't fully understand— but wanted to—and they dizzied her. He tasted smoky, and rich. She liked it, liked this. Maybe she shouldn't, but she did.

Only the sound of a mule wagon driving by—more specifically, the gruff call of "Get on, now. *Move,* you mules, move!"—distracted her from the pleasures of being held, being made love to . . . being wanton.

It must have had the same effect on Ross, because he leaned his face into her shoulder—despite how far he had to bend for that—and just breathed. Hard. She thought she heard the trace of a moan in his panting breaths.

She whispered, "We weren't supposed to be doing this."

He shuddered, perhaps because she'd whispered that against the back of his neck.

"I know," he admitted, his voice a bare rasp. But he turned his head on her shoulder, nuzzled into her hair, so that she shuddered too. "I warned you. . . ."

From the road, the unseen mule-driver yelled, "For Chrissake, *get on!*"

"No," she decided, her own voice unsteady. "If one of us is wicked, the other must be too."

She was a modern-thinking woman, after all. She rode a bicycle. And at that moment, being wicked seemed as attractive as being wanton, so she turned her head to find his lips again. But he sank sideways, bracing one shoulder wearily against the tomb, and didn't let her. His eyes burned down at hers for a moment. Then he took her shoulders and pivoted her around so that she was facing away from him, and he wrapped his arms around her from behind. As he held her against him, like a child with a doll, he leaned his cheek on her hair.

"Not you," he murmured, still breathless. "Never you."

"*I'm* the one who invited you here," she insisted, shifting in his embrace. She wished she weren't wearing so many petticoats. She wished she could feel more of him.

Wanton.

"You didn't invite me here for this," he pointed out. Then he leaned around her, so that he could better see her face. "You *didn't,* did you?"

She laughed at his sudden uncertainty, kissed his afternoon-rough cheek before he could evade her, then turned the rest of the way out of his arms. "What if I did?" she teased him, since she remembered now

185

why they weren't supposed to have done that. He wouldn't court her properly, that's why.

But she was giddily glad she'd forgotten for a while.

"What if I did? What if I slipped you that note just so that we could meet in private and you could ravish me?"

He opened, then closed his mouth. Nothing came out. He leaned more weakly against the tomb wall and looked dark and mournful and confused.

"Actually, I made a mistake," she admitted with a doomed attempt at dignity, smoothing out her weighted skirts. "I thought we might find a clue here, but now I'm afraid I misjudged the dates."

"A clue," he repeated blankly.

"To the mystery, of course!" With a deep breath, an attempt to clear her mind, Victoria set her shoulders and started toward the back of the cemetery and what would be its oldest graves. Comparatively speaking. "I read the newspaper accounts today. It's just awful, what happened to the Lauranovics. Especially if they weren't even really stealing cattle at all. But you know, even if they *were* rustlers, they didn't deserve that. You and Papa didn't treat Harry Smith that way."

"No." In a moment, he'd caught up with her. His long legs made it easy for him. The jangle of his spurs somehow made even his walk sound dangerous. "What sort of clue?"

"I thought how terrible it would be to lose three family members, so close to each other. That reminded me of the Olson children who took fever and died, two in one week, and how sad their funeral was. Then I wondered if the Lauranovic family would have *had* funerals, considering the circumstances of their passing, and it occurred to me that their graves might tell us something."

"Something?" he prompted, clearly doubtful.

"We might learn who paid for the grave markers for

one thing, since I imagine all the family's money went toward Drazen's defense. And whether anybody's been tending the graves. After all, just because Julia's rancher betrayed her doesn't mean he didn't care at all—just not enough. Maybe once she died, he regretted what he'd done, especially once he learned of the baby. I can't imagine he would have betrayed her if he knew about the baby."

Ross made a rude noise. "You know nothing about men."

Reaching the far end of the graveyard, Victoria decided to just start walking the rows, looking at names. It wasn't as fun as kissing Ross, but it was probably far safer. "I beg to differ. I know many decent men. My father and his partner. My brother and my brothers-in-law. And I know you."

"Obviously not well enough."

Oh? Her lips still tingled from his kisses. She still had his taste in her mouth, his scent on her skin. She wasn't wholly clear on how a girl went from such kissing to *knowing* a man, the way Julia must have done with her beau, but she feared it happened more easily than she'd thought.

She feared it—without feeling fear. It was her own boldness that unsettled her, not him. Him, she wanted in ways she'd never imagined. When she drew her lower lip into her mouth now, it was to taste him.

Victoria made herself turn toward the tombstones, heartened to see that some were older than the cemetery itself. Many people who'd originally been buried "on the farm" had been moved here, once the town had a respectable place of rest.

"Do you mean to tell me, Ross Laramie, that we could never forget ourselves like we started to by the creek?" A sly glance in his direction, registering a blush on his dark cheeks, confirmed that she was correct. They had come perilously close. "Do you mean that if I found I was in trouble and killed myself, you wouldn't even visit my—"

She stopped because his hand, hard on her shoulder, stopped her. "No," he said firmly.

She looked up at him, his desperate voice worrying her more than his answer. "No, you wouldn't visit my grave?"

"No." He shook his head, clearly struggling for words. "You would never do that."

"Kill myself?"

"Yes." But again he shook his head. "No. *Any* of that. Not you."

He spoke urgently, as if trying to convince himself. She wondered if his lips felt swollen, and if he had the taste of her in his mouth. She wondered then if it was possible to kiss him until neither of them could stop.

She was clearly wanton. But she turned with resignation back to the graves—and caught her breath. "Look!"

"What?" But she was already dropping to her knees between two simple stone markers bearing the same surname and date of death.

Josip Lauranovic
1845–1888
Filip Lauranovic
1870–1888

She looked up in triumph at Ross, but the way he was now staring at the graves, like at a ghost, she could tell he didn't see her at all. He didn't even offer his hand when she stood again.

Suddenly an intruder, and unsure why, she stepped back from the graves and the range detective. She looked beyond that pair—and found the clue she'd really wanted.

Explaining Herself

Julije Inela Lauranovic
1873–1888
"Lost and Gone Forever."

Beside that headstone stood a small, white marble block with a lamb carved on top of it—the standard marker for a baby.

And between those two sat a rusting tin can holding the remains of some long-dried roses.

"It doesn't mean anything," insisted Laramie weakly.

But he was lying. Maybe the flowers meant no more than the quote, which Victoria attributed to the song "Clementine." But seeing the graves meant something. Everything. It meant more than he could ever have guessed.

Poppa. Phil. Julije. They had respectable graves.

"They misspelled her name," Victoria said, kneeling on the far side of Julije's and using a handkerchief to wipe off the face of the tombstone.

"No," he said, shaken. He'd felt on edge since meeting Ward, since Lonny Logan spotted him outside the sheriff's office. What other excuse did he have for how he'd greeted Victoria, stealing kisses that weren't his? And now—

Poppa. Phil. Julije.

"Oh." Victoria gave extra rub to the second *j* in "Julije." "I thought you were saying *Julia*. What language *are* these names?"

Laramie sank stiffly into a crouch. "Bohunk."

"That's not a nice word."

"No," he agreed, and met her gaze, and felt more for this woman than he could remember feeling since he was twelve. He'd thought he owed her before this day? He owed her everything. "How did you know they were here?"

As if embarrassed by his gaze, she ducked her head.

189

"I must have remembered them from Decoration Day or something," she guessed, trying to straighten the roses in Julije's tin-can vase. One of the desiccated flowers crumbled under her fingers, so she snatched her hand back. "Either that or I heard my parents talk about them, back when they helped the town pay to move people into the new cemetery. I hear a lot of things I'm not meant to, you know."

Her parents. That dark suspicion returned to hollow out his chest, to chill his throat. "Your parents paid to move them here?"

She smiled, innocent of the truth. "They might have."

"Two rustlers and a suicide?"

A breeze picked up through the cedar trees at the far end of the cemetery. Ghosts again. *Isn't that what you are?* he thought at the graves, suddenly angry. *What we became? I'm no better.*

Victoria searched his face again, more cannily. "You said they were stealing their own cattle back. Isn't that what Drazen told you?"

She mispronounced "Drazen," but he didn't correct her. He didn't want it to sound any more like "Ross" than necessary.

He didn't want the name to sound like him.

"He believed that," he admitted finally, reaching out to pull a weed from Poppa's grave. His hand wasn't used to that. His hand understood guns so much better. "But they were his family. The boy could have been mistaken."

"Don't be silly." Victoria touched the stone lamb's head. "How could a person be wrong about his own family?"

She should know. "He was wrong about his sister. He never believed . . ." A spread hand toward the block she was touching, marking her never-born bastard, explained for him.

190

Good girls did not do that.

As if she read his mind, she said, "Any woman could make a mistake if she were in love. That doesn't make it right, but it's not . . ."

Not wrong? What did that leave?

Of course, Julije had once been strong-willed too, at least before . . . Before. She'd believed she would marry the man whose name and face he had yet to discover. The man she'd met in secret—perhaps in the same way he and Victoria had met in secret.

The idea only hardened his hatred against that unknown rancher. "A person might think the best of a loved one, but that doesn't make her—him—right."

Victoria shook her head, unwilling to believe it.

"There were not many men who could have done this," Laramie insisted, glancing from Victoria to Julije's grave and back, even now searching for an answer to fit her view of the world. "Not the Wards, or the deputy; neither of them was rich, and she said— How old *is* Alden Wright?"

"I don't think he's any older than you," she admitted.

Far too young. "Well, I doubt it was your father."

"Don't even say things like that in jest, Ross Laramie! Of course it wasn't Papa. And Colonel Wright is even older than him. So it had to be Hayden Nelson."

As if older men would not offer a great deal for a young lady's companionship. "It wasn't Hayden Nelson."

"He's the only choice left."

"Nelson had no family in the area to have threatened her." Laramie flexed his hands, scowled at the tin can with its crumbling roses. He disliked Victoria's idea that the man he wanted would leave roses on his sister's grave. "And he left town years ago."

"Oh." She looked at the roses too. "These can't be any older than late spring, early summer."

Which left the one person she would not see.

"That's everyone the newspaper listed as being on the posse, Ross," she insisted. "And if he wasn't in the posse, he could have been anybody. The Garrisons and the Wrights weren't the only successful ranchers in Sheridan."

Laramie took a deep breath and stood, torn. It seemed so clear to him. He did not want to be the one who did this, who said this, to Victoria. And yet here, before Poppa and Phil—no, *Filip* and *Julije*—he could not leave it. Not again. He'd avoided his vow for too long already. "Perhaps he had a relative on the posse," he prompted, desperate.

Victoria considered it, then shrugged. "I don't believe the Wards had any relations in town. And the deputy's name isn't familiar."

Laramie turned to escape toward that large tomb, toward where she'd left her bicycle. He did not want to hurt her, but he had to know. God help him—he needed her to at least consider it, so that he could finally know for sure.

Whether he could do anything about it or not.

When she followed him, a whisper of petticoats and a whiff of cinnamon, he simply said it. "Thaddeas."

Victoria stopped, blinked at him. "*What?*"

"Victoria, it was Thaddeas." The heir to the Circle-T, a fancy college student, must have seduced Julije, used her to send a posse after the rustlers. He'd destroyed Ross's world—then gone on to become a respected lawyer while Julije and their baby rotted in the earth.

Once again, Laramie had fallen victim to his world's cruel irony. It was Thaddeas Garrison who deserved to die.

And Laramie had fallen in love with the man's sister.

Chapter Seventeen

Victoria said, "My brother?"

Ross looked disgusted by the question, which made her angry—though his accusation might explain that, too. She pushed him, flat against his chest. "My *brother?*"

He did not budge. "Who else?"

"Anyone!" Clearly, he did not know Thaddeas. Despite Mama's gentling influence, Thad was pure Garrison—proper, stern, just. Papa's son from a previous marriage, Thad had lived with an aunt until Vic's parents married. Mama once said that part of him was still ten years old, desperate to justify his inclusion in the family.

She hadn't said it to *Victoria,* of course, or known Vic was listening, but she'd said it.

Thaddeas would never do anything so terrible!

Ross seemed convinced, though. "He was here after

the Die-Up," he reminded her. "He's got money. Your folks paid for lawyers, for tombstones."

Now she pushed him with both hands, so he stepped out of her way. She stalked past him and got her bicycle.

"Come on," she told him, starting to wheel her bicycle toward the gate, where his horse waited.

He didn't move, except to watch her. "Come where?"

"We'll go to my house and straighten this out."

"I'm not going there."

"Of course you are. You think my brother seduced some poor immigrant girl, and it's not true. He'll tell you so."

"He'll lie," he warned her.

She stopped and turned on him again. "So now he's not just a scoundrel, but a liar?"

Ross stood there, smoldering at her, but she could tell he didn't really see who she was, what kind of family she came from. He didn't even believe it existed.

"Ross, my parents paid to move *lots* of graves to the new cemetery. It was the right thing to do. I'm sure that's why my mother hired your friend's lawyer. She supports all sorts of causes—the orphanage, the Society for the Prevention of Cruelty to Children, the Ladies' Aid. If you come home with me, I can show you her desk, some of the letters she's received from organizations like that."

He looked dangerous again—and very alone. "No."

"Are you afraid for Thaddeas to see us together?" Heaven forbid anyone think they were courting! "I'll go home first, then, and you can visit later."

Ross shook his head. "No."

"Then I'll ask him and tell you what I find out."

Ross shifted his weight, flexed his hands with uncertainty, then faced her full on again, mouth set. "If

194

he *did* tell you the truth, would you want to know?"

"Of course I would, because the truth is that he didn't do anything."

"No." He squinted—or winced. "No, Victoria. If that *weren't* the truth. Would you still want to know the worst?"

She didn't understand. There *wasn't* a worst.

"Would you rather . . ." But whatever he meant to say, he gave up. He shut his eyes, tight, and clearly just gave up. "Never mind."

"Never mind what? Ross, you aren't making sense."

He lowered his head, looked down at the ground for a long moment. When he lifted his lashes, slanted his gaze back up, his eyes—those dusky green eyes—looked wounded again. "Go home, Victoria. Just . . . go home to your brother and be happy. Please."

She knew she was missing something. That worried her. But the sun was starting to set, and she hadn't brought Duchess with her, and she was too frustrated with him to know what else to ask. "Good evening, then, Mr. Laramie. I'll see you later."

But he didn't promise any such thing. Confused, Victoria pushed herself off and pedaled away from him.

She on her bicycle, returning to her family's modernized home in her turn-of-the-century town.

He standing in the cemetery with all the dead people.

When Victoria rode off on her two-wheeled contraption, she looked as if she were flying. Flying away from him. Laramie knew he should feel relieved. Less complications this way. She would never be the wiser.

Instead, he felt hollow. Empty. Beaten.

He loved her. Somehow he'd gone and fallen in love with her, and now he had nothing. He no longer had the vengeance that had carried him for so long, because he would not hurt Victoria that way. And he could not have her, because—well, because he would not hurt her that way, either. He was a rustler, a liar, a killer who wished her brother dead. He was a man who did not keep promises.

Clearly, he had no more business in Sheridan.

Laramie mounted Blackie from sheer habit. He'd almost reached the Red Light Saloon before he even knew that was where he'd headed. He didn't like saloons. But as with so much else in his life, it was someplace that would accept him. And it was where Lonny Logan would seek him out.

Laramie didn't know where he would go or what he would do, but he knew better than to alienate a Logan.

Bad companions were better than none at all.

The saloon was too damned full for sunset. He noticed a skinny whore looking him over, and he felt disgust.

Disgust that he could make up for nothing—and he'd taken this long to figure it out. Disgust that he could never sit in a parlor with Victoria Garrison, but he could easily take a whore upstairs and do anything he wanted with her. Disgust that while so many men headed home from a day's honest work to a meal prepared by a mother, or a wife, or a sister, he got a shot glass of rye and a pickled egg from the jar on the counter. Disgust that despite being exiled into this world of lawbreakers and bad men, he would never live up to his potential as an outlaw any better than he'd lived up to his potential as a cowboy.

Laramie wanted what he could not have. He had what he did not want. And he probably wasn't any different from half the men here.

That disgusted him most of all.

An hour later, he was nursing his second drink at the farthest table from the front when Lonny Logan finally pushed through the swinging doors, fully armed.

Laramie was fully armed, too. Firearms restrictions weren't tightly enforced on the edge of town.

Lonny approached the table, close enough that Laramie could hear the chink of his spurs over the guffaws and arguments and shrill laughter. Laramie waited.

When Lonny dropped into a scarred chair, signaling the barmaid for a drink, Laramie wasn't even sure he felt relief. So Lonny didn't mean to kill him for doing business at the jail. So what? It didn't give him anyplace to go, anything to do.

It sure as hell didn't win him Victoria.

Laramie finished his drink in one gulp, raising a hand to indicate he wanted another. Maybe the problem was he wasn't drunk. Maybe that would help.

"You hunting bounties now?" challenged Lonny.

It wasn't just conversation. Laramie knew the train robbers on sight, and he could find their hideouts—Brown's Hole in Colorado, the nearby Hole-in-the-Wall, even the snaking trail into Robber's Roost, down in Utah.

He would never turn bounty hunter and live.

So he told the truth. "Range detective."

He stared into his empty shot glass for a moment, remembering how Victoria had always said that—*range detective!* Then Lonny snorted, and he lifted his gaze.

The youngest Logan was grinning. "You?"

Range detective! Like he was the governor, or Santa Claus or something. Not for the first time, he wished Victoria's innocent world was his real one . . . but as her father had said on hiring him, this wasn't a frontier anymore. A man couldn't just leave his past behind and start over.

Especially not a man who'd jumped parole years before.

"Was," he clarified.

"Hell." Lonny paid for both drinks when they came, and Laramie let him. "You sure you want to give it up? I reckon you'd be good at it, considerin' how many strays you've moved yourself."

"I'm done." Laramie took another sip of rye.

It still tasted bad.

"Well, Harve will be glad to hear that," decided Lonny, tasting his own drink more enthusiastically. "He's got plans for you."

Laramie wasn't impressed. Harvey Logan was the meanest of the Wild Bunch. Some folks thought he was the leader of that gang, but Laramie never had. Only other Logans followed Harvey.

"Where's—" He almost said Butch, but the man-hunt was on, and not all the bad men in the Red Light Saloon were necessarily lawbreakers. "—Lowe? Still at the WS?"

Lonny looked pensive. "The law caught Mac, you know."

For the Folsom robbery? Laramie didn't know.

"Lincoln County, they got him. *Lowe* talked your old boss, French, into putting up money for bond, but it turns out train robbery's a cap-i-tal offense in New Mexico. Besides, looks like they'll throw in murder."

Laramie lifted an eyebrow.

"Some of the folks what went after them got themselves shot up," Lonny explained. "And one of 'em was a sheriff. Lowe's kind of busy right now."

Laramie once thought a fellow had to want something, and bad, to risk his neck outlawing. Only that had kept him straight. All he'd ever wanted couldn't be bought. Vengeance. Victoria. "Not interested."

"We need a shooter," said Lonny.

Laramie didn't have to make an effort to look bored as he reverted to instinct, eyeing the crowd, wishing he weren't there. If he ever *did* take up train robbing, it would be with a leader who tried to make your bail, not Harvey Logan.

Now, if Lowe lost his right-hand man to the state of New Mexico, and needed help, that might prove more tempting. Maybe instead of wanting anything, an outlaw just needed to lose that last thing of importance in his life.

Laramie took another sip of rye—and then he felt it. An awareness, almost like a hum. *Something was wrong.*

"Well, you know where to find us," said Lonny.

Laramie slid his left hand casually down to his thigh. His palm cuddled up against the smooth butt of his Colt. He continued looking bored.

"Alone," Lonny added. "We wouldn't want to—"

But then his instincts caught up to Laramie's. His eyes widened. He rolled toward the floor while Laramie stood.

Laramie drew and aimed at the glimpse of danger he saw reflected in the measly bar mirror. He squeezed his trigger in that grain of a second between looking down someone else's barrel and keeping anything from shooting out of it.

His Colt bucked in his hand with the blast, because double-actions pulled. Women screamed, men shouted, and everyone seemed to be ducking for cover. That's how he finally, clearly saw the man who was trying to shoot him.

The man who tried lifting his gun again, even now.

Laramie fired a second time, while recognition struck him so sharply, he thought he'd been hit.

Harry Smith, staring down at his chest, looked confused too.

The young, soft-spoken rustler he'd captured this morning stumbled back against the bar. Laramie stepped forward, aiming for the boy's freckled face this time to make the rustler drop his weapon, survival instincts overriding anything else.

Harry Smith?

To his shuddering relief, the pistol slid from Smith's hand to the sawdust floor. Laramie stepped close enough to kick the damn thing out of reach, then grabbed Smith's shoulder and looked into his face. The kid was so pale that his freckles seemed obscenely dark. His eyes swam with tears.

Laramie recognized the stench of blood, saw blood spattered across the bar behind the man—the boy— he'd shot, saw two bloody holes through the rustler's shirt front. He stared, confused, into the kid's wet, glazing eyes.

Why? He wanted to ask that, at that moment, more than he'd wanted almost anything in his life. *Why* did you try to kill me?

Why did you make me kill you?

But words never had come easily, especially not that one. And Harry Smith's body slumped to the blood-spattered, sawdust floor before the kid could have answered.

Folks began talking, lifting their heads again, and all Laramie heard amid the words that began to surround him was the single, repeated word "fast."

Hooray for him.

Then he heard one other noise—Lonny Logan's whistle. Laramie spun, followed Lonny's aim—the stairway above where they'd been sitting—and dropped to one knee as a burst of blue flame blasted from the bar's shadows. He heard the mirror behind where he'd been standing shatter. He shot back.

The second rustler—to tell by his hat—also fell.

At that, Laramie turned, pistol raised and ready, eyeing the rest of the stunned bar. He didn't understand the first attempt, much less the second, but there wouldn't be a third attempt on his life. Not tonight.

Not until he heard the drawled words from the doorway.

"Put the gun down and raise your hands, sonny boy."

Victoria knew she was in trouble when she turned the corner onto Elizabeth Street—Thaddeas stood on the sidewalk in front of their in-town house, in the dregs of a cloudy twilight, with Duchess beside him. Suddenly, all thoughts of walking with Ross, arguing with Ross—kissing with Ross—faded behind a more immediate situation.

She was late for supper.

Her brother resembled Papa at times like these—arms folded, eyes narrowed, head tilted with suspicion. When she coasted to a stop beside him, he sounded like Papa too. "Get in the house, please." Except for the please.

Then he turned and headed inside without even waiting for her excuse.

The kitchen table was set with a cold meal, as befit the late-summer weather. Thaddeas held out her chair, and waited until she sat before asking, "Where were you?"

"I rode to the cemetery," she told him, helping herself to a tomato. "I'm researching a story I'd like to write for the newspaper."

All of which was completely true. She could imagine no better punishment for the man who had abandoned Julije Lauranovic—a man who certainly was *not* Thaddeas—than to be exposed at last.

Her brother sat down too. "It's threatening rain, and you know better than to stay out this late. When the folks are away, I'm in charge of you."

Which was its own interesting topic. "Why?"

Yvonne Jocks

"Why?" He had the grace to look amused by that.

"I'm out of school," she reminded him, pouring them both some water. "I have a job. Neither of us is married. Why are you still in charge of me?"

"Because I'm older. And because I'm—" He stopped, and his eyes narrowed again. "Oh no you don't."

She tried to look innocent.

"I warned Mother about reading all those speeches to you girls," he said. "This is not about suffrage, Victoria Garrison, it's about common decency. And safety."

She leaned over the table and kissed his cheek. "I'm sorry I worried you."

He scowled at her. "You *did* worry me."

"Then I'm sorry." And she sat again.

Thad turned his scowl to his plate. "Apology accepted, but don't do it again. And if you'll be out after dark—"

"I wasn't out after dark," she reminded him.

"—take Duchess," he finished firmly. "You promised."

She smiled her sweetest smile. "I understand."

Thaddeas narrowed his eyes, having fallen for that dodge once too often, but to give him more would be to agree that he had the right to demand it of her. So, as casually as she could, she changed the topic. "Thad, may I ask you something?"

Her brother paused, sulkily buttering a slice of Mrs. Sawyer's good, thick bread. "Now I'm worried."

"Do you remember an immigrant family named Lauranovic?"

She saw from the flare of his eyes that he did remember. Right away. For a moment she wondered, *What if Ross was right?* But with all the headlines about the lynchings, the trial, and the suicide, why *wouldn't* Thaddeas remember them?

He put down his cold-meat sandwich and met her gaze, solemn. Worried, even. "Yes, I do. Why?"

"Do you remember *Julije* Lauranovic?"

When she asked that, he relaxed a little. Whatever worried him, it wasn't guilt over Julije. "You mean the poor girl who killed herself?"

She nodded.

"Again I ask, *Why*?"

Well, she guessed he *was* a lawyer. Though she hoped he didn't practice law with his mouth full. "Tell me what you remember about her first," she insisted. "Please?"

He looked suspicious—but he was also a pushover when it came to his sisters. "Really, Vic, I don't remember very much. I left for college at about the time the Laurences arrived."

"The Laurences?"

"It was only after the trouble that people started calling them by their European name. Julie was a tall kid with long black braids, and we never talked." He shrugged.

Victoria felt certain that if he had ever loved her— loved her enough to get her with child, enough to leave roses by her grave years after her death—he would not be able to shrug. Now all she needed was to figure out who *had* loved her . . . or at least pretended to. "Do you remember if she had a sweetheart?"

"She was a child when I knew her!"

"Later, after the Die-Up. She would have been about Audra's age then. Did she have a sweetheart before she died?"

Thaddeas opened his mouth, then decided against whatever he'd meant to say and shook his head. "No."

"No, she didn't? Or no, you don't remember?"

"No, I don't remember. I'm not always watching and noticing things the way you do, Vic."

"What about at her funeral?"

"Nobody went to her funeral. It was a big scandal."

"She was with child," Victoria agreed, since Thad was too proper to mention that. Assuming he'd known. "So she must have had a sweetheart."

The alternative, that the girl had been attacked, was too awful to imagine.

Thad frowned, wearing his lawyer look. "Why are you asking all this? And don't say you're writing a story; that's not all."

"And I'm helping a friend," she admitted, and made a face at his expression. "Someone who's interested in the Lauranovic family, and don't ask more, because I promised this friend to be discreet. I just want to find out who Julije Lauranovic's sweetheart was before her suicide, that's all."

"Victoria," demanded Thaddeas, "this wouldn't have anything to do with Pa's new range detective, would it?"

His question took her so by surprise that she hesitated, just a beat, before she managed to say, "Mr. Laramie? Why would it have anything to do with him?"

It was a beat too long.

"You've been talking to Laramie," accused Thaddeas, pushing his chair abruptly back. "I can't believe it. No, I *can* believe it, and that's what worries me."

Her brother's reaction was what worried *her*. She talked to almost everyone in town; Thad couldn't know about the kissing, or the secrets. "What if I have? He escorted me back to the ranch the day Kitty was attacked, remember?"

She was pleased by that feint, until Thad asked, "And you talked about Julije Lauranovic?"

He stood and started to clear their food. Victoria suspected he just wanted an excuse to pace. She wouldn't mind pacing herself. "Why would you think

Mr. Laramie is interested in Julije Lauranovic?" Did he know something she didn't?

"Is he?" Thad asked. "Just how good a friend is he?"

"Thad, he works for Papa. He saved Kitty's life, and he talked to me when I was upset. Why does that bother you?"

"So it's for him that you're asking about Julie Laurence." Thaddeas rolled his eyes at his own foolishness. "Of *course.*"

"Of course what?"

But Thaddeas said, "Listen to me, Vic. You aren't to have anything more to do with Mr. Laramie."

What? "Why aren't I?"

He folded his arms. "Because I said so. And because Pa will say the same thing, as soon as we tell him."

"Tell him *what?*" Thaddeas and Papa knew something about Ross, and they weren't telling her, and she hated it. Bad enough that he had secrets—she knew that much. But that her father and brother knew more about them than she did . . .

"Leave it alone," warned Thaddeas, heading for the sitting room. As if he could escape her questions that easily.

She followed. "I won't leave it alone. I want to know why you don't like Ross Laramie!"

Thaddeas slowly turned back to her, his eyes wide. "*Ross?* Trust me, Victoria. Don't get involved with Ross Laramie."

"Why *not?*" she demanded.

"I'm not telling you."

A knock on the front door kept her from protesting. *It's him,* thought Vic, relieved. Ross had relented from his stubbornness and would confront Thad with his foolish accusations, and everything would be set straight.

"I'll get it," warned Thad. "It's nighttime."

She sighed, but let him. When he opened the door

to a rain-swept porch, it wasn't Ross. It was a drenched Evangeline.

"Miss *Taylor?*" greeted Thaddeas, and looked at the clock. It was past eight. Only then did he take a look at her dripping clothes and say, "Please, come inside!"

She did, her gaze sliding desperately to Victoria. Clearly she had news. Rain had slicked her long, pale hair to her scalp. Her thin, wet dress clung to the slim curves of her body.

"Come back to the kitchen," offered Victoria quickly, putting an arm around her. "We'll make you some tea."

But Evangeline only shook her head, then spun, startled, when Thaddeas draped a blanket from the sofa over her shoulders. At least, she looked startled until she saw it was him.

"I'm sorry," she whispered, ducking her head.

"Not at all," said Thad—but of course, he would say that to anybody. "Is something wrong, Miss Taylor?"

Under the drape of the blanket, Evangeline's damp hand—slim but strong—found Victoria's.

"It's Mr. Laramie," she said. "He's in jail."

Chapter Eighteen

"Who are you?" demanded Bram Ward.

Laramie sat in the cell and said nothing. That the sheriff didn't recognize him was maybe the only thing that had gone right in the last hour.

Not killing the bastard in the saloon, when he had the chance, was just one of the many things that had gone wrong.

He stared at Ward and thought, *I could have taken you.* He'd wanted to. The gun had been in his hand! And yet he'd stood there in the saloon, the smell of blood and metal and gun smoke sharp in his nostrils, and somehow he'd known better.

Ward was a sheriff, no matter how corrupt. If Laramie were to twist around, like his body wanted to, or to shoot, like his hand itched to, it would be neither self-defense nor forgivable. There'd be no return.

So he'd set his Colt down on the bar with a gentle thud. He'd let Bram Ward drag his hands behind his back and secure his wrists with handcuffs. Then he'd been dragged back to the jail from this afternoon—sitting on the wrong horse.

Now, his shoulders aching from his still-cuffed hands, Laramie stared at the sheriff's increasing impatience and thought—there'd be no return to *what*?

He should have shot the bastard.

"You hear me, sonny boy?" The sheriff picked up a billy club, rattled it across the bars. "Who the hell are you, anyhow?"

Laramie would prefer not to be persuaded. "I'm Ross Laramie," he said yet again. "I ride for Jacob Garrison as—"

"What's your *real* name?" interrupted Ward.

Good question. He'd lost Ross Laurence somewhere amid the original violence. He wasn't Drazen Lauranovic anymore. The alias came from folks thinking he'd done time in the Wyoming State Penitentiary; it had been his for years. "Laramie."

Ward shook his head. "I know you from somewhere. Where the hell do I know you from?"

From me killing your pa, after you killed mine.

Bad answer. Laramie let nothing show on his face.

"You one of them train robbers we're hunting?"

Not yet. "I shot in self-defense."

Ward, backing away from the bars, twisted his lips in an ugly smile. "Broke firearms laws, too. Shame you did it on a Friday night. We might have to spend a few days together, afore all this gets cleared up, and you'd best not be any trouble." His eyes glittered hopefully. "Like that damned rustler you brought in."

Bastard.

Harry Smith wouldn't have escaped alone. Harry Smith would have run away if he had—not tried to do murder. And now Harry Smith's blood was on Ross's cuffed hands, his dark freckles in Ross's memory. . . .

So as not to seem challenging, Laramie lay awkwardly down on one shoulder, on the cot, and tried thinking of something other than how long it would take Ward to recognize him.

He thought about Victoria.

It was more than he'd had the last time he'd been here.

"I'm going with you," announced Victoria as Thaddeas slung on his mackinaw against the rain.

"No, you're not," said Thaddeas. "You're staying here with Miss Taylor."

The three of them stood in Mama's kitchen, where Vic had put water on for tea while Thad grabbed his coat. Evangeline, still holding the blanket tightly around her, like a hug, stood back and watched them through wary, pale eyes. Her feet were muddy. Victoria *did* want to make sure her friend was all right.

But she wanted to make sure Ross was all right even more. Two men had tried to kill him, and the sheriff was calling it murder. And he was in jail, and she wanted him to be all right.

"Evangeline can stay here on her own."

Evangeline shook her head, eyes wide.

Thaddeas looked at Victoria and asked, "Why?"

She blinked, startled. "Because he's my friend."

Thad didn't accept that. He took her shoulders, his grip tight. "Your friend? I don't think so, Victoria. I think you know this man better than you ought to, and it ends here. Do you understand me?"

She understood, but she certainly didn't agree. "You have no say in the matter. I'm going with you."

"Oh?" He folded his arms, set his shoulders. "Here's your choice. Either you agree not to come with me, or I don't go."

She stared. *He wouldn't!*

Thaddeas didn't even blink.

"But he needs a lawyer!" she protested. "You know

as well as I do that Sheriff Ward can't be trusted."

"If I have to choose between my sister's safety or my law practice, I'm choosing my sister. So you just choose."

"That's not fair!" If she hadn't been born female . . .

But he meaningfully began to unbutton his mackinaw.

Victoria wanted to hit him. Never in her life had she felt such fury toward another human being, much less her brother. But she loved Ross more. "Fine," she spat. "You win. Now go get him."

His hands paused on his buttons. "Swear it."

"I swear it."

Thad leaned nearer. *The whole thing.*

"I swear not to go with you tonight."

"And you'll stay here and make Miss Taylor comfortable until I come back," he added.

"And I'll make Evangeline comfortable. Now go help him!"

Even now, Thaddeas hesitated.

"Please?" Her voice broke on the word.

Her brother closed his eyes, took a deep breath, and opened them. "You don't know how much I hate it that I can't trust you."

If you would ever trust me long enough to stop telling me what to do, maybe you could. But that was asking a lot.

When he pushed out the door, through the rain toward the stables, Victoria tried to feel glad that he would help. She felt afraid instead. Drawn. *Uncertain.*

Why would anybody try to shoot Ross? Why would the sheriff arrest him for self-defense? Why was he at the Red Light, anyway?

She pressed a hand against her mouth and watched the stables out the window, and she wanted Ross to be safe. Stubborn and wrong or not, she wanted him safe—and with her.

Evangeline slid her arm around Victoria's shoulders. "Your brother will take care of him," she comforted. "That's what he does. He takes care of people."

Then the stable doors opened and Thaddeas led his horse out, closed the doors, mounted. He lifted one hand, acknowledging the girls in the lit kitchen window, then rode away into the rain.

Evangeline sighed.

"Come on," said Vic softly. "Let's get you comfortable."

Of course Evangeline protested, but Victoria pulled her upstairs, found her a fresh—if rather short—dress, and helped her dry her hair. Then she fixed Evangeline a cup of tea.

Then she put on her own cloak.

"What?" Evangeline put down her tea. "Victoria, you can't. You promised him. You swore!"

"I swore not to go to the jail with him. Well, I'm not with him. I swore to make you comfortable, and you're comfortable."

"But that's not what he meant. You're not being fair."

"He didn't play fair when he blackmailed me." She put on one of her mother's old cowboy hats. "Now I'm going to make sure Ross is okay. You stay here and be comfortable. Thad's orders."

Evangeline looked stricken, but Victoria hurried out into the rain anyway, toward the stables and her bicycle. She paused only long enough to whistle for Duchess.

It was after dark. And she'd promised.

Laramie had plenty of time to remember kissing Victoria, holding Victoria, not feeling alone.

Like he felt now.

Ward offered to unlock his handcuffs, then used the moment to push Laramie down so that his cheek cracked against the cot. The bullet wound in his side throbbed almost as badly. But Laramie rolled awkwardly to his feet and said nothing—by invoking Victoria's cinnamon scent, by imagining her eyes, her hair, and her eager, continuous kaleidoscopic of words.

Thoughts of her soothed him as nothing ever had.

Which was why he had to leave, while none of his memories of Victoria included her disillusionment.

Alone as he felt, Laramie was surprised when the door to the jail opened and Hank Schmidt, the foreman of the Circle-T ranch, sauntered in dripping rainwater.

"Sheriff," the older man greeted lazily as he took off his wet hat, slapped it against his leg. "Hear tell you pulled one of our boys out of some trouble tonight."

Laramie had already sat up, intrigued and confused. Someone had ridden out to the ranch? In a saloon full of folks he didn't even know, someone had gone to get help?

Ward said, "I arrested one of your boys for murder."

"The way I hear it, he was defending himself."

Ward hitched his thumbs into his suspenders. "I reckon the judge can decide that on Monday."

He was stalling for time, keeping Laramie locked up until he figured out how he knew him—and what to do about it. All the more reason for Laramie to get the hell out.

Schmidt looked over at the cell. "Why's he still cuffed?"

"Holding him for murder," repeated Ward. "Dangerous man."

"Didn't know you for a coward, Sheriff." Schmidt narrowed his already sun-squinted eyes. "Give me the keys."

Ward straightened. "You ain't takin' my prisoner. That's breakin' the law, Schmidt, and I won't have it."

"I'm not takin' anybody," said the foreman, disgusted. "I'm unlocking the handcuffs. Give me the keys."

Ward hesitated.

The Circle-T foreman leaned, dripping, over the desk. "You either give me the key, or you unlock those cuffs yourself, or you arrest me for the goddamned hell I'm about to raise. I won't see you abusing one of my boys, and I sure as hell won't let the boss think I did. *Savvy?*"

The two men stared, long and hard, and Schmidt won. With a swipe of the keys off the desk, Ward stomped over to the cell and said, "C'mere, boy."

Laramie doubted Ward had the balls to try anything in front of Schmidt, so he came to the bars, turned around, and felt the sheriff undo the cuffs with a few vicious swipes.

"There," announced Ward bitterly, as Laramie quickly stepped deeper into the cell, flexing his hands and shaking out his cramped arms. "You mean to give any more orders around my jail?"

"Brought a fellow out from the ranch," said Schmidt. "He'll help you stand guard, if you don't mind."

"I do mind. We already had one jailbreak today."

Schmidt smiled coolly. "All the more reason to accept the help, Sheriff. His name's Nate Dawson, and he'll stay outside in case anyone needs him." He glanced back by Laramie as he said that part. "Try not to shoot him. Fall roundup's coming on."

Then he nodded and turned to go. "Laramie."

Laramie felt . . . unbalanced. Not only had someone ridden to the ranch for help, but the man in charge had left his family to come to his defense. And Nate was outside.

"Sir," he answered weakly. When the door closed behind the foreman, he sank onto the cot. Was it even possible that he wasn't as alone as he'd feared?

"Goddamned cattle barons with their goddamned uppity ways," muttered Ward, staring with pure hatred at the door, then turning it at Laramie. "Think they're more important than everyone else. Well, don't you get any ideas that you're safe, sonny boy, 'cause this is still my jail. You hear?"

But Ward would have to wait a few lifetimes before Laramie ever called *him* sir.

The ride was dark, despite the gaslights along the streets. Rain skittered across Vic's hat, her clothes, and her bare hands. Her skirts weren't about to blow anywhere.

Twice, the bicycle wheels slid right out from under her, but somehow she caught herself with a foot before she truly fell. She reached the dark shops across the street and down from the jail pretty quickly—faster, apparently, than Thaddeas. She didn't see his horse hitched out front.

He was going to help Laramie, wasn't he?

She coasted her bicycle with a spray of puddle water right into an alley beside the Hot Dinner Café, Duchess loping along behind. Then she dismounted, propped it against the wall, and crept back to the mouth of the alley to see what she could see.

"Sit," she told Duchess. "Stay." The dog looked no happier about the orders than Vic had ever been, but the dog obeyed.

The first thing Victoria saw was a Circle-T ranch hand, standing outside the jail and staring at her with wide eyes.

She waved, then put a finger to her lips.

Nate Dawson spread his arms—*what are you doing?*—and then pointed firmly back down the street. *Go home.*

She shook her head, pointed at him in warning, then put her finger to her lips again. When he shook his head, she pointed more adamantly. She knew a few secrets about him and her sister Laurel, after all, and *she* had faithfully kept *those*.

Dawson widened his eyes again—but looked helpless.

When she heard horses approaching, Victoria sank back into the shadows of the alley. It was Thaddeas, leading Ross's horse. He had a number of men with him—and one woman, scandalously straddling a horse behind a man, her arms around the rider's middle and her skirts hitched up. On Main Street!

Victoria watched them head into the jail. Then she waited.

When Thaddeas Garrison brought a cluster of wet people into the jail with him, not a half hour after Hank Schmidt had left, Laramie felt sudden fear. What if he'd brought Victoria? What if she saw him like this?

Better to have let Harry Smith kill him than that.

That he didn't see her among Thaddeas's entourage—folks he now recognized from the Red Light Saloon—relieved him so surely, he could almost forgive the man for destroying his life. Not for destroying his family's, or Julije's. But his own. Almost.

"Howdy, Ward," greeted Thaddeas with casual, cowboy camaraderie. Now Laramie saw why a lawyer would wear dogging boots. "Word has it you've got one of my father's hands in here."

"Arrested him for murder," agreed Ward, looking particularly sour as four men and a barmaid dripped water all over his jail.

"The way I hear it, he shot in self-defense."

"He didn't just shoot," insisted Ward, still behind his desk. "The man's a gunslinger, Garrison."

"Last time I heard, being a good shot wasn't illegal

215

in the state of Wyoming. But incarcerating a man without just cause is."

Ward leaned forward, trying to look superior. "You didn't hear me right, boy. I ain't holding him for bein' good with a gun. I'm holding him for killin' two men."

"Both of whom were shooting at him." Thaddeas managed to look superior without trying. "One of whom allegedly *escaped from your jail* this afternoon. I believe I can make a decent case that this gentleman wasn't just watching his back, and might have done a service for the community. You don't want to be arresting folks for that, do you? And don't cry 'firearms ordinance' to me, either," he added. "We've both been in the Red Light before."

Huh? Thaddeas Garrison had been in the Red Light Saloon?

"The judge can decide on Monday," insisted Ward.

"I don't think so," said Thaddeas, and smiled—with just his mouth. "I think the judge will decide tonight, when I go wake him up. It'll annoy him some, sure. But he'll come down here, and he'll listen to what these eyewitnesses have to say about self-defense and escaped prisoners. And which one of us do you think will have most annoyed him by then—Sheriff?"

After what he'd discovered today, Laramie did not want to admire Thaddeas Garrison, but . . . *damn,* he was good! He was good enough that Ward stood up from behind his desk, trying to make up in brawn what he couldn't in brains.

"He ain't hired you as his lawyer," he pointed out.

"True." Thaddeas held up a hand. "Excuse us for a moment. Folks, you just make yourselves comfortable."

The witnesses he'd brought with him nodded. They'd come out in the rain—for Laramie. They were willing to risk getting on Ward's bad side—for Laramie. It was incredible.

When Thaddeas approached the cell, Laramie met him. He expected the lawyer to say something about policies, even price. Instead Garrison said, very low, "As soon as I get these charges dismissed, you're leaving town. Preferably tonight. Understand?"

Laramie only began to understand—with gut-deep dismay—when Garrison continued. "I don't know what's going on between you and my sister. She's a good girl and she knows her own mind, so I'll trust it's nothing needs killing for. But it's too much for my comfort even so, especially considering who and what you are. So I will get you out of here, and then you will collect your wages at the ranch, and then you will leave here."

It was what Laramie had meant to do anyway. It was what he wanted to do. But that the man who'd ruined *Laramie's* sister was now warning Laramie away from *his,* grated on him.

"And if I don't accept your help?" he challenged.

Thaddeas adjusted how he leaned his arms along the crossbar of the cell, as if to get more comfortable, and ducked his head even closer to the bars. "Take some advice. If I'm your lawyer, most of what I know about you stays our secret. But if I'm not, I might have to share some of it."

Then he met Laramie's eyes straight on, and mouthed, *Drazen.*

Nate Dawson had not, Vic noticed with some relief, told Thaddeas about her. In fact, the cowhand would not even look at her now, as if pretending she didn't even exist.

Good.

She had to wait a long time, there in the alley. Rain drummed on her hat, dripping off the brim and down her hair. Some of it trickled in under her shirtwaist, first cold and then itchy. She didn't care. She just

217

wanted to see that Ross was safe. It mattered to her more than she could ever have imagined.

And Victoria could imagine a great deal.

Just when she was beginning to think she should cross the street and listen in at the jail windows, the door opened. The crowd that had gone in with Thaddeas emerged, mounted their horses, rode off in the direction from which they'd come—even the woman who, again, showed her legs. Not too long after that, Thaddeas stepped out onto the boardwalk.

Then Ross Laramie. He was safe.

Victoria leaned against the brick wall of the Hot Dinner Café, weak with gratitude. He stood as tall and dark as ever. He walked just fine. He was safe, and Thaddeas had done it, and maybe she didn't hate her brother after all.

She heard Ross say something about "has my Colt," and Thaddeas say something like "count your blessings."

It wasn't enough. She lifted her wet skirts, circled behind the café, and crept up an alley almost across from the jail. She could hear a lot better then—a horse approaching, a train whistle, and Ross Laramie when he stiffly said, "Obliged."

See, she wanted to say, pleased. *Thaddeas isn't the bad man you think he is!*

But Thaddeas said, "You were innocent, weren't you?"

Ross stared. The longer he said nothing, the more nervous Victoria felt. He'd spent time at a reform school. He was good with guns. He'd been hiding unexplained wounds.

Thaddeas clarified, "It was self-defense this time, wasn't it?"

All Ross said in agreement was "This time."

"Then he shouldn't have held you," said Thad. "I got you out because it was the right thing to do, Laramie. Not for you. Not for my sister. And now I expect you to keep your word."

His word? What word? What had Thad made Ross promise?

Then, before Victoria could even work that out, her father rode up to the two of them on his buckskin.

Thaddeas Garrison knew who Laramie really was.

Jacob Garrison, reining back his gelding in front of the jail, also knew. According to Thaddeas, the rancher remembered Laramie's poppa, saw the resemblance right off, and hired him anyway. Of course, the cattle baron had also warned him against making trouble or trifling with his daughters.

Likely Elizabeth Garrison knew, too—but Victoria did not. Not yet. Maybe, if they were lucky, not ever. It was the one thing the three of them had in common, whether they knew it or not.

Not wanting to hurt Victoria.

"Well," said the older Garrison, nodding as he looked from his son to Laramie and back. "You're out."

Yet someone else "doing the right thing" by riding to Laramie's rescue. Not for Laramie, though. Just for justice.

He guessed justice had to be enough.

"He's out," said Thaddeas. "And now he's leaving."

Garrison looked at his son in silent question.

Thadeas just shook his head. Of course, that satisfied his father, no matter what ghosts haunted Thaddeas's past.

Laramie silently braced himself so he wouldn't show pain, then fitted his boot into Blackie's stirrup and swung himself into his wet saddle. He met Jacob Garrison's steady gaze and nodded silent thanks, for more than he could ever say. For the trust. For the daughter, no matter how briefly he'd known her.

He also nodded to Nate Dawson, who, standing on the corner, looked nervous about something. Whatever it was, it wasn't likely Laramie's business anymore.

"Good-bye," he said. With a soft clucking to Blackie, and the lightest touch of his spurred heels, he turned and headed down Main Street, into the drumming rain.

And that, he guessed, was that.

Except for one last stop.

Chapter Nineteen

Victoria *did* fall off her bike this time. Fleeing Main Street before either Papa or Thaddeas knew she was there, though, it wasn't her speed or the wet roads that took her down. It was sheer, blind fury.

Thaddeas had told Ross to leave.

Ross was going.

One moment Vic was pedaling wildly, blinking away rain and leaning into a turn. The next, the wheels of her bicycle skidded out from under her. She hung suspended—then slammed into the paved street. Pain shot through her wrist, her knee, her hip, and she cried out a word she wasn't even supposed to know. But the hurt was at least a distraction from the hollow ache in her heart.

She sat up and gingerly made sure nothing was broken, pushing a wet, concerned Duchess away from her. Too soon, she knew that her heart still hurt worse.

He wasn't even going to say good-bye?

Some of the rain felt hot on her cheeks, and she realized that she was crying. Sitting in a stream of run-off, Victoria drew the knee that wasn't hurt up against her and tried, for just a moment, to think.

They were clearly *making* him leave. But he wasn't gone yet. And maybe . . .

The idea wasn't clever at all. It was more instinct than sense. But she thought she knew where to find him.

Carefully testing her leg, she stood. Her knee still hurt, but she could walk on it. She picked up the bicycle and made sure it would roll; the fender rubbed against the tire only a little. *Good,* she thought, determined. *Good.*

If it were broken, she would have darn well limped her way out of town. Or stolen a horse, and forced Thaddeas to defend her at the resulting trial. But she was going after Ross.

Her friend.

Ross felt empty, numb, *hard* as he hitched Blackie beside Mount Hope's only lamppost, pushed open the gates, and walked into the cemetery. He didn't know who he was anymore. Outlaw? Cowboy? Vengeful brother? He didn't know what the hell he would do now, other than keep breathing.

But the least he could do was see the family once more, and apologize for failing them.

After this night, he wanted to apologize to *someone.*

Had he ever, even as a child, feared cemeteries? Tombstones and graves were nothing, even in the rain; a remarkably neat packaging for the ugliness of death. Laramie walked among them without a second thought—and had almost passed the tomb marked "McCrae" when he saw the bicycle leaned against it.

Staring at it, Laramie realized that maybe he *wasn't*

numb. Maybe he could feel something after all.

He just didn't dare name it.

He glanced toward the gates, just in case. Then he spun and wove his way past more headstones toward the back of the cemetery, splashing through puddles, tripping once over a child's small marker.

Victoria?

Maybe she'd left the bicycle earlier. Maybe he'd imagined her so hard tonight, he'd gone loco. Maybe the woman he spotted, huddled against the pale square of Julije's tombstone, was his sister's ghost, come to chide him for deserting her cause. That was no more foolish than to think . . . to think. . . .

A dog, lying beside her, sat up at his approach.

The woman looked up with Victoria's wet face. Her eyes burned with silent accusation, her mouth tight with the effort to hold back whatever she meant to say. And Laramie sank to his knees beside her, grateful, penitent, afraid to believe, afraid to doubt.

He'd wanted her so badly tonight. More than life.

Then Victoria blinked against the rain and asked, "You're leaving?" He didn't know how she knew, or what she felt about it, but she was real.

And here.

He'd come straight from jail, and before that, a bar. He'd come from killings. He didn't deserve her. But she was here, and he reacted to her nearness, not her words. He reached for her, sank into her arms even as he drew her into his. He curled around and into her, losing his hat in the grass, laying his head to her chest where he could hear her beating heart.

It was the closest thing to his own heart that he'd ever had.

Even if she was angry, she wrapped her arms around him—all curves and warmth and wetness—and she repeated her accusation. "You're leaving me?"

He blinked away rainwater, glad for its disguise.

"I'm sorry," he whispered, his voice broken. It became a chant. "Victoria, I'm sorry. I'm so sorry. I'm sorry, Victoria . . ."

She countered with hushing sounds, first hesitant, then steadier. Her lips brushed his temple, his jaw. The scent of soap and cinnamon surrounded him like a sacred incense—almost enough to mask the smell of blood. Almost. "Tell me what's wrong," she urged. "Please, Ross. Whatever's wrong, please just tell me."

"I . . ." But he didn't know where to begin, what to leave out. Why should he hurt her with the truth now that he was leaving? He did not want to leave her that way. He did not want to forever remember her disillusionment. So he dammed his words at "Sorry," and he held her.

"Ross," she pleaded, deliberately loosening her hold to sit up, to look at him full on. She didn't stop touching him, though, her fingers on his face, one hand drawing up and down his arm. She wasn't pushing him away. "Are you all right? What happened to your face? Why did they hurt you?"

She was not here because it was the right thing to do. She was here for him. Or the man she thought he was.

He closed his eyes a moment, to balance himself, then opened them to stare at the marvel that was the woman he loved. He touched her cheek with his fingertips, wondering if the dampness was tears. He almost wished they were, and hated himself for wishing it. "You shouldn't even be out here," he murmured, awkward. And yet even the awkward words came more easily when they were for her. "The ground's wet."

Victoria squared her shoulders. "It's barely September, and I have a cloak. And I'd best warn you, Ross Laramie, that I've had my fill of men trying to protect me against my will tonight."

She sounded serious. Good thing she wasn't dangerous. He no longer had his gun.

"At least . . ." He leaned back against Julije's tombstone and drew Victoria full into his lap so that he was the one sitting on the damp ground.

Snuggling more securely onto him, against him, she filled his arms with her warm curves, soothed his scarred heart with the balm of her concern. "Oh," she murmured, adjusting herself on him, and he could have died from the sensation. "This *is* better."

Better? It was heaven. Stolen heaven, true—but he would take what he could get.

"Tell me what happened?" she repeated as she looped her arms behind his neck and leaned more comfortably against his chest. Of course, she was hungry for information. To Victoria, truth equaled love. Truth—and shared secrets.

He could at least give her some of it.

So instead of asking his own questions, which he'd never been very good at, he confessed about tonight. He told her about the Red Light Saloon, and she didn't even chide him for drinking. He hated leaving out the part about meeting Lonny Logan, but told her about the first shooting as evenly as he could. As he spoke, he realized his voice was shaking.

But that's what guns did. He'd never once forgotten that's what guns did.

"Harry Smith?" Victoria lifted her head from his shoulder, though her arms stayed behind his neck. "But he was in jail."

He ducked his head to better see her, searching her gaze for condemnation. "He got out."

"But why would he want to kill you? He seemed like such a nice . . . rustler."

With one hand Laramie drew her head back to his shoulder, where he could kiss her forehead. Her cheeks. Her eyelids. Every kiss might be his last; he wanted to hoard as many as he could. But he knew she wanted information even more. "Maybe he was working for someone important. Maybe his boss got him out on the condition that he kill me."

Her eyes widened.

"So that I wouldn't look further," he explained. It was the only thing that made sense. Even in the wild West—the West that Jacob Garrison said was over—very few men killed for the sake of killing.

"That's all the more reason for you to stay here and not give them the satisfaction," insisted Victoria. Then her face paled, her lips rounded. "But then they might try to kill you again! Oh no, Ross. You *do* have to go."

"That's not why I'm going." If it was kinder to let her think that, why did he want to tell her more? "Not all of it."

She waited, asking nothing except with her eyes.

I'm leaving because the sheriff is gunning for me.

But he'd never been a coward before. That wasn't enough.

I'm leaving because your family will destroy me.

But he remembered what she'd said about her sister and the sheep farmer, and even that wasn't enough.

I'm leaving because I lost my first reason to be here, and the truth would destroy my second one.

And God knew if he stayed, Victoria would get to the truth. She deserved it.

Feeling inadequate, he went back to what he *could* tell her. "Smith drew down on me, and I killed him. Then another fellow shot at me, so I killed him too." He never did get a good look at the second man, though he assumed it was the gravelly-voiced rustler. It could have been an innocent saloon patron, itchy from the first shooting. He may have killed someone's husband, son, brother, pa.

Fast. That was him.

Maybe he shouldn't even have told her that much.

"Victoria, there are two men dead at my hands to-night."

"That," Victoria said, "was self-defense."

"It's still killing."

She drew back from him, just far enough to study his face—what little she could see of it by that one streetlamp. Now she would know what he really was.

Then she said, "Oh, Ross, I'm so sorry." And she kissed him.

He was so stunned, he could not move his mouth against her kiss. He simply stared until she drew back. Then he demanded, "*You're* sorry?"

"That must have been terrible." She stroked his hair back from his collar, drew her soft thumb over his injured cheek, kissed the corner of his mouth. "You poor thing."

Poor thing? "I killed them," he repeated.

"No," she insisted with a loyal nod. "They killed themselves. They just used you as their weapon."

At that, something deep in the recesses of his heart cracked and split open and let out too much, all at once. Out poured his grief at the killings—tonight, and twelve years ago, and three others through the years between. Out flowed his guilt. Out rushed his certainty that he could have done something else, been something else, if only he'd tried harder.

If only he hadn't taken up with outlaws. If only he hadn't run off from the boys' ranch in a futile search for his mother. If only he hadn't told Julije their poppa's plans in the first place.

It all shuddered up from him, filling his chest, burning at his eyes, closing his throat. He turned his face quickly into her softness, hiding from what he felt, what he trembled with the need to do.

Gunslingers don't cry.

But dear God, why had he become what he was?

He didn't cry—didn't breathe, didn't move, but at

227

least didn't cry. Still, Victoria held him and murmured sweet, blissful lies. "It's all right, Ross. It wasn't fair, but it's not your fault. It's all right, darling. It's all right."

But she only knew about tonight, only knew what little he'd told her. Even sinking under grief and guilt and *feeling*—more feeling than he'd endured in years—Laramie knew better.

More of it was his fault than not. Nothing would be okay.

But Victoria saying so gave him a few more blissful moments of imagining that maybe, maybe it could be.

At first Victoria thought Ross would cry, but he didn't. He'd been forced to kill two men. He *should* cry.

But although he closed his eyes against some great pain, and pressed his face into her bodice, until he was as much in her lap as she was in his, he did not.

Poor, rugged, bottled-up man.

She petted his hair, kissed his forehead, told him it was all right—it had to be, didn't it? Then, afraid that her attention just made him feel worse, she began to talk about other things.

"I heard you tonight," she admitted. "I was outside the jail and I heard Thaddeas tell you to leave. That's why I came here. I thought—I'm not sure why, but I hoped you might stop here. I'm glad you did."

He began to breathe again, a little more regularly. "You were outside the jail?"

"Earlier, I asked Thaddeas about Julije Lauranovic, and he barely remembers her," she continued. She loved his hair, so black, so sleek—even wet. Especially wet. "He remembers the family. He said their name was Laurence, which now that I think of it, the paper said something about too. But he doesn't know who Julije's sweetheart could have been."

Ross rolled more fully onto his back, looking up at

her from where his head was now cradled on *her* lap, and he seemed . . . shaken. Worn. And somehow, tragically amused.

"Believe him, Victoria," he said, raising a hand up to her shoulder and fingering a wet hank of *her* hair. The side of his wrist pressed against her breast. She liked it. "Believe the best of your brother."

She rolled her eyes, but was careful not to move her body. She liked her body where it was. "I'm not just believing the best of him, Ross Laramie. I may be angry with him, after the way he talked to you—and to me earlier, when he asked questions about why *I* was asking questions. You know, I'm afraid he's read more into our friendship than . . ."

It suddenly occurred to her how late it was for them to be alone. Much less together. Much less with Ross pillowing his head in her lap, his hand in her hair and his wrist on her bosom. Were anybody to see them like this, he would have to marry her or the scandal would linger for years. Even if they married, it would linger for months.

He looked amused—for Ross—and she touched his lips with her fingers, trying to draw them up farther at the corners. "Or perhaps not," she whispered. She'd never come close to feeling this way about any of her other friends.

"Perhaps he's simply a very clever brother," he agreed, just as softly, and withdrew his hand.

Her breast ached where he'd touched her.

With a deep, determined breath, she made herself ask the one thing she didn't want confirmed—but something she knew so deeply, *not* confirming it would eat away at her. "Oh, Ross, do you really have to leave?"

He closed his eyes, hints of hidden pain flashing across his face, and she realized it wasn't just words he shared with her. She felt honored, suddenly, to have been privy to so much about Ross Laramie.

"You do, don't you?" she asked.

He sat up then, much though she wanted him to lie with his head in her lap forever. He drew a knee up so that he could lean closer to her, and he took one of her hands in his own.

Their hands were almost dry. At some point, the rain must have stopped.

"I don't belong here," he told her.

"You could."

"I've never been a range detective before."

"Well, you're a good one."

He smiled a little then, his lips quirking even without help from her fingers, and he slowly leaned close enough to kiss her. His lips were firm, warm, adoring. Oh, she did like being adored. "At best," he conceded, "I *was* a good range detective."

She remembered then that he'd been fired.

"And someone's trying to kill you here," she admitted reluctantly.

"Which endangers whoever I'm near," he agreed. He spread her palm flat, then opened his hand and pressed it to hers. No fists. "The only reason I have to stay is you. And even you . . ."

She shifted her hand slightly, so that her fingers could curl between his and hang on. "Even I what?"

He whispered something that sounded like, "Just seeing make-believe."

She cocked her head, confused. "What?"

Ross searched her face—for what? Then he leaned in and kissed her, longer and harder and more desperate than before. She found herself sinking into him, pressing against him, melding with his mouth, wanting him to never stop kissing her like this.

But he did stop. He levered her gently back into balance with a hand on her shoulder, his eyes somehow wild, and he rasped out the desperate words,

"Even you wouldn't want me if you knew my real name was Laurence."

For a slow, stupid moment, while her lips throbbed and her body felt cold from not being snuggled closer to his, she thought: *Lawrence Laramie?*

Then other bits of information, settling so cleanly into place in a puzzle she hadn't even known she'd been working, began to force their truth onto her. *Ross Laurence.*

Except . . .

She looked at the tombstones beside him, trying to make out the names in the dark of night, but he answered for her.

"Originally it was Lauranovic," he told her. "I was born Drazen Lauranovic, and then I was Ross Laurence. I have been lying to you, and all of that and more is why I cannot stay."

Chapter Twenty

Victoria looked from the tombstone back to him, and she didn't appear angry yet. She still seemed confused.

Give her time.

Still, Laramie took advantage of her momentary silence. "I did not want you to know," he admitted shamefully. "Ever. The more I saw you, the more I wanted you to think I was . . ." *Anybody else.* But it was not that easy. "I wanted to be the man you see when you look at me. But I am not, and it was selfish of me not to let you know that. At least your father and your brother—"

Victoria raised a hand to silence him, pulling her other hand free from his grasp. "My *family* knows?"

He'd expected anger at the lies, the rustling, the killing. He hadn't thought of this. "What?"

"You told my family and you didn't tell me?"

She sat fully back from him now, her eyes bright,

her shoulders high. He would have laughed if it weren't for her pain—if it weren't for remembering how Victoria felt about secrets.

"No. I told nobody." He captured her hand again between both of his, tried to make her understand at least this. "Until you."

"But you said . . ."

"They guessed," he insisted. "Your father recognized me and told your brother. I only learned it tonight."

She stared, her brow furrowed, as if silently begging him to make this right. He knew he could not, but he had to try. He owed her that much. No, he owed her more. But this, he could give.

"I've been Laramie for years," he explained. "I was not lying about that. Not quite."

That sounded inadequate, even to him, which is why she startled him so when she finished, "You just did not tell the entire truth."

She understood?

He squinted at her, not believing it. She understood?

She repeated, "You're Drazen Lauranovic?"

He nodded, ready for the worst—and yet somehow, desperately relieved to have it done with. Anything she said now, be it soothing or angry, she finally said to him. For a few minutes at least, whoever he really was got to spend time with her. "I was."

"You used to live here?"

He nodded.

"And the Wards stole your family's cattle, and your family stole them back?"

He nodded. He couldn't ask her to say what came next, so he did it for her. "And Victoria, I killed Boris Ward."

"After he killed your father and brother in front of you. Oh, Ross." She wove her fingers through his again, holding his hand tighter, then looked up in confusion. "I mean . . ."

She actually cared what to call him? "Ross," he pleaded. "Hardly anybody called me Drazen until after . . ."

"After the lynchings. And the trial."

He nodded.

Her head came up at another realization. "Julie was your sister." He heard how she Anglicized the name, and he loved her. "Oh, Ross, no wonder you want to find who deserted her."

Betrayed her. But now was not the time to pursue that argument. If he did not finish this now, he would never again have the chance, much less the nerve.

"They sent me to a boys' ranch in Texas, on parole, but I ran away. As I grew, I took ranching jobs. That's where I met other outlaws."

She whispered, "And you went bad."

He could not correct her—except, perhaps, her faith he'd not been bad already.

She considered him solemnly. "Did you really rustle cattle?"

"Depending on my boss." *Ride for the brand.* That was the cowboy code.

"Bank robbery?" At least for that, he could shake his head. "Train robbery?"

"Just the rustling," he insisted. "But if folks were shooting at us, I shot back. I've likely killed men since '88, Victoria. Maybe as many as three—I wasn't the only one shooting, but maybe that many. I've done that."

She chewed her lower lip in thought. "Lawmen?"

He shook his head.

"Innocent bystanders? Feuds? Were you threatening people?"

"It was range wars. Men were hired to move cattle and shoot at us. We were hired to move cattle back and shoot at them. It—" He let go of her hand, so she would not have to take it back herself. "It paid well."

She frowned at her empty hand. "Who's we?"

He wasn't about to start naming names, even for her.

Victoria stood and stalked away some distance. Her skirts made a slapping noise, they were so wet. That's when he noticed that the rain had stopped.

He gave her a while to think about it, to understand what he'd done. In the meantime, he touched Julije's tombstone and thought, *My sister.*

My poppa. My brother. It was right that he'd told.

The dog, who'd sat up again when Victoria stood, lay down when she turned and came back. She was taking this far better than Laramie had feared. Maybe she just didn't understand.

He picked up his hat and stood to meet her.

"You shouldn't go," Victoria announced.

He stared. He'd expected a slap, or tears, or fury. "What?"

She took his arm, tugged him a little to make him walk her slowly back toward her bicycle. "You should stay here. This town once did a great disservice to your family. You oughtn't let that chase you away."

He stopped, made her stop, searched her face. She couldn't be serious, could she?

The words came harder this time, even speaking to her. "W—wouldn't it chase *you* away?" he stuttered. "*All* of it?"

Somehow she knew what he meant, even with him saying it so poorly. She ducked her head. "I don't know for sure," she admitted—not what he longed to hear, but far more than he'd expected. "Maybe if I had more time to get to know you as . . . as Ross Laurence."

Ross Laurence.

A fine, bright feeling came over him when she called him that. Laurence was who he'd been back when life was still hopeful, when he'd been loved. When he'd lived in a world far more like Victoria's.

Ross Laurence would just say *Yes, I'll stay.*

But could he survive the world Laramie—even Drazen Lauranovic—had built for him?

"I have no job," he reminded her. "Someone powerful is gunning for me. The sheriff is this close to figuring out why I look familiar. I've given up on the man who—"

But no, he wouldn't argue about who had ruined Julije again. Not tonight. Maybe never.

"My lawyer advised me to leave town," he finished weakly, gazing into her beautiful face, memorizing it.

"The hell with your lawyer," she insisted, which made him want to laugh. And to cry. But gunslingers didn't cry.

He laid his open palm against her cheek. "I have no reason to stay except for you. And your family would never let you get to know Ross Laurence."

"Then we'll make them," she said firmly.

He wanted to believe her. But what did he have to offer her, except danger and a bad reputation?

At least, that's all he could offer her here.

The idea stole upon him unexpectedly, maybe out of desperation, maybe out of sheer greed. He didn't know, didn't care. It—*she*—was all he had now.

"Come with me," he said.

Victoria stared up at him, her eyes going round.

"Tonight. We'll start somewhere new. You'll write home that you're safe, and—" *Oh.* He flushed, to have forgotten so important a detail. "We would marry. If you'd have me."

Had there ever been a worse proposal? He could see

from her face that this wouldn't be. Not in his world. Not in hers.

"Oh! Ross . . ." Now he'd forced her to reject him.

"Never mind," he assured her, taking her arm, leading her toward her bicycle. "I'm sorry, Victoria. I shouldn't—"

"No! It was . . ." Now she was the one who dug in her heels and stopped them. She laid her hands against his chest as if to steady him. Or herself. He felt so embarrassed, he hardly cared. "It's not that I don't want to go, or even to . . ."

He winced away from her kindness. "Please don't—"

But this was Victoria. "I do want to go. More than I would ever have thought. But oh, Ross. I—I don't really know you."

How could she? He didn't know himself.

When he said, "I understand," she began blinking away fresh tears. "Victoria?"

"No." She drew one hand protectively to her lips, held him from her with the other. "If you don't go now, I might not let you, and I guess I have to let you, except that it isn't right, and there's got to be something—see? You've got to go now."

He looked down at her, and he hated himself for hurting her, and he loved her beyond reason—and he knew he could not do it. "You go first."

She glowered at him through teary eyes. "Coward."

"Yes," he admitted, voice broken.

"Tell me you'll come back," she demanded suddenly.

"I—" *Come back?*

"I can't leave—let you leave—unless you promise you'll come back to me someday. In a few months you'll write to me, and I'll let you know how things are, and then you'll come home."

The closest he had to a home was her, and she deserved a better home than him. "I don't—"

"I've seen you read," she warned him. "You can so write."

He nodded. He *could* write. But from where? To where would she send her reply? What would he even be by then?

Surely he'd gone too far to start over, at least without breaking a few laws. A few *more* laws.

"Don't you dare leave me thinking I'll never see you again, Ross Laramie," she warned him, her voice thick with tears, and dug her fingers into his shirt. "Don't you dare do that to me."

He would give her anything. His life. His heart. His soul. Likely in half a year, she would have found a proper beau—but he would give her this.

"I'll write," he promised, leaning down to rest his forehead against hers. "I will find someplace safe. Then I will write to you and tell you where I am, and . . ."

"And we'll decide then," she whispered, with no idea how unlikely it was that they would ever get that far.

"We'll decide then." If he were in prison, or Argentina, there wouldn't be a great deal to decide. And if he were dead . . .

"Kiss me?" she pleaded, so he did. He covered her lips with his, held her and pretended he didn't have to let her go. He allowed all the precarious, vulnerable life in him, the emotions she'd awakened, to fill that kiss. His lips worshiped her, his hands cherished her. She buried her fingers in his hair, responded to him hungrily. Her bosom pressed round and firm against his chest, her hips flared and swaying under his hands, and oh, he wanted more. He wanted everything. There was more than one way to be considered married out west, and then even if he died . . .

But no. That crime he would not commit. If he

loved her enough to leave her, he must love her enough to leave her alone.

They kissed, long and longingly, until finally Victoria wrenched herself from his arms, grabbed her bicycle, and began to run with it, somehow mounting it as it rolled. She coasted out through the gates of the cemetery and pedaled, hard, out of sight. Staring after her, Laramie wished, more than he'd ever wished for anything, to be someone else. Someone who could stay with her. Someone who could love her properly.

But hell, he'd already been three people, and he wasn't even twenty-five years old. Besides, a fellow brought all those past selves with him. Prison and Argentina aside, the person he was now—whoever that was—might not even be alive in a year.

One more secret he'd chosen to keep.

Victoria was halfway home, nearly blinded by her tears and the gaslit darkness, before she realized the truth.

She was in love with Ross Laramie.

The thought surprised her so much, she almost swerved right into Duchess. She braked immediately and dismounted to find her balance. How blind was she? For mercy's sake, she'd been happily kissing the man for weeks!

Had she thought the excitement came from the rustling?

She looked over her shoulder, toward the cemetery, and she thought—*I* don't *know him.* She had too many unanswered questions. Who were his bad companions? Did he enjoy reading books? Was he a Republican or a Democrat—or did outlaws even vote?

And how had he hurt himself, when she first saw him bare-chested and bandaged?

But she did know Ross Laramie had a soft voice, a deliberate manner, a coiled control. He was impressive with a side arm but still didn't like using it. He was tall and angled and darkly handsome. He made her feel safe, cherished. Now that she knew who he really was, or at least had been—

Drazen Lauranovic!

—she also knew he'd come through awful adversity and, with few good influences, had grown into a man so decent that he'd comforted Kitty about the stallion's death. So decent that he hadn't taken advantage of how she kept meeting him alone like a regular hussy. So decent that he mourned his self-defense shooting of a cattle rustler.

She knew more than she'd thought—and she loved him.

And now she'd let him go?

"Idiot!" She said the word out loud, turning her bicycle to go after him. Then—again—she hesitated.

How long could he hold down a job? How heavy a drinker was he? Was there a price on his head? Did he believe in God, the rights of children and laborers, or women's suffrage?

She looked back toward the cemetery and wanted him. She wanted to get on her bicycle and go after him. But she couldn't seem to make herself move— until Duchess spun around, ears high.

Then she heard hoofbeats, coming fast. Someone was riding toward her at a trot, just this side of dangerous on paved streets. *Ross?* She spun hopefully in that direction.

Then she recognized her father's buckskin, her father's fury—and her heart took a header.

Papa reined to a stop and glared down at her, beyond words. Before she'd even reconciled herself to disappointment—that he wasn't Ross—he reached down, lifted her bicycle right up out of her hands, and hurled it in a high, heavy arc into the bushes beside the road. His horse started at that bit of business, but Papa just reined him in again, leaned out of the saddle, and caught her by the waistband. Her, he dragged up onto the saddle in front of him, facedown.

"Papa!" she protested. But she also grabbed on to his leg when he wheeled around and set off at a canter. "Let me up!"

"Keep your voice down," he cautioned, his own drawl dangerous. "Just might survive this night without ruinin' your reputation and the rest of ours."

Reputation? The man she loved had just left to God-knew-where, and her father was worried about her *reputation*? Only out of respect for her sisters, and *their* reputations through association, did she bite back further protests until they reached the in-town house. That, and apprehension. Generally, when one of the girls was old enough to ride sidesaddle, it was understood that they were too old for whippings. But Victoria's sister Laurel had disproved that understanding once or twice.

Vic wasn't about to submit to a child's punishment without a fight. But even Mama tiptoed around Papa when he got angry—and Victoria had never seen him this angry.

He rode right into the now-open doors of the stables and swung her none-too-gently onto her feet. Then he pointed at an empty stall. "Wait."

She drew a breath to protest, then saw his face. His brows slashed low over eyes that glittered with gray fury. His mouth was set tight. His movements, too, were sharper than he would normally make around a person, much less a horse.

She stood, silent and obedient, while he saw to his horse. But she regretted her obedience when he grabbed her by the arm and all but dragged her toward the house.

He made poor Duchess stay in the stables, like a failure.

"Papa, stop it," Victoria protested again.

She might as well argue with a mountain. He didn't let go until he'd shoved her down into a kitchen chair. Then he strode to the other side of the room, as if afraid of what he would do if he were close to her.

She sat up, head high, and waited.

Papa opened his mouth once, closed it, shook his head. It took him another few tries before he managed, "Where. Were. You."

So much for choosing home and family over true love. That hurt—that *anger*—made her fold her arms and demand, "Where do you think?"

Only then did she spot it, the flash of pain behind Papa's fury, the confusion at her disobedience of lifelong rules, the fear he must have felt. He turned away, before she could see more, and braced a forearm against the wall. "Gallivantin' through the night," he accused, aggrieved. "Riskin' your safety, your honor."

At that, he turned back to her. Or upon her. "*Family's* honor," he added with an accusing nod. "Thank God your mother and sisters weren't here. Still scair't your brother near to death."

And him. She'd scared him.

"I was fine," she assured him, more gently. "I had Duchess with me, like I promised, and I was safe the whole time. Although if Thaddeas had only taken me with him when I asked him to—"

From his expression, that had not been the best answer.

"I went to the jail to see what happened," she offered.

"Dawson said as much," Papa drawled, and looked disgusted. "When he got 'round to it."

She felt a stab of guilt for poor Nate. "When I heard Thad tell Mr. Laramie to leave town, I went to the cemetery."

"The cemetery," Papa repeated, confused.

"I had a hunch he might stop by there, and I was right."

"Met him at the cemetery." His breath was ragged.

"To *talk*, Papa. To find out what had happened, why he was leaving." That wasn't all they'd done, but it was why she'd gone.

Besides, Ross didn't need anyone else gunning for him.

"To talk," repeated Papa now, more than suspicious.

"Yes, to talk about why he was being ordered out of town by a local cattle baron and his son."

He angled a hand in her direction, a warning against that tone of voice. "Middle of the night."

She said, "Apparently, that's when he got his orders."

Thaddeas burst through the back door, breathless. "Thank God you're safe, you brat." Then he looked at their father. "I saw the light on the third floor. Thanks for the signal."

Victoria frowned. "Papa didn't go up to the third floor."

Thaddeas said, "Miss Taylor's still here. And weren't you a friend, leaving her to face us when we got in?"

Oh no. Poor Evangeline!

Where *was* poor Evangeline?

"Do you know what you put *us* through?" demanded Thad.

Papa said, "Met him at the cemetery."

Thaddeas made a face. "The *cemetery*?"

The back door opened again, and Nate Dawson skidded inside. "Oh, thank God," he said, seeing Victoria.

Papa said, *"Git."*

He said, "Yessir," and backed out the door.

Thaddeas said, "What were you thinking, meeting a man at night? And *that* man? I guess you *weren't* thinking!"

Victoria had heard enough. "I met him at the cemetery because I knew that he would stop there. He was visiting his family's graves one last time, since because of you he has to leave them." Not that she'd known they *were* his family, at the time, but it sounded better this way than, "I had a hunch."

Both her father and brother went so still, it would have been funny. Under different circumstances.

Nothing was funny tonight.

"His family," repeated Papa.

"The Lauranovics," she confirmed. "Yes," she added, to Thaddeas's expression, so grateful to Ross for telling her himself that she could weep. "I *do* know who he is. I know a great deal about him, and he understands me, too. More than you do."

Papa narrowed his eyes at the challenge. "He does."

"Yes. I'm glad to be your daughter, your sister. I'm sorry for risking the family, and for frightening you. But I have a life beyond being just Victoria Garrison, whether you like that or not. I have dreams that are worth taking chances on."

"Did you think you'd become Victoria Lauranovic?" challenged Thaddeas, his sarcasm thick.

"Laurence," she corrected him. "They wanted to be called Laurence. And I *would* be, if I'd said yes tonight. Is *that* why you two were so scared? You thought he'd beguile me with promises, then light out when it was too late? Well I'm not Julie Laurence. Oh, I could probably get myself into trouble like her, if I fell in love with someone less honorable than Ross," she admitted, aware that they were staring at her with almost identical expressions of horror. "But if some man misused me, I certainly wouldn't commit suicide. I'd go gunning for him myself. I wouldn't rely on my father or my big brother to do it!"

Or even wait for a younger brother to grow up?

Victoria had been leaning forward from the chair

in her zeal, but slowly she sat back with realization. "He was going to kill the man who ruined Julie, wasn't he?"

Thad raised his eyebrows. "Figured it out, did you? *That's* why we fired him."

"But he thinks *you* ruined Julie."

"What?" Sensing his father's silent question, Thaddeas spread his hands. "Wait, I barely even knew Julie Laurence!"

"That's what I told him, but he thought you were the only one left, and he didn't kill you." *He really* does *love me.*

Thad said, "Luckily for him, since I got him out of jail."

"He was innocent. It couldn't have been that awfully hard," she challenged right back. "And by the way, he made an excellent range detective, and you still have a rustling problem on your hands, because whoever's really behind the operation helped Harry Smith escape jail. You just consider that next time you feel all smug about firing Ross."

Papa shook his head in warning, clearly more concerned with her tone of voice than the loss of cattle. "Get upstairs."

"Gladly." She stood. His next words surprised her.

"Monday, you'll serve your notice and take yourself back home where we can keep watch on you." He narrowed his eyes in full accusation. "Since you ain't to be trusted."

What? "I will not!"

"As long as you are under this roof—"

"Then I won't *stay* under this roof." That took him by surprise, and she made the best of the moment. "By the time he was my age, Thaddeas had been at college in Virginia for almost two years. I can certainly manage living within a half mile of my family if I move out to a boardinghouse. So, if I can't go about my own

245

business without throwing this whole house into turmoil—if I feel I have to sneak around to entertain whom I choose—it may be our only compromise."

Rather than push her luck, she headed for the back stairs. There, reluctantly, she stopped. She did have responsibilities beyond her own heart. "Evangeline's here?"

"Reckon she's hidin' somewhere," admitted Papa. "This ain't decided."

"No, sir," conceded Victoria. And maybe that was a good thing. "It probably isn't. Good night."

Then she hurried upstairs, to where Evangeline waited.

"You're staying the night," Vic said. At this hour, it was her only choice. Besides, she longed to talk about Ross—about his truth, his proposal, the letter he would write to her.

She wanted to admit that she was in love.

"They're just scared," offered Evangeline solemnly. "They love you so much. They just want to protect you."

Victoria said, "Protection against one's will is sometimes called imprisonment." But it occurred to her, especially as an avid reader of Nellie Bly, that many troublesome women were committed to asylums for no more than what she'd done, under the assumption that any sane woman would behave herself. Despite Mama's work, such incarceration was still legal—and she, Victoria, was very lucky to have the father and brother she did. As she'd told Ross, she knew quite a few decent men.

She wished he knew he was still one of them. But at least she could tell Evangeline.

For once, gifted with all that Ross confessed to her, she could tell Evangeline everything.

Chapter Twenty-one

"I'll live with my family after all," confessed Victoria, using a gardening fork to turn up topsoil. "I know, I know—moving out was how I meant to establish my independence before Ross comes back. But Mama negotiated between Papa and me. He can be so single-minded about matters like independence and growing up . . . and men." She made a face. "True, both Stuart and Collier were something of a shock to him. I should think that, in contrast, he would be *glad* to welcome Ross back. Someday."

Someday soon? A whole month had passed. The leaves were already changing, and so far she'd received no letters.

She sighed. "But you know Papa. *There's a right, and there's a wrong.* Rustling and gunfighting—he sees those pretty much in the *wrong* column. Maybe a man can change enough to work for him, but not enough to court one of his daughters. I think Mama understands better because she sees *us* more clearly."

She considered that for a moment while she lifted some orange marigolds from the pot she'd carried to the cemetery. "Did you even know my mother?"

Of course, the silent graves of Josip, Filip, and Julije Lauranovic had no answer to that. With a shrug, Victoria scooped more dirt aside to make room for the flowers. The ground felt cool, even through her leather work gloves. "In any case, Mama pointed out that were I at a boardinghouse, I would still be in trouble. Respectable residences have a curfew, and Ross and I certainly broke that! She suggested that we try something similar to the arrangement they have with Thaddeas. I still live at home, where they can keep an eye on me; and really, I like that better. That way, I can also help with the household and watch after Elise and Audra—and Thaddeas—when our parents take Kitty to that nice specialist in Chicago. I had to pay to fix my own bicycle, which hardly seems fair, but I get to keep my job. And as long as I behave like a responsible adult, they will attempt to treat me like one. Papa wasn't particularly satisfied, but he did get some concessions. Didn't he, Duchess?"

The dog lifted her dark head, ears perked at the sound of her name. Victoria grinned at her, then settled the flowers and scooped some dirt back over their roots. She felt foolish—not just talking to the graves, which actually seemed natural, but presuming to pretty them up on her own. Ross had not asked her to. And although he'd offered to marry her if she left with him that night, she hadn't left with him; and he hadn't even promised to return, much less marry her later. Just to write.

And he still hadn't written.

Even after almost a month—a month of mulling over all her questions, a month without his embrace or kisses to remind her of the ways she knew him beyond mere facts—Victoria believed better of him than to think he'd been trying to lure her away to scandal and desertion. But he could have changed his mind. Golly, she still hadn't wholly made up hers! And on the chance that he did not intend to renew his proposal . . .

Well, wouldn't she look silly, having put this effort into prettying up his family's cemetery plot. Her sister Audra had already voiced concern. People might notice, and then they might talk. *Acting as if he'd given her a ring.* She'd heard enough gossip in her time to imagine it well enough. *And him no better than a gunslinger. Poor, abandoned Victoria.*

She realized she was chewing her lip, and slowly released it. He *was* better than a gunslinger. Once he came home . . . well.

In any case, she *liked* spending time in the cemetery.

"By the way, the fall roundups showed that ours isn't the only ranch losing stock." She assumed Mr. Lauranovic would find that particularly interesting. "The local cattlemen collected a reward for the capture of the rustlers, preferably alive. Papa doesn't want any more lynchings. I don't know if it will help, though. Nobody knows how Harry Smith got out of jail, though I have my—"

Duchess's head came up again. When Victoria glanced toward the front of the cemetery, cautiously craning her neck to see past the gravestones, she saw a man hitching his horse by the lamppost. It wasn't Ross; the horse wasn't Blackie, and even from the back, the man was neither tall nor dark.

He didn't seem to notice her bicycle, leaning against the back of the McCrae tomb. Perhaps it would be better if he didn't notice her either. For her scandal-shy sisters' sake, Victoria ducked behind Josip Lauranovic's tombstone. Then noticed how her skirts spread out beyond it, and swept up armfuls of weight-pinned material and petticoats—three times before she had them all—so they wouldn't give her away.

Duchess sat up, clearly intrigued, then looked back toward the cemetery's visitor, ears even more alert than usual. Victoria realized that the man was whistling to himself.

Well, that wasn't uncommon.

But he was whistling "Clementine."

She felt a shiver across her whole body—puzzle pieces! Of course, everyone knew the words to that song, which had gotten popular in the mid-'80s. *"Oh my Darling Clementine, you are lost and gone forever. . . ."*

But that line was engraved on Julie's tombstone!

As the whistling approached her hiding place, Vic tried to sink even lower, her knees practically pressed to her face. Duchess, still sitting in the open, glanced back at her and cocked her head with canine curiosity. It was probably too late to extend an arm and order her away.

Perhaps if she was very, very quiet?

The whistling faltered into a slow, descending note. "What have we here?" murmured a man's voice. About the flowers?

Then a shadow fell over her. Reluctantly she looked up, into the face she now recognized as Alden Wright's, heir to the Triple-Bar ranch.

"Well, hello," he said slowly, as if choosing his words carefully. "Aren't you Victoria Garrison?"

It occurred to her that she needn't keep on huddling like this, so she released her armful of skirting and slowly sat up, trying to regain her poise. "Yes, I am. Mr. Wright, isn't it? When did you get back to Sheridan?"

Alden Wright spent a great deal of his time in St. Louis. Even today he was dressed in a fine, single-breasted suit coat of brown worsted, complete with matching trousers, a businesslike watch fob, and fashionable cloth-topped shoes.

He looked older than she remembered him. Certainly older than Ross. Almost as old as Thaddeas.

Instead of answering her question, he glanced at the Lauranovic graves, the newly planted marigolds. "I—pardon my inquisitiveness, Miss Garrison, but are you the one who . . . ?" Then he noticed her dirty work-gloves. "Of course you are. But you're too young to have known Julie Lauranovic."

As if Victoria needed any more proof, he had a big, white chrysanthemum in his hand. Unlike Ross, Alden Wright didn't look at all dangerous. Or even annoyed. He just seemed curious.

That made two of them.

Victoria stood—he caught her hand to help her up, being a gentleman—and she took off her work gloves, just as glad when Duchess trotted to her side to sniff her hand. "Julie," she repeated softly, confused. He'd called her Julie. So she took a chance. "Mr. Wright, if you paid the undertaker to add that quote onto her tombstone, why did you still let her be buried under the name Julije?"

Alden Wright stared at her for a searching moment. Then he took a deep breath, and as he released it, his shoulders sank as if from under the weight of years of secrecy. "Because she matched her father and brother that way," he told her. "And Julije is three syllables."

She cocked her head, not understanding.

Alden smiled, a little sadly. "It fits better in the song, Miss Garrison," he explained evenly. "In place of Clementine."

Until that autumn, Laramie had never cared so he'd never noticed. But in under two months, he discovered why most cowboys "married" only ladies of easy virtue, and merely for a weekend at a time. Even saving every cent from the fall roundups, he had nothing to "write home" about—neither a place to stay nor a stake to start building any kind of a respectable life.

And when the roundups ended, so did all but the most secure cowboy jobs.

"You come back next spring," said the foreman at the Lazy-Z Ranch, down Thermopolis way, when Ross asked him about it. "We'll have work over the summer for a good hand."

His solid handshake implied that Laramie was, in fact, a good hand. It was a fair enough offer. But to dream that he might ever make a place worthy of Victoria Garrison—assuming she even wanted him to try, assuming some other man had not already made her a much better offer—Laramie at least had to dream up year-round employment.

Either that, or something that paid incredibly well on the short term. But he was trying not to think that way.

For the first time, he found himself regretting his flight from the boys' ranch for a reason beyond the parole violation. At least there, folks tried to teach the boys honest professions—carpentry, printing, shoe repair. Jobs that, if he'd begun in his youth, would now be paying enough to support a . . .

A family?

He could not think of it that clearly or he would want it too badly. It was still too unlikely, especially for his world. But such jobs would have paid enough to support a respectable life anyhow, which would be a good starting point. Since he had run off, he was more suited for frontier, bachelor jobs: cowboying, mining, logging, railroading.

Crime.

No, not crime. Victoria may have forgiven him a great deal, but surely she would never forgive him that.

Explaining Herself

By the time October was near over, Laramie was desperate. And he was back at Hole-in-the-Wall—at least, at Butch Cassidy's cabin on the Blue Creek, still in the red rocks, a few miles south of it—just to have a familiar place to stay.

Of the numerous hideouts on the hoot-owl trail, the best three spread across three states, playing merry hell on lawmen whose jurisdiction stopped at the border. The hardest to reach was Robber's Roost, down in eastern Utah. Then there was Brown's Park in Colorado, close enough to the Utah and Wyoming borders to spit. And finally there was Hole-in-the-Wall, beyond the red rocks in Johnson County—a day's ride, if a long one, from Sheridan. Laramie wouldn't mind running into Cassidy—not for any jobs, just to have company while he kept the snow off his head. Just to talk.

Instead, he rode up to the low, double cabin of logs to see Lonny Logan, slim, dark, and armed.

"Damn, Laramie!" exclaimed Lonny from the doorway of the main cabin. He lowered the rifle he'd been leveling at his intruder. "I'm seein' more of you than I am of Harvey lately. Come on in. I got coffee."

Laramie stared at the doorway, through which his friend vanished into the cabin, and he thought, *Bad companions.* But Lonny *was* his friend. He'd helped save Laramie's life, after Harvey had gotten him shot. He'd warned Laramie about that second gun, back in the Red Light Saloon. They were pards.

Which didn't say a lot for Laramie's future.

But it was cold out. So he watered Blackie in the creek that ran behind the cabin, then set him loose in the corral and went inside for coffee.

"Hear the news?" greeted Lonny, handing him a hot cup.

Laramie shook his head. He also found himself

253

fighting a smile. Lonny, he realized, reminded him of Victoria.

No insult to Victoria meant, of course.

"New Mexico gave Elzy Lay a life sentence. Actually, they're still callin' him McGinnis, but no matter his name, he's in the State Penitentiary in Raton for good. Cassidy's sick about it, and he's decided to go straight. He's got that lawyer fellow he likes, Preston, tryin' to get him amnesty—hell, the railroads are even thinkin' of hirin' him to guard the trains, if it keeps him from robbin' them."

Laramie took a sip of coffee during all this, then said, "That's why you haven't hit the Burlington and Missouri?"

Lonny nodded glumly. "That, and Harvey just isn't a planner the way Cassidy is."

Laramie agreed with that. He put down the coffee long enough to shrug off his black duster, take off his hat, and scrub a hand through hair that felt like it needed a wash. He wasn't sure why he was here anymore. It wouldn't get him the life he wanted.

If anything could. It was a big *if.*

But he sat again, and he asked something that surprised even him. "How's your boy?"

Lonny's head snapped up, and his black, Cherokee eyes widened. Then he ducked his head, scowling at his coffee. "Damn, Laramie. How the hell would I know?"

Folks didn't talk much about Lonny's son, ugly as the whole situation had turned out. From what Laramie had heard, Lonny took up with one of Pike Landusky's stepdaughters up in Montana. *Landusky,* Montana. Her pa got riled when she bore a natural son and named him Lonny Curry Junior. The bad blood between the families had escalated until first the oldest Logan brother, Johnny, and then Pike Landusky got shot dead.

Rumor was, Harvey's fight with Pike hadn't been a fair one—yet another reason why Harvey "Kid Curry" Logan had never led the outlaw bunch. Yet another reason why this was a dangerous topic to pursue.

Laramie wasn't sure what had gotten into him, unless somehow kissing Victoria Garrison had infected him with wordiness. But he asked anyhow. "Didn't you ever want to marry her?"

"Elfie?" Lonny shrugged. "I guess I *did* marry her."

That was news. "Legal married?"

Lonny laughed then—a harsh, not-quite-safe laugh. "Nah, not *legal* married. Hell, I'm an outlaw, ain't I?"

Oh. It wasn't that outlaws never married legally. Elzy Lay's wife, Maude, was one of those few nice women Laramie had met before his time in Sheridan. They had a baby daughter.

And now Lay was in prison for life.

Laramie put his coffee cup down, certain now. He should not have come here. He didn't know where the hell else to go, with only two months' wages in his pocket, but he had to find someplace that wasn't part of this life.

This world.

"You're thinkin' of that Garrison gal, ain't you?" guessed Lonny. "Hell, pard—*you* ain't an outlaw. Not of any real standin', anyhow. Go ahead and set up housekeeping if you want."

As if it were that easy. He couldn't forget the expression on her face when he'd asked her to come with him, to marry him.

Panic.

She didn't know him. The only chance he had, and that one slim, was to try to win her slow-like. And that would be nearly impossible without settling near her. He doubted anybody in Sheridan meant to allow a Lauranovic to do that.

He rested his forearms on his knees, hung his head,

breathed out a swearword. God, but he was tired.

"She's got a nice enough family," noted Lonny, refilling his coffee—clearly glad the conversation had moved off of him. "That littlest sister's a pistol, ain't she?"

Laramie lifted his head. "How do you know Elise?"

"Mrs. Garrison and Mrs. Pembroke fed me dinner after I stopped by to tell your boss you'd got arrested," explained Lonny with a smirk. "That little blond girl kept askin' the funniest questions."

Laramie stared.

"I guess he got you out all right," continued his friend, "you sittin' here and all. Never can tell, with Ward."

Laramie frowned. "What about Ward?"

"He's crooked, is all. Not in no honest way, neither." Trust an outlaw to distinguish—but Laramie knew just what he meant.

"You mean it's more than fining the whores?"

Lonny snorted. "Hell yes, it's more. Ward runs the biggest rustling operation in northeastern Wyoming."

Laramie stared at him. "You sound pretty certain."

"Why wouldn't I be? Harve, Johnny and me used to work with him, back before the Invasion." The Invasion was what a lot of the small ranchers called the Johnson County Cattle War, back in '92. "Before we moved up Montana ways."

It really had been Ward, all along?

Lonny shrugged.

Laramie said, a mite angrily, "You couldn't mention that in Sheridan?"

"In Sheridan," said Lonny, "you were a range detective."

Damn, but Laramie felt stupid. All the facts had been there—Ward's past as a rustler, his reputation for graft, Harry Smith's escape. But Laramie had been so shy of his own prejudices, he'd looked right past them, missing the chance to bring in the one man he most despised.

Besides Thaddeas Garrison, he reminded himself. He still hated Victoria's brother. How would that set for any future?

Lonny frowned, leaning forward. "You aren't thinkin' of goin' after him, are you? 'Cause, one, you ain't no range detective anymore. Two, it's none of your business. Three, it ain't like the cattle barons can't afford to lose some beef now and then. And four, Ward's managed to run his operation just fine. Folks don't get hurt unless they start nosin' around his business, and then you can't blame him."

Nosing around his business. *Oh God.*

Victoria.

"I've got to go," said Laramie, standing.

"Now? It's almost nightfall!"

"Thanks for the coffee." And the information. But since Lonny hadn't meant it to be used this way, Laramie guessed he'd just keep his gratitude to himself there.

"You're goin' to Sheridan," accused Lonny, starting to look sulky—and dangerous—even so.

"Yep." Shrugging on his duster, Laramie glanced toward his friend. "For the lady, Lonny. The lady noses around everyone's business. Any idea where I can hole up, that the cattlemen won't know I'm there right off?"

"The hell with you," said Lonny. "It had better be the lady. You ever come after *me*, don't think I won't shoot you dead."

Which at least meant he didn't intend to shoot Laramie dead this afternoon. "I won't," agreed Laramie. But he was already trying to think this through. Someplace the cattlemen wouldn't be watching for him. Preferably with someone who had his own grudge against the sheriff.

He wanted to see Victoria again so badly, the need almost suffocated him. But he could control himself better than that, especially if it was her he was worried about. So Laramie took his time saddling poor Blackie and heading out, north, across the desolate openness that was Johnson County. Riding across country like this, where the reds and oranges of the sunset seemed to mix right into the desert, Laramie thought maybe the frontier would never die. He holed up until the full moon rose, lighting the red-rock country into a silvery blue. With the moon, he could ride all night.

Back to civilization. Back to uncertainty. Back to Victoria's world, where he wouldn't likely be welcome—but he had to try. And the best place to start would be with other unwelcome types.

He rode into Stuart MacCallum's Double-M Sheep Ranch late the following morning.

Chapter Twenty-two

On the one hand, letting the townsfolk—and her dubious family—think Alden Wright was courting her was a sound idea. It provided them privacy to discuss the one thing the two of them really had in common: the Laurence family.

On the other hand, Victoria couldn't quite dismiss the niggling possibility that Ross, when he came back, might want to shoot Alden over Julie alone. Seeing him as a rival suitor might not help matters. She hoped Ross had finished with vengeance, back when he gave up on Thaddeas. But if he hadn't . . .

She had to know all of him, if she hoped to love him at all. It wouldn't do to forget that he was a dangerous man, whether she was the one in danger or not.

Still, she found herself hoping for quite a bit that autumn: a letter from Ross, a good newspaper story, someone to catch the rustlers. As the weeks passed, hope grew increasingly unfulfilling.

At least Alden had immediate answers, whether or not she dared ever share them with Ross.

Alden *was* Julie Laurence's secret sweetheart, though not so secret that he hadn't taken privileges only a husband deserved. Of course, Victoria did not discuss that part. Sixteen and terrified, he'd sat by while a lynch mob murdered Julie's family. Certain that she hated him, he'd never known his family was keeping her away. He claimed to have never gotten over her.

Victoria found him charming enough, but weak-willed. Even if she were interested in any suitor other than Ross, she would not choose Alden Wright. Still, Alden was as eager to talk about Julie as Victoria was to hear about her.

So he paid calls, and she accepted them.

As long as people thought they were courting, Alden Wright could stroll with her—and Duchess—along leaf-littered streets between their families' in-town houses, recounting what he remembered of the Laurences. As long as people thought they were courting, they could respectably ride out together on a brisk Saturday morning, without even the dog as a chaperone.

Nobody had to know that Alden was taking her on a tour of places important to the Laurence family.

"They had a well here, under these rocks," he told her, kicking some large, flat stones piled in what was now just woods. "We covered it so nobody would fall in, after Father bought the land. The cabin stood over there, where those saplings are."

Victoria opened her latest newfangled gadget, a Folding Pocket Kodak Camera, and snapped a picture of the area he indicated, with the Big Horn Mountains looming in the background. Though a luxury at $10, the camera delighted her. Once she used up the film, she would mail it to Kodak, along with a dollar, and they would send it back with new film and all her nice, round, black-and-white pictures.

If only she'd learned to use the camera before Ross left, she might have a photograph of him. She closed the camera and thought—hoped—*When he comes home, I'll take his picture.* Then she went to the cabin site and noted the nearly flat ground beneath mulch and pine needles, all that was left of his childhood home since the logs had been dragged off. She tried to imagine a young Ross, chopping wood or playing with a hoop, but it was difficult to imagine him as anybody but the tall, quiet man she loved. *A man with a gun.*

Even if he came back, he would still be a man with a gun.

"What happened to Mrs. Laurence?" she asked, unwilling to think about that—and feeling like a coward for it.

"I heard she moved back east." Alden clasped his hands behind his back and gazed past her, a brooding-poet pose. "Over there, that really big spruce—that's where I would hide and wait for Julie to meet me. We would hold hands and run together until we reached a field up that way, full of columbine and goldenrod. Would you like to see it?"

Victoria considered what he and Julie may have done in that field and shook her head. "No, thank you."

"You're right," agreed Alden with a sigh. "There certainly won't be any flowers, not this time of year."

No, there certainly would not.

"So where would you like to go next, Miss Garrison?" he asked, with a flourish of his arm toward the mountain vista, the blue sky. "Your wish is my command."

She took a deep breath, for courage. If she hoped to love Ross at all . . . "I'd like to see where the lynchings happened."

His charming smile faded. "What?"

"If I'm to understand . . . them . . . I should see everything."

A new smile stretched across Alden's face, too quickly to be genuine. "That place holds unpleasant memories for me, Miss Garrison. This may be simply a matter of history to you." She'd claimed to be studying Sheridan's history and the role the Wrights had played in it. "But what those men did there . . ."

He still hadn't realized that, in not trying to stop them, he'd *been* one of those men. "I understand, Mr. Wright," she said. "If you would just take me as far as you feel comfortable, and then tell me how to go the rest of the way . . ."

"What?" He said that a lot.

"I'm just trying to understand the Laurences, and what happened to them," she explained. "And if I refuse to look at the bad parts, aren't I somehow, well, *demeaning* them?"

He shook his head. "What do you mean?"

Ross, she thought, would have understood. "People's lives have both good parts and bad parts, don't they?"

"Not everyone's lives."

She remembered her horror at seeing Kitty crumpled in the stallion's corral. "Perhaps everyone's lives do," she suggested again carefully. "It's important to focus on the good, of course—like with my little sister Elise, to encourage how bright and bold and lively she can be. But if we loved her without even seeing that she can also be a brat, would we really love *her,* or just the person we want her to be?"

Ross had wanted her despite her chatter and questions and nosiness. She loved him even though he'd rustled cattle, had even killed people—as long as he'd reformed, of course.

And if he hasn't?

She disliked her relief that she need not yet decide whether to trust him with what she'd learned.

"I hardly see what little Elise has to do with lynchings."

"I won't feel as if I understand everything," she insisted, "unless I understand *everything*. Even the bad parts. I can't explain it better than that. Won't you please take me as far as you can?"

He frowned—no, *pouted*.

But he was also weak-willed.

"She's what?" Laramie had to force the question out through a closing throat. Surely he'd misheard.

Mrs. MacCallum cast her husband another concerned look, as she'd been doing throughout breakfast. "She told me she's not serious," she assured Laramie quickly. "But they've been keeping company for several weeks now. Some people have expectations. I believe this is the day they'd planned for their picnic."

Only moments before, Laramie had been admiring the kitchen of Stuart and Mariah MacCallum's new stone house. And pretty Mrs. MacCallum's resemblance to her darker-haired sister. And their baby boy. Their world fed him far more than did the oatmeal Mrs. MacCallum put in front of him, despite his long ride. But now . . .

Victoria was seeing the heir to the Triple-Bar Ranch?

What little money Laramie had saved felt embarrassing, in contrast. He'd been foolish to dream his hopeful, romantic dreams, to even pretend he could ever live in the world of the Garrisons and the Pembrokes and the MacCallums—the world where things sometimes went right for a fellow. Except . . .

Almost against his will, he looked back toward the MacCallums. Mariah had put a hand on her husband's stocky shoulder, and Stuart met her gaze with some shared, silent affirmation. MacCallum hadn't had an easy life either. But he'd worked his way out of the sheep wagon where he'd first brought his bride and into this handsome, stone ranch house. Now he had a healthy son in his arms, gurgling and waving his chubby hands, while his blond wife—her apron suspiciously round—oversaw breakfast for their unexpected guest.

He never broke laws, he reminded himself. But the man *was* a sheep farmer. That was almost as bad.

Seeing the satisfaction Victoria's oldest sister had brought to her husband, Laramie couldn't discount the possibility that sometimes good things did still happen. Especially where Garrison women were concerned.

At least, he thought, *if Victoria's seeing Wright, she's not getting into trouble.* Which is when he figured it out. Maybe. It was more hope than even instinct, but . . .

"Is it possible—"

Baby Garry squealed, and his poppa touched a thick, gentle finger to his cheek to silence him, waiting.

Laramie tried again. "Could Victoria be up to something?"

He almost winced, in expectation of their pity. Instead, MacCallum sent another of those unspoken messages toward his wife—this time with dry amusement—and Mariah laughed. "Well, you certainly *have* gotten to know Victoria, Mr. Laramie. That's what we're hoping. It would be better than her going sweet on a *Wright!*"

She didn't deny it. Victoria's own sister didn't deny it!

He tried another bite of oatmeal, and actually managed to swallow it. "You don't like the Wrights."

"They're the ones who hired that awful range detect—" Eyes widening, Mariah clamped her mouth shut too late.

"I've been worse than a range detective, Mrs. MacCallum."

"Well, I trust my sister's instincts," she told him firmly, lifting her son from her husband's lap and into her arms. "When it comes to people, that is. The way she takes chances, she needs a guard, not a dog. You don't suppose she's got Alden Wright helping her track down rustlers, do you?"

It surprised Laramie to realize that she wasn't just asking her husband. She was looking at him!

"I don't know Alden Wright," Laramie admitted. "And God only knows what your sister will do."

It unsettled him, how the MacCallums' shared smile now included him. Somehow either he or Victoria had misled them about his true nature.

But he savored that sense of being part of them, even undeserving. Then he asked, "Where were they going to picnic?"

If Victoria were pursuing Sheriff Ward, she needed help.

Even if he *did* risk interrupting her Saturday picnic.

Alden really did take Victoria only as far as he was comfortable, in the foothills about half a mile from the box canyon where the lynchings had taken place. Then he drew his horse to a stop. "I'm sorry, Miss Garrison. That place . . ."

She supposed it would be difficult to face one's greatest failure. "It's all right. Just tell me how to get the rest of the way."

Then she left him comfortably settled under a tree and rode on by herself. It bothered her that Alden might still come between her and Ross, not because she had any feelings for Alden, but because of Julie. No; more than that. She still hadn't decided whether to tell Ross about Alden and Julie, true, but how could she trust him with her own life, if she couldn't trust him with someone else's?

She and her sorrel gelding, Huck, rode comfortably together, picking their way around rocks and trees in the direction of the little canyon Alden had described. She tried to imagine what other people had ridden this direction. The Laurences, including young Ross, moving their stolen livestock back home. The lynch mob, with Boris and Bram Ward, the Colonel and Alden Wright. Papa, following the sound of gunshots to interrupt their fate.

She could imagine the ugliness of it all too well, so well she could almost smell the stench of burning hair from a branding iron on the shifting wind.

Then, suddenly, she was almost on top of it! The stench hit her full in the face, along with a cow's distressed lowing, the chink of spurs, and a voice that sounded far too close saying, "We've got to be gone by this afternoon, savvy?"

Startled beyond breath, she reined Huck back, lifted her leg from behind the curved horn of the sidesaddle, and slid quickly to the ground where she could better hide. Huck, tossing his head at the acrid smell, backed away some, and Victoria leaned against the trunk of a large pine and made herself think—all the more confusing a prospect when the wind changed and the noise and stench vanished with it.

Fall roundups were over. For a confused moment, she could almost believe that she'd ridden back in time, and was about to witness past horrors. Then sanity returned. So, along with another whiff of burning hair and the nearby bellow of an upset cow, did a clutch of fear. *Rustlers.* The wind shift had allowed her to ride almost on top of them. And now she had to creep away from here without any of them seeing her.

Whoever they were.

That question stilled her, even as she extended one hand to begin crawling back toward her horse. Someone very important, powerful enough to help a man escape jail, was stealing cattle not only from her father but all the local ranchers. This wasn't merely a case of a hungry family butchering a "slow elk," as Papa called the occasional loss of livestock to settlers—a loss most ranchers, himself included, bore without too much ill will. No, to account for the losses indicated by the recent roundup, this was practically a syndicate! And by accident, she found herself within crawling distance of seeing who was committing these crimes.

And she had a camera.

Victoria knew exactly what Papa, Thaddeas, Mama, Mr. Day, even Ross—pretty much anyone she could imagine—would counsel her. Run home and bring help! And yet over that fear, with every beat of her panicked heart, beckoned treacherous opportunity.

If they're in a box canyon, she thought, *they would have to look up to see me. Who looks up?*

The posse was able to ambush the Laurences because it was so easy to see them without being seen, she thought.

They're leaving this afternoon, she reminded herself. *If I go for help, there may be nobody left to capture.*

And, most damning, *If I leave now, without finding out, how will I feel later?*

Papa, Thad, even Ross would say, *You'll feel alive. You'll feel safe.*

But she also knew she would feel like a coward. The one thing that had ever mattered to her, beyond her family, her friends, and Ross Laurence, was knowing things. Who better to take a few careful pictures of the rustlers before riding back for help? Who better to make sure that the truth about this came out?

If she did not do this, she could never compare herself to Nellie Bly again.

Before she could lose her nerve, Victoria peeked out from around the tree, then crept in the direction from which she'd heard the noise. She saw the rock ledge well before she reached it, saw the orange of firelight playing across the other wall of the small canyon despite the daylight. Her hands felt clumsy as she retrieved her leather-bound camera from around her neck, extended the lens on its brass fittings, advanced the film. All she needed were a few shots.

I am a lunatic, she thought mournfully.

Then she thought, *I'm only four feet from getting it done.* So she crawled the last four feet and very carefully peeped over the edge.

It was a small operation, only three men. They'd tied a bull calf's legs and two were going about the ugly process of branding him with what looked more like a bent poker than a branding iron. *A running iron,* Victoria realized; in some counties, men could be hanged for even owning them. It must take longer than a regular branding, which made it crueler. Suddenly, she felt wholly justified in her reckless choice. She lifted the camera and started to quietly snap pictures.

Two men she did not recognize, and the back of a third. A bunch of other cattle held against the back wall of the box canyon, some of them wearing a brand she'd never seen. Horses, hitched near the arroyo's mouth.

And when he turned to pick up a coil of rope, Sheriff Ward himself.

Victoria's sense of satisfaction, as she snapped that picture, ranked among the best feelings in her life—even kissing Ross! Learning something this important felt like the first gulp of water on a dusty day, the relief of a feather bed after hard work—the fit of a puzzle piece sliding into place. She'd discovered the truth.

Her.

And now everyone would know.

Despite the temptation to finish off her film on this, the need to get to safety was stronger. Quickly, she folded the camera back into itself and crawled backward, careful to dislodge no stones, to make no noise. When she reached the cover of the trees, she breathed a heartfelt sigh of relief—and started to smile.

Nellie would be so proud!

She crept to where Huck waited, walked him a ways off until she found a fallen log, hooked her camera strap on the curved saddle horn, and mounted.

Then she reined Huck in the direction of where she'd left Alden—and found herself staring into both barrels of a double-barreled shotgun.

Chapter Twenty-three

This, thought Victoria nervously, as she rode ahead of Deputy Franklin and his double-barreled friend, *is why I should only take outings with men I trust.*

Not that Alden Wright had gotten her captured; he wasn't even there! Which was maybe the problem. Ross wouldn't be resting under a tree right now. Then again, Ross might have shot Deputy Franklin, which seemed a drastic solution. And he probably would have protested her taking the photographs. Which reminded her—

She subtly unhooked the leather carrying strap of her Kodak from over the saddle horn and used her fingers to inch the camera itself up into her grasp, all within the cover of her overfull riding skirts. Then, twisting around to see Deputy Franklin, she shrank with a frightened cry from a nearby pine tree.

Just as she'd hoped, Franklin fell for the distraction and aimed his shotgun at the tree for a moment.

Victoria used the time to toss her camera into some brush, well off the path, near a rock formation she hoped she would recognize later. Assuming nothing stepped on it. Assuming it wasn't broken in the fall. *Assuming she ever got back.*

But she had to.

Franklin quickly pointed the shotgun back at her. "Don't you go thinkin' you can make a run for it, Miss Garrison."

"Make a run for what?" she demanded. "Deputy, I have no idea why you're behaving so rudely, but I don't like it. I was out riding, is all. Is it—am I trespassing?" She assumed one of her innocent looks. She didn't have to feign concern; her mouth was dry with it! "I thought this was Colonel Wright's land, but if it isn't, I promise you I didn't know I was doing anything wrong."

He looked uncertain. *He isn't sure that I saw anything,* she decided, relieved. Then he told her to "Hold up," and whistled loudly, through his teeth.

Victoria reined Huck back and waited with him, her mouth drier with each passing moment. Overhead, a hawk screamed. Then she heard footsteps.

Sheriff Ward appeared around some rocks—pistol drawn.

Victoria let her shoulders sink dramatically. "Sheriff! Thank goodness you're here. I was out riding, and the deputy pointed his shotgun at me, and I don't know what to do!"

The sheriff looked from her to Franklin and back, clearly annoyed. "Well, hell," he said, catching his thumbs in his suspenders.

"She was comin' from the canyon," protested Franklin.

Victoria decided against asking, *What canyon?* Too obvious. Instead, she bit her lower lip and made certain to look confused and frightened and girlish.

271

Only the confusion was a lie.

"Well, hell," said Ward again. "Miss Garrison, I'm afraid you've ridden yourself into a bit of trouble."

"Trouble?"

"See," continued the sheriff, "you might be tellin' the truth, in which case we could've just sent you on your way. But I'm thinkin' you're here on account of you've heard tell what this arroyo gets used for. I'm thinkin' it has somethin' to do with how you've been spendin' so much time with them Bohunk graves down at Mount Hope."

Darned gossips, anyway.

"So," said Ward with a sigh, cocking his pistol and aiming it at her, "why don't you get down off your horse, nice and slow, and let us make you comfortable until we figure this out?"

For once, obeying seemed the better choice, what with two weapons pointing at her. She might still escape this, after all. Alden was bound to realize she'd gone missing, sooner or later. Once he did, he would either come looking for her or fetch her father and brother, wouldn't he?

She rather hoped the second. Alden was too benign to rescue her himself. Of the two evils, she preferred Ross's type. With every gun pointed at her, she preferred Ross's type even more.

"Why should you do anything about me?" she asked warily, going where the sheriff pointed, toward what she now recognized as the entrance to the box canyon. Scrub trees and an old rock slide naturally camouflaged it.

Rounding the bluff, she could see the whole operation—the horses, the two remaining rustlers, the fire, the rope corral holding the cattle. Were she still uptop the rock wall, she would be in her own photograph.

She also noted a large tree with high, heavy

branches, and felt a shudder in her chest. She could imagine it too easily—the night, the ropes over the tree limbs. It had really happened, and Ross had been forced to endure it. Why wouldn't he want vengeance? That he had any compassion at all was a miracle.

"I'm not being kidnapped, am I?" she asked, since kidnapping would be preferable to anybody getting killed. "Just because my parents have a great deal of money doesn't mean they'll take kindly to any ransom demands."

She felt hope when Franklin said, "You know, the Garrisons *would* pay an awful lot to get her back."

"Her and everythin' she's seen today," countered the sheriff, pushing her toward a large stone when she took too long looking around her. "You jest sit there and be quiet, Miss Garrison. Like a good girl."

A good girl? She glanced over her shoulder, at the mouth of the box canyon. If she picked up her skirts and ran very fast—

The muzzle of the sheriff's pistol appeared, just in front of her nose, to catch her attention. "If you try to get away, I *will* shoot you," said Ward. "And if we have to resort to that, your folks won't even get your body back. An accident would be kinder to them, now, don't you think?"

It didn't much sound like he meant to ask for ransom.

Victoria had to try more than once just to swallow. It was the fear. But imagining how her family would suffer if she died, she also knew building anger. How *dare* he!

Was this what it felt like to want someone dead? She sat stiffly on the rock Sheriff Ward indicated, and she understood Ross better than ever.

Ward smiled an ugly smile as the other men, clearly more nervous, went back to their branding. " 'Course, that might not be so bad a thing at that, honey girl," he drawled. "If they won't find your body, then it won't matter what we do to it before we kill you. Them high-and-mighty cattle barons been riding my tail long enough, it'd be mighty sweet to get some of my own back."

He meant to *molest* her? Now she couldn't swallow at all. She definitely wished him *very* dead—and she wondered whether she could, if given the chance, do it herself. A lightning strike or a stampede would be neater. *Or Ross . . .*

What she needed was Ross.

But the oak tree, nearby, reminded her that sometimes people didn't get what they needed.

The man Laramie assumed was Alden Wright seemed to be asleep on a checkered picnic blanket in the autumn sunshine. His boater tipped across the upper half of his face, and he was alone. One horse grazed nearby, and it wasn't Victoria's.

Dismounting, Laramie wasn't sure if he felt relief or building fear. He hadn't lied to Mariah MacCallum. He loved Victoria, but he couldn't predict what she might be doing.

Wright slept through a shadow falling across him, but sat up fast enough when Laramie extended a booted toe and kicked his foot, spurs jingling. "What? Huh?"

"Where's Victoria Garrison?" If Wright had already taken her home, or she was off seeing to personal matters in the bushes, Laramie would feel very foolish.

He was willing to feel foolish, to know she was safe.

"What?" Now the fellow sat up. Laramie's memories of Alden Wright, who hung back during the lynchings, were vague, but this man did resemble them. "Who are you?"

Surely Victoria didn't want this man. "You Wright?"

"I am." Alden Wright stood, then looked crestfallen

when his head came up only to Laramie's nose.

"You were with her, weren't you?"

"I don't see how that's any of your interest."

It was a fair enough protest, but Laramie didn't like lingering to explain, especially if Vic had given her supposed escort the slip. He leaned forward, putting them at eye level. "Where is she?"

Wright sighed in defeat, too soon for Ross's respect. "She rode ahead to a box canyon she wanted to see. Gruesome interests for a girl, but she's pretty enough."

Laramie glanced in the direction Wright indicated and felt his insides go still. *The* box canyon? The one where . . .

He remembered a pebble skittering down the arroyo wall, horses' cries, the hiss of ropes thrown across the thick branch of a nearby oak. And him, pulling the trigger on a human being. He swallowed, hard. *That* box canyon.

"The place has bad memories for me," Wright continued. "So I let her go on ahead."

Bad memories for YOU? "How long ago?"

Wright removed his watch from his vest pocket and checked it. Then he frowned, glanced up at the sun, and frowned down at his watch again. "Say, it's been almost two hours."

Damn!

Laramie strode back to Blackie, pausing only long enough to take off his spurs and shove them into his a saddlebag before remounting. "Come with me."

"What?"

He wasn't denying his instincts this time. No matter how disreputably he'd earned them, they clearly had their uses. "She's got to be in trouble. Come with me."

"But—" Wright picked up the blanket to fold, clearly torn.

"Now," prompted Laramie dangerously.

Yvonne Jocks

To his credit, Wright dropped the blanket and moved to tighten the cinch on his horse. "I'm only doing this because I am the lady's escort," he announced. "Not because of you."

So? Laramie rode in the direction Victoria had gone, following Huck's tracks.

"Whoever you are," added Wright, pushing the matter.

Laramie scanned the ground, noticed a broken twig here, some fallen leaves pressed into the dirt there. "I'm Ross Laurence," he announced, distracted, and spurred Blackie in that direction.

Alden Wright said, "Oh my God."

"Some folks call me Laramie."

That Wright had been there when Poppa and Phil were lynched tickled another thought in the back of Laramie's mind, but he pushed it away. He would have time enough to hate the man. For now, he had more important matters to pursue. The most important matter in his life. Victoria.

Even before they reached the rocky overhang of the arroyo—where the posse had gotten the drop on the Lauranovics, so long ago—Laramie knew something had gone wrong. He saw where Victoria had been walking her horse back from the canyon, saw that someone else's tracks intersected hers. He considered following the resulting pair, but then the breeze shifted, bringing with it familiar noise—words, cattle— and a burning stench. *Just like that night.*

He changed his mind and headed for the overhang, listening. It *wasn't* just like that night at all.

He would recognize that voice anywhere.

"So you've been rustling quite some time?" asked Victoria. As the afternoon crept past, she'd decided that if she might die anyway, at the very least she wanted answers.

276

It was either ask questions, or cry uncontrollably.

"You could say that," agreed Ward from where he kneeled by some bedrolls, packing what had clearly been a camp.

"Have you been working here all along?" she asked. "Since you helped lynch the Laurences, I mean. Wouldn't this be the first place anybody would look for rustlers?" She considered Alden Wright's earlier reaction. "Though I suppose bad memories might keep people away—those who know how to find it in the first place. As if it were haunted."

The two men she didn't know looked quickly up from brand-blotting a large Circle-T steer with a piece of wool blanket, just the way Ross had described—but smelling much worse.

"Finish the damned job!" bellowed Ward. Then he turned on Victoria. "And don't you go tryin' to spook my help."

"I didn't say it to frighten anybody," she protested. "Although if I were Mr. Laurence or his older son, and if I'd been unfairly hanged, this is where I would do my haunting."

"Unfair!" Ward spat. "They were murderin' rustlers."

"I've heard that they were stealing back their own cattle."

"Lyin' foreigners."

In the meantime, the two other rustlers were moving more clumsily, glancing occasionally toward the big oak tree. She wondered if they were new, since Harry Smith had died.

"Did Mr. Smith know about this place, Sheriff?" she asked. "I only ask because, if I were him, I might come back here to do my haunting, too."

Even Deputy Franklin looked nervous now.

Ward didn't. "Miss Garrison, if you don't shut your mouth right now, I'll gag it shut." He smiled, mean.

"At least until I want to hear you scream."

She pressed her lips tightly together, to show compliance. When the breeze shifted through the trees, sending another shower of red oak leaves down on the rustlers, they jumped.

"Good," Ward said, turning back to the cattle. From what she'd gathered, he meant to take a decent-sized herd of stolen livestock across the Montana line this evening.

"It's just," she added, and he turned back to glare at her. "It's just that it's all so interesting. That you've managed to run this whole operation, practically a syndicate, all these years and have never been caught. The sheriff! I just wish . . ."

He waited, impatience playing across his pliant face.

"It must be fascinating," she flattered, whether she wanted him dead or not. She didn't know how to kill him. She knew how to get him talking. "I wish I'd known how clever you were, before now. How did you ever conceive of such a thing?"

He stared at her a moment longer, then shifted his weight—and actually began to tell her. His father knew some rustlers. They'd made good money. The cattle barons monopolized the market. Between them and the foreigners, how else was a small rancher to earn a living?

It would have been fascinating, if she'd had hope of repeating it.

Then, as if at her wish, a disembodied voice interrupted Ward's. The voice said, "Victoria, duck."

And she must trust Ross Laurence implicitly, because she dove without question behind her rock— just in time to miss the gunfire.

First, Laramie fired just to let the rustlers know he was there. Then he fired immediately in their path, to dissuade them taking cover themselves. His aim, with his newest Winchester rifle, was perfect. "Hold it," he warned, loudly, and his voice echoed up at him.

To his relief, all four men fell still—even the one standing on one leg, whose toe he'd apparently just shot.

Near to perfect, anyhow.

The damned lynch mob had been right about one thing, anyway. This was one fine place for an ambush.

"Toss your firearms toward the girl," he commanded, using the momentary lull to feed more cartridges into his rifle. He was older now, he reminded himself. He could control himself better. This time, nobody would die in the arroyo—unless it was at their own insistence. "Carefully."

Deputy Franklin was the first man to comply. When one of the lesser rustlers followed suit, his pistol landed wrong and misfired. Its bullet ricocheted off the stone walls twice before spending itself into the oak tree—too close to where Victoria was hiding. Far too close.

Everyone except Ward and Laramie ducked, even Alden Wright. And Alden was kneeling safely up top.

"Carefully," repeated Laramie, letting every killing he'd ever committed—or partially committed—darken his voice. Then he noticed that Vic was starting to lift her curly dark head up over the rock. That she was still alive, and still curious enough to be interviewing the sheriff who held her hostage, had cheered him more than anything in his life—except maybe for some of the private moments they had already shared.

That she was still in danger terrified him. "Victoria Garrison, stay down!"

She ducked back down. Then she turned her face in his general direction, probably following his voice, and stuck out her tongue.

Laramie felt that tightness in his cheeks again, the one that beset him so often around Vic. At least she was still safe, mere feet from him, even if most of those feet were down. Her nearness was what counted. That, and her continued breathing.

"You too, Sheriff," he called after the third man tossed his revolver in with the others. "The rest of you, lie on your bellies and put your hands behind your heads."

Only two of them did it.

Alden just kneeled there, holding Laramie's spare revolver, staring into the box canyon, and doing nothing to help.

"Who are you?" demanded Ward. From the way he was turning, craning his neck, he was having less luck in guessing just where Laramie stood than Victoria had.

Ross considered the question a moment, took more careful aim—then shot off Ward's hat. "I said, drop it."

A third man quickly lay down on his belly and put his hands on his head.

"Who the hell are you?" demanded Ward, glancing back toward Victoria's hiding place.

Laramie considered shooting off something else—but he did not want to expose Victoria to either missing body parts or another ricochet. She was what mattered, nothing else.

Just her.

"I'll take any moves toward Miss Garrison as a personal invitation," he warned. There was one good way to prevent his next shot bouncing off rock, after all—burying it in flesh. *"Now."*

Laramie would have liked to feel relief when Ward lifted his revolver from its holster with two fingers and tossed it over with the rest. It would show he'd made progress.

Instead, he felt disappointment.

*   *   *

"May I *please* look now?" demanded Victoria.

"If you're careful." Ross's voice sounded clearer. When she looked up, he was descending the arroyo wall in small, sideways steps, still pointing his rifle at— she peeked—at Sheriff Ward.

Ward was still alive, but without his gun, she didn't want him dead quite so badly. As long as he didn't get hold of another one. And Ross wouldn't let him.

Ross wore a long, black duster that, with his black hat, made him look more dangerous than ever. And tall. And dark. She particularly loved the easy way he held that rifle.

"I'm always careful!" she protested, sitting up as he reached the canyon floor.

Ross gestured briefly with one spread hand at the arroyo around them and made a disbelieving sound.

"This was *not* my fault!" she protested, hurrying to his side. It took all her control not to dive onto him, clutch him, perhaps get them both ambushed. She refrained from grabbing anything he needed. But she stood close enough to feel his warmth, to smell his horse on his coat.

She stood close enough to feel, from his tension, that this wasn't close to over. But he was here. It was close enough.

"Well, *probably* not my fault," she admitted unevenly. "The deputy might have caught me anyway, but I guess we'll never know. I'm so glad to see you. What should I—"

Ward interrupted her. "Laramie. You son of a bitch."

"Watch the lady," warned Ross, about Ward's language.

"He doesn't think I *am* a lady." Safe behind him, Victoria found she could swallow again. "He said he would do rude things and make . . . me . . ."

281

Then, watching Ross's profile, she stumbled into silence—too late.

"Make you what?" he demanded. The way Ward paled confirmed that Ross was looking his most dangerous. She almost told him, like a child tattling. *He said he wanted to hear me scream.* And why not say so? It was the truth, and he should pay for it.

And yet, now that she was safe again, she wasn't so sure Ward should die. Maybe the important part was her life, not his death. Besides, she loved Ross too much to press him into doing that just because she was angry. Just because she hated.

"I'll tell you later," she promised. *When you're not holding a gun on him.*

"Victoria," Ross said, sweeping her behind him as he edged toward where the rustlers had thrown their guns. "Can you use a pistol?"

"Of course I can! When Laurel was homesteading, we had to kill our own snakes. Well—I think we scared more of them than we killed, but we did kill some. Once, Laurel forgot that she'd already loaded the shotgun, so she loaded it again. When she fired, she actually flew backwards—it was the oddest thing to see. We couldn't even find *pieces* of that rattler."

Was she babbling? The sheriff was staring at her, and so were two of the men from where they lay in the dirt, their hands still on their heads. Ross's vigilant gaze was still darting darkly between them and the sheriff. Unless she was mistaken, he was smiling his ghost smile.

She had to be mistaken, didn't she?

"Perhaps before we arm you," he suggested, an odd note in his voice, "you could go to the sheriff's horse and check his saddlebags for his handcuffs?"

She did so, found the metal circlets, and held them up. "Here."

"The key," instructed Ross of the sheriff.

His expression murderous, Ward dug into his pocket, then tossed the key to the ground at Ross's feet.

"Victoria," said Ross then, "please pick up the key and cuff the sheriff's hands behind his back. Take your time."

He was finding words just fine now, she thought proudly, quickly figuring out how the handcuffs worked. And if he meant to kill Ward, he wouldn't handcuff him, would he?

Then the sheriff widened his eyes and said, "Boo!"

Vic caught her breath, then spun to face Ross's approach.

Ross drew his pistol with one hand, slung his rifle over his back with the other, and came at the sheriff pistol-first. When he reached Ward, he yanked the sheriff's head back and shoved the muzzle of his revolver right into the man's mouth.

She was about to see a murder. And she didn't want to.

From the sudden, embarrassing smell of urine and the dark spot spreading into the man's pants, Sheriff Ward must have thought the same thing.

"Wright!" Ross called out, now that the sheriff was quiet. "Fire into the air so the others will know you're here."

Alden Wright was there? Victoria didn't remember Alden even carrying a gun. Ross probably had spares. Sure enough, a gun discharged from the ledge over the arroyo wall. Everyone flinched that direction except Ross and Sheriff Ward. Ross hardly seemed to hear, and the sheriff was standing very still, his mouth open painfully wide around the penetrating gun barrel.

"I think," said Ross, low and even, "that he will hold still while you cuff him now, sweetheart. Please stay low, in case I have to shoot through the back of his head."

So she crouched way, way down before putting the cuffs on the sheriff's trembling wrists and cinching them tight. Then she stepped clear, and Ross slowly withdrew the revolver from the man's mouth—and nobody had died.

And she thought, *Sweetheart?*

She liked it.

Ross touched her again, a steadying hand on her shoulder as he guided her back from the sheriff, then pressed his revolver gently into her hand. It had spit on the end of it, but she didn't let herself wipe the muzzle. Instead, she obediently held the gun while Ross patted his hands across the sheriff's arms and legs—and she hoped she would not have to use it. From the man's boot Ross withdrew a nasty-looking knife, which he tossed over with the other weapons.

"Who the hell *are* you?" demanded Ward again, even as Ross shoved him over against the rock wall, away from the others, and beckoned Alden Wright to join them.

He might not deserve to die, but he deserved to be frustrated. So Victoria almost groaned when Alden, scrambling down the steep side of the arroyo in his impractical shoes, ended the sheriff's misery. "You might want to rethink whether this place is haunted, Sheriff," he called, starting to tie up the men who were still lying on the ground. "It's Ross Laurence."

Ward's head swiveled back at Ross, eyes wide and disbelieving. Then he looked accusingly at Victoria, maybe remembering the care she'd given the Laura-novic graves, or Ross's casual use of the term *sweetheart*. With a wrench, he turned back to Ross. "You god-damned bastard."

"Watch the language," warned Ross.

"You murdered my father!"

"And you murdered mine." Ross's gaze never wavered. "Maybe we're even."

Were they? Encouraged by the fact that almost all the bad men were securely tied, and nobody had died, Victoria reached out a needy hand.

To her soul-deep satisfaction, Ross took it. He drew her tight against him, her back against his front so that he could keep watch over her head as he slid one arm around her. He kissed the top of her head and even teased in a low voice, "I brought your beau."

"He's not my beau," she protested happily.

"Lucky for him," he said. Her gaze crept to where Alden Wright had finished tying the hands of the men on the ground. Alden was the one Ross had wanted all along. The one thing she still feared sharing with him.

But surely Ross was teasing. She wrapped her arms over his, and leaned back against him, and tried to trust him.

"Even!" spat Sheriff Ward. "We'll never be even. My father was worth the three of you I killed and more!"

Victoria said, "Three?" And she felt suddenly ill.

Was that why his mother had vanished?

Chapter Twenty-four

Three? Laramie hadn't fully absorbed that part of the sheriff's boast before Victoria questioned it. Poppa, Phil . . . and who?

Then Ward said, "You think your sister killed herself?"

And with slow loathing, Laramie understood. Maybe not Victoria's sigh of relief. Maybe not how Alden Wright spun in their direction, blanching.

But he understood the evil that was Bram Ward. He knew it in himself. Maybe it was just a matter of degree.

Reluctantly, Laramie let go of Victoria.

"Oh, Ross," she protested, reaching for his arm, but he dodged her touch. He could not touch her goodness and ever know, for sure, just how deep his own evil went.

"She went to Sheriff Howe about our rustling," continued Ward with desperate sadism as Laramie

stepped nearer him. "Said she had proof. But Howe
was a pard of my pa's. So we waited 'til your ma was
at the jail—"

Laramie reached behind his head and unknotted
his oversized silk bandanna which cowboys wore
against dust and weather.

"—and we rode over to that stinkin' cabin of
your'n—"

Laramie began to flip the dark cloth into a loose
coil.

"—and we strung the bitch up, same as her pa,"
gloated Ward. "I done in three of you Bohunks, damn
you! Whether you put me on trial or you murder me
right here can't never even us up. *I won.*"

Then Laramie struck, looping and tightening the
cloth around Ward's neck in one smooth movement.
"Like this?" he rasped into the man's ear. "Is this how
you won?"

Ward tried to hold his smile, but within moments
his lips had parted in an attempt to draw air. Still, he
gasped the word "Yeah."

It was easy, easy as Laramie remembered. He
wanted this man dead. He had the ability to do it. He
cinched the scarf tighter around the man's neck, tried
not to imagine his once-pretty sister fighting for her
life, her baby's life. "You think she felt like this?"

An odd, abrasive sound began to stutter out of the
sheriff's mouth. His wide eyes bulged; his face red-
dened. He dropped to his knees, his arms beginning
to yank against the cuffs, but Laramie just kneeled
right beside him. He felt the man shudder, his ugly
life fighting to continue even now. Life was tenacious,
after all. Even bound and helpless. Even as dark a life
as this.

And Ross respected that.

In a quick move, as Ward's eyes rolled up in his
head, Laramie dug his fingers between the silk noose

287

and the man's throat and yanked it loose. He scooted back from his own horror, on his butt, as the sheriff crumpled to the ground, pants soiled, hands still cuffed behind him. Only then, drawing his knees under him, did he really look at the filth this man was.

So that's what winning looked like, was it?

Ward could have it.

"If you don't want a trial," he warned, beginning to shake, "find someone else to kill you."

And he stood. His heart raced; his head spun. History had almost repeated itself—but with Laramie in the role of Boris Ward. It wasn't self-defense this time, only vengeance. And vengeance wasn't enough.

He wouldn't let a Ward make him kill again.

Laramie looked down and saw that his hands only felt like they were shaking. Then he looked at Victoria—*I didn't kill him!*

And his heart sank.

She stood, her hands covering her mouth, staring in horror at the unconscious sheriff—and Alden Wright was clutching her shoulders with white fingers, as if protecting her from Laramie. And she let him.

There was something between the two of them after all.

Laramie should never have started feeling again, because that realization almost destroyed him. When Vic lowered her hands to say, "Oh, Ross," he couldn't bear to hear what would surely be a lengthy explanation, so he turned away and focused on just doing what he had to do to get her home.

Careful, closed, he made sure their captives were gagged. He hitched the rustlers' horses to a lead rope and made Alden Wright help him hoist the tied men, one at a time, into their saddles.

Wright kept sneaking glances of building fury toward him, the whole time. Was he jealous that Ross had called Victoria "sweetheart," or angry that Ross had helped bring such ugliness into Vic's world? Only when the unsightly heap that was the sheriff groaned back to muffled consciousness did Wright finally say, "You had him!"

Ross squinted at him, confused. "What?"

"You could have killed him!" Wright's voice cracked. "You're a killer—"

"Alden!" protested Victoria sharply from where she was packing weapons into a saddlebag. *She called him Alden.*

"—why didn't you kill the son of a bitch?"

Wright *wanted* Laramie to kill the sheriff? Laramie shook his head, disgusted. "That's what he wanted."

And Victoria was there. But that wasn't a good enough excuse, even if she *weren't* involved with Wright.

"Then don't tie the bastard onto his horse; drag him behind it!" Wright insisted. "Damn it, Laurence, he killed your sister; how can you let him get away with jail time?"

"Alden," warned Victoria again.

Laramie just shook his head and left the two of them, went to throw sand on the rustlers' fire. Something tickled at his awareness again, and he eyed the arroyo for danger, then conceded that it wasn't that sort of instinct. This was more what Victoria would call puzzle pieces.

The area looked clear, the horses calm, the bad men tied. Whatever it was could just remain a puzzle for now. The ruin of two months' worth of dreams sufficiently distracted him.

Laramie felt Victoria's gaze on him once, her confused gray eyes begging him to speak, to react, to do *something*. He wasn't sure what. Likely something to do with talking, something beyond his capabilities. When he returned from dousing the campfire, she and Wright were arguing by the horses. So the man wasn't just wealthy and presumably respectable—he had words, too. So what?

That's why it surprised him when Victoria turned away from Wright and asked *him*, Laramie, "May I ride behind you?"

Laramie looked at her gelding, still wearing her padded sidesaddle. The horse didn't seem hurt. When Victoria put an insistent hand on his arm, the sensation flashed through him like standing too near to a lightning strike. He closed his eyes against it. He could not do this, not here, not today. If he started feeling it all now . . .

"Please?" she insisted, as if he could deny her anything. "I don't want to ride alone."

So Laramie offered his hand and boosted her onto Blackie, glad his bullet wounds had finally healed. Her skirts rode up on her legs as she straddled the horse, behind the saddle's cantle. She wore high, soft-leather shoes with little bone buttons that traced the curve of her ankle. Her stockings were knitted with an intriguing, zigzag weave that stretched for her calf.

Laramie mounted, careful not to kick her. While he found his stirrups, he felt Victoria draw one side of his split-tailed duster into place, and stiffened. It seemed so proprietary, so *right*. Then she wrapped her arms around his waist. Her bosom and jaw pressed against his back through his duster, and he realized what a bad call this had been. He could hardly *help* feeling her, this way! And if he began to allow one sensation, God knew where it would end. Hope?

Hope was more dangerous than firearms.

Not surprisingly, Wright protested. "Really, Miss Garrison! That's hardly proper." God pity any beau of Victoria's who presumed he could direct her behavior.

But she'd said Wright wasn't her beau.

"I'll move onto Huckleberry before we reach town,"

Vic assured them both, her tone cross. "For now, I am riding with Ross."

"Ross?" challenged Alden.

Instead of arguing, she said, "I want to go home." So they rode out.

Laramie tried to ignore the sensation of Vic's fingers across his abdomen and ribs. Her words seemed to vibrate into his spine when she asked, "Where will we take them?" Then she shifted behind him, perhaps to eye their prisoners. "Considering that we've captured the sheriff and the deputy, who watches them in jail?"

Don't. Feel. Anything. Ross carefully shrugged.

"And we left the cattle," she noted, leaning a different direction. Every time she moved, her hands gripped another bit of him, warm and sure. "Will they be all right until someone fetches them? They won't get too hungry in there, will they?"

She paused after that question. Since Wright said nothing, Laramie assured her, "No."

"Good." She squeezed him a little more tightly, resting her cheek against his back, and he felt something anyway. A falter in his reserve. A cracking in his guard. It was all that the blows from this day—Julije's murder, Wright's interest—needed to gain a fingerhold.

He took a deep breath, struggled to regain his balance against the eddying, swirling emotions in him. Then Vic cried, *"OH!"* and he nearly leapt out of the saddle.

"What?"

"We have to go back!"

Ross reined in Blackie, called "Whoa" to the train of horses following him and Wright, and twisted in his saddle to better see Victoria. "Why?"

Her hands slid innocently down to his hips, and he *definitely* felt that. "My camera," she explained, eyes pleading. "I dropped my camera when Deputy Frank-

291

lin captured me. We have to go back for it!"

Wright made a frustrated sound. "For God's sake, I'll buy you a new camera! Could we just get this day done with?"

Victoria glared at him. Then she turned her bright gaze to Laramie. "But I took photographs," she pleaded. "Pictures of the rustlers blotting brands."

Sheriff Ward, though tied and gagged, turn to glare silent accusations at his deputy.

Laramie stared down at her. She'd put herself at risk to take photographs of the rustlers? *Was she a lunatic?*

If so, she was a lunatic with what might be important evidence, assuming photographs were admissible in court. She was exactly the kind of lunatic he had figured her for, both at Hole-in-the-Wall and Stuart MacCallum's sheep ranch. And she was a lunatic asking *him,* not Alden Wright, for help.

"Please let's go back?" With him turned back in his saddle and her leaning around to better meet his gaze—with her hands still on his hips, fingers brushing the crease where his dungarees folded onto his thigh—the moment felt almost intimate.

Ross looked at Alden Wright. "Cover them."

"Me?" Wright's surprise hardly inspired confidence. Ross stared him down. "Do not get close to them."

Then he reined Blackie back in the direction they'd come. Just him and Victoria Garrison.

He wondered if she knew how tightly she was holding him.

He didn't kill the sheriff, Victoria reminded herself. *And the sheriff even murdered Julie. Surely Alden—*

But she *wasn't* sure. That's why telling Ross posed such a risk. Staying silent, though, risked no less than *his* trust. Ross had kept his promise and come back, at the best possible time. He'd saved her from a fate she feared to imagine. How could she *not* trust him?

"Ross?" Victoria bowed her head so that her fore-head touched his spine, through his long, black duster. *Like praying.* He filled her arms, her heart, every dream she had.

If that didn't deserve prayer, what did?

He did not say *What?* But she felt his interest in the shifting tensions of his body against hers.

"I have to tell you something. I don't want to tell you, because I'm afraid of how you'll react. But as long as I'm afraid of how you'll react, then it's not right to pursue anything further, and I've *got* to pursue this further. Sensible or not, I've got to. So I have to tell you."

He tensed beneath her hands, so taut that he almost vibrated with it. But he also managed to say, low and raspy, "Go on."

"It's just that, after you left, I realized . . ." She felt like a traitor, even to hesitate. "I realized that you wanted to know who seduced Julie in order to get revenge. Didn't you?"

It felt like hugging a tree, all hard muscle and hardened heart. "Yes," he admitted.

So much for explaining that away. "But you decided not to."

He hesitated before admitting, "Yes."

See? She took a deep breath of him. "Because of me."

He said nothing.

"Well, I'm going to ask you to do that again. I mean, to *not* do anything. Because of me. I—" Oh God. If she were wrong, and got Alden Wright killed, how would she live with herself?

But if she let her need for proof get in the way of what her heart already knew, insulted him with her distrust, how could she live without him? She loved Ross. Beyond words, beyond reason. She loved his support when Kitty was hurt. She loved his protection when they surprised the stranger by the creek, when he rescued her today. She loved his wounded heart and his steady spirit.

So she told him. "I want you not to hurt Alden."

Now it felt like hugging a rock. He said nothing. His only movements were the tiny adjustments in his arms and legs as he guided the horse to retrace the route of her capture.

Victoria considered asking him to promise before she said anything more. That would be safer for Alden. But it would also be manipulative; she would never know his real decision unless he had full freedom to kill Julie's lover.

He didn't kill the sheriff, though. Ward deserved punishment for what he'd done to Julie, far more than Alden did, but Ross hadn't executed the man himself. He was good.

"You should know that after you left . . . ," she began—then recognized a rock formation. "There!"

Ross's body jumped beneath her hands. Feeling cowardly to welcome the distraction, she quickly slid off Blackie's rump and hurried to the base of the rocks, searching through undergrowth. It had to be here. She knew this was the place—

Ah! With a cry of triumph, she lifted her prize by its leather strap. "Here it is!" she exclaimed happily, turning back to Ross. "We've got proof—"

But she stopped at the sight of his blank face.

Nothing about how he'd schooled his features hinted at emotion. His brows, his mouth, how he held his head as he watched her seemed more indifferent than the first time she ever saw him. But the brightness in his deep-set eyes, behind his indifference, and the pallor of his dark face shook her.

She saw the pain behind the mask. "What's wrong?"

He looked sharply away, so that she had only a profile of sharp nose, angled jaw, high cheek. A muscle in his throat twitched, giving him away, and she stepped to his side, reached up to touch his leg. "Ross, what's *wrong?*"

He shook his head, reached down to lift her back up onto the horse.

She backed away from his hand. "No. I'm not going until you tell me what's wrong."

He glared at her then, and his dark, greenish eyes were bright. Bright with agony. Bright with accusation. Bright with despair. He swallowed and managed to say, "I'll go."

What? She wished she understood. It felt cruel, after his obvious effort, to ask him for even more words, but she had to know. "Go where?"

He glared.

"Go to town without me?" she tried as she looped the camera up over her shoulder. Maybe if she gave him options—

But he just looked angrier.

"Go . . . ?" Where else was there? "Back to the arroyo, to let the cattle loose?"

He tipped his head back, turned his face to a glimpse of sky through the trees. When he parted his lips, an almost inhuman cry shuddered out of him.

She'd never heard anything so hurt as that cry. Somehow, it shook with every bit of ugliness—lynch mobs, and dead girls, and murderers; range wars and self-defense and missing mothers—that had tried to destroy him. As the pain of it washed past her, through her, she wondered if anyone else could have endured as long as he had and *not* want to commit murder.

Then, as if he'd cleared a dam, he talked—leaning out of his Texas saddle to bend over her, throwing the words at her like rocks. "I'll go *away*, Victoria. From here. You can have your Alden Wright, your—your cattle fortunes, and—and all his educated words. If you want them, take them. Just get your beautiful butt back up on this goddamned horse and let me bring you home first, all right? I want . . ."

He looked sharply away then, and muttered the last of it. "I just want to see you safely home."

She stared up at him, speechless. Not because he'd taken the Lord's name in vain. Not even because of how many words he'd strung together. Because he believed—

"You think I want Alden Wright?"

He peeked quickly back at her, dark eyes wary. "You—"

"Alden Wright?" she repeated. "If you could see my list of why I would never seriously consider Alden Wright, even you could not say that with a straight face. How could you think I would want Alden Wright?"

Ross searched her face, as if for a hint that she was lying. About *this?*

"Get down here," she told him.

"You don't want me to hurt him," he reminded her, an accusation. "You said you want to pursue it further."

Clearly, words would not work for this. "Ross Laurence, you get off that horse right now."

He seemed reluctant now, as if she would attack him.

Wise man. "If you love me," she warned, "you'll get off that horse."

To her delight, Ross slowly lifted his leg over Blackie's rump and dismounted. Then he turned to face her, all planes and hardness and walls. Walls against her. Walls against his own feelings. Walls against all their possibilities.

But he got off the horse.

She stepped up against him, reached for the back

of his neck, and drew his head down to where, on tiptoes, she could just barely kiss him. "I love you, too."

It felt wonderful, kissing him again. It felt right. But the fact that he didn't move his mouth against hers—that she was the only one doing the kissing—left something to be desired.

"I don't understand." But he said it leaning toward her. He didn't straighten to where she could not reach his mouth again.

Since he was at least cooperating that far, she wrapped her arms around his middle instead. She liked that better because she could slide her arms inside his duster and pull herself more tightly against his shirt—feel his ribs against her breasts, brace her skirted leg against his own. He'd come back to her, and they loved each other, and when she kissed him this time, he kissed her back.

But he was still hesitant. *Controlled.*

"I don't—" he protested, and when she tried to kiss him a third time, he actually straightened away from her. Well, away from her mouth. She was affixed to the front of him. "Please, Victoria," he protested, his voice caught somewhere between a laugh and a sob. "Please talk to me."

"I don't want Alden Wright," she confirmed, craning her head up to keep looking at him. He'd tipped his face sharply down to look at her, too.

"Then why would I want to hurt him?"

"Because . . ." Oh dear. But if she could trust him with anything, she had to trust him with this, no matter what Alden had begged. "Because I was wrong about his age. Alden was sixteen when Julie was fifteen. Ross, *he's* her sweetheart."

Ross stood very still within her embrace, staring down at her, expression blank. "He what?"

"That's what I found out, after you left. He's the

297

one who brought flowers to her grave, and he bribed the undertaker to add that line from "Clementine" to her tombstone. He swears he loved her, and he didn't know about the child, and he never knew she tried to see him after the lynchings. And I believe him. So I'm asking you not to do anything to him, because you're a good man and because if you do now it will be partly my fault for telling you. But I *had* to tell you. I—I have to trust you, and I *do,* even with this. Or else it's not really love at all, and it *must* be. I don't want you to go anywhere. And if you have to go, I want to come with you. So that's what—"

"Victoria," interrupted Ross softly.

At least he was blinking again. She balanced on the very tip of her tiptoes, trying to get closer to the face bent above her, and wished she were even a little taller. "What, Ross?"

He kissed her.

Chapter Twenty-five

Alden Wright seduced Julie?

After eleven years, that simple answer shattered into a rock slide of further questions. Victoria didn't want him taking vengeance, but she also believed Wright's overdue claim of love. Last time Laramie checked, true love did not impregnate, betray, and abandon. His own responsibility to Julije's memory had kept him alive, had brought him to Sheridan. And yet . . .

He'd come to Sheridan for a different reason this time.

Victoria didn't *want Alden Wright?*

Two worlds dragged at him, promises from his past, dreams for his future, equally complicated. But Wright wasn't here and Victoria was, saying his name, lifting her earnest face toward his—and she wanted *him*.

She loved him.

Laramie covered her beautiful, sweet mouth with his own and chose her, worshiped her with his kiss.

Her affection tasted—felt—so delicious that he trembled with it. She really wanted *him!*

He felt such relief, gratitude, such joy that he laughed into her mouth.

She drew back, startled. Then she laughed too.

"Sorry," he whispered, ducking his head.

"I love your smile," she said, and caught his cheek with one soft hand and guided his mouth back down to hers. "Thank you, Ross. Thank you."

"Thank you?" he asked in blissful confusion, just before their lips met. Thank you for his *smile?*

Then he was kissing her again while she sighed, "Uh-huh" against him, and his thoughts began to stutter.

She wants to—

We'll be—

He couldn't finish the thoughts for fear of jinxing them. This sort of thing didn't happen in his world. But he'd pushed that world aside; he did not want it. He preferred to stake a claim in hers. Because she allowed someone as unworthy as him in, he would love her forever.

When she hugged him, she'd slid her hands inside his duster to do it. One of her hands drifted down his denim-covered spine, then the small of his back, then past his belt and onto a less proper venue, and her wanting to stay with him awoke erotic possibilities as well. He had not intended to think of her that way. *Carnally.* She was his sweet Victoria. And yet he no longer felt merely itchy under her blessedly curious hands. He felt downright hot.

Lifting her into his arms, even as they kissed, Laramie took awkward steps until a tree scraped the back of the hand cupping her head. Then he slowly slid her down his aroused body, pressing himself into her buttoned-up, petticoated softness. He slid his tongue into her hot, willing mouth. She parted her lips wider for him, let her head fall back—a move that lifted her jacketed breasts generously up and into his ribs.

"Uh-huh," she either repeated or encouraged, muffled and happy. Her hands found his butt again, under his coattails, and all of his hard-won control couldn't keep his body from pushing greedily against hers where he'd braced her against the tree. To tell by her sigh, she didn't seem to mind.

She *loved* him? The truth of that was a blanket around them, wrapping them together, sheltering what they did here. He thrust deeper with his tongue, and she drank him in, her breath catching in little whimpers.

He combed his fingers through her thick, curly hair and drew his hands over her shoulders, down the round softness of her arms in their coat sleeves, his thumbs testing even less decent curves. *So hot.* Suddenly frustrated that his tongue could not bring closure to the matter, he slid his kisses from her mouth, across her jaw, down her cinnamon-scented neck. She released his rear end to reach up and pull off his hat, drop it somewhere, then dig her fingers in his hair as if to insist that he continue kissing her there. When he trailed kisses down her throat, then to the collar of her coat, she let him do that, too.

Drugged with pleasure, with satisfaction—with sheer, blinding hope—he could barely think enough to wonder if it was possible to undo buttons with his teeth.

"Oh, Ross," Victoria sighed, squirming against his need of her. "Oh—keep doing that."

He slid a hand off her arm and directly onto her breast, round and firm and tempting even through too much material, and she arched eagerly into him. "And that!"

His fingers began to dig into the serge of her riding coat, but somehow he forced them to close into a fist instead. He would not tear her clothes. He would not, must not be violent to her in any way.

Ever.

Just in case, he turned his face into the welcome shelter of her shoulder, gasping for breath.

"You'll marry me?" he pleaded, desperate. This was more than he should ever do with a woman he would not marry, probably not with a woman he hadn't *already* married. He'd never known anything as blissful as this, just this, and oh, God, he had to be sure.

When Victoria blew out her breath, he felt it feather across the back of his hair. "You don't think I would go away with you and not get married, do you? Now kiss me."

Demanding, wasn't she? He loved that about her. He loved everything about her. If she was willing to marry him, it was only because she'd given him reason to change.

He even straightened, resting the crown of his head against the tree trunk, over hers, and said it. "Victoria, I love you. Beyond life. Beyond . . . beyond anything."

She ran her hands up and down his chest, somehow admiring, but ducked her head into his chest.

"I love you, too," she said to his heart. "I wouldn't go away with you without that, either."

Either . . . ? Confused, but happily so, he stared down at her dark, now-wild curls and felt his own smile stretch his mouth, uncertain on his face. He should practice. He might end up smiling around her a great deal.

Then she looked back up at him, somehow petulant, and reached up for his face. "Ross," she insisted, drawing his face invitingly back to her bosom. It had to be the roundest, most fetching, most glorious bosom he'd ever seen, much less touched, even under layers of her wine-colored coat.

She would be his. Even her bosom.

But she deserved better than to have him doing anything about it at this point in their engagement.

Their engagement!

So he tried to kiss her again instead—and then had to turn his head back into her shoulder.

"What's wrong?" she demanded, her cross tone exacerbating the problem.

He tipped his face to hers. "I cannot kiss you," he confessed, his words uneven. "I cannot stop smiling."

"But I love your smile," she reminded him with teasing solemnity, touching the bend of his cheek with curious fingers, seeming to savor even his beard stubble. "You need to smile more."

"I love you, Victoria," he repeated, just to prove that he could say it more than once, just to see her delight upon hearing it. "But I am not taking you away with me."

Her eyes narrowed dangerously, so he hurried to add, "I am staying with you. I won't take you away from your family, or your town, or your newspaper. I am finished with running. Somehow I'll stay, unless—" *Damn.* This part came harder, particularly with the fear that crept back. But didn't she say they had to trust each other? "Unless I get jail time for breaking my parole. But if . . . *if* you still wanted me after that . . ."

Her lower lip began to tremble before she caught it between her teeth. Her eyes, searching his, glittered suspiciously, and his gut clenched up. She had not realized he might yet be in trouble with the law. Of course, she wouldn't wait for him to serve time. She deserved so much better.

Then her lower lip escaped into the brightest smile yet, and she threw her arms around him and pressed her face into his chest. "Thank you," she said again, even if it was muffled, then drew back, still in his arms. "For being willing to do that. That has to be the nicest present anyone's ever given me! Of course, Thaddeas will keep you out of jail," she insisted. "But even if he didn't, I would visit you every day. We could do a jail-house interview! You could introduce me to the other prisoners, and I could write about their stories too, but I'm sure yours would be the best."

He stared down at her and knew he wasn't dead only because he would not deserve the heaven of having Victoria Garrison love him. "It would have the best ending," he whispered.

Suddenly her eyes widened. "Ross! There's a bounty!"

His gut clenched tighter. "On me?"

She laughed. "On the rustlers. The Sheridan Cattle-man's Association gave themselves an official name just to raise the reward. Personally, I don't think Al-den should get an even split, since you did all the work, but—" Her mouth opened in realization. "Al-den!"

He might end up confused around her a great deal, as well. He doubted he would mind. "Alden?"

"How long have we been here? He must think I lost my camera in Colorado! And him all alone with that awful sheriff, knowing he killed Julie, and worrying about you—Ross, we need to tell him it's all right!"

He shook his head, lost. And in love. "All right?"

She kissed his jaw, rolling her eyes at his thickness. "That you forgive him for being Julie's lover."

Julie's lover? He blinked down at her, trying to fit that thought into the wonder that had been his world for the last ten or fifteen minutes. The puzzle piece did not match, so he looked at the information with-out trying to fit it anywhere, and he remembered. "Al-den was Julije's lover."

Victoria, in the circle of his arms, said, "I *told* you. Sixteen years old. Undertaker. Flowers."

He ached not to leave this world for that one. But

staring down at where he held her in the loose circle of his arms, he knew he had no choice. "Yes," he agreed. "Of course you told me. I just . . . forgot."

She widened her eyes. "You *forgot?*"

The man he'd hunted for so many years had a face at last—Alden Wright's face—and Laramie had no idea what to do about it. *Wait,* he guessed. *Wait, and think, and see.* And love Victoria. "I was distracted."

Before he could lean down to kiss her again, she'd reclaimed her own lower lip between her teeth, and her brows had drawn together. "But it's all right," she prompted him. "Because now you know Sheriff Ward is the one who killed her."

"After Wright led him to us in the first place," he reminded her—and felt the first stirrings of uncertainty when Victoria *stopped* talking. She'd been afraid to tell him, he remembered, almost too late. She would feel responsible if anything happened to the son of a bitch. It hurt, to think that she still thought that of him. It hurt that she didn't realize she'd become far more important than any vendetta. "I won't kill him, if that's what you're afraid of."

"I didn't say you would." She pressed her lips together, as if trying to understand—but what? What was there to grasp? *He seduced my sister. He led a lynch mob to us. He abandoned her during the worst days of her life.*

Did she want him to forgive the bastard? If so, then there existed one thing he might not be able to do after all, even for her. That frightened him. Couldn't she still love him, even if he hated Alden Wright to his dying breath?

Isn't it enough that I don't kill him?

They both startled at a single gunshot from the direction where they'd left Alden Wright.

Suddenly Laramie's two worlds blurred yet again.

* * *

Victoria flinched at the familiar report. *Alden!*

"Stay here," instructed Ross, striding toward Blackie. "I'll see what happened."

She dodged ahead of him and boosted herself up and across his saddle, on her stomach. "No!"

"Victoria!"

She had to struggle to get her leg up and over Blackie's rump, weighted down in a riding skirt like it was. "You said that you wouldn't leave me!" There! She had a leg on either side and sat up.

"That didn't mean I would carry you into gunfire!"

But she grabbed onto his saddle's cantle and hung on, warning him with her eyes that he would have to fight to make her get down. Ross groaned, deep and heartfelt—and mounted in front of her. She wrapped her arms around his slim waist and held on while he urged his horse ahead, in the direction where they'd left Julie's lover. She felt glad to have something, someone to hold. If the sheriff had killed Alden, while she and Ross were misbehaving in the woods . . .

Ross reined Blackie to a stop before they'd quite reached the clearing where they'd left the others. Dismounting, he reached for her. She slid off the horse and into his arms as if she belonged there—even if he did then set her aside, behind a tree. With an ominous *whoosh*, he drew his rifle from its scabbard. "Wright!" he called loudly after taking several deliberate steps away from her.

Her heart clutched to realize that he was drawing off any possible gunfire. He didn't want her to be hurt. Oh, she did love him. He wasn't a murderer. Why should it matter whether he believed her about Alden?

She hated that it mattered—and she sank against the tree, with relief, when Alden called, "Laurence? It's safe. We just had a little . . . trouble."

"Good," called Ross. But he was drawing his pistol

at the same time. One-handed, he popped the cylinder, spun it to check for bullets, snapped it back in—all while walking back to her—then gave it to her. The weapon seemed to float in his hand. When it reached her hand, the reality of its weight and bulk almost made her drop it. "Watch from here."

But— "He said it's safe."

He shrugged one shoulder, a gesture she finally placed as vaguely European. "They put a gun to his head, he might lie. I love you."

What? But before she could protest, even reassure him that she loved him back, he called, "I'm coming out," and strode into the clearing.

Victoria waited, terrified, for more gunfire. Sheriff Ward certainly did seem to want Ross dead, after all. Every second drew her tighter, until Ross called, "Victoria, it's safe. Just try not to look."

She could imagine Alden lying to save his life. Not Ross; never Ross. So she led Blackie into the clearing, where Alden stood alone and Ross was carefully catching hold of a spooked, riderless horse's saddle. Only after looking twice for some sign of trouble did Victoria realize that the horse wasn't riderless at all—and why it was spooked.

She pressed a hand to her mouth, hard, while her nausea rose in proportion to her slow comprehension.

Sheriff Ward hung half off the mount to which he was still tied. His mouth was still gagged with Ross's black bandanna. His arms, still cuffed behind him, hung at an awkward, upside-down angle.

"It was self-defense," said Alden numbly while Ross cut the body loose so that it could slide to the ground. "It was."

He wasn't holding the gun they'd left with him. It lay in the grass beside him.

"Self-defense," he repeated, and she turned back to stare at Sheriff Ward. Ross, kneeling beside the body with one hand on his neck, met Alden's eyes and shook his head. Alden had killed him.

He was still wearing the handcuffs she'd put on him. The key was still in her pocket!

A slow cry began, deep in her, and she pressed her hand harder against her mouth, making a fist to keep it all in. She didn't want to be around guns anymore. She didn't want to be around dead people. She didn't want to notice that the horse must have been spooked for several minutes, because Sheriff Ward's head—

The cry came out of her anyway, and Ross glanced sharply up. "I said don't look!" he commanded, more sharply than he'd ever spoken to her, but she couldn't turn away.

She had to know things, even now. She had to know the grim ease with which Ross wrapped the corpse in the picnic blanket, then tied it onto the horse. She had to see the way he paused to look over their other three prisoners, in case one of them had been hurt. She had to watch him pick up Alden's gun and, instead of giving it back, unload it and slide it into a saddlebag. He'd had to learn all of that, she thought. What kind of a life had Ross lived, that he'd had to learn all of that?

She forgot she was even holding his pistol until he came to her, took it from her hands, and seated it gently back into his holster. His head was down the whole time. Only after she said nothing did he slant his gaze up at her and his green-brown eyes, through his dark lashes, seemed naked. "I'm sorry you had to see that," he apologized.

She said, "I'm not."

At least now she knew what she must try to make up for.

Laramie asked Victoria to ride her own horse, with her own sidesaddle, the rest of the way into town. Considering that their little parade now included a corpse, he figured they could use all the respectability they could get. Not that he meant to use her for that respectability. When they reached town, he sent her to the telegraph office not just to wire for a marshal from nearby Big Horn, but so that she wouldn't have to ride the gauntlet of Main Street with him, Wright, and the rustlers.

But it probably helped that she wasn't sitting straddle behind him, like before. And until they resolved what they'd been discussing, before Alden's sudden bent for murder interrupted them, he wasn't sure he should enjoy the heaven of her arms around him anyway. He wasn't sure she would want his, either.

"The . . . undertaker?" murmured Wright, uncertainly, when they reached the jail. He still seemed dazed. Killing did that to a fellow—even a son of a bitch.

"He'll be here," Laramie assured him dourly, cutting the sheriff's incongruously wrapped, red-and-white-checked corpse down from its horse. "Help me carry him inside."

Once they dumped the thing in its own cell, Wright just stood there, staring at it. So Laramie had to herd the other rustlers in by himself. He gave pennies to excited little boys to run and fetch the local ranchers—and Thaddeas Garrison—to the jail.

"I'm going home now," announced Wright then, suddenly turning for the door, but Laramie caught his arm and pushed him into the deputy's chair instead.

"It will look better if you stay," he warned.

"Look better." Alden Wright stared up at him, both confused and somehow insulted. "I said it was self-defense."

He was an idiot. Laramie just wasn't sure how he *felt* about the man's idiocy. Wright had clearly murdered the sheriff in cold blood. Gagged, Ward couldn't even have taunted him. Cuffed, Ward hadn't likely threatened him.

You could have killed him, Wright had complained back at the box canyon—trying to make things easy on himself, Laramie guessed. *Why didn't you kill the son of a bitch?*

Then he'd been forced to sit there, waiting for Laramie and Victoria's return, watching the sheriff and maybe thinking through everything Ward had said about Julije, over and over. Maybe Ward had smiled. Maybe he'd even laughed. Either way, Alden Wright had snapped, and become a killer himself.

Assuming he wasn't already, at the least, an accomplice.

Alden Wright was rich. A rancher. A bachelor. He'd seduced Laramie's sister, led a lynch mob to them, and abandoned Julije during the worst days of her short life. Laramie tensed with more than ten years of slow-burning fury, to think of it. And now that they were more or less alone, except for the captive rustlers, he finally managed to do what he'd been failing at since arriving in Sheridan.

He asked a question. "You think you loved her?"

Wright's head came up, and some of the glazed look to his eyes cleared. "I *did* love her."

"She told you where our hideout was, and you told—"

"My father!" Wright stood, turned angrily away, ran a hand down his face. "Just my father. Do you think I haven't regretted that, every day?"

Laramie stared at him and thought, *Not the way I have.*

"I was so angry that year. My father wanted to send me to college, but I was going to prove what a great rancher I made, so that I could settle down and marry Julie. He said he'd use the information to straighten things out between your family and the Wards. He said nobody would get hurt."

God, what an idiot. He'd also been young; Laramie admitted that to himself with extreme reluctance. But . . .

"You sat there." His voice shook on those words—the drawback of allowing himself to feel things again. "You sat there and watched them do it."

"And a twelve-year-old boy showed more grit than I did," Wright agreed, and spun to face him again. Tears glittered in his wild eyes. "Yes, I did that. I betrayed her, and I let her father and brother die, and I never confessed it to anybody until Victoria, and *her* only because . . ."

He gestured with one confused hand, and Laramie found himself nodding agreement. *Because she was Victoria.*

"I was a coward, and a fool, and—and a libertine!" Wright planted both hands on the desk between them. "If you want to kill me for that, you go right ahead. I probably deserve it. But don't you dare say I didn't love her. Maybe I didn't love her right, or enough. God, she went to Howe instead of me! If she'd just come to me . . ." He shook his head. "I didn't deserve her. But I loved her."

Laramie stared at him and felt a final shifting, a final cracking, deep inside where the hatred had protected him all these years. The last of his heart's shell seemed to fall away—and it hurt.

God, it hurt. That was the problem with stopping. Stopping was when a fellow remembered to hurt. But his family had been murdered, and he'd wasted his life ever since. Maybe it was long past time to hurt.

He glanced back toward the cell where they'd put the dead sheriff. "Did it make you feel better?"

Looking confused again, Wright shook his head.

"No," he said, voice hollow. "I thought I would, but I just feel . . ."

Ugly. Used. Worthless. Humiliated.

"She's still dead," explained Wright. "So it didn't really help at all."

"It never does." Laramie took a deep breath, rolled some of the kinks out of his shoulders, exhaled. Julije—Julie—*was* dead, but not at her own hand. She hadn't died of a broken heart. "It doesn't look like self-defense," he offered.

Wright shook his head, a spectrum of emotions from betrayal to resignation shifting across his face. "What?"

"I wasn't there," Laramie warned. "But when I rode in, it looked more like he'd been trying to escape."

The front door of the jail creaked open, and he spun to face the intrusion, afraid someone important had overheard. Someone important *had* overheard. Victoria.

Despite that he had said nothing illegal, offered no alibi, Laramie felt guilty. She believed in right and wrong, not in helping a killer—

But she said, closing the door behind her, "I thought that, if he was trying to escape, maybe he moved fast and scared you into *thinking* he would hurt you. Not that I was there, either."

Between them, she probably had the most clever criminal mind. When she came to Laramie's side and slid her arm around him, gazed approvingly up at him, he knew he wouldn't care if she *was* a criminal. He loved her, every curious, contradictory, troublesome inch of her—and from the way she was looking at him, he must have somehow stumbled back into the world where she loved him, too.

Or maybe he'd never left it.

"Yes," said Wright, slowly. "I'll try to remember more . . . carefully."

Laramie ignored him to gaze back down at the most beautiful face in all the world. The one he still wasn't sure he deserved. The one who'd helped him come closer than he'd ever expected.

I heard, Victoria mouthed up at him, and maybe he looked confused, because she sighed, ducked her head, then seemed to force herself to face him. "I listened outside the door. I'm sorry—for everything. Forgive me?"

He stared down at her for another long minute. Forgive *her?*

Then he laughed.

Laramie had a rusty, uncertain laugh. Victoria adored it. She adored him. She adored him even more when he sank onto a bench and pulled her into his lap with him, his arms tight around her, her skirts draping across him to his knees, and overcame his smile just long enough to kiss her.

Oh, but he had to be the best of kissers.

"Uh, excuse me," interrupted Alden from where he sat remembering. "I'm not quite sure of proper etiquette in such circumstances, and I'm loath to deny Mr. Laurence anything at this point, but as the lady's actual escort, it does seem I should register a protest. No offense."

It was Ross, his arms still tight around her, who unleashed another of his beautiful smiles and made it real. "We are engaged to be married."

His eyes searched hers, as if even now he had any doubt. She bit her lower lip and nodded encouragement. Yes, they were. Engaged. To be married.

If it was a respectable engagement, they would have plenty of time to collect proof to support all of her instincts about this man she loved. It might put her family's mind at ease, whether she needed it anymore or not.

"Oh," said Alden. "She, er, hadn't mentioned that before now. My apologies."

Ross shrugged, and Victoria draped her arms over his hard shoulders. She'd never felt him so relaxed.

"And thank you for not killing me," added Alden, his laugh only a little uneven.

But Ross looked at Victoria when he said, "I should have gotten the whole story first."

The door to the jail opened and Victoria's father walked in. As soon as he saw Vic and Ross, he stopped still, stiffened. His gray eyes began to narrow.

Ross stood so quickly, only his arms around her kept Victoria from falling onto the floor. "Boss," he greeted. "I—"

Then he just stared, an almost amused look of helpless resignation stealing onto his dark, angled face. He'd lost his words again.

"Ross wants to speak to you," finished Victoria quickly.

Papa glared from him to Victoria—who wriggled her feet back to the floor and tried to convey in her smile how very happy she was—then back to Ross.

Then her father turned around and walked back out.

"He'll get used to the idea," she assured Ross confidently. "It's not like you're a sheep farmer," she reminded him, sliding her hand into his, weaving their fingers together.

Ross looked doubtful. "Just a gunman and cattle rustler."

"A *reformed* gunman and rustler."

Alden Wright mused, "I wonder if it gets easier or increasingly difficult for him each time one of you chooses a husband?"

Victoria considered that and said, "Even if he *doesn't* get used to the idea, I'll still marry Ross. So he might as well."

"I'm not sure it works that way," cautioned Ross, eyeing the doorway as if noticing that it provided the jail's only exit. But then he saw her watching him and managed a smile, if not one of his better ones. "But we'll make sure it does."

She nodded happily and whispered, "I love you, you know."

He bowed his head to hers, worshiped her with his eyes. "Beyond life," he reminded her. "Beyond anything."

So she stretched up for a kiss, which, after one last, wary glance at the door, he gave her. She sank into his embrace, warm and melting all over again.

Which was when Thaddeas walked in. Stopped still. Stiffened. His brown eyes began to narrow.

Victoria whispered, "And I really will visit you in jail."

Chapter Twenty-six

"Please state your name for the court," instructed Thaddeas from the front of the room. He looked his most proper and lawyer-like in a three-piece suit. Evangeline, seated beside Victoria, seemed more than content to simply watch him from the gallery, but Vic, leaning sideways to get a better view, wished he wouldn't keep standing between her and the witness. How was she supposed to report on this trial if she couldn't see?

It particularly frustrated her that the witness looked so handsome in his Sunday go-to-meeting clothes, and she hadn't spent time with him for two whole days!

"Ross Laurence," answered the man steadily.

To Vic's satisfaction, Thaddeas turned to face the jury, and she could finally better see her fiancé. Ross's tanned, angled face and shiny black hair made him look as dangerous as ever; she suspected that perhaps he still was. But Thaddeas had cleared him of any lingering childhood charges. He was a good man, and he was now helping to convict a no-good rustler.

Surely the jury would see that!

Thaddeas said, over his shoulder, "And your profession?"

"I am the range detective for the Sheridan Cattle Association." Nobody would ever wonder who he worked for now. Despite the shoddy reputation that range detectives had, Ross had told her, he meant to uphold the law.

And he had experience in overcoming shoddy reputations.

"How long have you held this job?" Thaddeas was a good lawyer. He never sounded annoyed asking questions for which he full-well knew the answers.

"Since November," answered Ross. "Eight months." And finally, almost against his will, his gaze touched Victoria's. She liked how his lips pressed together with a brief mixture of pain and amusement. *Eight months* since he'd saved her from Sheriff Ward, since Thaddeas had cleared his name, since he'd come home to stay! If circumstances had been different, they would be married already.

But Papa had insisted on a long engagement and Ross had gratefully agreed, as if marrying her was worth any price. The only person who complained about the wait was Vic. And oh, she'd done her share of complaining. After all, Ross had been a model citizen!

Then again . . .

"Would you characterize yourself as *familiar* with the way cattle rustlers work?" Thaddeas managed not to make a face while asking that.

He and Papa hadn't gotten past that minor point quite yet.

"Yes," agreed Ross steadily. "I would."

"So your initial suspicion of Mr. Price was based on experience and real evidence."

"It was."

The defendant—a forty-year-old man from Ohio, new to town that spring—scowled at them from where he sat with his own lawyer.

Thaddeas said, "Please tell us what led you to request that Sheriff Jones take a look at Mr. Price's livestock."

Ross did so. Since Victoria had heard the story more than once, she nudged Evangeline, then tapped the little watch neatly pinned to her friend's best skirt. Mama had given Evangeline the watch for Christmas, and Evangeline seemed to enjoy opening its cover to show Victoria that it was only ten-thirty.

They had plenty of time, yet. So Vic jotted notes for her latest newspaper story and, only partly listening, simply watched the man she loved.

The man she would marry next week.

In eight months Ross had been everything, done anything anybody could want of him. He'd practically become part of the family, sitting beside her at church, coming to the Garrisons' increasingly awkward but always interesting Sunday dinners. He'd rented the apartment over Thaddeas's law offices to live in—maybe in part so Thad could keep watch on him and see his innocence.

That winter, Ross had even helped Audra.

Of all the Garrison girls, nobody had thought proper little Audra would cause their first real scandal. Her beau, a seemingly respectable banker's son, had taken her on a carriage ride and kept her out well after nightfall—cause enough for rude speculation, especially when Audra then refused to marry the scoundrel. Despite that she'd practically been kidnapped, poor Audra had taken her compromised reputation to heart. She hardly left the house except for church and school. Once she finished out her levels, in May, she mainly went out for church. She hadn't even argued when the Sheridan school board chose not to hire her as a teacher, the one thing she'd ever really wanted.

Victoria wanted to argue. She wanted to argue plenty! But Audra begged her, and Laurel, and their mother to leave it alone. Reluctantly, they did.

No such luck with the menfolk, thank goodness. Forced into unnatural silence, Vic had felt all the better to learn that Ross had personally helped Papa, Thaddeas, Stuart MacCallum, and Collier Pembroke put the fear of God into Audra's former suitor.

Of the five of them, Victoria knew which one most bankers' sons would least want to meet in a dark alley.

Yet one more way she was nothing like a banker's son!

Now Audra was taking a teaching position with a widowed aunt, down in Texas where nobody knew her. Victoria didn't want to see her go. But in the meantime, Papa had allowed her and Ross to marry this summer, so that Audra could attend.

Next week, she told herself happily, and shivered. In a week, Ross would really be part of her family, and she—

Vic turned back to her friend, and Evangeline surreptitiously opened the watch again. Barely ten minutes had passed since the last time Vic checked. Even with Thad's questions to guide him, Ross was not particularly talkative.

Good.

Vic loved that Ross was now earning a living protecting cattle interests from bad men. She loved writing newspaper articles about it; her editor now joked that rustlers were her specialty. But what with her plans for the afternoon, she hoped Thaddeas would finish his questions, convict the greenhorn to a fair judgment, and let Ross finally spend some time with her.

In public.

With Duchess.

"Mr. Laurence, do you have any further proof that the cattle were in the defendant's corral?" asked Victoria's brother, and Ross nodded.

Thad went to his table and picked up a handful of round, black-and-white photographs, returned to them by mail from Rochester, New York the previous week. "Please tell the court what these pictures show."

"Judge," protested the defending attorney.

Ross said, "Cattle in Mr. Price's corral."

Now the other lawyer stood. "Judge!"

"Mr. Nicholson, we've been through this before." But the judge glanced wearily toward Victoria as he said it. "Photographs count as legal evidence."

Thaddeas handed the pictures to the jury.

The photographs that Victoria had taken of Sheriff Ward, back in the box canyon, had created a sensation in Sheridan. They'd helped convict the rustler's accomplices and stained the sheriff's reputation to the point that nobody bothered investigating Ward's death. Since then, photographs were appearing in court more and more often. Especially since Kodak had recently started selling Brownie box cameras—*You push the button, we do the rest*—for a dollar.

Victoria had bought Ross one for his birthday. Of course she would rather take any pictures he might need herself. But he'd gotten frustratingly stubborn about her not putting herself in danger.

Well, any more danger than necessary.

Not that she liked the story of how Mr. Price had threatened to shoot him rather than letting him ride away after taking the pictures. Apparently, Ross had ridden off anyway. He'd reassured her that he had a good eye for whether a man had killing in him.

Mr. Price had not shot him.

"As you can see," Thaddeas was telling the jury, "this is clearly Mr. Price's cabin. The cattle in his corral bear brands from several area ranches. And lest my colleague argue that the defendant was unaware of their presence, in several of them, Mr. Price himself is standing among the stolen livestock."

Ross, still in the witness box, deliberately refused to look at Victoria. He was probably afraid he would smile.

Safe in the gallery, Vic smiled anyway. She seemed to be smiling all the time lately. They made a good team.

And she knew about the surprise.

Ross deliberately did not voice his concerns about Victoria's latest scheme. Whatever it was, she was enjoying it—and he adored her.

"Hurry," she insisted, dragging him onto Sheridan's railroad platform by one tightly held hand. She was walking backwards, trusting him to keep her from falling or backing into unsuspecting townsfolk. "It's a surprise."

Not only did he adore her, but next week she would become his wife . . . assuming no *surprises* got in the way.

"Oh, don't scowl like that," she chided, reading his expression despite his silence. "It's not the kind of surprise that could result in you accidentally shooting someone. It's my wedding present to you, and I'm sure you'll like it."

Only then did she bite her lower lip in further thought. "Well, almost sure. I hope. I mean you'll like *it,* but you might not like that I didn't tell you earlier. I found out so close to the wedding that I thought it would make a good present. But . . ."

Frowning now, she pushed his chest with one hand.

"Stop being so gloomy—now you've got me worried too."

"Don't worry," he assured her. It was the surprise part that concerned him, not the gift. Whatever she gave him would only add to the gift that was her hand, her heart, her future. Her world. Even after eight joyous months, he sometimes shook his head in wonder at how he'd ever become part of her world.

Compared to all that, she should not have bothered to get him anything, much less something special-ordered. But he would not argue that with her, either. He chose his arguments with Victoria carefully.

She was far better at words than he would ever be.

So he said, "Anything from you, I will love." And she rewarded him with one of her bright smiles, all the brighter for now knowing all of his secrets and still loving him.

"But this is special," she promised, turning anxiously toward the train that was pulling into the station.

Special did not comfort a cautious man like Ross much more than *surprise*. Still, he caught her hand with his and tugged her gently against his side, weaving their fingers together. Some bystanders noticed, and a few whispered. If she did not mind, he refused to.

They had the dog with them, didn't they? And she was *marrying* him. Thanks to poor Audra and her unfortunate scandal, he and Vic hadn't even had to wait the entire year!

Sometimes, he thought as the train huffed and chugged to a reluctant stop, things really did happen for the best.

And then sometimes, one of the meanest outlaws Ross had ever known stepped off the train—barely a week before his wedding.

Taking in Harvey "Kid Curry" Logan's dark coloring and handsome, amoral face, Ross fell into his old, cautious posture without even thinking. It matched Logan's. When the outlaw's Cherokee eyes brushed across Ross, they widened in recognition, then narrowed with suspicion.

Ross set Victoria firmly to one side. "Stay here."

"But your present—"

"I won't be long," he assured her, and warned her with his eyes that she'd best not risk following him. He trusted that she would not. They'd had to come to *some* agreements over the past months. The joyful, loving, full months he'd had with her.

Maybe part of him had feared all along that his world wouldn't let them make it to the altar.

Assured of her safety, if not his own, he crossed the platform to stand in front of Harvey, poor Lonny's brother, the toughest gunman in the Wild Bunch. Unsure what name the man was going by today—Logan? Roberts? Curry?—Ross contented himself with nodding a greeting. "Howdy."

Harvey nodded suspiciously back, but said nothing.

"I was sorry to hear about Lonny," said Ross. And he was. Apparently his friend had tried doing what Ross had done—going home. For Lonny, home meant Missouri. Just that February, Pinkertons had shot him dead in his aunt's house. Ross heard they'd found him by tracking bills from the Wilcox robbery.

"Damned sons of bitches," agreed Harvey. Flat-Nosed George, another member of the Wild Bunch, had been killed by a posse in April. Elzy Lay was still in prison. Rumor was, even Butch Cassidy was struggling to go straight—and failing.

The frontier was really ending. Looking at Harvey Logan's hatred, Ross marveled at how close he'd come to ending with it.

"Ross!" called Victoria, down the platform, and Ross glanced over his shoulder. She was standing with a thin, gray-haired lady.

He looked back at Harvey and caught the outlaw's curiosity, so he laid his cards on the table. "I'm marrying her."

Harve Logan shook his head with a grimace of a smile. "Guess you ain't lookin' for a job, then."

"I've got one." He took a slow breath. "I catch rustlers."

Harvey raised his eyebrows, almost in challenge.

"In Sheridan County," Ross added. He'd refused to take the job without limiting the geography of his already unofficial jurisdiction. Unless someone from Hole-in-the-Wall or Robbers' Roost came after him or his, he didn't want to have to go after them. And he wouldn't take a job he couldn't do well.

The train blew its whistle, a warning for folks who were stretching their legs or grabbing a bite from the vendors to climb back onboard.

"I guess we're done, then," said Harvey.

"Yep," said Ross, shifting his weight more comfortably. He did still carry a gun. He did still know how to use it.

But they'd been done for a long time.

They didn't shake hands. But when Logan climbed back aboard the Burlington and Missouri train, Ross couldn't help but feel part of himself leaving as well.

Luckily, it was a part he was just as glad to see go.

He backed up, watching for Harvey through the windows out of both habit and instinct. When the train chugged away, with the outlaw safely on board, Ross's shoulders sank in relief.

Maybe fate would let him get married after all.

"Are you done chasing away the bad men?" asked Victoria at his elbow. He'd grown so accustomed to her over the last months, he didn't even jump. Instead, he smiled at her teasing.

"For today," he assured her, turning—and now he saw Victoria's gray-haired lady friend up close.

Ross tried to swallow, and couldn't. He opened his mouth to speak, but no sound came out. He'd known Victoria had been searching, but he'd never believed that even she . . .

"Ross?" asked the woman, her voice still accented, her green eyes crinkling into a delighted smile. "Can my little Draz be so tall?"

He managed to mouth the name, even if his voice hadn't returned. *Momma?*

She nodded—as if she could be anyone else! "Your Miss Garrison, she writes to my brother Goran in Chicago and says, *Do you know her? I must find her.* Goran brings me her letter, and I ask him to write back, and she sends me tickets for the train, so I can come see your wedding. She is an angel, your Miss Garrison."

But he'd never doubted that.

Dizzy with the shifting of his worlds—his recent past leaving on the same train that had brought his true past—Ross gave up words for action and drew his mother into his arms. He held her carefully at first, afraid that she was an illusion, or a ghost, and might vanish at his touch. But she wrapped her arms around him, tight and real—arms that had rocked him to sleep as a child, hands that had tended his boyhood wounds.

"My baby," murmured his mother, despite that he now towered over her. "My sweet baby. I never stop looking. I save money, I hire detectives, but they find nothing. Laurence, nothing. Lauranovic, nothing. I am so afraid for you. Then Goran brings me Miss Garrison's letter, and again my life is whole."

My life is whole.

He pillowed his head on her gray hair—and, his eyes still open, he took in the sight of Victoria and wished she could know even a portion of the joy she'd given him.

She was happily crying for the three of them.

When he held out an arm for her, she joined their embrace, and his world became something he'd never guessed even existed.

Someday, he would make Victoria explain how she'd done it.

Epilogue

Victoria's friend Evangeline played piano, as she had at Mariah's and Laurel's weddings. Kitty, now with only a slight limp, hovered adoringly at Ross's side until the ceremony. Alden Wright spoke earnestly to Ross's mother, perhaps discussing the new tombstones they'd purchased for "Joseph," "Philip," and "Julia Laurence"—or perhaps just discussing Julie.

Papa—as Mariah and Laurel had warned he might—said little more before the service than a quiet, "You don't have to do this, Victoria Rose."

"Trust me, Papa, I do," she assured him. Then, as his concerned gaze sharpened into suspicion, she hurried to clarify herself. "Because I love him, not because we have to! Golly, you and Thaddeas and Duchess have certainly seen to that."

Mariah had pointed out, rather sulkily Victoria thought, that at least Papa hadn't had Ross beaten, although Ross probably deserved it more than Stuart.

Luckily, by their wedding day, the sisters were back on speaking terms. Mariah's new baby boy, hers and Stuart's second, had helped smooth that reconciliation.

Even if Ross *was* still a range detective.

When Vic saw Ross waiting with the minister, she almost ran across the room to take his hand. Once Papa reluctantly delivered her to him, Ross spoke his vows clearly and confidently. So did she—except for having to stop midway and bite her lower lip, to keep from crying her happiness. Once, he couldn't promise her anything. Now he promised her everything. And oh, that was so much more than she'd ever dreamed.

Mrs. Victoria Laurence.

Ross, Vic's hand in his, made sure to seek out her father during the reception. "Thank you," her new husband said. "Thank you for allowing me to marry your daughter."

Papa, behaving himself with Mama on his arm, still snorted. "Allowin'."

As if Victoria were as headstrong as that! Although, from the way both Mama and Ross smiled over her head, she wondered if they thought so too.

"Thank you anyway," said Ross softly, looking at Victoria as he said it.

"You hurt her," warned Papa, "you'll regret it."

"I thought the West wasn't a frontier anymore," challenged Victoria.

Mama smiled. "I think it may always be, where daughters are concerned. The boss tends to change his mind on the topic, depending on which answer suits him better."

Then Mama kissed them each on the cheek, assuring them that she had no qualms about Ross at all, and let them get back to their guests.

"Ain't your boss," Victoria heard Papa complain, behind them, and she and Ross shared happy smiles.

Sometimes she loved his smile most of all.

*   *   *

Ross doubted even Victoria could ever report the fulfillment that was their wedding night—and not just because it would fly in the face of both common decency and the Comstock Law.

It couldn't be described because it transcended words, an erotic wonder of buttons coming undone, mouths seeking and finding each other, careful hands exploring private places—what they'd started calling "married places," during their lengthy courtship. It couldn't be described because surely she could never explain how she so clearly enjoyed something that he feared would hurt her, despite his best efforts.

And after he lost control at last, shuddering his completion into the purity and acceptance and trust that was his Victoria, he doubted his loyal wife would ever tell anybody about the wetness that she kissed off his cheeks. Everything he'd gone through in his life, and he hadn't cried. Now, at this . . .

She was his own untainted piece of the world. She cleansed him, whole and holy, a completion unto herself.

And not even *her* excellent words could describe that.

In their bed together, naked and damp and still intertwined, Vic drew her soft cheek across the scratch of his, and Ross knew happiness. Every breath tasted distinctly like her, of soap and cinnamon and Victoria. Her breath and heartbeat serenaded him.

And they were even home.

At her urging, he'd kept the rooms above Thaddeas' law office. In two years, the money that they'd save would buy them a far better house than anything they could afford now, even with his bounty money—and Victoria said she liked the apartment, that it made her feel modern. She had insisted that they come here instead of going to a hotel for their honeymoon. "I

329

want to go home with you," she'd said, as if she understood.

She understood him better than he understood himself sometimes.

"Are you all right?" she whispered now, before he'd even regained the strength to move after . . . well, afterward. He did not mind the paralysis, as long as he got to keep a naked leg between hers, an arm draped across the tuck of her velvety waist. As long as he got to gaze at her in the nighttime shadows, her pretty face framed by the dark, wild hair spread across the pillow, he welcomed his fate. "Oh, Ross, is it as wonderful for men as for women?"

He might not be able to move his body, but he managed to widen his eyes, both relieved and amused. Surely she owed anything wonderful about their marital relations to her enthusiasm more than to his skill. And more than that, on both sides, to their love for each other. But oh, he had tried. He wanted to please her so badly, he'd tried very hard.

Now he could let more fears slide away.

"Now I guess I know everything," she admitted, tracing her delightfully curious fingers across the corded muscle of his shoulders, down the length of his arm. "What's this scar from?"

Damn. He'd forgotten about the scars. "Bullet."

"And this one?" Her hand found his side.

"Bullet." *From my other life.*

"And this one?" The white mark sliced across his midriff.

"Knife," he admitted, and when she started to lift the blanket to investigate more of him, he laughed and found he could move after all, and kissed her. Levering himself over her, he kissed her flawless collarbones, then the round tops of her beautiful, luscious breasts—and then the rest of them, until she moaned. Then he kissed lower. . . .

"I like your scars," she admitted, between encouraging sighs. "They make you seem dangerous."

He paused in kissing her gently curved belly—the belly that, God willing, would someday carry his children—and looked back up at her through a fall of hair, uncertain.

"But not dangerous to me," she assured him. "Can we do this every night?"

He kissed his way back up her body, then tucked an elbow under his head to better watch her. "We can try."

"Good," she decided, "I knew when we were kissing sometimes that it—this—must be wonderful, as badly as I ached for it, and that was before I even knew what it was. Well . . . in detail."

He'd never known women ached for it too. Trust Victoria to admit to something like that.

"Ross," she said solemnly, and he raised his eyebrows and waited, loving her. "Do you know how I feel right now?"

He shook his head, just a little.

She said, "I don't either. What I feel is so big, there aren't words for it."

He considered that, considered her. He took a deep breath to steady himself in a world of such happiness. "I have a word."

"Love?" she suggested, then smiled, wanton. "Lust?"

He smiled back, waiting patiently for her to finish.

"Happy? Married? Wife? Husband?"

He particularly liked those words.

"What?" she demanded finally, climbing on top of him, heaven in a little, curvy body—and a dangerously bright mind.

"Home," he said.

She folded her arms on his chest, gazed down at him. "Because the apartment's our home now, yours and mine."

Partly that. But he shook his head.

"Because you're back in Sheridan, as a Laurence."

That too. He had family buried here, and family visiting. He had a job, and he'd made friends. But he shook his head.

She bit her lower lip for a moment, suddenly shy. She knew him well enough to guess, after all. "Because of me?"

He nodded, wrapped his arms carefully around her, and rolled her onto her back, illustrating that they could possibly even do this more than once a night.

He loved how her eyes shone up at him.

"Welcome home, Ross Laurence," she whispered.

Then he kissed her, long and hard, and settled into saying the same thing back to her.

Without any words at all.

Author Notes

Thank you for sharing the world of *Explaining Herself,* Vic and Ross's story, which immediately precedes *Behaving Herself,* bringing the saga of the Rancher's Daughters full circle . . . not that Jacob Garrison doesn't have a few daughters—and a daughter-in-law— to worry about in his future!

Sheridan, Wyoming, really was a booming city at the turn of the century. I "invented" the *Sheridan Herald,* where Victoria works, in order to allow myself more poetic license; in reality, the city had two papers. As of '94, at least, the *Sheridan Post* (Republican) and the *Sheridan Enterprise* (Democratic) were edited by J. W. Newell and Joe DeBarthe, respectively. And the end of the nineteenth century was important for advancing the idea that child offenders should be treated differently.

Wild Bunch scholars may picture Lonny Logan differently than I did. I tried to choose a lesser-known outlaw, to avoid annoying too many legitimate historians. But one of the few pictures I've found of Lonny—as part of a large group in front of a Rawlins, Wyoming, saloon around 1896—shows a slim, inoffensive-looking fellow with big ears and a derby hat. Appearances may be deceiving, but I'm convinced the guy in the picture *could* be my version. All details regarding the outlaws are as accurate as possible.

Legend has it that much of Butch Cassidy's loot from the Wilcox Train Robbery is still buried somewhere in Wyoming. But, as Victoria's father would tell you, it probably *still* belongs either to the state or to the Union Pacific Railroad, should you happen to find it.

I love to talk about my stories and characters. Feel free to e-mail me at Yvaughn@aol.com, check out my website at www.ranchersdaughters.homestead.com, or write to me at P.O. Box 6, Euless TX, 76039.

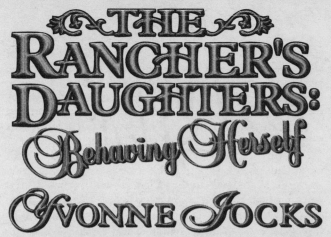

THE RANCHER'S DAUGHTERS: Behaving Herself

YVONNE JOCKS

There are so many things that a girl shouldn't do, and for a teacher, there are even more. Miss Garrison is learning them all by doing them. No sooner has the hapless beauty escaped scandal in her Wyoming home by taking a Texas teaching job than she meets up with "Handy" Jack Harwood—a handsome gambler who will surely do her reputation no good. She knows she can get on track, if only she can ignore the unladylike excitement he stirs in her. She'll gamble one last time—on the goodness of Jack's rakish soul and that they are meant to be together. After that, she'll start behaving herself.

___4693-8 $5.50 US/$6.50 CAN

Dorchester Publishing Co., Inc.
P.O. Box 6640
Wayne, PA 19087-8640

Please add $1.75 for shipping and handling for the first book and $.50 for each book thereafter. NY, NYC, and PA residents, please add appropriate sales tax. No cash, stamps, or C.O.D.s. All orders shipped within 6 weeks via postal service book rate. Canadian orders require $2.00 extra postage and must be paid in U.S. dollars through a U.S. banking facility.

Name_____
Address_____
City_____ State _____ Zip _____
I have enclosed $ _____ in payment for the checked book(s).
Payment <u>must</u> accompany all orders. ❑ Please send a free catalog.

Lori Morgan
Autumn Star

Morgan Caine rescues Lacey Ashton from a couple of pawing ruffians, feeds her dinner, and gives her a place to sleep. He is arrogant, bossy, and the most captivating man she has ever met. He claims she will never survive the wilds of the Washington Territory. But Lacey sets out to prove she not only belongs in the untamed land, she belongs in Morgan's arms.

Morgan is completely disarmed by Lacey's innocence and optimism. Like an autumn breeze, she caresses his body, refreshes his soul, invigorates his heart. At last, the hardened lawman longs to trade vengeance for a future filled with happiness—to reach for the stars and claim the woman of his dreams.

___4892-2 $4.99 US/$5.99 CAN

Cinnamon and Roses
Heidi Betts

A hardworking seamstress, Rebecca has no business being attracted to a man like wealthy, arrogant Caleb Adams. Born fatherless in a brothel, Rebecca knows what males are made of. And Caleb is clearly as faithless as they come, scandalizing their Kansas cowtown with the fancy city women he casually uses and casts aside. Though he tempts innocent Rebecca beyond reason, she can't afford to love a man like Caleb, for the price might be another fatherless babe. What the devil is wrong with him, Caleb muses, that he's drawn to a calico-clad dressmaker when sirens in silk are his for the asking? Still, Rebecca unaccountably stirs him. Caleb vows no woman can be trusted with his heart. But he must sample sweet Rebecca.

Lair of the Wolf

Also includes the second installment of *Lair of the Wolf*, a serialized romance set in medieval Wales. Be sure to look for future chapters of this exciting story featured in Leisure books and written by the industry's top authors.

___4668-7 $4.99 US/$5.99 CAN

Dorchester Publishing Co., Inc.
P.O. Box 6640
Wayne, PA 19087-8640

Please add $1.75 for shipping and handling for the first book and $.50 for each book thereafter. NY, NYC, and PA residents, please add appropriate sales tax. No cash, stamps, or C.O.D.s. All orders shipped within 6 weeks via postal service book rate. Canadian orders require $2.00 extra postage and must be paid in U.S. dollars through a U.S. banking facility.

Name_____
Address_____
City_____State_____Zip_____
I have enclosed $_____ in payment for the checked book(s).
Payment <u>must</u> accompany all orders. ❑ Please send a free catalog.
CHECK OUT OUR WEBSITE! www.dorchesterpub.com

A Promise of Roses

Heidi Betts

Spunky Megan Adams will do almost anything to save her struggling stagecoach line—even confront the bandits constantly ambushing the stage for the payrolls it delivers. But what Megan *wouldn't* do is fall headlong for the heart-breakingly handsome outlaw who robs the coach, kidnaps her from his ornery amigos, and drags her half across Kansas—to turn *her* in as an accomplice to the holdup!

Bounty hunter Lucas McCain stops at nothing to get his man. Hired to investigate the pilfered payrolls, he is sure Megan herself is masterminding the heists. And he'll be damned if he'll let this gun-toting spitfire keep him from completing his mission—even if he has to hogtie her to his horse, promise her roses . . . and hijack her heart!

Heidi Betts
ALMOST A Lady

Pistol-packing Pinkerton agent Willow Hastings always gets her man. Until handsome, arrogant railroad security chief Brandt Donovan "gallantly" interferes in an arrest, costing Willow a collar and jeopardizing her job. And now she is supposed to collaborate with the dashing, distracting bachelor to catch a killer? Never! Brandt is shocked yet intrigued by this curvy, contrary, weapon-wielding brunette. Willow's sultry voice, silken skin, and subtle scent of roses make him ache to savor her between the sheets. But go undercover with the perplexing Pinkerton? Chastely pose as man and wife to entrap a killer? Such unthinkable celibacy could drive a bachelor to madness. Or to—shudder!—matrimony. . . .

___4817-5 $4.99 US/$5.99 CAN

Dorchester Publishing Co., Inc.
P.O. Box 6640
Wayne, PA 19087-8640

Please add $2.50 for shipping and handling for the first book and $.75 for each book thereafter. NY, NYC, and PA residents, please add appropriate sales tax. No cash, stamps, or C.O.D.s. All orders shipped within 6 weeks via postal service book rate. Canadian orders require $2.00 extra postage and must be paid in U.S. dollars through a U.S. banking facility.

Name_____
Address_____
City_____ State_____ Zip_____
I have enclosed $_____ in payment for the checked book(s).
Payment <u>must</u> accompany all orders.☐Please send a free catalog.
    CHECK OUT OUR WEBSITE! www.dorchesterpub.com

WALKER'S WIDOW

HEIDI BETTS

Clayton Walker has been sent to Purgatory . . . but it feels more like hell. Assigned to solve a string of minor burglaries, the rugged Texas Ranger thinks catching the crook will be a walk in the park. Instead he finds himself chasing a black-masked bandit with enticing hips and a penchant for helping everyone but herself. Regan Doyle's nocturnal activities know no boundaries; decked out in black, the young widow makes sure the rich "donate" to the local orphanage. And the fiery redhead isn't about to let a lawman get in her way—even if his broad shoulders and piercing gray eyes are arresting. But caught in a compromising position, Regan recognizes that the jig is up, for Clay has stolen her heart.

___4954-6 $5.99 US/$7.99 CAN

Dorchester Publishing Co., Inc.
P.O. Box 6640
Wayne, PA 19087-8640

Please add $2.50 for shipping and handling for the first book and $.75 for each additional book. NY and PA residents, add appropriate sales tax. No cash, stamps, or C.O.D.s. All Canadian orders require $5.00 for shipping and handling and must be paid in U. S. dollars. Prices and availability subject to change. Payment must accompany all orders.

Name_____

Address_____

City_____ State_____ Zip_____

E-mail_____

I have enclosed $_____ in payment for the checked book(s).

❑Please send a free catalog.

CHECK OUT OUR WEBSITE! www.dorchesterpub.com